MW00526509

Also available from Camphor Press

EVERLASTING EMPIRE, BY YI IN-HWA

FORMOSAN ODYSSEY, BY JOHN GRANT ROSS

LORD OF FORMOSA

Published by Camphor Press Ltd
83 Ducie Street, Manchester, M1 2JQ
United Kingdom

www.camphorpress.com

Copyright © 2018 Joyce Bergvelt

First published in Dutch translation (author's own) in 2015 as *Formosa, voorgoed verloren* (*Formosa, Forever Lost*) by Uitgeverij Conserve, the Netherlands.

All rights reserved. This book or any portion thereof may not be reproduced or used in any manner whatsoever without the express written permission of the publisher except for the use of brief quotations in a book review.

The map of Tayouan Bay on page 51 is adapted from *Lost Colony: The Untold Story of China's First Great Victory over the West* by Tonio Andrade. Copyright © 2011 by Princeton University Press. Reprinted by permission.

ISBN 978-1-78869-139-0 (paperback)
978-1-78869-148-2 (cloth)

The moral right of the author has been asserted.

Set in 11 pt Linux Libertine

Except in the United States of America, this book is sold subject to the condition that it shall not, by way of trade or otherwise, be lent, re-sold, hired out, or otherwise circulated without the publisher's prior consent in any form if binding or cover other than that in which it is published and without a similar condition including this condition being imposed on the subsequent purchaser.

Lord of Formosa

Joyce Bergvelt

A Camphor Press book

Contents

	PROLOGUE	xv
	The Explorer	xix
	PART ONE	1
1.	Son of a Pirate	3
2.	Fatherland	23
3.	Migrants and Colonists	53
4.	Pirate, Merchant, Mandarin	63
5.	Seeds of Rebellion	85
6.	The Young Mandarin	95
7.	Daughter of the Samurai	103
8.	The Imperial Surname	115
9.	A Question of Loyalty	125
	PART TWO	159
10.	Leaseholders, Merchants, and Missionaries	161
11.	The Uprising	187
12.	The Physician	219
13.	A Lack of Trade	245
14.	Merchant, Interpreter, Intermediary	255
15.	His Father's Fleet	281
16.	An Unreasonable Admiral	293
17.	Crossing the Strait	317
	PART THREE	325
18.	Hostages	327
19.	The Siege of Fort Zeelandia	357

20. The Demise of He Ting-bin 383
21. A Defector of Value 391
22. The Fall of Zeelandia 405
23. The Loss of a Colony 425
Epilogue 441
Author's Note 445
A Word of Thanks 449
Sources 451

Maps

East and Southest Asia XVII
The Strait of Formosa 49
Tayouan Bay 51

In memory of my father

In order to win a war, one must first know one's enemy.

Sun Tzu, *The Art of War*

LORD OF FORMOSA

PROLOGUE

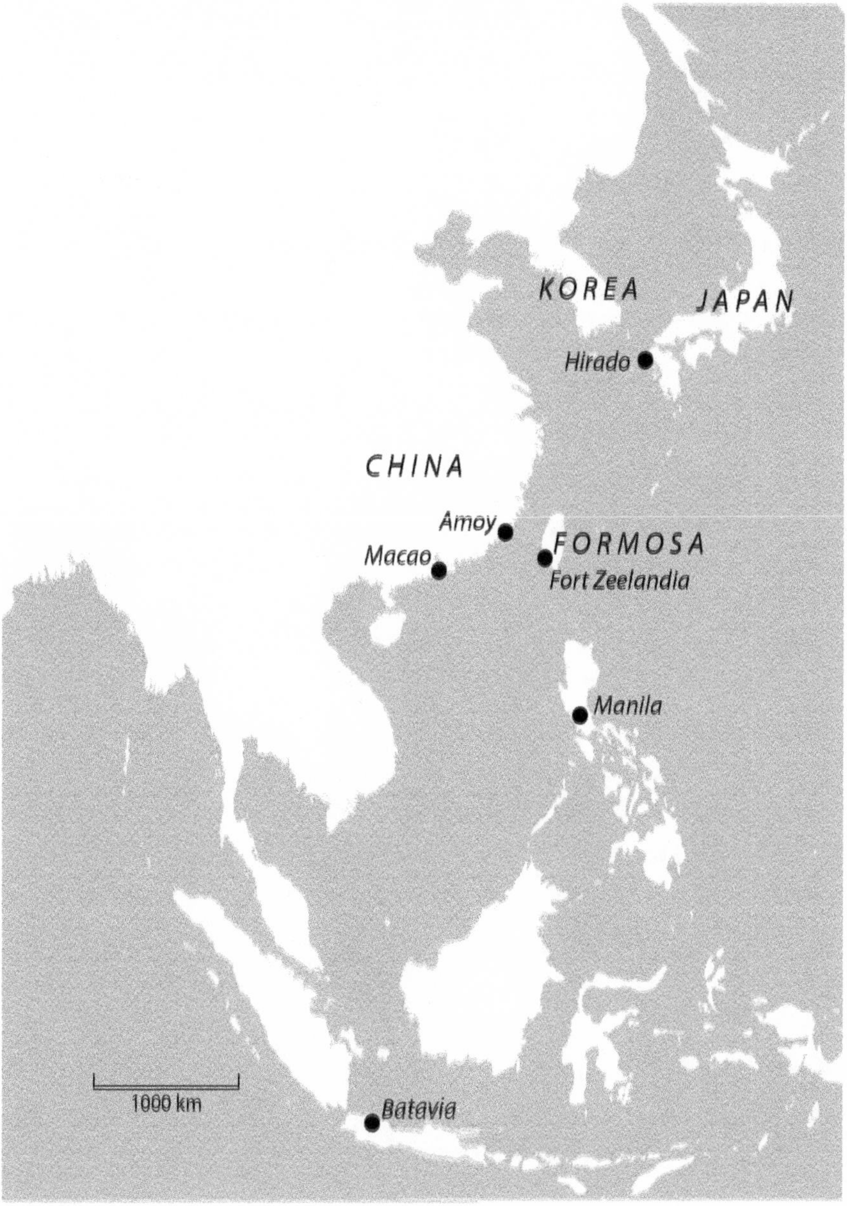

KOREA
JAPAN
Hirado
CHINA
Amoy
FORMOSA
Macao
Fort Zeelandia
Manila
1000 km
Batavia

The Explorer

THE STRAIT OF FORMOSA, MING DYNASTY, 1430

THE first typhoon arrived unseasonably early, lashing the fleet of ships, the taut sails straining under the powerful gusts that pushed them forward. On the flagship, Admiral Zheng He held on to the railing as well as he could while trying to make his way to the captain, his clothes sodden. The hard rain beat onto his face, mixing with the salt spray of the waves crashing over the sides, stinging his eyes and rendering him almost blind.

"Captain!" he shouted, the harsh winds practically ripping the sound from his lips. It was no use as he saw the captain's back still turned to him. He would have to get up close. "Captain!"

Feeling the hand on his shoulder, the captain swung round.

Zheng He leaned forward, placing his lips close to the captain's ear. "We've been blown off course!" he shouted at the top of his lungs. "We have to turn back!"

The captain squinted at the admiral as he considered their situation "No, it's too late to go back! We'll have to try and weather the storm!" he bellowed.

Zheng He grasped the railing again with his hand as another monstrous wave lifted the junk on its side. "Where are the other ships? There's no sight of the rest of the fleet! We've lost them. And the storm is only getting worse!"

The admiral looked around but saw nothing, the horizon lost behind a moving wall of waves. Again he felt the contents of his stomach churning, and he turned his head to vomit over the side. Momentarily weakened by the violence that had taken hold of his body, he waited for his strength to return.

Above the din of the storm came the sound of splintering wood. He looked up, his eyes focusing on the first mast of the middle deck. The flagship had no fewer than nine masts, the tallest of which were on the middle deck. He knew that if one mast went down, the other masts would be hit and damaged. The crew had seen it too, and all eyes were fixed on the main mast, which was bent like a crossbow. The sailors pointed and shouted, yelling instructions at one another while trying not to get swept overboard.

Again the dreaded sound of wood stressed to the point of breaking.

"It's coming down!" someone shouted in warning. The reduced sail whipped like the wing of an injured dragon as the powerful storm pushed into whatever it could find with a fury, adding further strain to the already damaged mast. Zheng He watched with horror as the taller part of the mast finally broke away and came crashing down. But the mast did not tear into the others, as he had expected. One of the cables to which it was attached held, stopping its fall, causing the mast to bounce heavily in mid-air. The thick, oiled cable snapped under the weight of the mast and lashed out with a zing, hitting one of the sailors against the head, killing him instantly. The broken section went crashing down over the side, its ropes entangling it and causing it to head straight for the hull.

The heavy mast crashed through the boards, creating a gaping hole in the side of the junk. As if on cue, a large wave lashed into its side, washing into the hold, its liquid tentacles enfolding all in its path.

The captain shouted his orders futilely into the wind, knowing that his seasoned crew knew what to do. A team of sailors rushed to the side and began to haul in the heavy mast, struggling with its weight. One man slipped and fell, losing his hold on the security cable. The junk's violent roll threw him to the side, where he lay, stunned. Without endangering his own life, Zheng He could do little to help him. As the junk rolled again, he grasped the security cable firmly and felt himself lifted off his feet. He watched helplessly as a wave washed onto the deck, receding again, taking the wounded sailor with it over the side. The man's last cry was cut off abruptly as he was engulfed by the waves.

There was no time to pay heed to one drowning man. Their faces grim, both the captain and Zheng He rushed forward to aid the struggling sailors as the solid timber shaft was finally lifted over the railing and dropped heavily onto the deck. Others had already jumped into the hold to bail out the water coming in.

The injured vessel lurched helplessly as huge waves lifted it and let it crash back onto the waves as the full force of the winds pushed it eastward, farther from the sanctuary of the Chinese coast.

"How far have we been blown off course?" the admiral shouted at the captain, his voice an uncharacteristic soprano for a man his size, betraying his status as a eunuch.

"Roughly thirty *li** to the east, sir," the captain repeated at the top of his voice.

"We are too far away to make it back in this state," Zheng He yelled. "We will have to ride the storm in the direction it takes us. We have no choice."

He held onto the railing tightly, his legs splayed to remain standing on the rolling ship as he considered the dangers that faced his beloved flagship. On its seventh voyage of discovery, the magnificent junk had withstood many tests over the years; but the storm had revealed its true age and found its weaknesses.

For three hours, the heavily injured junk struggled to stay afloat in the midst of the typhoon. Just when Zheng He began to believe they would never set foot on firm ground again, the storm subsided.

As the size of the waves decreased, lookouts searched for the other ships. Visibility was still poor due to the heavy sheets of rain that melted into the seas, but it was evident that they had become detached from the rest of the fleet. No other ship could be seen or heard.

While the captain and admiral tried to get their bearings, the crippled, formerly imposing junk that had once sailed as far as the waters of Arabia limped on. They would have to wait for the storm to die. Perhaps then

* One *li* = just over a quarter of a mile.

they would be able to spot land or be guided by the stars at night once the heavens had cleared. Meanwhile, the sailors below continued to bail water in shifts. Zheng He thanked Allah that the hole the mast had smashed in the hull was well above the waterline. As long as they did not encounter another heavy storm before reaching land on which they could repair the damage, they might just make it.

It was just before sunset when one of the lookouts spotted land. Stuttering with excitement and relief, the boy repeatedly jabbed his finger in the direction of what he had seen. Agile as a monkey, he clambered down. Zheng He was immediately at his side, where he peered into the distance, his eyes no longer as sharp as the lookout's. Then a rapt expression appeared on his face as the distinct outline of an island loomed through the haze of rain.

"I have heard of this land," he whispered in awe. "An old legend speaks of an island several hundred *li* from our coast. This could be the same. We will be safe. Allah be praised!" The passion of the Muslim naval explorer shone through his eyes, which were now wide with excitement at the thought of discovering new land.

This is what he lived for: great journeys of exploration. Emperor Xuancong had personally dispatched him: it was his job to establish diplomatic relations with sovereigns in undiscovered lands, offering them gifts and getting them to open trade with the Chinese empire. His ships had been specially made to transport foreign representatives, exotic creatures, and large amounts of valuable goods back to China. He would return to bring with him the latest medical and astronomical knowledge, passed on to them by people living as far away as the East African coast. Scientists and physicians from foreign lands would accompany them to exchange their invaluable knowledge in many a field that would make the Ming dynasty even more glorious than it already was.

Strong currents caused the heavily damaged junk to drift southward as its crew struggled to avoid the rocks that lay strewn along the island's western coastline. The current finally carried the vessel toward the reefs along the south, pushed by the residual strong gusts of the typhoon. Out of control and in unfamiliar waters, the ship ran aground against the shallows, tearing open its timber bottom with a sickening crunch.

"Look!" someone shouted. "There are people down there!" From behind the foliage that lined the beach, human shapes cautiously emerged. Zheng He stared down at them, fascinated. Around him the crew members reacted differently. Some were relieved that the island was habitable, others were skittish, muttering words of fear and suspicion, wondering if these were peace-loving folk. The islanders looked up in awe at the prow of his flagship, which was carved to resemble the body of a dragon.

He started as the huge junk rolled once more in rhythm with the surf, and waited for the inevitable. For a moment there was an eerie silence. Then the ship's timbers groaned one final time as the vessel ran aground along the shallows, immobilized. Frantically, the sailors tried to abandon ship as water filled the hold of what was now a mere carcass.

But Zheng He remained where he was, observing the islanders with interest. He suspected that this was not the first time that these people had watched from the shore, patiently waiting for disaster to happen. During the past many Chinese junks would have beached along the shore. How many Chinese vessels had been stranded here along these coasts over the centuries? How many of his countrymen had ended up on this island by accident, driven by storms or strong currents, or were simply lost at sea? If sailors had returned from this island to China, he would surely know of it. "So none must have returned," he said to himself. The mere thought brought him a tremor of excitement.

A dozen pairs of human eyes watched from behind the foliage as the Chinese sailors struggled to save themselves.

One of the natives, an elderly, stocky man with a dark, deeply lined face, rose from his squatting position in an easy movement that belied his age. Gesturing and shouting, he spurred his companions into action, the men emerging from their various hiding places as they walked onto the beach.

The admiral watched with interest as the dark-skinned figures brought out their canoes from seemingly nowhere, the prows of the vessels piercing the surf with determination. Some waded into the surf toward those struggling in the water, their dark skins glistening in the sun. Others deftly jumped into the canoes in pairs in the direction of the inert junk. Sodden, gasping sailors were pulled onto the small vessels, which then ferried them to the safety of the beach. As more natives, intrigued by all the commotion on the beach, emerged from the woods, the number of canoes increased. They ferried Zheng He and the rest of the crew across with remarkable efficiency and finally assisted in bringing their valuable cargoes ashore.

With the help of two sailors, Zheng He stepped into the water from the canoe that had carried him ashore. Intrigued, he observed the flurry of activity on the beach that had seemed so deserted. When most of the shipwrecked sailors had been brought to safety, the seasoned, motley crew from various parts of the Chinese empire and the natives of Formosa regarded each other with mutual curiosity.

Zheng He, a seasoned diplomat, lost no time in showing his goodwill and gratitude toward their rescuers, and bowed with respect to the barely dressed men. His crew followed his example without hesitation.

"Gifts! Bring them gifts!" he ordered imperiously, while he attempted to remove his sodden clothes.

Three sailors scrambled around the crates which had been stacked on the dry sand, and prized them open. Hands delved in and came out holding necklaces of luminous beads, colorfully woven cloths, and strings of copper coins. They approached their local rescuers, who eagerly accepted the novel items with outstretched hands, their eyes shining.

In the days that followed, Zheng He and his crew were warmly welcomed. The natives showed them around the island, provided them with food, helped them build shelter, and served as their guides in the heavily wooded hills. As he and his men followed the guides in search of timber for the ship's repairs, they were greatly impressed by what they saw.

They watched as fishermen along the shore hauled in their nets, heavy with luscious, shiny fish. Drying pools of salt dotted the sandy shoreline. The hills and mountains were covered with lush green forests of valuable timber and teemed with deer. The pungent odor of sulfur, prized as an ingredient for the production of fire sticks, gunpowder, and medicine, permeated the hillside. The soil was soft, damp, and fertile, while the trees were heavy with exotic fruits.

As Zheng He and his men explored the south of the island, they paused often to gaze in wonder at the spectacular sight that greeted them. They were entranced as the rays of the early-morning sun pierced the thin veil of mist that lay draped over the green hills, giving the place an ethereal kind of beauty. They followed the native people as they hunted the deer, downing them with their bows and arrows and deftly skinning them with simple tools. They watched with appreciation how the island people worked as they felled timber and helped them to repair their ship.

Zheng He and his men remained on the island for several months as they waited for their ship to be seaworthy once more and for the wind and tide to turn in their favor. When they finally left, the hold of the ship was filled with precious goods and items of interest gathered on the island.

Later that year, at the court of Emperor Xuancong, the exploring admiral told tales of the island he had discovered some three hundred *li* off the Chinese coast. He waxed lyrical about its wild beauty, the fertile lands, its seas rich with fish, and presented the emperor with bags of salt, dried venison, and clumps of yellow sulfur. He spoke of the island's aboriginals with affection and admiration, and his enthusiasm was contagious.

The emperor, fascinated by Zheng He's stories of the island's magnificence, was impressed; and the island became of topic of conversation and speculation at court for months to come. The deep-rooted traditional Chinese belief that the oceans formed China's southeastern border, however, prevented Xuancong from embracing the island as part of his empire. Zheng He died in 1435 during an ill-fated voyage, and through a twist of fate the emperor died that same year. In his place, an eight-year-old boy took the throne. But the boy was left entirely in the hands of scheming relatives and courtiers, men and women with agendas of their own.

With the deaths of the explorer Zheng He and Emperor Xuancong, the court, embroiled in intrigues and feuds, forgot all about the island. Unclaimed and forgotten, it once again fell into isolation.

During the centuries that followed, the place became a haven for pirates, adventurers, and traders — both foreign and Chinese. The Portuguese were the first Westerners to discover it, and it was they who named it for its beauty. Thus, the island became known to the West by the exotic name of Ilha Formosa, a name that was picked up by early Western cartographers, who placed it firmly on their maps.

Formosa continued to be used as a rendezvous for smugglers and pirates, who hoarded their goods on the island. Merchants traded their wares there to avoid paying taxes, while Japanese merchants rested along Formosa's shores as an interlude during their travels. Only occasionally did minor mandarins visit the island; but the court in Peking never did bother to station officials there. No one was willing to relocate to the backward, humid, and uncivilized island; and the court did not press them to do so.

But after millennia of isolation, another sovereignty would finally take possession of Formosa. Not the great empire a mere hundred miles away, nor any neighboring country. The first nation to lay a claim to the island was of the West.

PART ONE

1

Son of a Pirate

1631, HIRADO, NAGASAKI, JAPAN

"FUKUMATSU!" his mother yelled angrily, clutching her bundled, sleeping infant in her arms. She had not arrived a moment too soon. In the deserted garden courtyard, her son straddled a plump boy, his fists beating down upon a face she recognized as Yoshi's, the son of the chief merchant, the richest man in Nagasaki. The boy's nose was bleeding profusely. Yoshi began to cry piteously the moment he saw her.

"Tagawa-*san*!" the boy wailed, sounding like a girl. Fukumatsu's fist froze in mid-air, his face flushed a furious red as he met his mother's eye. He hesitated.

"Fukumatsu! Leave the boy alone! Now!" The tone of her voice was stern and full of warning. Her seven-year-old son slowly lowered his fist, standing up over the blubbering boy as he did. For a moment it seemed as if he was considering giving his victim one last kick; but he changed his mind when he saw his mother's expression, whereupon he deftly lifted his foot over his victim's flabby stomach.

"Help him up," Matsu Tagawa told her son. Fukumatsu obeyed, extending his arm to the boy on the grass, who was by now sobbing pathetically.

He had to put all his weight behind him to lift Yoshi to his feet. Yoshi was almost a head taller than her son, and almost twice in girth, yet Matsu knew that if her maid Junko had not alerted her in time the damage would have been far worse than the nosebleed the boy now nursed.

"Apologize to Yoshi-*san*," she commanded, her eyes cold, even though she did not like the boy, just as she did not like his malicious, gossiping mother.

"No." Fukumatsu looked at the ground as he pursed his lips in grim determination.

"Tagawa-*san*! Fukumatsu attacked me for no reason at all!" the taller boy wailed as he wiped the blood off his face with his sleeve. He grew pale at the sight of the red stains.

"Yoshi-*san*, I must apologize for my son's behavior if he will not. Now please leave us," she said firmly.

"But –"

"Leave us, Yoshi-*san*. Go home."

The boy hesitated for a moment. Then he saw the look on Matsu's face. He threw a sly, sideward glance at Fukumatsu, a nasty smile playing at the corner of his lips. Undoubtedly he thought that Fukumatsu was in for it, and made off quickly, satisfied. Once he was out of sight they heard him wailing once more to draw as much attention to himself as he could. Matsu winced. She could just imagine the fuss his mother and maids would make over him, and knew she would eventually have to face them.

She turned to her son. "Why?" she asked. It was the third time in a month that Fukumatsu had gotten into a fight, she just couldn't understand it. He didn't answer but simply continued to stare at the ground in front of him.

"If you cannot even explain why you are behaving in this manner, then I have failed you as your mother." She sighed. "And you are doing your father's name a great injustice." The truth was that the boy's Chinese father had not shown his face for almost five years, and even in those days the visits had been brief. She had practically raised the boy on her own. Her words had the desired effect: the mention that he might bring shame on his parentage always did.

He lifted his head and looked her straight into the eye. "He was saying bad things about Zaemon-*chan*. And about you, Mother," he whispered as he looked down at the face of his sleeping baby brother.

Matsu swallowed. Of course. Her son was now seven years old, and of an age that he would hear things. Things about his father and his baby brother, Shichi-Zaemon – but most of all about her. She should have known better than to try to protect him from the malicious gossip that was bound to escape people's lips. Especially from the mother of that little shit, Yoshi.

"What...." She found it difficult to ask the next question. "What bad things did he say?"

Fukumatsu looked around him to make sure no one could hear him, and then looked her in the eye. "That Zaemon is a bastard and the son of a whore."

Matsu gasped and closed her eyes, a familiar pain squeezing her heart. As she opened her eyes they were filled with tears. Tenderly she began to stroke her infant's cheek as if to gain strength from his innocence. Then she looked at Fukumatsu, who was shocked to see her grief.

"Do you understand those words?" she asked softly.

"Yes," Fukumatsu said, now shamed. "Yoshi-*san* told me what they mean." He spat on the ground, and Matsu almost jumped at his vehemence.

"He called you a whore!" His mother winced at the word. He fought to control the tears of anger and frustration that threatened to flood his eyes. Matsu put her hand gently on his shoulder and kneeled down so that she could face him.

"Do not believe everything people say," she said. Her son looked up at her, not understanding.

"There are many things that you do not know. Things that I thought you would be too young to understand. I was wrong. I should have told you."

Fukumatsu made as if to walk off, his head hanging down, afraid of what he might hear. His mother expertly placed her sleeping baby in the crook of her arm and took hold of her son's arm, willing him to look at her.

"You know that Zaemon is your half-brother," she began. "I am mother to you both, but your father is not his father."

Fukumatsu nodded. She took his hand and sighed. Though he might be too young to understand the implications of her words, he had always known that Watanabe-*san* was not his real father. She had told him long ago who his real father was.

"In our society, when a woman has children by more than one man, no matter what the circumstances, people tend to talk. They say bad things about her, especially if the woman marries someone who is not Japanese."

"My real father is Chinese, right?"

"Yes, your father is Chinese. He is a powerful and influential man in southern China, which means he is an important man to the merchants here in Hirado and Nagasaki. I married your father in secret after I met him through Lord Li Dan. He was your father's mentor and employer. Lord Li Dan had made a promise once to look after your father's interests. Yet there was more. Your father...." She searched for the right words, not knowing quite how to explain. "I believe your father truly had feelings for me. But he had to return to China. His family is very powerful, Fukumatsu-*chan*. From what I hear, I don't think they even know I exist. We were both very young when I had you. But things happened, things that have kept him away from me. He has not been here for so many years...." She lowered her eyes sadly as her memory trailed back in time.

Zheng Zhilong had not even been her first husband, but her son didn't know that. She had been married off at the tender age of fifteen to a young Japanese officer of junior rank. The youth had been killed in combat within months of the marriage, hardly given the chance to consummate it, leaving Matsu widowed at barely sixteen. When she first met Zheng Zhilong at one of Lord Li Dan's official functions, she had been smitten at the sight of him. She had actually been one year his senior, but Zhilong was quite mature for his age. And so very handsome! Their romance and the quiet, very private wedding ceremony that had followed seemed a lifetime ago.

"When your father returned to China, he sent funds for our upkeep; but for some reason the money stopped coming. Things became difficult. You would be too young to remember, yet there was a time when I had to turn to my family for money and food." She fell silent at the memory, lost in thought. Her son stared at her in confusion, and she wondered if he was able to absorb what she said.

"I was very lonely, Fukumatsu-*chan*, and still young. Watanabe-*san* is a good person. He was willing to take care of us. I accepted gladly. He is Zaemon-*san*'s father – that you know. We are lucky. It is because of him that we are not poor. He takes care of us. Can you understand that?"

The boy nodded. "Where is my father now?"

"In Fujian, in southern China. People say he has become quite wealthy from trade. From what I understand he also has a great deal of influence as a mandarin these days. I also know that your father has at least one other wife there, and you probably have more half-brothers and sisters there too."

The boy's brow knotted in a frown as he tried to imagine his Chinese half-siblings.

"Why? If he wants to be with you, then why does he marry someone else?"

"It's just the way things are. Men are like that. Especially if they are away from a woman for a long period of time. They, too, have to obey their parents' wishes. They probably arranged for him to marry the daughter of an important man. I waited for your father for many years. But I believe he has forgotten us." She sighed while Fukumatsu pressed his lips together in a gesture of disappointment. She lifted a hand and stroked his cheek. "However, I do know that you are his oldest son, his firstborn and heir."

Fukumatsu stared ahead in silence, a perplexed look on his face. Matsu wondered if her last words had gotten through to him. More likely than not this information would be too much for him to take in.

"Funny," he said, tilting his head slightly as he pondered her words. "Zaemon has always seemed like a whole brother to me. Just like a normal brother."

His choice of words made Matsu smile. Gracefully she straightened herself. "He is your normal brother. He is your brother, no matter what anybody says. Like I said, some people will always talk badly if a woman has children by more than one man. Do not listen to them. These people don't know the truth. Yoshi doesn't know the whole truth, nor does his mother. Do you understand?" Fukumatsu nodded wordlessly. They both looked again at Zaemon, innocent and still asleep in his mother's arms.

"Right. Now you are coming with me and you will apologize to Nagata-*san*. And to his mother, for causing this inconvenience."

Fukumatsu had almost forgotten about the fight. He was about to protest when he looked up to see a mischievous glint in his mother's eye. It puzzled him, but he closed his mouth and obeyed, falling in step beside her.

By the time they reached the wealthy merchant's imposing residence, the whole Sato household knew of the beating their master's oldest son had received at the hands of the half-Chinese boy. The spoiled brat had probably wailed so loudly about what had befallen him that none could have remained unaware, even if they had wanted to.

Matsu knocked on the door, which stood half ajar. A stern, middle-aged housekeeper was standing in the doorway, as if expecting them.

"*Konnichiwa*. Good afternoon, Yuki-*san*." Matsu bowed slightly toward the older woman, who bowed back respectfully, flashing a false smile that exposed a terrible set of teeth. Matsu knew that the respect with which the woman greeted her was because of her foreign husband. She might have married a *gaijin*, a Chinese, but she had married one with influence. Apart from that, everyone knew that her father – even though of *ashigaru*, lower samurai rank – had been employed by the great shogun in his personal army. And that, too, was something worthy of respect.

"Excuse me, Yuki-*san*," Matsu said. "We would very much like to see the lady of the house and Yoshi-*san*, please." The woman nodded with a grunt, walked across the room and slid open the rice-papered door. Fukumatsu and his mother waited patiently as they heard a woman's sharp response and Yoshi's typical, nasal whine. The door slid open again and the housekeeper emerged, followed by a severe-looking woman in a richly embroidered silk kimono, her fat son trailing behind.

Fukumatsu glanced at Yoshi, who had taken up a safe position behind his mother, his bulky body partly obscured. Matsu didn't like Mrs. Sato. She was the type of woman who always made sure everyone around her was constantly reminded of how important her husband was.

Matsu and Fukumatsu both bowed respectfully. "My son has something to say to you," she said, subtly prompting Fukumatsu with her elbow. The boy stepped forward hesitantly.

"Mrs. Sato, I am sorry I beat your son. It will not happen again. It's just that —" He would have said more, but his mother threw him a warning glance.

Matsu took his arm as if to leave, then she suddenly turned around as if she just remembered something. She looked at the haughty woman with an innocent expression.

"Oh! I nearly forget. I would also like to take this opportunity to thank your son for teaching Fukumatsu some fascinating facts of life, and some very interesting additions to his vocabulary," she said sweetly, gently patting her baby's back. "Thank you so much." She inclined her head politely to emphasize her words.

Her ego tickled, Mrs. Sato smiled crookedly for the first time, unaware of what was to come.

"Oh? And what words might those be?" she asked.

"'Bastard' and 'whore.' Good day." Matsu inclined her head respectfully and saw how the woman's jaw dropped, her face flushing crimson. Pleased with herself, Matsu turned and walked away, Fukumatsu following behind her. They soon heard a sharp slapping sound, followed by a howl of pain from Yoshi. They quickly walked on, both biting their lip to stop themselves from grinning.

"Do you think Father will come?" Fukumatsu asked his mother as the tailor fussed over him to make sure the hems of the kimono were not too long. The boy was half-dancing, hopping from one foot to the other. Matsu grabbed hold of him to keep still, the tailor's tsk-tsks of exasperation growing ever louder. The sleeves of the boy's new kimono were far too long and flapped like a bird's wings. It was obvious that his arms were tiring from holding them up for so long.

Matsu did not answer. Her Chinese husband had not shown his face in Nagasaki in many years, and she heard from him only sporadically. When he did send letters, it was mostly to inquire after his son, and whatever was directed at her was businesslike and curt.

She hoped for her son's sake that her husband had not forgotten the importance of their child's seventh birthday. In these times of plague, disease, and other misfortune, a boy turning seven was a good reason to celebrate.

"Mother?" her oldest son pressed as she didn't answer. "Will he come?"

She could not lie to him. Not anymore. "He has not written that he will. I have not heard from him. We shall have to wait and see." Matsu pressed her lips together. She very much doubted that Zhilong would come. She could only hope that he would at least remember his son's special birthday with a gift.

Disappointed, Fukumatsu dropped his arms down his side, only for them to be pushed up again by the increasingly irritated tailor. The boy sighed and stared at the screen opposite. Matsu felt sorry for him. He had not seen his father for such a long time that she wondered if her son would even recognize him if he bumped into him on the street.

"Is my father a pirate?" he asked suddenly, bored with having to stand still. The tailor, only too aware of the identity of the boy's father, nearly swallowed the pins that were sticking from between his lips.

Matsu smiled in spite of herself. "No," she said. "In China, your father is a mandarin, an important official, as you well know. And he is a merchant." Then she cocked her head to one side and regarded him seriously. "Although it might depend on your point of view. Some might consider him a pirate."

"Really? Who?" Fukumatsu asked, fascinated.

"Gaijin. Foreigners. The Portuguese and the Dutch. They regularly attack his merchant ships and steal his goods in their war for wealth. However, when he attacks their ships to get his goods back, they are angered and call him a pirate."

"So the Dutch and Portuguese are also pirates, then?"

"They would never think of themselves in that way. They would say they do it for their king and country. But, yes, they do act like pirates sometimes."

Fukumatsu was silent again as the tailor finished pinning his garment. Matsu assumed that his head was filled with images of angry-faced pirates with large noses and long hair the color of straw. He had seen the Dutch often enough in the harbor of Nagasaki; he even played with their children.

Noticing her son's increased restlessness, Matsu hoped that the tailor would be able to finish pinning the kimono in one sitting. Finally, the old man was done. He straightened up and nodded, satisfied. Fukumatsu sat down gratefully and took the cross-legged position of grown men. Zaemon squealed on the tatami next to his mother, moving his tiny hands in an agitated way. Matsu inched her knees forward to pick him up, bundling the infant deftly onto her back.

At the tailor's insistence she paid a small advance for his work. Fukumatsu had already run out, impatient to release his pent-up energy.

"I hope he comes," Fukumatsu said as they walked out of the tailor's shop, more to himself than to anyone else. Matsu said nothing. She hoped Zhilong would never come — for more reasons than one.

As they walked down the hill together toward the harbor she saw a ship moored that she didn't recognize. She could not discern its origin, but a crowd had gathered on the market square alongside the harbor. The locals milled around several stalls that had been erected, examining the goods with interest. One of the stalls displayed the characters that indicated the services of a fortune-teller.

"Mother, look!" Fukumatsu shouted, excited. He, too, had seen the stall. "A fortune-teller!" He ran down ahead of her, toward the harbor. "Perhaps he can tell us whether or not Father is coming," he yelled over his shoulder.

Even before she could answer him, he had reached the market stalls. She sighed, smiling. Fortune-tellers had always held an attraction for him. She seldom gave in to his pleas: most of these people were cheats, and the fees that they asked for their services were often ridiculously high. Only when Fukumatsu was born had she relented under social pressure to have his numbers read, based on his date of birth. The woman who had read his numbers had told her that he was meant for great things and that her son would one day provide her with grandsons. But these were happy tidings that every young mother wanted to hear, and something they gladly paid for.

"Mother! Come!" Fukumatsu stood waiting for her, impatient. The crowd had diminished, more than likely discouraged by the fee it would cost them to have their fortunes told.

Under the canopy sat a bald old man with tattooed eyebrows and a forehead that was remarkably free of any wrinkles. Only the crow's feet around his eyes betrayed his advanced age. His head was free of any form of hair, save for the small white goatee beard that bobbed up and down as he chewed on something that stained his teeth a dark red. When he spotted Fukumatsu, his jaws fell still. With eyes black as obsidian he fixed his stare upon him, his expression curious.

"Mother, may I? Please?"

Matsu hesitated. She did not believe for one second that this old man could possibly tell him whether his father would come to visit him or not. But when she thought of the length of time the boy had needed to keep still at the tailor's, she relented. It wouldn't do any harm, after all. From personal experience she knew that people like this were always deliberately vague in what they said, telling you only that which you wanted to hear.

"All right then," she said, and nodded her consent.

The old man grinned, displaying a frightening array of discolored, rotting teeth, and resumed his chewing. Matsu could tell that he was not from around here. More likely he came from the northern part of Japan, or maybe he was a foreigner.

He beckoned toward Fukumatsu and pointed to his hand. The boy glanced at her, hesitant.

"Go on then, show him your hand," she encouraged him.

Fukumatsu held out his hand, whereupon the man grabbed it and pulled him closer. He stared into the boy's eyes and brought Fukumatsu's other hand to his face, carefully feeling the contours of his cheekbones, jaw, and temples. He squinted his eyes in concentration, as if trying to determine the symmetry of Fukumatsu's face.

"When he born?" he asked in an odd accent, gesturing in Matsu's direction. She gave him the details and told him that his place of birth was Hirado Island.

"Ah so," he said. "A rat. You smart. Opportunistic. And a charmer." He grinned lustfully, and turned his back on them to pore over a stone tray containing what looked like bone chips with inscriptions. He busied himself with the chips, moving them to and fro with a frown of concentration.

Fukumatsu was beaming with pride from the compliments he had just received, his excitement evident.

"Element is wood," the man continued. Matsu said nothing. She knew all this, having been told this at the time of his birth.

"From wood come fire, but need more to get fire. Cannot do alone. Rat, wood, rat, wood. Hmm. Is good. You have talent, you know what people think. You very good convincing others. This will bring you great success, great success. You be great leader one day." Once again he took Fukumatsu's hand and squeezed it, never taking his eyes off the boy's face. "I feel ambition, big confidence and … forcefulness. Yes! Forcefulness." He made a fist to emphasize the word. Then he closed his eyes. "You will strive high morality, all your life, is good, is good!"

He then pulled the boy toward him, picked up a needle and, without warning, pricked it into Fukumatsu's forefinger. He caught a few drops of blood on a small tin saucer. Fukumatsu looked at the scarlet drops, unmoved, but Matsu stepped closer, somewhat disconcerted at this unusual turn of events. She had never seen any fortune-teller do this before.

The man spat onto the saucer, pressed Fukumatsu's hand palm over the mixture of saliva and blood and massaged it into his palm. Then he lifted the boy's palm and brought it so close to his face that for a moment Matsu thought he was going to lick it. But all he did was look.

He grinned. "Many women," he said lasciviously, peering into her son's face with glee. "But price. You will pay price for this." His face creased in distaste, as if something disgusted him utterly.

Fukumatsu blinked, confused. It was obvious that he had no idea what to make of this information. "I only want to know if my father will come to Hirado for my seventh birthday."

The man's jaws stopped chewing. "Father?" Once again he peered at the boy's blood-smeared palm, which he was still holding in his veined hands. "No. I no see father. Your yin, your aura too strong, too powerful. I think…." He shook his head uncertainly. "No. But you will make a journey, soon. Across sea, faraway place. New life."

Matsu froze at the sound of those words. Dizziness took a hold of her as the blood drained from her head. She did not want to hear this. She suddenly felt a powerful urge to grab her son by the collar and drag him away, yet she could not.

"You want very much, can do very much. Big ambition!" The man continued, his tone excited.

"You be careful! Must not want too much. You must learn see truth." He squinted his eyes again. "I see island. Big island. Not here, far away, foreign place."

"Island?" Fukumatsu asked, his interest piqued. "What island, where, to which country does it belong?"

The old man frowned, rubbing his fingers into the boy's palm once more, holding it close to his eyes for further inspection. He looked up, a surprised look on his face. "Know not," he said with obvious annoyance at not knowing the answer. "I don't see. Is unclear. I see strangers, *gaijin*? Yes, foreigners. They not belong." He drew a breath, a hissing sound as he considered this. "Not easy, is difficult situation. But your fate is on island. This island. The strangers will leave one day. Then island your destiny. But pay price. Big price." He took one last, long look at Fukumatsu's hand and finally nodded, satisfied. For the first time he looked up at Matsu and released the boy. His state of concentration was broken, his task done.

"Come, Fukumatsu-*chan*," Matsu said. She wanted desperately to leave that place, away from that awful man, away from what he had told them.

"But mother, I want to know —"

"No! We are leaving right now!" She had not expected this. Her son had asked the man a simple question but had instead been given details of a future that was still too remote, a future that she did not wish to know about, and one she liked even less. She placed a couple of coins in the man's greedily outstretched hand and walked off as fast as she could.

Just as Matsu suspected, Zheng Zhilong did not come for his son's birthday. He was not there to see how handsome his firstborn son looked in the new red kimono that had been specially made for the occasion. He did not witness the Shinto ritual of prayer to see his son clap his hands with his eyes closed in order to awaken his ancestors' spirits. Nor would he be able to shower his son with small gifts and sweets, and take pride in the fact that Fukumatsu was the image of his father.

A month later, she received a message that her brother-in-law Zheng Feng had arrived in Hirado and wanted to see her. Her heart sank. Feng often came to Nagasaki to do business on his brother's behalf, but rarely did he come to see her in person. Letters and gifts for her and Fukumatsu were usually brought to him by one of her husband's clerks or numerous couriers, as her brother- in-law was normally too busy to come himself. That he intended to see her could only mean one thing.

Matsu finished feeding Zaemon and bundled the by now sleeping infant before placing him behind the screen, out of sight on the tatami, and readied herself for the visit. Fukumatsu was having his martial arts lessons, something in which he excelled. He would not be back for more than an hour, giving her time to discuss whatever Feng wanted in private. Feng was five years older than her husband and although he had a good head for business, he was far less ambitious and not quite as charismatic as Zhilong. Having met him only infrequently she did not know him well enough to feel comfortable with him. At least his Japanese was reasonable. As Matsu sat in the simple but elegant room where she received her guests, the rice-papered door slid open and her maid's head popped through.

"Tagawa-*san*, you have a guest," Junko announced. "The Chinese gentleman Zheng Feng is here and wishes to see you." Matsu got to her feet, smoothed the obi that encased her kimono around the waist, tucked a loose strand of hair behind her ear, and took a deep breath.

"Let him in," she said as she could perceive her brother-in-law's silhouette against the rice paper. She bowed to him as he entered the room, her heart racing.

"Zheng Feng-*san*. Welcome, I am honored by your visit." Junko made as if to slide the door shut, but left it slightly ajar and stayed close as instructed. Feng nodded his head curtly, probably feeling as uncomfortable as she did. Matsu hardly recognized him. He had grown a beard and moustache and had broadened in every sense of the word.

"Please sit down," she motioned to the cushions that were laid out on the tatami floor, and he settled on them with his legs crossed. Matsu slid down onto her knees, her hands tightly clasped in order to still the trembling.

"Zheng Feng-*san*, I hope you are in good health. You bring news of my husband? He is well?"

"Yes, he is well and sends his respects. He apologizes for not coming to you in person. Official business and military matters keep him very busy. Things are not well in our country, as you may know." His brow furrowed as he said the words.

Matsu nodded. Zhilong had written her of the increased unrest in China. She knew of the threat the country faced: the warmongering Manchus who had been troubling the northeast for years.

"I have brought letters…." From his outer garment he retrieved a thick envelope of silk and handed it to her. She took the parcel from him and laid it in front of her. She had no intention of reading the letters while under the scrutiny of her brother-in-law.

"With due respect, Zheng Feng-*san*, your couriers could have brought these to me. Why have you come to see me in person?"

Feng blinked at the unaccustomed directness coming from a woman. He pursed his lips and motioned to the envelope that lay between them.

"Read the letters," he said. "They will explain."

Reluctantly, Matsu picked up the parcel and took out several letters. There was one for her and one for Fukumatsu. She glanced at her brother-in-law before giving the letter her full attention, not at all happy to have the man's eyes on her while she read. It was written in simple, halting Japanese, probably translated by one of her husband's people. The message, however, was clear. And so was the reason Feng had come to Nagasaki.

Matsu's hands shook as she lifted her gaze to her brother-in-law.

"You have come to take Fukumatsu." She could not stop her lips from trembling. She had no need for a fortune-teller. This was exactly what she had feared all those years. In her heart, she had always known that this day would come, but she had pushed it away to the back of her mind. The fortune-teller's words were still ringing in her ears. 'You will make journey, soon. Across sea, faraway place. New life.' This was the price she had to pay for bearing a son to a foreigner, especially a powerful man like Zheng Zhilong.

Feng nodded. "Yes. And yourself, if you should wish."

Matsu's heart skipped a beat. For years she had waited for this moment, longed for it. Now it was too late. She had not written to her Chinese husband about Watanabe, the other man in her life, let alone that she had given birth to a child that was not his. Zhilong would never allow her to bring her other child, her baby son borne to another man. Yet she knew she would be unable to leave Zaemon. Her stomach churned at she thought of the choices she would have to make.

"But ... what about the travel restrictions? The shogun has decreed...."

"Your son has been given permission to travel. All the necessary documents have been issued. You forget your husband is a man not without influence. He is Chinese, so these restrictions do not apply to him ... or his oldest son. I am to accompany him on the journey. The boy is to be educated in China. Those are his father's wishes."

Matsu struggled for breath as her stomach flipped inside of her. She took a deep breath and lifted her head to look Zheng Fen in the eye.

"I ... I need some time to think this over," she said.

"I'm afraid you don't have a choice," Feng said, not unsympathetically. "The boy is his firstborn son, and my brother wishes for him to come to China. He expects you to come along. Surely your place is with your husband and oldest son?"

Matsu sighed. "You forget that Japanese women are restricted from travelling outside the country. I fear I will not be able to join him."

"I think we will be able to arrange something. There is the possibility –"

A loud gurgling sound from behind the screen interrupted him. Feng looked at Matsu, startled, but she dropped her eyes to her lap in shame and could not look him in the eye. Without a word, she got up and picked up a bundle from behind the screen. Then she sat down again opposite him. Feng stared at the child in her arms and looked back at Matsu, bewildered. Matsu met his gaze head-on.

"What about my other son? What about Fukumatsu's half-brother?" she asked softly as she offered her little finger to her baby, who encircled it gratefully with its tiny hand. Feng was still staring at the child in her arms, then he looked back at her, completely at a loss. He knew this could not be his brother's child. Zhilong had not been back to Japan for years.

"This is rather unexpected," he managed to blurt out.

"You must know I have not seen your brother – my husband – for many years. His letters have come sporadically, the funds for our upkeep stopped coming a long time ago. Things have been difficult. I ask of you not to judge me too harshly."

Feng recovered quickly, and looked her in the eye with an expression of compassion. "I do not judge you. But you cannot take the child with you. My brother would never allow it. I could not allow it."

"Then I have no choice but to stay here," Matsu said, the tears filling her eyes. "Do you really have to take Fukumatsu away from me?" she asked, knowing the answer. Feng nodded. They both knew that his brother would be mortified to hear that his Japanese wife had a child by another man. She could no longer join him now, even if she were granted permission to leave the country.

"Wh ... when will Fukumatsu be leaving?" She wiped away the tears that threatened to roll down her face.

"In a week. I must ask of you to prepare him for departure. How is his Chinese?"

Matsu regained her composure somewhat, glad to be able to speak of practical matters.

"He has been tutored in the Chinese language since he was four years old. He speaks, reads, and writes your language quite well, I can assure you."

"That is good, that is good," Feng said, satisfied. The boy's father had hand-picked his son's Chinese tutor himself, determined that he should learn to speak the language properly.

"Where is the boy? Please summon him, I wish to speak to him."

Matsu looked at him, horrified. If anyone was going to tell her son that he was to leave her and the country of his birth, it was to be her, and not this man, who was no more than a stranger to the boy.

"Please, Zheng Feng-*san*, I do not wish to offend, but I respectfully ask of you that you allow me to tell him the news. I am his mother, after all."

Her brother-in-law sniffed with displeasure, unaccustomed to being opposed by a woman. He regarded Matsu for a moment.

"Very well. I will not speak to him of the matter and leave this to you. But I do wish to see him now. Summon him."

Matsu welcomed the chance to get to her feet, relieved to be able to escape the Chinese man's presence. Her throat felt dry, constricted. She slid open the door. "Junko-*san*," she managed to say, her voice hoarse with emotion.

Junko edged forward on her knees, her face as white as a sheet, her eyes big as saucers. Matsu knew that she had been listening in on the conversation. Junko did not have to look at her to know how she was feeling. She handed the baby to her maid and instructed her to fetch Fukumatsu.

"Tell him his uncle wishes to see him."

"*Hai, oksan*," the girl said, shaken, before she disappeared.

Before long, Fukumatsu spilled into the room in his martial arts gear, unable to contain himself at the news that his uncle, his father's brother, was waiting to see him. His *sensei* followed right behind him, admonishing the boy for his boisterous behavior, intrigued to find out why his charge had been summoned so suddenly.

Feng turned at the commotion caused by the boy's arrival.

"Uncle Feng!" Fukumatsu bowed down low. His mother looked on with pride and love as her brother-in-law regarded the boy with amusement.

"Fukumatsu. You have grown. You look like your father," Feng said in Japanese. The boy beamed at what he thought was a great compliment, eager for his uncle's approval. Feng gave him a brief smile and reached out to ruffle the boy's head.

"We are honored and happy to see you, uncle." Fukumatsu articulated carefully in Chinese. His tutor, who was still hovering in the doorway, prodded him in the back, urging Fukumatsu to speak some more, but Feng overruled him with a wave of his hand.

"Please! Leave us." The balding little man apologized for his presence and withdrew, bowing repeatedly as he did. They could hear Junko criticize him loudly through the thin rice paper for his lack of manners.

Feng turned to the boy. "Your Chinese is not bad, Fukumatsu. Your pronunciation is excellent."

Fukumatsu grinned to display the gaps where his milk teeth had once been.

"Your father sends you these gifts," Feng said, handing the boy two parcels wrapped in green silk. "There is also a letter for you from your father, Fukumatsu, you may read it later." The smile of pride on Matsu's face disappeared at the thought of its probable contents. She would have to tell her son that they were to part. The thought made her heart contract with pain.

The moment Feng had gone, Fukumatsu scrambled to open his father's letter. His mother snatched it from his hands and snapped at him sharply. He looked at her, startled. He could not understand what could be more important than his father's letter. His mother took a deep breath and dropped down so they were at eye level and took his hands in her own, something she always did whenever she had something important to say to him.

"Fukumatsu." She cleared her throat. "There is something I have to tell you. Something that involves you." She paused as she tried to find the right words. "Your uncle has come to Nagasaki to take you to your father's family home in China."

The boy's eyes grew wide. "I get to go to China? To see my father?" Matsu nodded, not trusting herself to speak as she watched her son's face shine with excitement.

"Yes. But there is more. Now that you are seven years old, your father wishes for you to be educated properly. You are old enough now, and China is the land of your father's ancestors. And yours." Matsu waited for the information to sink in. She dropped her eyes, looking sad. It did not go unnoticed on the boy.

When the truth dawned on him, his face crumpled. "You mean I won't come back here?" His voice was incredulous. Matsu swallowed as she fought the tears that welled in her eyes.

"No, Fukumatsu-*chan*. I don't believe you will," she murmured. "To visit, perhaps, but no more. Your home is in China now."

Fukumatsu looked at her, unable to believe what his mother had just said. He was born in Hirado. He had never even travelled outside of Nagasaki. Now he was to leave his country to join a family he did not know.

He stared at her in wonder. "Mother, this is just like the fortune-teller said. That I would make a journey. Overseas. To another country, to start a new life."

"Yes" was all she could say.

"Will you be coming with me?" he asked, his voice a higher pitch than usual. Matsu slowly shook her head, the tears streaming down her cheeks. The boy stared at her in shocked disbelief. "Is Zaemon-*chan*?" he asked, his voice now high-pitched with emotion.

Matsu shook her head. She picked up the letter that had his name on it and handed it to him.

"Read the letter from your father."

Fukumatsu took it from her hands and looked at it with an odd expression on his face, and then, with an angry gesture, threw the letter across the room. "I'm not going," he said, twisting out of her embrace, stepping back to create a distance between himself and his mother.

"Fukumatsu...."

"I'm not going!" he shouted. "I'm not leaving here without you and Zaemon-*chan*."

"Your father –"

"I don't even know my father. Or any of my Chinese family. I'm not going!" And with that, he ran from the room and out of the house, avoiding Junko and the cook, both of whom had been listening in on their conversation.

Matsu dropped to her knees despondently and sat still, staring ahead, her eyes unfocused. No longer able to master her emotions, she wailed in anguish, covering her face in her hands and cried. For herself, but most of all, for her firstborn son.

2
Fatherland

QUANZHOU, FUJIAN PROVINCE, CHINA

IN spite of his exhaustion, Fukumatsu rode his horse straight-backed, relieved and happy to be on solid ground again after spending weeks at sea. He had arrived in China at last, the land of his father. He felt at ease on horseback. Riding rejuvenated his spirits, even though he was nervous of what was to come.

Uncle Feng dropped back, allowing two of the armed guards to pass by so that he could ride next to Fukumatsu. They had a fair-sized armed escort: the captain thought it necessary to bring the boy in safely. The captain had also insisted that Fukumatsu change into more subdued clothing than the bright-blue tunic he had donned that morning to make a good impression on his Chinese family. According to his uncle, the hills of Fujian were crawling with bandits, and the richly colored cloth would be too conspicuous and attract unwelcome attention. He did not want to take any risks.

With the exception of politely answering any questions his uncle or the captain asked him, Fukumatsu spoke little, his face growing more solemn as they neared their destination. After a while his uncle left him with his thoughts.

It was less than a month since he had shouted at his mother that he wasn't going to China without her or his brother. He had run away, disappearing for two hours. Junko had offered to look for him, but his mother said that he was best left alone and that he would return when he was ready. She was right, of course, as she always was. He had returned, worn and tired, his eyes red from crying, but resigned to the fact that he had to do what his father expected of him. His mother had instilled in him a strong sense of duty, and he knew, in spite of his youth, that this was the path he had to take. His father was waiting for him: his leaving Japan was predestined, just as the fortune-teller had told him.

As he took in the stunning views around him he thought about his father. He had not seen him since he was a toddler and scarcely remembered him: Zhilong's visits to Fukumatsu's Japanese birthplace Hirado in Nagasaki were infrequent and never long, hardly giving the boy a chance to imprint his father in his memory, let alone forge a bond.

Fukumatsu's arrival in Anhai had been expected for some time. The typhoon season had begun earlier than usual, delaying the ship's departure from Nagasaki more than once and, even between storms, the seas had been violent, causing many of the passengers to be ill. What made the voyage even harder was the fact that he missed his mother and half-brother. His mother had made an admirable effort not to show her emotions at his departure, but he knew that her heart was breaking, as was his. His baby brother had squealed at him happily, oblivious of the torment his mother and brother felt at his forced departure. His mother had vowed to him that she would not rest until she could get permission to travel and come to China, and she made him promise to write to her every month. He had told her he would write to her that very same night.

He turned in his saddle to look at his uncle, his face an expression of awe as he took in the spectacular view from the mountain pass.

"It's beautiful here," he whispered. His uncle nodded his head in encouragement, pleased that his nephew was able to appreciate the physical beauty of his ancestral land.

During the sea voyage, which took more than two weeks, his uncle had often grilled him on the names of his father's family members, a family that was as yet unknown to him.

Although Fukumatsu knew from his mother and Chinese tutors that his father was an influential, powerful man in southern China, the size of the armed escort that had awaited them in Fujian still impressed him. He also knew that his father had a Chinese wife. His mother had mentioned that it was even possible that he had concubines. These thoughts had kept him preoccupied during the trip, especially during the last couple of days.

As their journey had progressed, the reasons he had to leave his mother and the country of his birth gradually dawned on him. He had been told that, as the oldest son, he was expected to join his father's household, to have a "proper Chinese education" as his father had written him in his letter. His Chinese was more than passable, but he believed it to be still lacking. He had also picked up a smattering of Dutch and Portuguese from the traders' children that frequented the ports, languages which, his mother informed him, his father spoke well. His mother had told him it was these very language skills that had made his father invaluable to the Dutch traders as an interpreter for the VOC, the Dutch East India Company. He wondered if he would be able to live up to his father's expectations.

They descended from the hillside only to have to climb again. On the crest of the next hill, the front guard stopped for the others to catch up. Fukumatsu had already noticed the increase in settlement, the traffic of carts drawn by horses and donkeys passing them on both sides. After repeatedly asking the captain how much longer they would have to travel, he was informed rather gruffly that they would arrive at Anhai within the hour. Fukumatsu spurred his horse onward, impatient to see what lay ahead, only to find the horse was as eager as he was to return to its home. He had to lean well back into his saddle to temper the animal's enthusiasm.

Fatigue was so beginning to overcome him that for a brief moment he dozed off in his saddle. The sound of raised voices woke him. He looked around him and brought his horse to a halt. Staring down, he knew that the sprawling compound in the valley beneath them was his father's ancestral home. He could not help but feel an almost religious sense of awe.

Shouts filled the air once members of the household had spotted them on the hillside. Fukumatsu sat up straight in his saddle, his heart thumping. The time had come to meet his Chinese family. He looked at his uncle for reassurance, his heart racing. Feng nodded at him encouragingly and pulled up alongside his horse, discreetly reaching out to squeeze the boy's shoulder. Embarrassed by this uncharacteristic show of affection, Feng jarred his horse with a harsh cry and galloped ahead down the hill.

A swarm of men and women emerged from the gate to greet them, bantering with the guards good-naturedly. While Feng dismounted, one man reached out to help Fukumatsu off his horse. Too proud to accept the help offered him, he lowered himself off his horse with ease.

It was a chaotic reception. There was raucous laughter all around him, tinged with relief that the men had returned unharmed. Orders were barked. And then he suddenly found himself surrounded by unfamiliar, curious staring faces.

Feeling self-conscious, he smoothed his garments as several servants rushed forward to receive him with titters of excitement. The women giggled and cackled with pleasure as they led him toward the residence. They fussed over him loudly in the harsh, guttural dialect of the province, spoken at a speed that made it difficult to understand. For one confusing moment there was a vacuum of authority, and he felt somewhat overwhelmed. No one seemed to take charge, until a stout, round-faced woman walked up to him with purpose from across the large courtyard. The talk and laughter ceased almost at once.

"Welcome, welcome!" the woman called out to him, the words articulated with exaggeration. Fukumatsu looked at her dubiously as she bore down on him, and he glanced around him to find his uncle. But Feng stood on the other side of the courtyard, in conversation with several of the men who had greeted them at the gate. With some hesitation, he bowed his head toward her. There was a sly, amused look on her flat, round face before she inclined her body with equal measure. Fukumatsu took an instant dislike to her.

"You must be young Master Zheng!" she exclaimed, her face upturned in order to observe her new charge as she bowed. "We have been awaiting your arrival for a long time. We are grateful to see that you are safe. I hope you and your uncle have had a good journey and that you are in good health?" The words, spoken in the local Fujian dialect showed the necessary respect, but her tone implied a certain underlying arrogance that Fukumatsu could sense rather than hear. For the first time in his life, he was grateful for the Chinese lessons that had been forced upon him since he was four. Now he understood why his mother had insisted on the language classes. She had done so to prepare him for this day.

"My journey went quite well, and my health is good, thank you," he said, wondering who she was.

"My name is Liu," the woman said. "I am your father's housekeeper. I will show you to your quarters and see to it that your things are brought to you." She turned briskly, walking ahead as Fukumatsu followed the woman, trailed by two servants carrying his possessions.

Passing through several gates in silence, he took in the surroundings. The compound was a sprawling complex, the gardens boasting full-grown trees, some of them entangled with the thick, latticed walls, a sign that they had been there for at least a century. As he passed through a third gate, he found the vegetation to be younger, the paint on the walls less weathered, which suggested that this was a later addition to the house.

At a freshly painted door near a low building, Liu stopped and turned to them.

"These are your quarters. I will show you your rooms." She waited by the door as Fukumatsu stepped inside, not knowing what to expect.

The quarters, comprising three separate rooms plus a servant's room, were not luxurious but more than comfortably furnished with all the necessities, including handsome screens, low beds, and a low dining table. There was one room to sleep in, another for dining and receiving guests, and a third for study and work.

"Your father is away," Liu informed him, speaking slowly to make sure he understood. "He is travelling and is expected to return within the next few days. However, your grandmother wishes to meet you in about an hour. In the meantime the servants will arrange for you to bathe. I'm sure you will wish to refresh yourself." She wrinkled her nose as if to hint at the necessity of the bath.

"Could ... could I have something to eat, please?" Fukumatsu's hunger overcame his shyness. He had had nothing to eat since an early breakfast that morning, and it was way past noon. Liu clucked her tongue, reprimanding herself for the oversight.

"Of course! How thoughtless of me. I will have something brought to you straight away."

"Thank you, Liu *taitai*," he said. Liu, pleased with the respect that he showed her, looked at him and for the first time they met, smiled at him, if stiffly. Then she left. For a moment he just stood there, lost, as two female servants set about unpacking his trunks. The girls worked efficiently laying out his clothing in neat piles.

When they were gone, Fukumatsu ran into the next room, surveyed it and ran to the next, where he climbed onto one of the chairs shaped like a horse-shoe. He swung his legs to and fro, enjoying the unfamiliar sensation of being seated on furniture instead of squatting on the tatami mats as he was used to. Back in Japan, Watanabe-*san* had a pair of Chinese chairs just like these, in the room where he occasionally received his foreign guests. That room had always been out of bounds to him. The memory of his mother and Zaemon came flooding back, and his exuberance faded. He wished desperately that they could be with him now. His legs no longer swung but hung motionless, just inches above the ground. He was terrified of meeting his grandmother in this unfamiliar place. Would he please her? Would his Chinese be up to it?

As he sat on the chair, taking in the details of the room, he suddenly spoke. "Mother?" he called aloud into the empty room as if she were there. "What do you think my grandmother will be like? Do you think she will be very strict? I think Housekeeper Liu is strict, don't you?" The empty silence slowly filled with the last words that she had spoken to him.

"Fukumatsu," his mother had said before he had left Japan, grasping his hands in her own.

"Listen to me. From now on, you will have to listen to your father's family. Your loyalty now lies with them, and they will expect you to behave like a Zheng. I know you haven't seen much of your father the past few years, but he is a good man, and powerful. Your future is there, in China. That is your country now. You listen well to your elders and they will reward you for it."

The door opened with a creaking sound. Startled from his trance, he jumped down as a servant entered with a tray of food. He waited until he was alone once more, pouncing on the dishes laid out for him and savoring the unfamiliar taste of the flavorsome items in his mouth.

After the meal, which he had eaten far too quickly, the door opened once more. It was the same young male servant who had helped carry in his luggage. The boy, no more than a teenager and whose face was covered in acne, gestured to him to allow him to help him undress, leading him to a tub of warm water. Tired and grateful, Fukumatsu allowed himself to sink into the tub. The servant was all smiles, happy that he had been given the task of looking after him.

"You speak Chinese?" the youth inquired as he folded the garments and laid them on a bench. Fukumatsu looked at him with interest, glad to have the company of someone closer in age. He had been surrounded by adults throughout the entire journey.

The servant boy looked at him expectantly. Suddenly Fukumatsu realized he had been asked a question.

"Yes, I speak Chinese. But not very well," he added.

"Ah! Your pronunciation is excellent!" the youth exclaimed, grinning broadly. "My name is Hong," he said as he helped him into the bath. "It is my happy task to be able to serve you. From now on, I am your servant." His face an expression of rapt happiness, he proceeded to wipe Fukumatsu down with a cloth. Fukumatsu sat in silence, enjoying the sensation of the backrub, unsure of how to respond.

In his eagerness to help, Hong selected what he believed to be appropriate attire for his young master's first meeting with the family's matriarch. His mother had seen to it that he had a selection of Chinese-style gowns before he left Japan, and Hong now helped him into a deep-burgundy tunic embroidered with a yellow pattern at the sleeves.

He held out his arms and stared at his warped reflection in the polished bronze mirror, Hong clapping with delight. He actually looked Chinese in these clothes.

"Young Master Zheng looks very handsome," Hong said, beaming. Fukumatsu looked at him with wonder. It was the first time anyone had called him "Master Zheng," and he liked the sound of it.

Liu kept her word in that she came within the hour to fetch him. "Master Zheng? Please come with me," she announced primly as she walked in, ignoring Hong. Fukumatsu followed her obediently. They crossed two large courtyards, Hong trailing behind, bashful. Fukumatsu had to make an effort to keep up with Liu but tried not to show it. Although he might be only seven years old, he did know that Liu was trying to intimidate him, and it annoyed him. His face was all seriousness, almost scowling, suddenly aware of his roots. His mother had instilled him with a sense of pride, stemming from the fact that his grandfather had fought in the shogun's personal army. His mother was of ashigaru heritage, not full samurai perhaps, but still something to be proud of. Although the other servants might regard Liu with awe, to him she was no more than his father's housekeeper.

They were brought into a room with two high windows that let in the daylight. No one was there. The room was almost bare of furniture, save for two low wooden benches and two intricately carved chairs. The walls were painted a deep indigo blue and boasted several long scrolls yellowed with age but showing fine calligraphy, probably by the hand of some relative long dead.

"You are to wait here for Lady Zheng," Liu answered his questioning look, motioning to the low wooden benches. "She will come when it pleases her," she added with satisfaction before leaving the room. Hong lowered his eyes, somewhat embarrassed, and sat down on the ground in a far corner of the room. They waited for almost half an hour before Lady Zheng finally arrived, preceded by several female servants. Fukumatsu got to his feet the moment they walked in.

Lady Zheng was a forty-seven-year-old woman with a stocky build and slightly coarse features. Her jaw was square and broad, and she had a large forehead and a flat, snubbed nose. Crow's feet marked her shrewd eyes, and her jet-black hair was drawn tightly behind her head. She walked right up to Fukumatsu, trailed by an entourage of young women, children, and nannies. She examined him closely.

Fukumatsu assumed that others were his blood relatives, but he kept his eyes in front of him and blinked, very self-conscious of the many curious stares directed at him. Lady Zheng gestured to two of the servants, dismissing most except for one girl, who went to stand in the back.

"So you are my oldest grandson," the old woman announced with considerable volume. "You look thin. Did your mother not feed you enough?"

Fukumatsu didn't answer. His first instinct was to defend his mother, but he held his tongue, unsure whether defying this severe-looking woman would be a wise thing to do. Lady Zheng peered at him and grunted, then walked to one of the chairs that stood against the wall and sat down. She motioned to him with her hand. "*Lai, lai.* Come here, boy." He edged forward hesitantly, stopped, then edged forward again as his grandmother beckoned him to come closer still. "What do they call you in Japan?"

"Fukumatsu, Grandmother," he mumbled, his heart racing.

The woman clucked her tongue with disapproval. "That's a Japanese name. You are in China now, and you are a Chinese boy. Your Chinese surname is Zheng, and you will use the name 'Zheng Sen' from now on. Is that clear?"

"Yes. Of course, Grandmother." He had already decided it would be wise not to cross this woman. "My name is Zheng Sen," he added, this time more forcefully.

"*Hao, hao*, good, good," Lady Zheng clucked again, slapping her fan into the palm of her hand as she said the words. "Zheng Sen, Zheng Sen." She cocked her head to one side, as if a sudden thought had crossed her mind. "You are a Hakka, not Han Chinese," she said. Fukumatsu looked at her blankly. "Zheng Sen, do you know who the Hakkas are?"

"No, Grandmother," he replied, quite sure that the answer would follow.

"We Hakkas are a despised people. We have always been despised. Despised and persecuted for centuries by the Han Chinese. We did not have the same rights as Han Chinese. For centuries we could not even own our own land." She paused, draping her arms casually on the chair's armrests. She was obviously enjoying the attention from her new audience and continued her monologue. "No one really knows why. Possibly our ancestors allied with enemies of the Han at some time, and they could never forgive us. No matter now. We have integrated ourselves well, adopted Chinese ways; we even marry Han Chinese. We may have been chased down to the south, but we Hakkas have always been strong people ... and smart enough," she tapped her temple with her fan to emphasize her point, "to survive. Your father has brought this family honor and wealth by being smart, as did my husband, your grandfather. Are you smart?" she asked.

"I don't know, Grandmother. I will try to be. My teachers have taught me about the *Analects* and the teachings of Laozi. I can recite some passages, if you like?" Fukumatsu offered.

His grandmother held up her hand and cackled softly. "That won't be necessary. We will know soon enough. At least your Chinese is passable. You must have had good tutors; they have taught you well. My compliments to your mother, Matsu Tagawa, to ensure this."

He looked up, surprised and pleased at the compliment that she had given his mother, even mentioning her by name. "Thank you, Grandmother. I have always tried to do my best. Mother always insisted I learn to speak the language of my father. I also speak some Dutch; I picked that up from the Dutch children in the port of Hirado."

His grandmother snorted with contempt. "Hah! Those big-nosed people with the yellow hair." Then she looked thoughtful. "This could be useful, though. Your father speaks the language. He even worked for those foreign devils for some time. There are so many of them scavenging around our coastline these days. They sniffed at the money the Portuguese are making by trading with us, and now they are coming for their share. No matter. They provide opportunity for your father's business," she said, tapping the tip of her fan against her nose, her eyes shrewd. "There is one thing that can be said about the Dutch, though. They do persevere. They may not have succeeded in taking Macao and making the trade enclave their own, but they don't give up. They even settled on Formosa, after they tricked the magistrate of Fujian into allowing them to take the island. That happened the year you were born. Since then they have proceeded in colonizing the entire island. Your father even had to leave Formosa because of it, the Dutch gave him no choice." She stood up and started pacing up and down in front of him. He followed her movements closely; she had his full attention now that she spoke of his father.

"No matter. Trade is trade, and it gives our family business a good opportunity to grow. Your father is a businessman. These barbarians call him a pirate, but they are the pirates! The impudent foreign devils!" she said, simulating an angry spit. "No matter," she repeated, calm again. "He is a respected man, your father, respected even by the Dutch. He has a considerable fleet and controls most of the trading in the area, also for the VOC." She stopped in front of him and put both hands on his slim shoulders. "You are his oldest son. It is your duty, your destiny, to follow your father. You understand that?"

"Yes, Grandmother," Fukumatsu said, somewhat overwhelmed by all the information and the old woman's grand expectations of him.

"Let me introduce you to your father's principal wife, your stepmother. Lady Yan!"

A carefully coiffed young woman, heavy with child and perhaps slightly older than his own mother, stepped forward from the line of women and gave him a small smile. In her arms she held an infant that Fukumatsu guessed to be about the same age as Zaemon.

"Du! Meet your big brother!" his grandmother called in a honeyed voice. A small boy of about five stepped forward, regarding the newcomer with suspicion. Lady Yan prodded him on, upon which the boy suddenly blurted, "*Dage!* Big brother, welcome, welcome! Your new family welcomes you to your new home!" The women giggled at the enormous volume the child produced saying the obviously rehearsed phrase. Lady Zheng smiled, pleased at the display.

"Thank you, *didi*, little brother," Fukumatsu said.

"And this is your younger brother, Shiyin." With her fan, his grandmother pointed to the toddler that clung to the skirts of a nanny, snot dripping from his nose. "We will forgive him for being too young to speak for himself, but I am sure he would welcome you if he knew how." The women laughed to please the old matriarch. "And these are your aunties and cousins."

Lady Zheng pointed at the women and children huddled together toward the far end of the room. The young girls looked at him shyly, while his "aunties" regarded him with suspicion. His mother had warned him of this: his arrival would probably affect their status in the household. Fukumatsu bowed in their direction.

"Zheng Cai!" His grandmother's voice piped again. "You are about the same age as Zheng Sen. You will be taking your lessons together. Greet your cousin!" A stocky boy stepped forward, scrutinizing Fukumatsu as he did.

"Welcome, cousin. I look forward to sharing my classes with you." The boy said dutifully, but from the look on his face Fukumatsu could tell that he wasn't at all happy about the fact.

"Excellent!" Lady Zheng snapped her fan closed, deciding there had been enough introductions. "You will get to know your new family in due time. Good. Education." Zheng Sen followed her with her eyes as she started pacing across the room again. "Education is the most important thing right now. Because we Hakkas could never hold public office or make money from land we could not own, we have always turned to education for survival. I have arranged tutors for you. You are to start tomorrow morning." She made for the door as if to leave, her young servant scurrying behind her. Then suddenly she stopped as if she had forgotten something, the young girl nearly colliding into her. The poor girl received a look of disdain from the older woman for her clumsiness. "Your father is expected home this week. He will wish to see you, of course." With that, she headed for the door one final time and was gone.

That first night, Zheng Sen was left alone in his quarters with Hong, who followed him everywhere like a loyal dog, eager to please his new charge. His meal was brought to him shortly. Overwhelmed by all the information he had had to take in on this first day, he retired early, and as he lay back on his bed he listened to the unfamiliar sounds of his new home. He could hear laughter and voices, a dog barking nearby, a woman scowling, the sound of a baby crying. From the small room next to him he heard Hong snoring softly, curled up on a mat. He must have fallen asleep the minute he lay down.

As he lay on the uncomfortable wooden bed, he thought of the strangers he had met. Lady Zheng, his stern, unsmiling Chinese grandmother. Lady Yan, his father's Chinese wife, who had given him such a false smile. Some of his "aunties," probably his father's concubines, had looked at him with downright animosity. He thought of those small boys, Du and Shiyin, who were his half-brothers; and then there was his cousin Cai. So many eyes on him, curious, some of them friendly, but most of them unsmiling and suspicious. They were supposed to be his family. It certainly didn't feel that way.

A new life, the fortune-teller had said to him. He had never wanted this new life. He wanted to go back to Japan, to Hirado. Tears streamed down his cheeks as he thought of his mother and brother, missing them so badly that it took his breath away. There he was, alone in these empty rooms, in a house that he barely knew. His chest heaving with sobs, he finally slept, exhausted by the day's events.

* * *

For many years Lady Zheng had not known about Matsu Tagawa's existence, or of her half-Japanese grandson's. Of course she was no fool: she had known that her son had his women, just as her husband had had his. Men were men, and her son was no different. She had her own loyal servants who kept her informed: there was little that went on in her household that she was unaware of.

She remembered well having to part with her favorite son. When Zhilong was eighteen, her husband had died, leaving her a widow and mother to six adolescent children. Lord Li Dan, her husband's business associate, had agreed to look after her interests in return for her occasional company, to join him for a game of mahjong, or to share his bed.

Shrewd as she was, she had planted the thought in his mind that he might take her oldest son under his wing as an apprentice. Convinced that it had been his own idea, Li Dan had taken him to Macao, where he taught the youth all about trade. Zhilong was quick to learn; and within a year Li Dan had sent him off to Nagasaki, where he had his business interests.

It had hurt her to part with her oldest son, but eventually it turned out best for everyone. She had seen with her own eyes how cleverly Li Dan played on the ambitions of the foreigners who hoped to do business in the area. Their arrival had made him one of the richest and most influential men along China's southern coast. And it made him the ideal mentor for her youthful, reckless son.

Two long years passed before she saw the boy again. She well remembered when Zhilong had returned home from Nagasaki on leave for the New Year celebrations. At the time, she had noticed that something had changed. Of course she knew well that this was a logical result of his travels abroad, but there was something else too. A certain kind of absent-mindedness in her son, as well as a sense of secrecy. Instinctively she knew that he was no longer hers, that he now belonged to another woman, someone she did not know. With a stab of jealousy she sensed his eagerness to return to Japan. She had recognized it for what it was: infatuation, perhaps even love; but she had dismissed it as inconsequential and unimportant, and did not press her son about the woman in question.

Within a year, she had summoned him home, insisting it was time that he married. The spouse she had selected for him was the young Lady Yan, niece to Lord Li Dan and daughter of one of Li Dan's close business associates. Her son would be smart enough to realize that such a marriage would be advantageous to all parties concerned. Moreover, it was time he started a family of his own.

In spite of his obsession for his secret, Japanese lover, Zhilong had agreed. Even at that young age, he already possessed a keen sense of business acumen and he was smart enough to see that his marriage to Lady Yan would bring him even closer to Li Dan. He fully realized that such a liaison would be very much in his interest.

Lady Zheng encouraged her son's young wife to make sure he stayed home as much as possible. Her ploy worked: Zhilong left for Nagasaki less frequently, which caused his love for the Japanese mystery woman to diminish and fade.

There was, however, little that she missed. All money matters that involved the household were her direct responsibility, and every coin was accounted for. She discovered a steady stream of unexplained expenses that were made whenever Zhilong, and later Feng, left on their visits to Japan. It was Feng who accompanied him on these trips, and who later travelled to Nagasaki in his stead.

She soon found that Feng knew everything. Of all his siblings, Zhilong had always been closest to Feng. Devious as she was, she finally managed to trick Feng into telling her that his brother Zhilong had a woman in Japan. For the first time, she also learned of her six-year-old grandson. Not altogether surprised, she pressed Feng for details. He spoke of an intelligent, gentle woman of good birth with strong character. But it was the existence of her hitherto unknown grandson, a bright, sharp-eyed boy who showed promise in horsemanship and the martial arts, that she had been more interested in.

For two days, Lady Zheng dwelt on the matter. She thought of her daughter-in-law Lady Yan, who was of excellent birth and gentle of nature, but unfortunate enough to have only half a bird's brain. The sons she had produced did not show a great deal of promise either when it came to intellect. Du, the oldest boy, had been clumsy and sickly from the moment he had entered the world, while the younger Shiyin had an unpleasant tic. No, she had no great expectations for those boys. New blood would do no one any harm, even if it were half-Japanese. And so, she finally summoned Zhilong to her side.

"I think it is high time that you bring your oldest son and that Japanese woman to Anhai," she announced.

* * *

Zhilong had been away for almost a month when he returned to Fujian. If someone had not brought to his attention that his son had arrived at his home, he would have clean forgotten about it. He had not seen the boy since he was a toddler. In a way his heart went out to him, knowing that it must be hard to be separated from his mother so brusquely. He had had the good fortune himself of spending his childhood with his extended family until the age of eighteen, when his father died.

After his father's funeral, Lord Li Dan had taken him to Macao, where he was taught the business of trade, learned the Portuguese language, and, at the insistence of his mentor, was baptized a Catholic. The Portuguese much preferred to do business with Catholic converts, Li Dan had told him.

Two years later he was sent to Hirado, Japan, where he ended up as a tailor's apprentice for the VOC. It soon became apparent that he had a way with languages, not only learning Japanese quite easily but also becoming proficient in Dutch. The yellow-haired Hollanders, together with the Portuguese and Chinese, were the only nations permitted to trade in Nagasaki, and for him that meant opportunity.

Due to his language skills and quick intelligence, he was soon promoted to become an interpreter for the company, until Li Dan discovered his other talents. As a wealthy Chinese merchant, Li Dan had considerable business interests in Hirado, and he had good use for someone like Zhilong. So he recruited him to come and work for him there, taking him under his wing to learn all there was to know about trade.

It was Li Dan who had introduced Zhilong to Matsu Tagawa at an official function where he acted as interpreter. Six months later, Zhilong married her. Knowing that his mother would never approve of a marriage to a Japanese woman, and a widowed woman at that, he decided to keep it a secret. At the time, he was still too young to have the courage to face up to his mother's iron will and fiery temper.

Matsu had soon fallen pregnant and given birth to a son. In awe of her and his firstborn son, Zhilong remained loyal to his young wife while in Japan, living with her whenever he was not travelling. Not only was Matsu a lovely woman, she also proved a devoted wife and mother with a strong sense of honor and a quiet strength that were a part of her ashigaru heritage. Widowed at a tender age, she also had a good dose of life's experience and an equal measure of common sense.

Over the years, Zhilong kept his Japanese family a closely guarded secret from his mother. While Lady Yan bore him the children that his married state demanded, his work required his travel elsewhere and it became increasingly difficult to stay in Japan for long periods of time. His visits to Matsu became less frequent, while their duration became briefer.

Eventually, Li Dan sent Zhilong to Formosa to represent him there. With no official authority to speak of in Formosa, the island had become an attractive location to merchants like him, offering him free rein of movement for his lucrative activities. More importantly, there were no magistrates or tax collectors demanding payments. And that made Formosa an interesting place to operate from. By then Li Dan had become such a well-known figure to Western traders in the area that they referred to him as "Captain China."

But then something happened that would change everything. A ferocious plague descended on the Japanese isles, leaving Li Dan and many of his senior company officials dead in its wake. Because Li Dan left no sons to succeed him, the survivors scrambled in a bid to lead his large trade imperium. Zheng Zhilong was one of them.

By this time Zhilong had acquired two ships and enough valuable trade ware to fill them. It was a modest beginning, and nothing compared to the sizeable fleet and wealth that his benefactor had built up. Yet his instincts told him that if he moved quickly he could turn this to his advantage

While his rivals bickered among themselves on who would lead Li Dan's organization, Zhilong made his move. Paying two local officials bribes so handsome they almost equaled half a year's salary, he had arranged to see Li Dan's will. A few hours later, it declared Zheng Zhilong as the sole beneficiary of his fleet, company, and worldly assets.

Although his rivals strongly contested the validity of the testament, quite a few people were willing – either because of sheer intimidation or the promise of financial reward – to support his claim. After all, they said, it was well known that Master Zheng had been close to Lord Li Dan, who was himself childless. It was only natural that he had chosen Zhilong to succeed him. Had he not already shown his leadership qualities?

And leadership qualities he had. He had also developed the necessary instincts to know who to bribe and when to bribe them, along with who to intimidate or charm in order to win the necessary support. Some of his challengers, however, remained unconvinced. They were unwilling to accept Zhilong as the sole heir to one of southern China's largest commercial enterprises, and they confronted him with force.

Those who did soon found that his power and backing had grown, and they had little choice but to accept Zhilong or leave the organization.

And thus he inherited Li Dan's substantial business and fleet. Nevertheless, the power struggle continued for several years until the original imperium finally collapsed. Still, Zheng Zhilong's "inheritance" formed the backbone of a commercial empire that would rule the waters of the South China seas for decades to come.

Not long after Zhilong had set up his offices in Formosa, the Dutch arrived under the guise of the VOC, the Dutch East India Company. They had initially taken control of the Pescadores by force; but the Ming court in Peking had bristled, as it considered the Pescadores part of its territory. The Dutch, however, were permitted to operate from Formosa, since that did not fall under Chinese sovereignty. The authorities informed them that there would be no trading until the last Dutchman had left the Pescadores. Still, a full naval fleet was required to ensure that they really left.

The pale foreigners had then proceeded to take control of Formosa, driving away all Chinese traders, pirates, and other undesirables that the island had attracted over the years. The VOC had made it abundantly clear that it intended to gain full control of Formosa. Much to his chagrin, Zhilong was forced to leave Formosa. He moved his working quarters to the Pescadores, from which he continued to run his enterprises.

The Dutch invasion of Formosa had alarmed many in the region. Initially, Zhilong too saw their presence as a hindrance to his commercial activities. To him, the Dutch were little more than aggressive invaders who had trespassed into his area of trade. But if he were able to benefit from their fervent wish to trade, then that was something he was more than willing to accept. When it became obvious that they were in Formosa to stay, he realized he could turn things to his advantage. His considerable negotiation skills, his knowledge of the Dutch language, and his keen business instincts persuaded the officials of the VOC to enter into deals with him that were to prove highly lucrative.

The arrival of the Dutch brought prosperity to the region. During the years that followed, Zhilong watched his fortune grow. He did not shun the use of force. His ships now dominated the trade routes between Japan, Formosa, and China, regularly preying on and attacking foreign ships. Sometimes he felt it was necessary to block the VOC's trade routes, if only to remind the Dutch of the power he held. His junks often attacked Dutch merchant ships that passed through the Formosa Strait, claiming the valuable cargoes as his own. That the Dutch accused him of piracy did not bother him in the slightest.

Besides, the mood in China was changing, and one could never tell what the future might bring. Through his numerous influential connections he managed to stay well-informed of what was happening inside the court walls of Peking. The continuous wars with the enemies along China's northern borders had proven costly, weakening the once-powerful empire. He knew only too well that the great Ming dynasty, one that had ruled over China for nearly three hundred years, was beginning to crumble. What had been a great age of cultivation, development, and exploration under strong emperors had begun to rot from within. A succession of less competent emperors had sat on the throne and allowed themselves to be led by advisors who had their own agendas, embroiling the court in an atmosphere of rivalry, intrigue, and corruption.

Meanwhile, Japanese ships continued to harass the coastal cities. The Portuguese, who had long since gained a serious foothold in China and forced the empire into trading agreements, had even managed to obtain Macao as a trade enclave. Harried and distracted, the court had failed to see the very real threat of the Manchus. But Zhilong had been aware of the danger that these aggressive northerners posed to the weakening empire for quite some time.

With the advent of war, Zhilong had sworn his allegiance to the Ming. After all, his connections with the Ming royals had contributed significantly to the accumulation of his wealth and power, and he vowed to defend the dynasty and do everything in his power to prevent it from falling. Still, he was realistic enough to realize that this might not be feasible, even for him. Time would tell, he told himself.

A young, startled deer buck crossed his path and bolted down the hillside toward the woods, breaking his track of thought. He smiled. The young animal reminded him of his seven-year-old son, who would be waiting for him at his residence. The thought of seeing the boy after so long made him urge his horse to quicken its pace. He thought of Matsu Tagawa, his first love, and, if he cared to admit it, his only love.

His brother Feng had come down to meet him the day before to inform him of the latest developments. It was from Feng that he learned that Matsu would not be joining her son to come to Anhai and that she had decided to stay in Japan. He had been insanely jealous when he had learned the reason for this, and felt betrayed. The mere thought that she, the first and only woman he had truly loved, had given birth to another man's child, hurt his manly pride to the core.

But after a long, sleepless night tormented by bittersweet memories, he knew that he had no right to judge her. Through his family's machinations and his marriage to Lady Yan, he had deserted her a long time ago, and he knew it. She was not to blame.

Now his oldest son and heir was waiting to meet him, and that brought an unfamiliar sensation. In his lifetime he had dealt with all kinds of men: merchants and soldiers, mercenaries and mandarins, even members of the imperial family. But he had little experience with seven-year-old boys. Admittedly, he had never made much of an effort with Du, his five-year-old son with Yan. But he told himself that this was because of his judgement of the boy: Du had always been slow of understanding, which was trying on his patience. And Shiyin was still too young to warrant his attention.

He wondered how his mother had received the boy. The old woman had become hardened since the death of his father. She could have a sharp tongue, but Zhilong believed her to be fair and just. If Fukumatsu was anything like his mother Matsu, he would be clever. Clever enough not to get on his grandmother's wrong side.

He also wondered how Lady Yan had treated his son. Yan had been absolutely horrified when she first learned that her husband's oldest son was borne to him by another woman, and that she was, in fact, not his "first" wife. It wasn't surprising. Fukumatsu's existence was a threat, not only to her position as wife but also to that of her own sons as heirs to his growing fortune.

For weeks, she had been cold and distant. Until the moment when she heard that her husband intended to bring the boy to Anhai. She had been livid. A great deal of chinaware had ended up in shards that afternoon. Despite a whole night of wailing and crying in protest, which simply led to his spending the night with a concubine, she had no choice but to accept his decision.

As they reached the hill's crest, the horses laboring heavily from the climb, Zhilong stopped and looked upon the house that had been the family residence since the Song dynasty. It had been there for five hundred years. Most Hakkas had left China in those days, seeking refuge from their persecutors and fleeing to Formosa or the lands of Southeast Asia; yet his ancestors had decided to stay in Quanzhou. They had eventually settled here, in Anhai. It was here that they had slowly built an existence through various trades and professions, extending the house to the sprawling complex it had become.

Zheng spurred his horse, which broke into a gallop for the last mile of his journey. His men followed his example, the sound of their hooves alerting the household that their lord and master was home.

A manservant greeted him, rushing forward to take the reins of his horse. Zhilong nodded, acknowledging him with a grunt. As he jumped off his horse, he saw housekeeper Liu hurrying toward him from the main building.

"Welcome back, Lord Zheng. I hope your journey was a successful one," she said in a honeyed voice, her face wrinkling in a smile.

"Liu, where is my son?" he demanded, ignoring her question. He had never had much patience with the sugary sweetness she used as a front when addressing him. He was well aware of how vicious she could be to the other servants.

"He is here, my lord. Young Master Zheng is doing his studies. I have assigned Hong to look after his needs," she answered smoothly, unaffected by his gruffness.

"Hong? That weak-brained fool?"

"Would you rather I assigned someone else? I apologize if I offended —"

He silenced her with his hand, reconsidering. "No. Leave it as it is. Bring him to the main hall. I wish to see him."

"Will you be requiring refreshments, my lord?"

"Yes. Bring me something to eat and drink, I will have it in the hall."

"Very good, my lord," Liu said, and disappeared across the courtyard.

* * *

Fukumatsu followed Liu to the great hall, prodded by his tutor Wang, whose impatience to witness his pupil's reunion with his father was palpable. He walked quickly, gradually beginning to know the way, especially since his cousin Cai had shown him around the compound the previous afternoon.

His heart had skipped a beat when housekeeper Liu interrupted his lesson to summon him to meet his father. No matter how hard he tried, he could not remember him. He could only conjure up a memory of a serious and sober man, and it made him nervous. Would he live up to his father's expectations?

When they arrived at the hall, his father was already there. Still in his travel clothes, his short sword still girdled at his side, Zheng stood in the hallway, a cup in his hand. There was no doubt in Fukumatsu's mind that this man was his father.

Zheng wore his long hair in a ponytail and had a strong, youthful look about him. Fukumatsu thought he looked tough and impressive in his travel clothes. His eyes went to the sword, and he thought he saw the beginning of a smile on his father's lips. He so desperately wanted to make a good impression on him.

"Fukumatsu-*san*!" his father cried, walking up to him and putting a hand on his shoulder.

"Greetings, Father. My name is Zheng Sen now. It is the name Grandmother has given me," he said solemnly, hoping that his father would not be able to hear the pounding of his heart.

"Zheng Sen! Of course, of course! Your grandmother is right. You are now in China. So a Chinese name is more appropriate. Zheng Sen," he repeated, his hands still resting awkwardly on his shoulder. "Zheng Sen, tell me. How is your mother?" he asked.

"She is well, Father." He lowered his eyes to hide the strength of his emotions when he thought of her. "She wanted to come with me, but she could not." He wiped at his eyes angrily. He missed her so very much.

"I know." His father's tone was not unsympathetic. He placed a gentle hand on his head. "You look like her, Zheng Shen," he said. "Perhaps she will be able to join us sometime in the future."

Fukumatsu nodded, not daring to speak lest his voice quail. It was then that he realized his father had addressed him using his new, Chinese name. That made it real, that truly made him the person he was about to become: Zheng Sen. So this was the new life the fortune-teller in Hirado had spoken of. It even meant having a new name.

An uncomfortable silence filled the space between them, and he felt a sudden need to say something, to break that silence. He raised his head to look his father right in the eye.

"My little brother, Shichi-Zaemon, is also well, in case you wish to know."

His father stared down at him frowning, momentarily at a loss. Then he laughed out loud. "Of course." He nodded, pleased at the boy's forthrightness. "You are now seven years old. It is time that you learn about such things. Have you met my wife Lady Yan and your other brothers and sisters yet?"

"Yes, Father. I have also spoken to Grandmother. She saw me yesterday." He tried not to stare too much at his father, whom he thought handsome and grand.

"Good, good. I will go and change now. I will see you later. Tonight we will eat together." And with that, he left.

Zheng Sen watched him in awe until his father turned the corner and disappeared from sight. For a moment he just stood there, slightly at a loss, until he saw Teacher Wang standing in the courtyard, his cousin Cai grinning by his side. The old man's expression was stern, but he could see a glint of pleasure in his eyes. Only that morning, Teacher Wang had complimented him on his Chinese and his willingness to learn. He had said that it was probably a good thing that he had joined the Zheng household. According to Teacher Wang, Cai was a lazy student. Having Zheng Sen as classmate might just prove to be the necessary incentive for Cai to make more of an effort to keep up with his peer.

Zheng Sen had been worried that Cai would be jealous or even dislike him. During the morning lessons Cai had not spoken one word to him. But that had changed since that afternoon. Upon finishing their classes, the boys had left the school building to find themselves confronted by a large, lean dog. The animal stood as high as his waist, and Cai had muttered beneath his breath that he didn't know the beast, that it didn't belong. It must have entered the compound unawares, hungry and looking for food. It had stood there, growling, his beady yellow eyes honed in on Cai's younger sister, who stood rigid with fear with her back to a wall. Cai had been unable to move, petrified.

Zheng Sen had acted on instinct. He had stepped between the dog and the girl, shouting at the animal in order to distract it. His ruse worked, and the dog's menacing attention turned to him instead. Cai had backed away in alarm, but Zheng Sen had remained where he was, undaunted. Careful not to look the growling animal in the eye, he reached for a branch on the ground and stepped in the dog's direction. The gurgling, warning sound that had come from deep inside its throat signaled danger, even before it launched its huge lumbering body in his direction. Zheng Sen had deftly dodged the animal and smashed the branch against its head even before it landed. The creature came down with a thud, only half-conscious. It got up groggily, upon which Zheng Sen had charged, shouting. The dog ran off, with him in hot pursuit, until it had disappeared through the gate, its tail between its legs.

He had returned, still holding the branch, to find a greatly relieved Cai, a protective arm draped across his sister's shoulder. Cai had been very impressed, and had been won over completely. From that moment on, Cai was rarely away from Zheng Sen's side.

For a while, he forgot his mother and Zaemon. He had been reunited with his father, who had not been unkind to him. His family appeared to be wealthy. And even his lessons with Teacher Wang were going well. But the most important thing was that he had found himself a friend. The future suddenly looked less bleak. Things might turn out all right, after all.

That night, his father had arranged for a banquet to celebrate his arrival. All the family members attended, including his grandmother, who played the part of the stern but not displeased matriarch, a wisp of a satisfied smile on her lips.

After dinner, they all attended the family shrine to worship their ancestors. He had felt his father's eyes upon him as he lit the incense and clapped his hands according to Japanese Shinto tradition to awaken the ancestral spirits, his eyes closed in prayer. His grandmother had looked sharply in his father's direction, expecting him to take corrective action. Zheng Sen knew then that he had done something wrong, that this ritual was out of place. But his father said nothing. He only looked at him, the pride in his eyes for all to see.

For the first time since his arrival, he felt truly happy, honored that he belonged to a family such as this. There he was, in the family shrine of his Chinese ancestors, to mark his new life. It was a momentous occasion, and one that would stay with him for the rest of his life.

CHINA
EAST CHINA SEA
Fuzhou
Fujian
Province
Tamsui
Quanzhou
Zhangzhou
Amoy
Strait of Formosa
FORMOSA
The
Pescadores
Fort Provintia
Fort Zeelandia
PACIFIC
OCEAN
SOUTH CHINA SEA
100 km

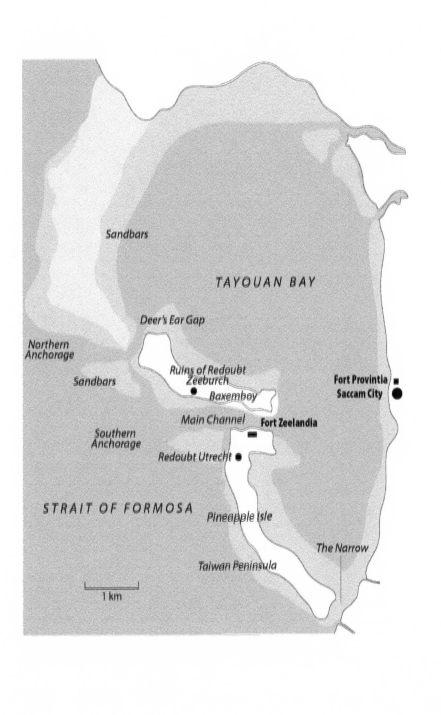

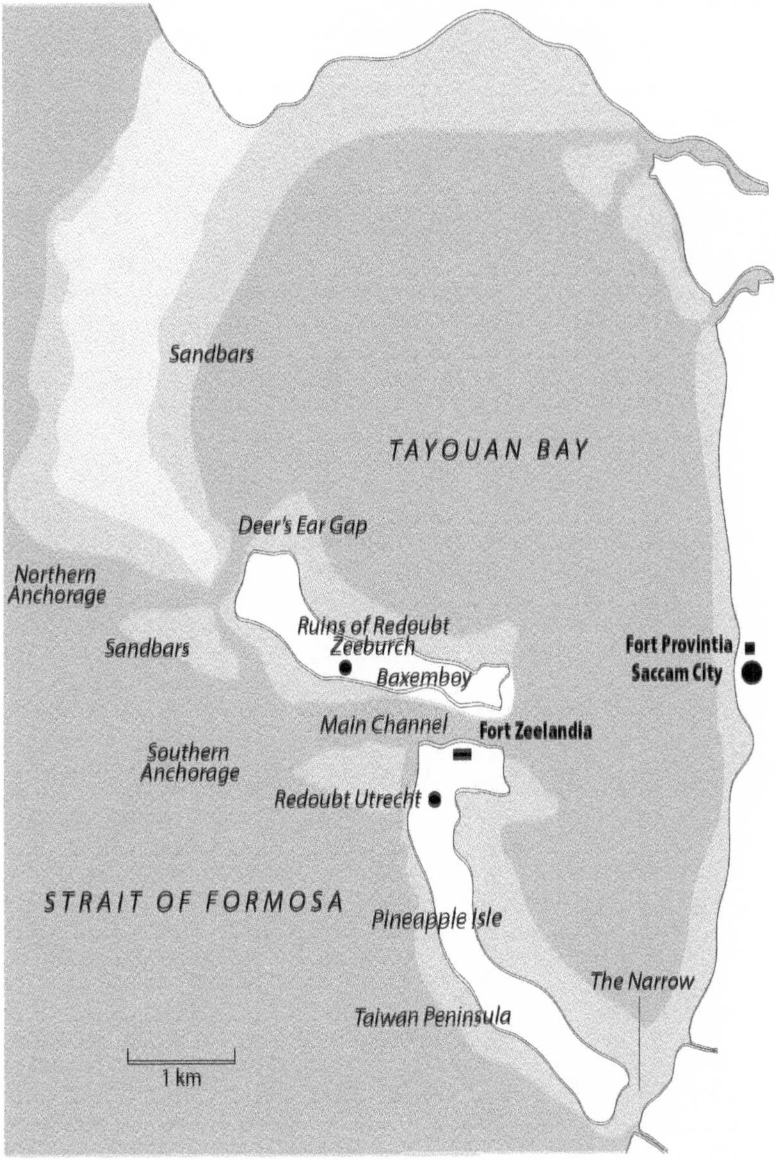

Sandbars
TAYOUAN BAY
Deer's Ear Gap
Northern Anchorage
Sandbars
Ruins of Redoubt Zeeburch
Baxemboy
Fort Provintia
Saccam City
Main Channel
Fort Zeelandia
Southern Anchorage
Redoubt Utrecht
STRAIT OF FORMOSA
Pineapple Isle
The Narrow
Taiwan Peninsula
1 km

3

Migrants and Colonists

FORMOSA

"WHO do they think they are, these barbarian devils, coming here like this and demanding our money! They really think they own the island!" Guo bellowed, still trembling from the encounter, even long after the Dutch were gone.

"Quiet, quiet. They will hear you. It's too dangerous," his wife tried to placate him, her hands on her husband's wrists in an effort to get him to calm down. "Listen," she whispered. They heard shouts coming from the next hovel on the hillside. Cautiously they peered out of the opening in the wall that served as a window. They saw their neighbor in the doorway, gesticulating wildly with his arms and shouting insults at the Dutchman.

"Piece of turtle dung! Egghead! Why don't you work yourself instead of sucking us dry of our hard-earned money?" The man hawked and spat noisily at the missionary's feet. This was too much of an affront for one of the soldiers, who reacted by hitting the man across the jaw with the butt of his gun. The man stumbled from the blow, his hand flying to his face to protect himself. The soldier then kicked him hard in the small of his back and looked down on his victim with disdain. The Chinese man rolled over in anguish. The soldier would have kicked him again if the missionary had not grabbed him by the arm. His expression was hard, the tone of his voice commanding.

The soldier shrugged his shoulders and fell back, obviously caring little for what the Dutch missionary had said to him. The missionary looked distressed and helped the poor man to his feet, mumbling something of an apology. Then he shook his head wearily and walked on to the next house, the bored soldiers following in his wake.

"You see!" Longfei hissed in Guo's ear after witnessing the scene. "We have to be practical. There are too many of them, their weapons are too powerful. That could have happened to you if had you denied them the money!" She looked at her husband, desperate that he understand their plight. Guo still stood hunched at the window, his eyes on the receding backs of the tall foreigners making their way up the path. Only after they were gone did he stand straight again, then realizing how deep his fingernails had dug into his hands. His wife was right. There was nothing he or any of them could do for now.

When he had first set foot on Formosa, the Dutch had treated Chinese migrants such as himself more than fairly. Back then, they did not have to pay taxes. The VOC had welcomed him and many others like him with open arms, even giving them start-up money. That was when the VOC needed all the laborers it could get. But once the number of Chinese coming to the island's shores reached into the thousands, the company had changed its policy.

Like so many others, Guo had left China to escape the threat of war. Manchurian forces had succeeded in breaking Ming strongholds, gaining an even firmer foothold in northern China. As the Ming empire flailed out its limbs ineffectively, the Manchu presence only grew stronger. Those who felt the cold winds of change found it wiser to leave while they still could. Although it was commonly known that the big-nosed, pale foreigners from the West occupied the island of Formosa, people knew that the Dutch did not turn them away. They were free to settle on the island, where there was plenty of work for them. It gave him a chance to start life anew. Guo had been one of the men who had left China, arriving on one of the merchant ships of Zheng Zhilong, who cleverly made use of the exodus by ferrying Chinese migrants across the Formosa Strait for a fee. A strong, smart farmhand, he had arrived on Formosa about three years ago, hardly a possession to his name.

Soon after his arrival he had married Longfei, a Hakka woman from his own native village. The couple had a two-year-old son and his wife was now heavily pregnant with a second child. Guo had been conscripted as a construction laborer by the VOC, while his wife worked the company fields to grow rice or sugarcane, lucrative export commodities that were grown in abundance on the island.

Together they worked long hours of physical labor, pushed hard by the overseers. The wages they were paid were low, but they had little choice, as returning to China was not an option, even if they could afford the fare back.

And now, the foreign devils had appeared at the door of his shabby accommodation, demanding a tenth of their wages as a head tax. At first he had refused to pay, in spite of the intimidating soldiers who accompanied the missionary man they called "Juni." Still spluttering with indignation, Guo had extracted the due amount from the tin container and paid the money only at the urging of his wife.

The following evening, the missionary returned to the hill with his entourage of armed men. This time, Guo's neighbor, now cowed into submission, handed over the required amount of money with a trembling hand. Longfei was right. There was little that they could do.

* * *

The VOC had done well in Formosa since its annexation of the island. Nine years ago it had been a wild, almost inhabitable place rife with swamp fever; but once they had begun to settle they discovered that the mosquito-borne disease was less prevalent along the coast, and the number of Dutch settlers grew steadily. There were now more than a hundred houses inhabited by Dutch settlers along the coast of Tayouan Bay. The first settlers lived to the east of Fort Zeelandia, which had been strategically built on a small island, which the Dutch called Pineapple Isle, named for the pandanus, a fruit that grew there and somewhat resembled the pineapple.

Pineapple Isle was one of two small islands, Baxemboy being the other. Both were no more than thin stretches of duny landscape that bent inward toward the mainland. These isles almost enclosed the bay, save for three inlets. The northernmost inlet was located between a thin stretch of dunes attached to the main island and Baxemboy, leaving a channel for the currents to mingle freely. Even at high tide, however, it was too narrow and shallow for vessels of any significance to enter.

Pineapple Isle was the more southern of the two islands. Its northern tip just missed Baxemboy's southeastern extremity, turning sharply to the east to point at Formosa's mainland like a gnarled finger, allowing an entrance to the bay large enough for bigger ships to enter. Its high dunes provided the perfect location for building Fortress Zeelandia, as from here, they could protect this entrance. The fort's formidable walls faced the sea both to the north and west, so that it could blaze its guns at any enemy bold enough to try and enter the bay. There was also a defensive tower on Baxemboy facing the Formosa Strait; that also served to keep any enemies at bay. In this way, the only entrance to Tayouan Bay could be defended from both sides.

The southernmost inlet, which the Dutch called the Narrows, was no more than a width of shallow water between the southern tip of Pineapple Isle and Formosa's mainland. It was here that the colonists living in Zeelandia could wade across to the main island to join their brethren there.

Some company employees were accompanied by their wives and families, with higher company officials marrying Dutch women brought from Holland or Batavia. These senior officials also brought in a small number of slaves who had been purchased in the East Indies or the Asian subcontinent: they were primarily for their personal, household use. Settlers of lower rank often married local women of aboriginal or Chinese descent.

The company management had been pleasantly surprised at the agricultural possibilities on the island, the soil proving most fertile. Both sugar and rice were now growing in abundance, a third of the sugar crop meant for export. On a smaller scale, tea was grown on the less fertile slopes for local consumption.

Where the native islanders seemed rather inept at working the fields, the Chinese settlers were very capable. Besides, there seemed to be more of them coming to Formosa every day.

The company organized the few hundred villages into farm groups of thirty to forty households, with each group appointing a village head. Every elected village headman was made responsible to the Dutch governor for local peace and order. These headmen also had to answer to him for any mishaps or incidents that occurred, in effect forcing them to police their own people. The village heads were mostly wealthy and powerful merchants from Fujian Province with good connections in China and high standing among their countrymen on Formosa. It was an efficient system, and agriculture flourished as a result.

The colonists treated the semi-civilized native aboriginal tribes reasonably well. Many of the natives proved to be open to conversion and thus, in the Dutch way of thinking, favorable and receptive to their way of life.

The Chinese, on the other hand, were a different matter. Those Chinese who had been on the island long before the Dutch had set foot on the place were stubborn and proud, going their own way as they had always done before the colonists had arrived. The Dutch could not tell whether they were Han, Hakka, or of other ethnic origin, and treated all Chinese immigrants as one folk, all of whom had to pay taxes.

With the population growing by the day, the Christian mission on Formosa became more important. The missionaries had become closer to the natives, whom they attempted to convert and tried to teach to read and write. Schools popped up across the island to ensure that the growing number of migrants were given an education. Because of the lack of educated Dutchmen, the reverends were regularly used for various tasks, including the collection of taxes. This often led to conflicts: the missionaries complained that such a task was not part of their jobs; their work was to spread the word of God. The governor would remind them in no uncertain terms that it was the VOC, not God, that paid their salaries. Such statements did little to improve relations between the two.

The local Chinese were the first to refuse to pay the head tax. They were born on Formosa. They would disappear for a while when taxes were due, usually in collaboration with the pirates that roamed the coast. The company authorities saw this as resistance and felt compelled to use force in order to collect the taxes that they believed were their due.

In the meantime, company headquarters in the Dutch East Indian capital of Batavia demanded that Formosa become financially independent. New sources of income had to be found in order to fund improvements to the island's infrastructure. New laws were passed, one of which was to deny any Chinese the right to own land. The Chinese were now forced to work the fields belonging to the company, for which they were paid low wages. With the newly applied head taxes, the conditions in which they worked were dismal.

They were, however, allowed to lease land. The VOC allotted them plots, and they were given production quotas, a large part of which was confiscated by the company. The land leases soon proved to be quite lucrative source of income. Unfortunately for the Dutch on Formosa, the company still had to forfeit most of its income to the council in Batavia, which was stingy and unforthcoming with funds. Requests for necessary improvements and development of Formosa were invariably turned down, Batavia only investing the bare minimum while pushing the Formosan council to work harder in order to generate more profits.

Batavia, however, did give permission for the construction of Fort Utrecht, a small redoubt to be built on a high dune just a stone's throw from Fort Zeelandia's southwesterly walls, so that it would be able to protect the main fort from that side with its guns in the event of an attack.

Military advisors had convinced the council that this had to be completed, advising its members that the tower might come in useful one day in defending Zeelandia. The construction seemed to be going according to plan, even though it was delayed somewhat due to the heavy monsoon rain. Not that the workers were allowed to stop work during the rains; the work simply became more difficult and dangerous when it came to moving the heavy stones and logs of timber on the muddy slopes.

Trade flourished. Local produce such as dried venison and salted fish did well in the Japanese market, as did deer antlers, which were ground to a powder used as an ingredient for medicine. Cotton and spices such as pepper came from India, as did tin and lead. Trade with China, for which the VOC had so fervently lobbied, finally began to develop, resulting in warehouses filled with goods. Some 1,500 pounds worth of silk bales lay stacked in the warehouses, most of which was destined for the European market, hungry for foreign wares. Profits were finally being made.

* * *

The following spring, Longfei had just given birth to a baby boy when Guo was nominated head of the village. His village was not among the ten major districts, where the village heads were rich and powerful, nor did he belong to a wealthy merchant family. But as one of the older and most respected among its inhabitants, the people chose him.

It was not a position he had craved, as it meant that he would have to deal with the Dutch authorities more than he cared to. If he became village head, he would be forced to report any damage, losses, or thefts to the Dutch authorities. He had no wish to tell on his fellow countrymen, as he knew the circumstances in which they lived. Yet if he failed in his duties as head of the district, he would be held accountable himself.

He had heard stories of stubborn village heads who had refused to cooperate with the Dutch in pointing out guilty parties. Those village heads were either fined or beaten in their stead, and sometimes imprisoned. Yet again, those who had carefully toed the company's line had ended up as powerful, even wealthy, men.

For the ordinary Chinese villagers, things didn't improve. Not only did the "men of God" as they called themselves return on a monthly basis to collect their cursed taxes, they were also worked harder than before. The hours they labored were becoming longer, while their meal rations remained the same. A growing number of Dutch troops had landed on the island, and they seemed to patrol the districts more regularly, limiting the villagers' freedom even further.

"At least you will have some authority in the village," his wife had said to him, her eyes glinting. He knew Longfei: she was in favor of his becoming village head. It would mean status and influence, and in her eyes, more money. It was something they could use with the additional mouth they now had to feed.

"Yes. I will have authority to tell on my own people," he said bitterly. "That is something I will not do." He looked at her with despair. "Do you honestly think I will have any real say? Not with the foreign devils. They will continue to treat me as dirt." He stared out of the window, lost in thought. "We will just have to be patient."

Longfei said nothing, her eyes returning to the infant feeding at her breast. Her milk supply was already waning; she knew that she wasn't eating enough to provide the nourishment her new-born child needed. She would have to persuade her husband that it would be to their benefit if he became village head. There was simply no alternative.

A few days later, Longfei stood ankle deep in the muddy water of the rice paddy, just as she did every other day of the week. After several monotonous hours of planting seedlings in the sodden earth, she straightened to adjust the position of her baby on her back. The additional weight of her child added heavily to the burden of her labor, causing a sharp pain in her lower back. For a brief moment she stood, her child against her hip as she waited for the pain to subside.

A chagrined Dutch overseer, who had spent most of the night emptying his parasite-invested bowels, spotted the woman standing idle in the field, and strode up to her. He shouted at her in his own language, his words incomprehensible, but his gestures were more than clear.

Seeing the Dutchman advance toward her, Longfei fumbled with the adjustment of the wrap, which only further delayed her in resuming her work. The next thing she knew, her foot slipped, causing her to lose her balance and land on the sodden earth on her side. As she struggled to get to her feet, she found herself covered in mud, her hair plastered and her cheeks smeared. One of the women working at her side made as if to assist her, but the Dutchman put up an imperative hand to stop her. The woman glanced apologetically to her friend and quickly resumed her task.

At the sight of the Chinese woman covered in muck, the burly overseer burst into peals of laughter, which caught the attention of his colleague surveying the neighboring field. He joined in, jeering her.

Burning with humiliation and frustration, Longfei wiped the soil from her face and furiously got back to work. She hardly noticed the looks of compassion from the other women in the field. She could only feel hatred. Hatred for the yellow-haired barbarian colonists.

4

Pirate, Merchant, Mandarin

GOVERNOR PUTMANS strode through the halls of the fort, his two officers trying to keep up with him as he swore like a common sailor. "That godforsaken pirate!" he growled. "I knew the man couldn't be trusted! Bloody Chinaman!"

Commander Boenck had also suspected for some time that Zheng Zhilong had breached their agreement. The Chinese merchant had hindered their trade ever since the VOC had taken possession of Formosa. Time and time again he had harassed company ships, on both sides of the strait. The man called himself a tradesman; but in the eyes of the company he was no more than a pirate. At some point they had come to an arrangement in which they agreed to leave each other alone and not trespass on the other's trading waters, and so far he seemed to have complied.

But trade had been strangely lacking of late, and the shipments that did come were often found to be wanting. Lucrative deals had suddenly been backed out of by the merchants in the Chinese ports, and large amounts of goods had a tendency to disappear while the ships lay in harbor.

Their suspicions had finally been confirmed. It turned out that Zheng had been actively obstructing their trade for at least a year. It seemed that Zheng knew exactly which merchants to bribe to obtain the goods that were originally reserved for the company. He had been trading only for his own benefit, often claiming the traded wares as his own. If that wasn't bad enough, they now knew that at least three of their merchant ships, their cargoes full of precious wares, had been pirated by ships that belonged to one and the same man: Zheng Zhilong.

"We have to stop the son of a whore. He has been stealing from us. We cannot allow this to continue any longer!" Once he stepped into his office he slammed the door hard against the wall.

"How soon can we attack?" he demanded of Boenck, commander of the military presence on Formosa. Boenck was startled at the suddenness of the decision, having expected more deliberation on the matter. An attack without true provocation? He exchanged glances with Lieutenant Caldenhoven, who remained silent.

"Sir, would it not be prudent to consult with the Formosan council on this, as –"

"I'll be the judge of what would be prudent, commander," the governor retorted. "Such insolence needs to be addressed without delay. We cannot waste any more time. So I will ask you again, commander. How soon?"

"Well, within two days we could –"

"Two days it is. We have suffered enough losses due to his intolerable actions. He must be stopped. This cannot continue!"

Boenck recovered swiftly. Duty was duty. "Sir, we could have the ships and troops ready within two days." He hesitated, which did not go unnoticed.

"Well, what is it? Is there a problem?" Putmans snapped.

"It's typhoon season, sir. It's just that it could be perilous this time of year." At that, Putmans jumped up from his chair and strode to the window. He looked at the sky, which was a bright, clear blue. There was hardly a breeze. He glared at Boenck with disdain.

"The weather seems fine to me. We attack in two days. Make sure not a single vessel leaves Formosa. I want him to get no warning. I want to surprise him. We will destroy this man's fleet once and for all. That will teach him. Is that understood?"

"Yes, sir." Boenck stood to attention. He had done his duty and warned his superior. The decision was not his to make.

"Good. Now go and do what needs to be done!" Irritated, he flicked his wrist for the men to be gone, which they did without hesitation, glad to escape the wrath of his foul mood.

The Dutch warships sailed out at dawn, the final preparations having taken place under cover of darkness. Boenck kept a close eye on the weather conditions: the seas were calm, the skies still clear. Governor Putmans stood next to him, his face eager with anticipation.

The coastline receded in the distance as the wind picked up, taking the great warships toward the Pescadores, which lay halfway between Formosa and the Chinese mainland. Spies had informed them that most of Zheng's fleet was lying at anchor at the island chain, from where Zheng ran most of his enterprises.

After a day's sailing, the islands came into view. The various junks and merchant ships that lay anchored there seemed almost deserted. Skeleton crews manned the few war junks at rest. Little or no activity was taking place on the other ships, apart from the day-to-day business of loading and unloading their cargoes.

Commander Boenck checked the sails: they were drawn tight and caught the wind at full speed. Then he ensured that the cannons were ready for use. This would be an easy strike, he knew. But somehow it didn't feel right.

* * *

Zheng Zhilong was attending a meeting with some of his trading partners when he heard shouts of alarm and the clamor of alarm bells. He hurried outside and nearly got knocked over. People were running, shouting warnings and pointing at the horizon.

What he saw sent a chill down his spine. An imposing fleet of Dutch warships was bearing down at them at full speed, the numerous sails taut with wind, the guns out, ready to fire. He drew in his breath at seeing the ships heading toward the island, cursing himself for not having expected this. He should have known that this would happen – he knew that it would be a matter of time before those ugly foreign devils discovered what he had been up to, but this he had not foreseen. They should have given him an ultimatum. There was no honor in this: these foreigners did not understand the art of diplomacy, they had left no room for negotiation or inducement. This attack was nothing but barbaric.

Around him, sailors and soldiers scattered. Many fled their vessels for the relative safety of the shore. The air filled with shouts. Brass bells clanged urgently, alerting all of the unexpected attack. He yelled his orders, striding toward his flagship, where its crew of sailors, pirates, and mercenaries hurriedly tried to prepare a defense. It was either that or flee. But there was no avoiding the fact that they were cornered.

The smaller trading junks in the harbor emptied themselves of a steady stream of half-naked prostitutes and their merchant customers, all of whom fled the scene in haste. Panic filled the air. Some ships headed in the other direction, their captains taking the risk with their priceless cargoes, nearly colliding with one another in their bid to get away.

Some of the war junks, their deep red sails raised like dragon's wings, had already drawn in their anchors and turned to face their attackers. Others were still in disorder, their crews not complete and ill-prepared for what was to come.

The minutes that they had from the moment the Dutch warships had been sighted had now become seconds. Then the deafening sound of the cannons rang out. Two vessels took a direct hit, followed by cries of pain and terror. One war junk responded in kind, but its cannon fell many feet short of its target. The Dutch fired at it in retaliation, blowing it to smithereens. The wounded jumped into the boiling sea, screaming with agony from the wounds they sustained. The next round hit a fleeing merchant vessel, its cargo flammable, turning it into a floating ball of fire. The nauseating stench of burning flesh soon wafted ashore as the flames devoured its dry timber.

The Dutch warships bore down along the damaged ships in order for their soldiers to board them. A few of the Chinese tried to ward off the embarking attackers; but they were gunned down, no match against the firearms of the Dutch.

The midmast of the junk that carried Zheng had broken, its top half lying shattered across the deck, its fall barely missing him but crushing the skull of a sailor. The railing at starboard had been smashed away, while a gaping, jagged hole was left in the deck where the point of the mast had entered it.

In less than an hour, Zheng's fleet had been mortally wounded. A number of junks had managed to flee or enter the refuge of a sheltered bay; those still able to sail limped off in retreat.

* * *

"Sir, we have succeeded in our mission," Commander Boenck announced unnecessarily as they witnessed the carnage. "Three enemy vessels were seen fleeing for the mainland. Do you wish to give chase and overtake them?"

"No, no, let them live to tell the tale. It will be a lesson to them all," Putmans said. Boenck surveyed the burning and sinking ships around them, the penetrating smell of gunpowder filling his nostrils. The cannons were finally silent, but the air still rang with the sound of guns firing and the wails of the dying. His fleet had taken several hits, leaving two of his ships badly damaged, and there had been a number of casualties and several wounded. But they had done what the governor had wanted: they had delivered a crushing blow to their enemy. Was it worth the price they had paid? They had no way of knowing whether Zheng Zhilong had been on board any of the ships, nor whether he had survived the onslaught. They would find out soon enough, he thought grimly.

As the victorious fleet gathered itself to turn and head back to Formosa, Governor Putmans remained at the railing, his shining brass telescope pressed against his brow, scanning the Chinese ships that were still afloat. After a few minutes he passed the instrument to Boenck, who lifted it to his eye and peered at the few remaining junks, some of which were surprisingly unscathed. For a moment he imagined he saw a man staring across at him from one of the larger junks, but the distance was too great, so he shrugged off the feeling as the ship gathered speed, dragging down the splintered remains of Chinese vessels in its wake.

* * *

The attack on Zheng's ships was devastating. Nearly all of his ships that had been harbored at the Pescadores were destroyed. Hundreds had been killed, and many more were certain to die because of their wounds. Many of the goods had been damaged in the attack, the cost considerable. But worst of all, Zheng had lost face. He had lost face because those wretched barbarians had caught him by surprise. He had lost face in front of his enemy, and in the eyes of his allies.

During the days that followed, he managed to salvage what was left of his fleet. Fortunately, not all of his vessels had been stationed at the Pescadores at the time of the attack. Some had been on trading missions on their way to Japan and Vietnam, or anchored further along the Chinese coast. He would never be foolish enough to put his entire fleet at anchor in one place.

Unexpectedly, he received many messages of support after the news of the attack reached the mainland. The hatred and distrust for the Dutch colonists among the Chinese had only intensified. Within days, a steady stream of able men came to him in person, applying to sail under his banners. His reputation preceded him: to many, he had become a leading figure in the fight against the Manchus. Many were eager to enlist with him to avenge the attack.

Still, Zheng did realize that with the decimated state of his fleet, any attempts to attack the Dutch on Formosa would be futile.

A week later, Zheng was visited by an envoy sent by the magistrate of Fujian. The envoy insisted that he had an urgent message that was of utmost importance. Curious, Zheng received the man between efforts to supervise the repair of his ships.

"Magistrate Xiong sends his good wishes, Lord Zheng," the envoy said courteously. "He has heard of your misfortune and it will hearten him to hear that you are safe and unharmed."

Zheng listened to the man's words, waiting for him to continue. The envoy stroked his goatee, relishing the moment and enjoying the attention that his office deserved.

"My master condemns the cowardly attack from the Dutch on your fleet, and would like to offer his support in avenging your enemy."

Zheng looked at the man intently, his interest piqued.

"Your enemy is also my master's enemy," the man continued. "You will remember he lost face in a most humiliating way when the foreigners tricked him by occupying Formosa." His speech was slow and deliberate allowing Zheng to take in his words. "This was a great loss of face, and he has not forgotten."

Zheng nodded gravely. Indeed, he had not forgotten, either. The Dutch had first taken possession of the Pescadores and had then refused to leave until they were granted permission to trade in Fujian. They had then threatened, blackmailed and even held Chinese officials hostage until they were finally given what they wanted. Exasperated, Xiong had eventually conceded, on condition that they would leave the Pescadores for Formosa. But no one had expected them to colonize the entire island.

"Magistrate Xiong also feels that a cowardly act such as this, by foreigners, no less, cannot be left unanswered." He stroked his goatee absentmindedly, but his eyes were shrewd. "That would be a further loss of face. Would you not agree, Lord Zheng?"

Zheng nodded his understanding. "What kind of support does his excellency have in mind?"

"Magistrate Xiong has his connections, as you well know." He gave a slight smile. "War vessels. Soldiers. Weapons. It is also in the interest of the Ming empire, after all, to rid our waters of these foreigners."

"Tell your master that I will accept his offer of help. When I have enough men and vessels sufficient for an attack, I will declare war on these people." His voice dropped an octave with his next words. "I will not lower myself to their standards. I am a warrior, not a pirate. I have the mandate of the emperor to fight all nations invading our territory. If they want war, they shall get it!"

Pleased at hearing his words, the elderly man smiled. "Lord Zheng, I will return to his excellency with the news of your acceptance."

"Thank you," Zheng said gruffly. "This is indeed good news. Please convey my sincere gratitude to his excellency."

During the following weeks, junks of all shapes and sizes arrived individually or in small groups at the Pescadores. In order not to cause suspicion among spies that the Dutch might have sent, Xiong had been careful to instruct his powerful connections that the ships were to sail in sporadically, not in full force.

On an almost daily basis, Zheng Zhilong received a steady stream of captains, all of whom came to report to him. They had been instructed by their superiors to assist Lord Zheng and that they would be under his command.

Many of the vessels that arrived had stashes of weapons and ammunition hidden in their holds. There were muskets and short-range pistols that had been stolen or captured on raids from Dutch, Portuguese, or Spanish ships. And all carried troops, even if they were motley. Within a month, Zheng had a sizable fleet at his disposal. It might not be as powerful as the one that the VOC kept in the region, nor its men as well trained as the Dutch soldiers, but the men showed a fiery willingness to fight for a cause they believed in. The time was right for a declaration of war.

* * *

Boenck ran up the stairs of Fort Zeelandia, taking several steps at a time. An interpreter followed at his heels, lifting the hem of his robe in order not to trip. Both men were out of breath by the time they reached the office. Boenck almost fell into the room in his haste to see the governor.

"Mr. Putmans! One of Zheng's war junks has just been captured by our troops at Tamsui."

Putmans looked up, surprised. Usually the captains on Zheng's ship stayed well clear of the Dutch, their infinitely better knowledge of the waters giving them the advantage.

"It allowed itself to be captured purposely, sir," Boenck said. "They were carrying a message for us. Zheng Zhilong has declared war upon the Dutch on Formosa." He handed Putmans the document he was carrying. The bold, elegant characters jumped off the pale background, but they meant nothing to the Dutchman.

"It has already been translated and confirmed, sir. It is a declaration of war. He means to attack us."

"It is true, Governor Putmans, sir," the interpreter piped. "That is indeed what it says." Boenck looked at him sharply. For a moment he thought he could discern excitement, even admiration in the man's voice. Not for the first time, Boenck wondered if the governor was aware of Zheng Zhilong's popularity among the Chinese in Formosa.

Putmans looked at him, incredulous. "So Zheng survived?" Then he laughed. "And with what does he intend to attack us with? Chopsticks?" he chuckled at his own humor. "Come on, Lieutenant! The man is bluffing! We virtually annihilated his fleet. There was nothing left! You saw that with your own eyes."

"That might be true, sir. But our spies inform us that there has been increased movement of ships between the mainland and the Pescadores. Now we know why. Apparently Zheng has obtained the backing of others powerful enough to supply him with ships and arms."

"I still think he is bluffing. Even if he did manage to get a decent fleet together, he would never succeed in doing us serious harm."

Boenck said nothing, noticing that the interpreter looked dead ahead, his face impassive. He wondered if he knew more than they did. Whatever the case, the man wasn't volunteering any information.

Putmans sat down, a frown creasing his forehead. Then he looked up at Boenck. "Summon Caldenhoven and Van Deurzen. I wish to speak to them on this matter right away."

The commander hurried off, glad to be able to leave the governor's office. That way he would be able to brief the two men. And to gather his thoughts. He felt that the governor had been much too impulsive so far, handling matters on his own, without counsel. At least now he seemed open to the thoughts of others. He quickly headed to the inner offices of the fort, finding Caldenhoven and Van Deurzen poring over maps.

"The governor wants to see you. You are both to come with me." The two men, both in their early thirties, exchanged glances across the desk.

"That Chinaman, Zheng, has declared war on us. Turns out he isn't merely the pirate the governor thinks he is, as he seems to have friends in high places. Managed to get quite a fleet together, or so it seems."

"My God! So it is true then," Caldenhoven said. They had all heard the rumors, but the governor had dismissed them as simply that: rumors. They strode in silence through the cool, damp halls of the fort.

"Sit down. Caldenhoven. Van Deurzen," Putmans acknowledged as they entered his office. They both took their seats. Boenck preferred to remain standing.

"I take it the commander has already briefed you?"

"Yes, governor, he did," Van Deurzen said.

"First of all," Putmans began, leaning forward, "I don't believe Zheng is seriously contemplating attacking us. I believe he is bluffing." The three men said nothing. "But we cannot afford to take any chances, as we don't know for certain what his true capacity is right now. Gentlemen, your thoughts?"

Boenck breathed a sigh of relief. The governor was actually taking counsel. Lieutenant Caldenhoven stepped forward, clearing his throat. "If I may, sir?"

"Of course," Putmans said, sitting back in his chair.

"We all know that there is a war going on between the Chinese empire and Manchuria. Apparently this Zheng is an ardent Ming loyalist who is willing to fight for his emperor. When he isn't interfering in our trade, he keeps himself occupied with his military campaigns against the Manchus."

"Go on," Putmans said, nodding.

"We could offer a truce, sir. Perhaps we could offer our support to uphold their cause, supply them with weaponries and a small number of troops to fight these Manchus," Caldenhoven suggested.

"You're suggesting we aid them in their war."

"It's not such a terrible idea, sir," Van Deurzen said. "Lieutenant Caldenhoven is right. By offering our alliance — even in a minor way — Zheng can focus on fighting these Manchus instead of us. That might get him off our backs."

"But can we trust him?" Boenck asked. "How do we know he won't use our own weapons against us?"

"Of that, we can never be certain," Putmans agreed, his eyebrows furrowing in thought. Then he leaned forward again, his elbows on his desk as he looked at them. "There is something we could ask for in exchange." His eyes glinted as an idea began to take shape. "In exchange for our aid in this war against these Manchus, not only could we make the arrangement that he allows us to trade in peace, we could also demand a trading base, say in Fuzhou?"

"We don't know if he has the authority to grant that, sir," Boenck said with a frown.

"No, we don't. Yet he did manage to scrape together a decent fleet in a short time, so he must have some standing over there. Time we found out how well connected this man genuinely is. It's worth a shot, isn't it?"

Caldenhoven and Van Deurzen traded glances, Van Deurzen nodded. Although it was rather ambitious, the governor was right. They did not have much to lose.

But Boenck, ever the military man, hesitated. Up to now, Zheng had been highly unpredictable. His gut feeling told him that the conditions demanded might be too much of a provocation. He had found it difficult to gauge the emotions of the Chinese, and he felt that this elusive man, who had so far proved a worthy foe, should not to be underestimated.

"Sir, we have attempted for decades to open a trading base there. Why should he —" He corrected himself: "Why should the emperor consent to it now?"

"Because," the governor paused for effect. "This time we have something to offer by means of repayment." He smiled confidently and sat back with his hands behind his head, a clear sign that he had made up his mind.

"Very well, sir. What are your instructions? Do we release the junk's crew?" Boenck asked.

"Yes. Arrange for the necessary documents and translations to be signed by me. Then we will permit these men you captured to return to Zheng with our proposal. They have been treated well, I trust?"

"Yes, sir. They have been held captive on board their own ship. We didn't harm them in any way."

"Good," Putmans said. "I expect we'll soon be hearing some kind of response from our Chinaman friend." Then a thought struck him. "Boenck, prepare six ships for sailing at dawn. We will provide the junk with a proper escort." He grinned at his own remark.

"Governor, with due respect, the winds are changing. Would it not be hazardous to...?"

"The weather will be fine. Haven't you ever sailed in turbulent seas before? What kind of a sailor are you?"

Boenck pursed his lips in an effort to stop himself from retorting.

"No," Putmans said, determined. "Let us make this pact while we can. We have lost too much time as it is with all this nonsense. And have my cabin prepared. I will be coming along. I would very much like to see the rabble that this pirate has managed to scrape together. Perhaps I can negotiate with the man myself."

Boenck looked doubtful. His reservations were not just about the weather. He did not share the governor's confidence in how things would turn out. Putmans might be his superior, but Boenck had been among the Chinese for longer than the brief two years that the governor had, and he seriously questioned his judgment.

"Sir, what if it doesn't work and they attack us? Six ships might not be enough if –"

Putmans' eyes blazed at being questioned. "Just do as I say. Prepare six ships. We leave at dawn. I make the decisions here, not you. Is that understood?"

Boenck didn't flinch. "Of course, sir, as you wish."

"Fine. I believe you have a job to do."

The following day, the six designated ships sailed with the smaller Chinese vessel leading the way. The junk's crew was jittery with the large Dutch warships right on their tail, and like Boenck, they had also noticed the subtle change in the weather.

When they reached the main island of the Pescadores where Zheng had his headquarters, Boenck gave orders to lower the anchors within two miles of the shore. The war junk sped away from its imposing escort to the safety of its home harbor, the captain keeping a nervous eye on the idle guns that the Dutch had aimed upon them throughout the voyage.

Putmans stood at the bridge peering through a telescope, scanning the shoreline for enemy ships. Boenck stood next to him, his unaided, trained eyes taking in more of the scene than Putmans could with the help of the brass eyepiece.

"Impressive," Putmans admitted with a grunt at the sight of the Chinese fleet. "Not quite as substantial as we were made out to believe, but still."

Boenck said nothing as Putmans continued to look through the instrument, watching as the Chinese envoy's vessel docked into harbor.

"We'll see what our Chinese friend will have to say to what we have proposed. I don't think there will be a fight. I am certain that he will accept what we have put forward," he added as he handed the instrument back to the captain. "Keep me abreast of developments." Putmans said, before disappearing to his cabin below.

Boenck remained on deck, too agitated to stay in his cabin, his telescope useless at his side in the dark of night. Even though he thought he could discern some activity in the harbor, they were anchored at too great a distance to see what was happening there. He glanced up at the masts above his head, feeling slightly uneasy. There were no stars by which to measure the ship's roll; the skies had been overcast even before the sun had set. But he had felt the winds pick up and noticed that the sea had grown restless. Once again he questioned the governor's confidence. He simply wasn't sure what to expect.

* * *

Zheng Zhilong sat on the floor, lounging casually against some silk cushions, a tray of leftovers between him and the retired general he was entertaining.

"Lord Zheng! Your envoy has returned," one of his lieutenants announced.

Zhilong remained seated, but his relaxed demeanor changed at the sight of the envoy he had sent to the Dutch, eager to learn their response to his declaration of war. The messenger dropped to one knee, carefully averting his eyes.

"You have returned. That is good. What news do you bring from the Hollanders?" he asked. Dispatching the war junk had been a risk, but he had calculated correctly that the Dutch would capture it and subject the passengers to questioning. He had worked for these people long enough to know how they thought. It proved once again how invaluable his employment with these people had been.

"My lord admiral, I have with me an answer from our enemy." The man quickly handed over the documents that the Dutch had entrusted him with. "They are here, awaiting your reply. Their *zhangguan*, their governor, is here. They anchored six of their ships off the coast."

Zheng immediately got to his feet, snatched the documents from the man's hands and strode to the door that faced the harbor, his eyes searching for the Dutch ships. He could vaguely make out the flickering lights of lanterns on the distant decks. Behind him, the messenger withdrew to await further orders outside. Zheng's brow furrowed as he read the contents, inhaling sharply between his teeth.

"They wish to negotiate," he said, the tone of his voice ominously low.

The old general chuckled. "Of course," he said. "That is to be expected, they are a stubborn people. What do they want?"

"They expect me to act as intermediary with the Imperial Court to arrange for trading rights. They wish to have their own trade enclave, just like the Portuguese. Pfff. The mere thought of it."

The general nodded, apparently unsurprised. "Those red-haired barbarians have been pestering the authorities for a trading base for decades. Do they offer something in return?"

"Weapons. Weapons and troops for the Ming cause."

"Ah," the old man said. "Your powerful benefactors have offered you their ships and troops to fight the Hollanders. You have declared war on these people and they still believe they can negotiate a deal." With his chopsticks he selected a morsel from the platter in front of him and popped it in his mouth, eating noisily and with relish.

"Yes," Zheng said, nodding. "They are blinded by their stubbornness and greed. These people do not understand the concept of face. And I have the mandate of heaven to fight them."

"War it is, then," the other man said, laying down his chopsticks across the top of his bowl. Zheng nodded, standing lost in thought for a brief moment before striding out of the building, into the darkness.

The fleet under his command had been ready since he had officially declared war on the Dutch. The crews were on full alert, the junks fully armed. Under the cover of darkness, the order was given to attack the Dutch ships lying at anchor while they waited for his answer.

Tens of junks were sent around the main island of Penghu to surprise the Dutch. Once they had cleared Penghu, the rest of the fleet would advance and attack. No torches were lit on the moving ships, not a single lantern. These sailors knew these waters like the back of their hands, and they used this to their advantage. They also knew that a storm was coming. There was no time to lose.

Two hours later, the Chinese vessels sailed around Penghu, unseen and unheard. The large Dutch ships, their sails down, rolled ungainly on the choppy waves, oblivious to their stalkers. With most eyes focused on the harbor, few members of the crew had seen the attackers appear from behind, and when they did, it was too late. In the blackness that was night, scores of enemy warships advanced ominously on the six ships.

Once within range, the Chinese fired their weapons on the ships, the sound alerting the other vessels waiting in harbor to join the attack. Even in their mighty warships, the Dutch were unprepared for the onslaught. They had been waiting for an answer, but they did not expect to be attacked. Within minutes, the small fleet was surrounded by war junks, their guns pointed ominously in their direction.

The scene on the decks of the ships was one of chaos. The Dutch sailors scrambled to hoist the sails, but they were surprised by Chinese who had managed to board the ships. Those men paid for their inattention with their lives, their torsos penetrated with cold, hard steel.

Anchors were raised frantically. The waters surrounding the great ships were now black with hostile vessels, a staccato of gunfire from both sides shattering the eardrums. The pungent odor of gunpowder could be smelled with every ringing shot, and before long the ships were shrouded by a stinking cloud of blue smoke. The guns of the Dutch were superior; but with every enemy vessel that went down, a new junk would appear in its place.

Bewildered, the governor gave the order to retreat. Boenck shouted the command into the wind, and soon the other five ships followed, their decorated prows turning in an ungainly dance of flight. Heavily under fire, the first ship managed to break through the attackers, firing salvos at random, vulnerable to attack on the bow side as they had to break through the line of fire.

By the time the Dutch ships had found the open seas to leave their attackers far behind them, two of their ships had been seriously damaged.

Seventy-one men had lost their lives in the attack; many more were wounded.

As the ships limped back toward Formosa, another typhoon gathered strength.

Exposed to the onslaught on the open seas, the majestic ships now battled with the fury of nature. Of the six ships that had sailed for the Pescadores, only four returned to Zeelandia Bay, a third of their crews gone.

* * *

Boenck was in a somber mood, like everyone else on Formosa. The colonists had suddenly been drawn into a war, the outcome of which was by no means certain, and there was little time to mourn those lost at sea. The typhoon that had ravaged the ships on their way back had done damage to the island as well, killing several Chinese workers and one Dutch settler with flying debris. Trees had been uprooted, and although the stone forts had withstood the fury of the storm, the bamboo scaffolding surrounding the buildings under construction had mostly been destroyed, as had many wooden houses.

Boenck hadn't seen the governor for several days when he was summoned by him. Putmans had probably needed the time to pluck up the courage to face him after the ill-fated battle at sea. Boenck had no real desire to see him, either. He had warned the governor, and the man had chosen to ignore his advice. The fleet had taken a costly beating and many lives had been lost, and it was all Putnams' fault. Boenck was still fuming.

Putmans received him in his private rooms, nursing a bruised shoulder that he sustained the night of the sea battle. As the other two men entered Putmans' quarters, he sat at his writing desk, looking sober.

"Gentlemen." He motioned for the two men to be seated and took a deep breath. "We have made a mistake." Then he shook his head. "No, *I* have made a mistake. I misjudged our adversary. Batavia has always been clear that we should make use of any opportunities to establish trade relations with the Chinese empire. However," he paused, a dramatic sigh. "It appears that our offer to aid Zheng and his fellow Ming loyalists in their fight against the Manchus does not weigh up to their reluctance to give us a trading post. It now seems as if we will have to accept this for now." He picked up his quill, dipped it in the inkwell and began writing. Boenck said nothing, still angry.

"What do you intend to do about Zheng, sir?" Caldenhoven inquired after a long silence.

"We struck him, he struck us back in retaliation. It looks as if we are on a par. Unfortunately, they also had nature on their side. Arrange for me to meet with this Zheng. Maybe we can come to some kind of covenant if we accept them on his terms. See to it." Despondent, Putmans handed the note he had written to Caldenhoven, who took it and left the room.

Putmans looked at Boenck, who returned his gaze, still saying nothing. There were many things that he wanted to say to the governor. As a military commander, as a man. But he restrained himself. With a nod of his head, but unable to hide a last look of contempt, he was gone.

* * *

After a week of envoys' comings and goings in which carefully written communiqués were exchanged, both sides finally came to a settlement. Zhilong agreed to meet Putmans at his headquarters on the Pescadores, but on his terms. Only two ships were permitted to approach the harbor, and no more than four men would be allowed to disembark. This was his territory, so he could set the rules. He now held the balance in this struggle for power, and he intended to use this to his advantage.

Accompanied by a VOC interpreter and a clerk, Putmans and Van Deurzen left their ship to meet Zheng. They were received by an armed escort, who led them to Zheng's official hall.

Fully aware of the psychological advantage that he now had, Zheng sat on his lacquered high-backed chair, dressed to impress in his blue embroidered tunic. Several aides stood to one side, two servants kneeling in the background. The armed guards that had taken the Dutchmen to their commander remained by the door, not taking their eyes off the foreigners for a single moment. Zheng looked at them with indifference before giving brief instructions to his interpreters.

"Our lord and master welcomes you. He trusts you had a good journey?" the chief interpreter asked cordially. More ritual pleasantries followed, the words first translated into Portuguese and then relayed into Dutch by a second interpreter. There were very few men who were able to translate Chinese directly into Dutch, or vice versa, resulting in lengthy interpreting rituals.

It was Putmans who eventually asked the question, impatient as always. What did Zheng propose?

Zheng smiled at the governor's discourtesy. The Dutch were so blunt in their ways. It was something he had grown accustomed to when he had worked as an interpreter for the VOC. He wondered if the man in front of him had any idea that he understood most of what he said. Apparently he did not, and he intended to take full advantage of the fact.

"There is no more need for further hostilities," Zheng offered in Chinese, in a calculated, conciliatory tone. "I am convinced that if we help each other in some way, we can come to an arrangement that will benefit us all." He waited patiently for the interpreters to translate.

Putmans mumbled something in agreement.

Zheng watched him, amused. The governor was sweating profusely, the strands of his dark hair stuck to his forehead. This man refused to adapt his clothes by shedding layers in the humid, subtropical climate, dressed in the heavy black uniform that befit his station as a VOC official. Discomfort was the price that he paid.

Zheng sensed the man's unease and allowed a deliberate silence to fill the hall. He found the Dutchman next to Putmans, presumably his second in command, more difficult to read, and suspected that he was the shrewder of the two.

"Your trade must be very important to you and your king," Zheng continued. It was a statement rather than a question. "It seems our country has many worthy products that you desire. That is good. We can come to an agreement that will benefit your revered company."

Putmans blinked as they waited for the translation.

"I am a businessman, Mr. Putmans. As you know, I have a fleet at my disposal and I have valuable contacts in all the important ports of China. I know what products you seek and I can obtain these for you at a good price. For a small fee I would be willing to trade on behalf of your company. As your exclusive agent, of course," he added with a hint of a smile.

He watched as Putmans nearly choked in consternation even before the interpreter had finished speaking, his expression betraying his feelings.

"*Verdomde piraat*! Damned pirate!" he heard him mutter to Van Deurzen. "Who the hell does he think he is? For the life of me we cannot allow some greedy Chinaman interfering in our business," he whispered, so the interpreter wouldn't hear. But Zheng had heard, and he observed the foreigners with cool amusement, enjoying himself.

"I think we have no alternative," the other man said. "If the only way we can trade with China is through him as mediator, then so be it. We're not getting anywhere the way things are now. Maybe we should consider it."

"Well, I certainly don't intend to take this decision without involving Batavia." The governor snorted in frustration, unwilling to take sole responsibility. "We shall have to try and win time."

Putmans turned back to Zheng. Speaking with slow exaggeration in a loud voice for the interpreter's benefit, he told Zheng that they had to consult with their superiors on the matter and that he would need a month to come back with an answer. In the meantime, they agreed to a truce in which the Dutch would temporarily halt their trading activities. Zheng summoned his scribe to record the agreement in writing. A writing table was brought inside the hall, and several clerks efficiently set to work. Within minutes, the documents were translated and signed by both parties.

* * *

By the time he was back on his ship, Putmans knew that he had been outsmarted by Zheng. In his cabin he feverishly wrote to his superiors in Batavia, formulating his arguments diplomatically. He reasoned in favor of granting Zheng Zhilong the trade on behalf of the VOC, stating that this was the only way in which the company could obtain the volume of Chinese goods that it desired. Zheng's influence had increased considerably during the past year, and they could no longer bypass him.

It took more than two months for Putmans to receive a reply from the council in Batavia. They agreed to allow Zheng to act as their agent. They did reprimand him for having failed in his mission to obtain free trade without having to involve "a notorious Chinese pirate," but they relented. Some members of the council had been strongly opposed to the idea, but the company's ambition to increase the trade volume with China won over its scruples and Putmans' well-formulated arguments gained him more advocates than opponents.

Once the deal was struck, there followed a frenzy of communication between the Pescadores and Formosa to make it official. Zheng Zhilong was now the VOC's exclusive agent for trade with China. But after all that had happened, relations between the two parties remained strained. The Dutch felt cheated, coerced to enter into a deal with someone they did not trust, while Zheng was more wary of the rude and aggressive Westerners than ever before.

As part of the conditions that Zheng had set, the Dutch merchant ships were now no longer permitted to enter China's ports. This resulted in less activity of the Dutch fleet in the Formosa Strait, and with his own fleet enjoying increased freedom of movement, his own spies could keep him informed on what the Dutch were up to.

Now that he could operate in the area unhindered, Zheng's ships started taking passengers from the Chinese mainland. With the threat of a Manchu invasion becoming very real, many wealthy and influential Chinese families decided to leave. Many left for the island nations of Southeast Asia, but the majority headed for the relative safety of Formosa. Nearly thirty thousand Chinese migrants reached the island, most of them carried by his ships for a fee. Mass migration had begun.

The sudden increase in migrants did not go unnoticed by the VOC. Not fully aware of the events taking place on the mainland, they welcomed the Chinese, as they needed the laborers. Some members of the Formosan council did point out the risks of such explosive population growth to the governor, but Putmans could see just the benefits: the bigger the population, the more laborers they would have at their disposal.

Now that they were no longer actively trading, the company had more time for other matters. It began to focus on developing the island as an independent source of revenue in its own right and looked closer at Formosa's potential as a mature colony. The steady supply of Chinese laborers did not merely boost agricultural production, it could also be put to work on the island's infrastructure. The arrival of wealthier Chinese gave an additional impetus to the local economy.

With less money coming from Batavia and more pressure to become financially independent, more taxes were introduced. Fishermen were taxed for permission to fish along the coasts. Permission to hunt for deer and wild boar was only granted after acquisition of a hunting license, which had to be paid for. Those who were caught hunting without a license or fishing at night in order to avoid the high taxes had to pay hefty fines. Although some warned Putmans of increased unrest among the poorer Chinese, he paid little heed. In every migrant farmer he saw not only cheap labor but also a source for additional income.

The story of Zheng Zhilong's naval battle and victory against the Dutch had spread on the island like wildfire. As discontent under Dutch rule grew, so did Zheng's heroic status; the Chinese were whispering about his exploits in awe. Many began to regard him as an ally against the Dutch authorities, even as a symbol of hope.

The stories of Zheng's heroism also reached the ears of the governor. The whole war business with Zheng had wearied him, and he still felt he had been outfoxed by the crafty Chinese pirate. Zheng's unforeseen attack at sea had decimated his fleet and soldiers. But what disconcerted Putmans the most, were Zheng's ever-increasing activities. There were even reports that he had ordered a fort to be built in northern Formosa. The man had become his nemesis – someone who made his blood boil and kept him awake at night. One thing he had learned over the past months was not to underestimate Zheng ever again.

5

Seeds of Rebellion

"AIYA!" the customer cried out in consternation. "Piece of turtle dung! You are trying to cheat me! Last week a bag of rice cost me just over half of what you're asking now. Do I look like a fool?"

Longfei strained her ears, curious. She stood halfway along the disorderly queue, waiting to buy rice. It was still early in the morning, the market crowded as usual. She pushed ahead in order to follow the argument more closely. The other waiting customers turned around, annoyed at being so jostled; but when they saw it was her, they let her pass.

The market salesman held up his hands in a gesture of helpless apology, glad to be separated from his customers by the trestle table that bulged with the weight of the bags of rice.

"I'm sorry, I have no choice. My boss has been ordered to apply a ten percent tax." He looked around nervously, uncomfortable with the unpopular tidings he was forced to bring.

The woman's eyes grew wide, her jaw dropped open.

"It is not for us," the salesman hastened to add. "It is to be handed over to the company authorities. Sorry, sorry, I'm really sorry." He had been dreading this from the minute the store's *thau-ke* had told him to raise their prices.

The customer's face had frozen like some grotesque mask. Longfei had listened in on the exchange with growing indignation. She pressed forward to intervene.

"Ten percent! Ten percent! How can we afford this increase? They cannot do this! What are they trying to do, starve us?" she raved.

Several other market goers, intrigued by the commotion, joined the growing crowd of onlookers.

"They also put ten percent on sugar," a man said. "And meat."

"*Siamih*? What?" Longfei turned on him, annoyed that he had drawn all the attention to himself at her expense. All eyes were now fixed on him.

"They also placed the same taxes on sugar and meat. And probably on other things too," he added.

The scene that followed was one of chaos. Women raised their voices, their faces flushed with anger. The rice seller shouted back in self-defense, concerned for his wares and his own safety.

"My husband should hear of this," Longfei declared. "He is the village head, after all. He will talk to the officials." She gathered her parcels and walked briskly toward her home, her round, pregnant belly protruding defiantly. Others followed her, still expressing their outrage as they went.

Guo Jinbao was startled and unprepared when his wife returned home accompanied by a crowd of peasants.

"Jinbao! You won't believe this! They've raised the prices by ten percent —" his wife began, but she was shoved aside by the disgruntled woman customer.

"A sales tax! They've imposed sales taxes on all the goods. We barely survive as is it!"

"My husband is a fisherman," a red-faced woman piped. "He can hardly pay the fisherman's tax. And now this!" Others began to shout in an attempt to make themselves heard, their complaints numerous. Jinbao's hands went to his ears in a helpless gesture.

"We must all go to the fort!" one man cried. "These foreign devils cannot do this. How are we supposed to feed our families?"

"Do they want us to starve?" another man asked.

"If they want us to work for them, they should treat us better!" someone suggested. "No taxes on daily goods!"

As they stood arguing on his doorstep, a group of seven farmers brandishing their tools passed along the dirt road. "Join us!" one of them called. "We are going to the fort!" Without hesitation, four of the men at Jinbao's door left and added themselves to the group, picking up sticks, spades or any other tools that could double as weapons along the way.

"If you won't join them, I will," Longfei told her husband, her expression fierce. Jinbao hesitated. As village head appointed by the Dutch, he knew he could easily be made responsible for not controlling the villagers if things went wrong. He looked at the growing band of men walking away, he saw the grim determination on their faces. He knew that they had little to lose. He nodded at his wife, and stepped outside.

"You stay here," he told her.

The growing mob, emboldened by his support, began to draw attention. Men and women returning from the marketplace, still bewildered by the news of the unwelcome sales taxes, stared at them dumbly, especially when they recognized Jinbao.

"Come! Join us!" their foreman cried out. "This time the red-haired barbarians have gone too far! We will not accept these new sales taxes!" More people joined. They passed the various houses and sheds, yelling encouragement to those who emerged from their houses, curious to see what the commotion was about.

"*Ei*, what's happening?" a woman called out as they passed a rice paddy.

"The red-headed barbarians have thought up even more taxes to pester us. Ten percent on rice, meat, sugar. Even cooking oil!"

The workers in the paddy exchanged glances. In an instant of silent understanding, they offloaded the baskets from their backs and made to join the mob, ignoring the startled Dutch overseers, who were powerless to stop the laborers from leaving the fields, no matter what threats they shouted after them. An overseer grabbed the arm of a woman about to quit the paddy.

"Where do you think you're going?" he snapped in rudimentary Chinese. "You stay! Get back to work!"

Bolstered by their increasing numbers, a couple of men stepped out of the crowd, angered by the Dutchman's interference. They advanced upon him scowling, their sticks and tools raised in threat. The overseer stiffened. He let go of the woman, suddenly aware of the danger the mob posed. The woman turned and spat at his feet before joining the others. Stumbling, the overseer fled for Fort Zeelandia. This was new: he had never experienced anything like this before. The Chinese ignored him and continued toward the fort.

By the time they were within a mile of the fortress, they had passed through four villages, collecting more disgruntled peasants on their way. Three Dutchwomen backed away in alarm at the sight of them.

Each and every one of them had a story. Among them were peasants who lived in poverty, their meager wages further reduced by the various taxes; they were hardly able to provide their families with two meals a day. There were the frustrated farmers, who had petitioned for years for permission to buy their own land, only to be told that they would have to pay rent for the land that they tilled. There were fishermen and hunters, who hardly broke even with the additional license taxes imposed on them. And then there were those who had become sick or injured during their work for the company, but who were left untreated at the risk of death. They were people who had little left to lose. By the time they reached the fortress, the crowd had grown to almost a thousand.

The sentries at the small redoubt of Fort Utrecht, which overlooked Fort Zeelandia, had a good view of the surroundings. They had seen the crowd heading toward Zeelandia from afar and knew straight away that something was amiss. They quickly reported what they had seen to their senior officers.

The menacing crowd of Chinese had arrived at the gates of the fort. The square in front of the gate was milling with people, their mood volatile. Someone voiced a slogan of protest, and others joined him, repeating his words over and over again. But this time, words were not enough. They rushed at the gates in unison, shouting and raising their improvised weapons in the air as they did. A woman stumbled, falling against a young Dutch soldier guarding the gates, his musket held across his chest. In his panic, he accidentally shot in the air, the sound reverberating against the fortress walls.

The gun blast triggered a dangerous reaction. A collective surge of adrenaline rushed through the veins of the Chinese, who were no longer in control of their heated emotions. In sheer panic they pushed toward the gate, where they faced a small band of stunned guards which they attacked with the weapons they brandished. They turned on the Chinese company employees who were despised for their easy jobs, shoving them to the ground to leave them spat upon and humiliated. Bales of silk that had yet to be taken to the warehouses were slashed and damaged, and precious porcelain was reduced to shards. Crates of spices were smashed to splinters, their fragrant contents spilling out onto the ground, trampled upon, and rendered worthless.

Several men managed to enter the fortress, but they found themselves staring at the muzzles of guns. They died with the first volley of shots. The demonstrators were so caught up with the fury of the moment that none of them noticed the Dutch troops that had gathered and advanced on them from behind.

Taking up their positions, the Dutch soldiers fired. At first, the sharp staccato of the guns could hardly be heard above the din. The protestors didn't become aware of the danger until blood began to flow and when they saw the look of disbelief in the eyes of the dying.

The reasons for their uprising were suddenly forgotten, their anger replaced by fear and the primitive, all-consuming desire to survive. As gunfire seemed to come from all sides, they fled in every direction, colliding into one another as they did.

Guo Jinbao stumbled in a desperate attempt to get away from the fort. He dashed for the safety of the mission schoolhouse, where he rested against the wall, trying to catch his breath. He turned to look back in the direction from where he had just come, only to see people getting shot and dying before his very eyes.

* * *

Reverend Junius was in the middle of teaching a class of aboriginal children the rudiments of the Old Testament when he heard the commotion through his open window. The small schoolhouse in which he taught was within a mile of Fort Zeelandia. He opened the door of the makeshift building, and what he saw outside made his blood run cold.

"*Mijn God*!" he breathed. He had always known that this would happen. How many times had he and his colleagues not warned the governor of the growing discontent among the Chinese? This had been long in the making. Yet Putmans had not listened to them, discarding their advice as nonsense. And these were the consequences.

The crowd drew ominously nearer. He remained where he was, in the doorway, despite the danger that he might face. At one time, they might have liked him as the man of God he really was, as the man he wished to be. They all knew him as Reverend "Juni." But now the sight of him was likely to remind them only of the despised tax collector the company had forced him to become.

Members of the crowd began to shout insults at him. His Chinese was sufficient to understand most of the insults.

"Son of a turtle head!"

"Piece of turtle dung!"

"*Lin nia*!" He wrinkled his nose in distaste as one man implied he had fornicated with his own mother. But no one stopped to bother him, unwilling to become detached from the relative safety of the crowd. He breathed a sigh of relief as he shut the door and ran to the window facing the fort, oblivious of his curious young students, whom he had momentarily forgotten.

His face ashen, he watched the Dutch troops emerge from the fort's back entrance, enclosing the protesting Chinese from behind. With the crowd's focus on the front gate, it seemed unaware of the danger that encroached it. He felt utterly helpless as he realized what was about to happen. If there was any way that he could have warned them, he would have done so. With trembling lips he prayed to God for those about to fall. He knew what easy prey the emotional, disorganized crowd with its improvised weapons would be for the armed Dutch soldiers. Against the superior firearms of these trained men, they would not have a chance.

Then Junius caught sight of movement just outside the window. He peered out to look directly in the startled eyes of a Chinese man. He blinked as he recognized Guo Jinbao, the head from the neighboring village. For just an instant, their eyes locked. Then the reverend broke eye contact and moved to the window facing north, where he made sure the coast was clear. He quickly returned and signaled with a slight movement of his head that it was safe for him to go. Jinbao nodded his thanks and disappeared into the woods.

Guo Jinbao fled for the hills, where he hid with the help of a local hunter, not daring to return for fear of reprisals. He didn't go home for over a week. When he did return he was picked up for questioning, but Reverend Junius intervened. The missionary had arranged to be present during the session, using his influence and authority over the lower-ranked officials to make sure they treated Jinbao with respect. "He was with me," he told them with authority, providing the village head with an alibi without having to tell a complete lie. Jinbao was lucky: he was soon released.

What had begun as spontaneous revolt had evolved into the first major riot in the colony's sixteen-year history. Putmans felt he had no choice but to strike down hard. The very next day, Dutch troops gathered the corpses of those hit in the crossfire and dumped them unceremoniously at the marketplace, where they remained for all to see in a grotesque display of power. An example was made of those captured during the riot. Others were taken from their homes and brought back as scapegoats to be subjected to the humiliation of public beatings. Many were imprisoned, some of whom were tortured to give the names of possible ringleaders. Because of the impromptu nature of the protest, there were no real leaders; but the governor was determined to punish those responsible for the disturbance and pursued his quarry with wrath.

The number of migrant Chinese continued to grow and eventually vastly outnumbered both the native islanders and the Dutch colonists.

Even though the riot had been easily quashed by the army, it did serve as a warning to the VOC council that the ever-increasing Chinese population could easily be a threat if not properly restrained. Now that

Formosa had become a significant source of income in its own right, the council in Batavia agreed that certain measures had to be taken to protect its interests. More troops were sent to the island.

In order to better control the Chinese, the VOC introduced a *hoofdbrief* tax, a head tax for all Chinese living on the island. It was a personal license with all kinds of limitations, for which a monthly fee had to be paid. Officials on the island diligently set to work to ensure that each Chinese paid the tax. Every month when the payments were due, the Dutch raised a flag on the fort's newly established tax office so that no one was left in doubt that it was time to pay. *Hoofdbrief* inspections could be performed by any of the Dutch settlers, and were done on a regular basis. Any Chinese not found in the possession of a valid *hoofdbrief* license was heavily fined. Those unable to pay the fine were beaten or imprisoned at Fort Zeelandia.

It soon became clear that the system was susceptible to abuse. Most of the Dutch colonists were poorly paid, uneducated ruffians who had left their motherland in search of employment overseas. They had absolutely no scruples about extorting money from the Chinese. Some of them began harassing Chinese for the *hoofdbrief* license wherever they saw them: in the fields, on the road, practically anywhere. Some even resorted to raiding Chinese homes at night. Soldiers confiscated the permits in order to demand bribes, seizing chickens and livestock, rice, or any other household items that they might desire.

It wasn't long before the Chinese started to complain. They turned to their village headmen about this latest grievance, and these went to speak to the governor, warning him that things could get seriously out of hand if the corrupt system were allowed to continue. Some members of the Formosan council suggested abolishing it altogether, but it had become too lucrative a source of income to discard. In order to avoid major riots, the governor changed the policy. Now only specially assigned *hoofdbrief* inspectors wearing special insignias would be allowed to perform the inspections. Unfortunately, these measures didn't stop the lowly paid Dutch employees from carrying on with their corrupt practice, and the humiliating raids and cruel harassment continued to take place.

The company then turned to the wealthier Chinese on the island. They were businessmen, entrepreneurs, and merchants – men of means. It was to these men that the VOC began to sell so-called village leaseholds. For a price, they could buy the exclusive right to exploit certain commercial activities within a village district, such as farming plots of land, issuing hunting and trading licenses, trading in a particular aboriginal village, or buying and selling certain products. These village leaseholds were sold at annual auctions, and the successful buyer would thus obtain the sole right to that particular commercial activity for the duration of a whole year. Inevitably, this system created trade monopolies, with the leaseholders able to set any price they wanted. The aboriginals now had no choice but to sell their goods at unfairly low prices, their income halved. Tensions between the two population groups mounted as a result.

During the seven years that Hans Putmans served as governor of Formosa, the company continued to develop the island, ruling over its people with an iron hand. A new governor was appointed and in turn succeeded by another. Within the space of sixteen years, thousands of Dutch settlers came to Formosa. Encouraged by the ease with which they had quelled the 1640 riot, the Dutch had by now subdued the entire island. Colonization had reached its peak.

Meanwhile, on the other side of the strait, the great Ming dynasty was slowly drawing to a close. The powerful forces of history gathered momentum, urging even more Chinese to take their chances and seek refuge on Formosa.

6

The Young Mandarin

1643, FUJIAN PROVINCE

THE size of the armed Black Guard that escorted Zheng Sen back to his home in Fujian was significant. Years ago, his father had explained to him why he preferred these men over his own countrymen for his personal army. From bitter experience, his father had learned not to trust anyone, not even his own brothers, and found that employing these hardened, foreign soldiers had its advantages. The Black Guard consisted of a motley crew of Africans and Moluccans from the East Indies, most of them mercenaries and former slaves of the Dutch. Recruited as strangers from other lands, they played no part in the intrigues that were rife among his Chinese officers or even his own family, all of whom had their own agendas. These people had no history of conflict or loyalty to any particular Chinese lord. The only loyalty they felt was to the wages he paid them.

Zheng Sen understood the value of these men, whom he treated well, just like his father had always done. As he rode, he noticed that they all seemed in robust health and were well dressed, a sign that, in spite of the mounting unrest in the land, the Zheng family business had not suffered. His father had long proven his worth and loyalty to the emperor, who had made him commander of his southern armies as well as an official custodian of the Ming. In that capacity, the emperor greatly respected his counsel, for which he was paid handsomely. The appointment had done him no harm, giving him additional status and providing him with even more influential, powerful contacts. He had become a well-known figure in southern China and someone with a considerable army under his command.

When Zheng Sen had protested in a manly show of confidence that he did not require such an escort, his father had become furious, saying that if he were to fall into the hands of the enemy, they might decide to hold him ransom, even kill him. It was a risk he was not willing to take.

Zheng Sen had acceded and apologized to his father without further comment. Even now, at the age of nineteen, he was still in awe of him. His father was a magistrate of influence, an important military leader, and a successful merchant. How often had his stepmother, grandmother, and "aunties" told him stories about his father's integrity, his feats of heroism, his wisdom and noble deeds? Not to mention his undying loyalty to the Ming and the emperor, both of which he had sworn to support to the end. So often he had listened to his father's conversations in admiration – conversations held with his uncles and military officers, impressive-looking men who frequently visited his home to discuss their campaigns to defend the Ming.

Zheng Sen's father had always allowed him to sit in on these talks when he was young, as long as he kept his mouth shut. "That way you will be able to learn something of value," his father had told him. The language he heard the men use was strongly worded. They were words of undying loyalty, about their duty to the emperor to help him in his fight against the enemy from the north. These men were his heroes, just as his father was. They were the custodians of the Ming. And that was something worthy of his respect.

Sitting in on these meetings was seen as part of his education, the importance of which his father said he could never emphasize enough. He had the best tutors available, which he could appreciate, as he had an aptitude for learning. It came to him easily, and he never found it wearying.

He loved the poems from the Song and the Tang; his teachers even said he had talent for writing poetry himself. Confucius' *Analects* he memorized with ease, as he did the works of Laozi and Mencius. But the writings of Sun Tzu especially appealed to him. He could recite and discuss *The Art of War* in detail, so that even his father was impressed.

He never stopped missing his mother. He had continued to write to her faithfully over the years, sending letters to her almost every week. In those letters he told her in detail about the members of the Zheng family, especially his stepmother Lady Yan, his grandmother and "aunties," who had eventually come to accept him. In the first six months following his arrival Lady Yan and his father's numerous concubines would have little to do with him; some were even openly hostile. But after this disrespect came to his father's attention, things had improved.

He wrote on the progress of his lessons, and told his mother about his half-brothers, Du and Shiyin, and his cousin Cai, with whom he had become fast friends. In order to keep up his Japanese, he wrote her poems: entire pages on the pain of separation, the beauty of the coming of spring, the grief he felt when he watched the sun go down, thinking of her and the country of his birth.

In turn, his mother answered his letters with poems of her own. He wrote to her with pride about his father, informing her of his ever-expanding trade imperium and the exotic destinations to which he travelled.

Zheng Sen realized how truly privileged he was. His father was a wealthy, respected merchant, which meant that as the oldest son he, too, was treated with respect by everyone. He had always had the best instructors in the martial arts, in which he could lose himself with a passion. That he had a talent for these was apparent from the satisfied faces of his stern tutors, as well as from the envious and admiring looks that he received from his brothers and cousins. On the occasion that his father and uncles attended the training sessions, he noticed that they would become instantly alert whenever it was his turn to perform. As he progressed, his instructors were replaced by others, more advanced and specialized than their predecessors.

His family's good intentions, however, also had drawbacks. The status that the Zhengs had gained was acknowledged by all and was therefore carefully safeguarded. This led to great scrutiny as far as his responsibilities were concerned, even when he was young. His father believed it was imperative that his son marry well. In order to cement their social position further, he had instructed his mother and wife to find Zheng Sen a suitable, high-born bride.

Zheng Sen hadn't been the least bit interested in marriage. Having just completed the Imperial Exams and possessed of a voracious sexual appetite, he was far more interested in bedding the local girls. His grandmother and Lady Yan, however, took their new task very seriously. During the past months it had been housekeeper Liu who had been compelled, her lips smacking with relish, to inform Lady Zheng and Lady Yan of the young master's sexual vigor. They all agreed that now he was a grown man, it was important that he marry soon. Besides, his grandmother intended to make it a matter of some urgency, in the hope that her grandson would sire her great-grandchildren.

Grateful for something to break the monotony of everyday life and the chance to use their influence, the two women had set upon the mission with relish, calling in the services of the province's most reputable matchmaker.

Due to the standing, wealth, and growing power of the Zhengs, many families came forward to suggest their daughters as brides to the matchmaker. The old woman, her face painted in the grotesque mask of white powder and red cheeks as a symbol of her trade, became a regular visitor to the Zheng household, where she would confer with the matriarch and Lady Yan for hours.

After two months of talks, divination rituals, and a variety of bribes and gifts from the girls' families to the matchmaker, the names of two suitable candidates for marriage were finally put forward.

Both marriage candidates were young, not-unattractive girls with similar backgrounds, their families rich and influential. After further divination of the girls' and Zheng Sen's birthdates, the matchmaker finally presented the name of Deng Cuiying.

The Zhengs had accepted. With an indomitable grandmother and a stepmother determined to have some say in the matter, Zheng Sen had no choice but to agree to marry the girl, however reluctant he might be.

With the coming of the new moon, Cuiying was transported to the village of Anhai in a litter of red and gold splendor, the wedding palanquin swaying with the bearers' every step. The Zhengs received the girl with honor, while the young bridegroom met her with a mixture of anxiety and physical excitement. He had felt immensely relieved at her gentle good looks and apparent modesty when he lifted the thin red veil from her jeweled headdress, delighted with her appearance.

In spite of the fact that he had to return to the Imperial Academy in Nanking to resume his studies, Zheng Sen had quickly gotten his bride with child, much to the delight of the old matriarch, who insisted on all kinds of diet restrictions and prescriptions to ensure its gender.

As Cuiying's pregnancy progressed, those around her soon discovered her true nature. Born to a wealthy household, the girl had never wanted for anything. An only child, her own mother had coddled and protected her, dressing her in fine garments, adorning her in jewels, and shielding her from life outside the walls of her ancestral home. Her pampered upbringing had done little to prepare her to adjust to the realities of married life, let alone to join a household as someone's daughter-in-law.

She spent long hours on her beauty routine, quickly irritated when things did not go her way. Unable to deal with old Lady Zheng's sharp tongue and the intervening Lady Yan, she often vented her frustrations on the many servants she insisted she needed. That didn't change after giving birth to her first son, Jing.

With Zheng Sen, she always played the part of the wronged and innocent. Pouting her lips and batting her eyelashes, she tried to have things her way. Although Zheng Sen initially had been flattered by her attention, he soon found her tiresome and dull of spirit, and unable to converse on anything that mattered. He did, however, enjoy her physical beauty, so he often came to her bed to fulfil his marital duties, her presence offering him easy and legitimate sexual release.

During his visit the previous Chinese New Year he had gotten Cuiying pregnant once more, and now her protruding belly was as round as a melon. In the meantime, his interest in nubile servant girls returned undiminished.

He had not wanted to break off his formal education at the Imperial Academy, but in the end he didn't have a choice. Many of his fellow students had already left the academy to join their families, their parents fearing that their sons would fall prey to roaming Manchu troops. He had suspected for some time that he, too, would be summoned home. The Imperial Academy had already begun to lose its best teachers and had become a potential target for the advancing Manchurian army, which saw the university as a breeding ground for Ming loyalists.

The academy had become too dangerous a place to be. Besides, his father had announced that it was time that Zheng Sen took on responsibilities, as he now had a family of his own. It was high time that he put all his learning to practice and become involved in the family trading business.

Zheng Sen didn't really mind. He was far too impatient to enter the real world, to trade and to travel; but most of all he wanted to fight against the Manchus. He couldn't wait to play his part on the battlefield, to show everyone what he was worth, to be able to put all those hard years of training to good use. Perhaps he could become a custodian of the Ming, like his father.

He sat in his saddle as he rode, flanked on both sides by members of his father's Black Guard. Looking around him, he realized that the men escorting him were no luxury. The Ming forces had failed in their efforts to the stem the tide of deserters, and the mountain passes were crawling with bandits and desperate people fleeing from the advancing Manchu armies, who were fast gaining ground up north.

They made their way down the hill at a leisurely pace. The peasants working the rice paddies glanced up as they passed, bowing low as they recognized the oldest son of their master, who owned most of the land that they tilled.

Zheng Sen nodded to an old man, who gaped at him in awe and then smiled, displaying the few teeth that he still had left. An official of the Black Guard shouted a command at two young boys poking their sticks at a dead snake along the roadside. One boy dropped his stick and raced ahead of the horsemen toward the Zheng residence, the other boy in pursuit, his filthy bare legs bounding away. Zheng Sen smiled. It reminded him of the time when he and Cai were just boys. The two of them would often sneak out of the gate after their lessons, in search of snakes, toads, and crickets, which they would catch with their bare hands and place in small cages to take home. During his time at the academy, he had missed Cai. Zheng Sen spurred his horse forward. It was good to be home again.

7

Daughter of the Samurai

HIRADO, NAGASAKI, JAPAN, 1645

MATSU found it difficult to remain calm now that her departure drew nearer, her emotions ranging from excitement, fear, hope, and at times, sheer panic. She spoke to no one of her plans save for her immediate family, and even that was a risk. Travel restrictions under the Shogunate were tight, especially for women.

Watanabe, her aging Japanese common-law husband and the father of her youngest son, Zaemon, had died the year before. He had suffered a serious stroke, leaving him paralyzed from the waist down. From that moment on, the life had fast drained away from his frail, old body. Watanabe's small inheritance went to his now three adult sons by his first wife, meaning that Matsu and her fifteen-year-old son were left to fend for themselves. Her benefactor and lover had left her with some funds, but they were sufficient to last them for only a short time. Matsu had made a serious attempt to find suitable work, but without any success.

Meanwhile, Zaemon had grown into a tall, gangly, and rather quiet teenager who closely resembled his father, whom he had adored. Like his half-brother, the boy had excelled in the martial arts, but a bad fall from a horse in his early teens had left his walking impaired. Fortunately, he had a good brain, which he had put to work assisting his father in keeping the books for his modest but successful business selling calligraphy brushes, paper, and ink.

From the moment Fukumatsu had left Japan, he had written his mother faithfully, a habit that he continued over the years. She knew that he had been given the name of Zheng Sen long since, but to her he would always remain Fukumatsu. His letters gave her a detailed account of his life in China, of the progress he made with his studies, his concerns for the future, his dreams, and of the antics of his precious young sons, Jing and Xi. He also included lengthy poems in which he spoke of his nostalgia for Japan. She cherished the poems, often reading them in the lonely hours of the evening, which only made her long for him even more.

In his letters, he often asked her to come to China and live with the Zhengs, stating that he often spoke to his father about the possibility. He wrote that his father had long forgiven her for her relationship with Watanabe-*san*. Even though his father had been bitter and angry at first, he had come to understand that it would have been too much to ask of her to remain alone all this time.

The years had indeed been difficult for Matsu. The loneliness, the lack of a regular income, and her son's departure for China had all taken their toll. When Watanabe-*san* had expressed his wish to take care of her, it had seemed a practical and not altogether unpleasant solution, and one that was necessary with regard to her own safety. The country had fallen prey to xenophobia, marking the beginning of an era of fear, especially for those who were in any way associated with Christians —Matsu among them. Her Chinese husband, who often did business with the Portuguese and Spanish and who had fathered a child with her, was known to have converted to the Catholic faith. That he had done this for practical reasons mattered not. It was something people tended to remember. After Fukumatsu had left, that intolerance had become even more extreme. In some parts of Japan this had led to major rebellions by Japanese Catholics; but the shogun's forces had struck down hard. The shogun had finally given orders to forcefully expel all foreigners, with the sole exception of the Protestant Dutch, who were forced to relocate to the small, fan-shaped island of Deshima, where the authorities could keep a wary eye on them and where they were greatly restricted in their freedom.

Her previous relationship with Zhilong thus posed a risk. She, too, had feared for her own safety, and she had been glad when Watanabe-*san*, who had never flirted with Christianity, expressed his wish to support her as his mistress. But now he was dead.

She soon found that the mantle of protection and security her older lover and benefactor had provided was gone. As a widow, she was easy prey for the local officials, who had begun harassing her. Remembering her liaison with the Chinese pirate and papist, and suspicious that she might have Christian beliefs of her own, they would drop by from time to time, hinting that she could pay them if she wanted them to leave her alone. In spite of her frugality, her money was fast running out, and she could not afford the additional costs to keep the corrupt officials at bay.

When Fukumatsu learned of his Japanese stepfather's death, he renewed his arguments for her to come to China. There was now nothing to keep her from coming, he wrote; and his father, who by now had eight concubines, had no objection. She would simply be another member of the Zheng household, and she would be safer in Anhai. Besides, he wrote, he needed her counsel. And he missed her.

At first, her oldest son's wish for her to come to China seemed no more but an unrealistic dream. Travelling outside of the country was virtually impossible and she simply could not leave Zaemon. Moreover, Fukumatsu had a wife and family of his own. The thought of holding her two grandsons, the children of her firstborn child, taunted her dreams, only for her to wake up with sad, exquisite longing.

And yet, her son's requests for her to come to China were constantly on her mind. With Zaemon spending his days with his uncle as an apprentice at the shop, she was often by herself. When yet another letter from China arrived with fresh attempts from Zheng Sen to get her to come to China, she came to realize that she should consider his request more seriously.

The first time she showed Zaemon his brother's letters on the subject, the boy had simply shrugged his shoulders. He, too, had received such letters from his older brother, although he didn't really remember him. He believed that his invitations to come to Anhai were no more than polite words and not to be taken to heart. The mere thought of leaving Japan, even Hirado, was something he would not even consider.

One cool evening, Matsu sat across from her youngest son, Fukumatsu's letters resting on her lap.

She had made up her mind. Zaemon must have sensed it from her silence.

"You are not really considering going, Mother. Are you?"

She looked at him without answering, assessing his reaction.

"You're not serious," the boy said. Then he shook his head slowly, his voice dropping to a hoarse whisper. "I'm not going. Hirado is my home. I belong here."

"I know you do." She lowered her eyes to her lap, faced with a terrible dilemma. She understood that he wasn't willing to leave everything behind for something unknown, a life among strangers in a country where he didn't speak the language, and frankly, where he didn't belong. After all, Fukumatsu had his relationship with his father to build on. But Zaemon had nothing. He would have no life in China as her Japanese bastard child.

"You would really leave without me?"

She could not bear to look him in the eye. "Yes," she breathed, her heart breaking. "There is nothing left for me here. Zaemon-*chan*, you have your apprenticeship. I know your uncle is very fond of you, he sees you as his own son. I love you and I will miss you terribly, but this is something I must do. I miss Fukumatsu."

He had stared at his mother for what had seemed a long time, tears springing in his eyes. "Yes," he said, a sob choking him. "I know you do." Matsu embraced the boy, who clung to her in despair at her decision.

She wrote to Fukumatsu of her intention to come to China. Discreetly she began selling some of the jewelry Watanabe had given her over the years. The money she raised she stacked away carefully, and with the help of her extensive network of family and friends, she began to gather information about the magistrate of Nagasaki. Through bribery and blackmail on account of the man's sexual preference for young boys, she finally obtained the official documents necessary to leave Japan.

She did not know when she would be leaving. She would have to find passage on a merchant ship, and those came to Nagasaki only every two or three months. The most recent departure had been just weeks before, so she would have to bide her time.

Eight weeks later, the next VOC ship finally came into port. After weeks of waiting and monotonous routine, the bay of Nagasaki and the tiny island enclave of Deshima came to life. Dutch and Javanese deckhands mingled with local laborers to offload the goods into small boats, which maneuvered across the shallow waters to land at the water gate of Deshima. Teams of customs officials ran to and fro, shouting orders to keep up with the stream of crates and boxes that emerged from the ships' cargo holds. Market stalls were quickly erected and Japanese buyers streamed to the city port to sample the incoming goods. Deerskins from Formosa, silks, camphor, and fragrant spices all exchanged hands to enable the buyers to place their orders.

The ship remained in port for about two weeks, giving Matsu enough time to secure passage, gather her possessions, and prepare for her departure.

On the day the ship set sail, the harbor teemed with workhands loading the last crates and barrels of merchandise while inspectors checked those boarding against their passenger lists. As people milled about her on the dock, Matsu turned to her family, and finally her son.

Zaemon's lip trembled as he faced his mother, her eyes filling with tears. No longer a child, she could not hug him in public. The boy's uncle nodded uncertainly, not quite knowing how to deal with the emotion that threatened to overwhelm them all. He placed an arm around the boy's shoulder awkwardly, and nodded to Matsu that it was time for her to go. One final time, she bowed low to them. As she was about to step onto the gangplank, Zaemon broke away from his uncle, forgetting all decorum and embraced his mother one last time. Matsu clung to him in anguish. "Write to me," she whispered. "*Sayonara*, Zaemon-*chan*."

Only when the ship had left the port, its sails fully hoisted, did Matsu allow her feelings to take hold of her. Standing on deck, she stared at the fast-receding coastline of her homeland. As she wrapped a shawl over her head to protect her from the chilly wind, she knew, instinctively, and with a pain in her heart, that she would never set foot there again.

Two weeks later, Matsu arrived in Fujian, exhausted and slightly apprehensive of what lay ahead. She stayed at an inn in Fuzhou, from where she sent word to the Zhengs that she had arrived. Matsu had no real desire to spring a complete surprise on her husband's family, as they had not yet received word of her impending arrival.

After gawking at her with unabashed curiosity, the innkeeper lost little time in sending a messenger to the village of Anhai to alert the Zheng family of the arrival of Lord Zheng's Japanese wife.

The following day, three horsemen arrived at the inn with two spare horses and a donkey. With a tingle of excitement, Matsu searched the faces of the men, but her son was not among them; they were obviously no more than servants. She felt a pang of disappointment, having secretly hoped that Fukumatsu would have come to get her personally. She reprimanded herself for harboring such foolish expectations.

She mounted the horse she was given, while her modest amount of luggage was placed onto the donkey's saddle bags. Matsu's nervousness increased as they neared their destination. When they finally reached the crest of the hillside overlooking a sprawling residential compound, one of the men drew up alongside her and pointed.

"There?" she almost gasped. "That's Lord Zheng's house?" The man nodded. She could feel a chill running down her spine. So this was where her son lived. This very sight must have greeted him when he arrived from Japan thirteen years ago, just as it greeted her now. She felt awed when she realized this. The man at her side regarded her with mild amusement before he spurred his horse to move on. Matsu followed in his path, her heart racing.

Apparently Matsu's arrival had already been heralded: a crowd had gathered at the entrance, everyone stood gaping at her. Then she saw him. He was standing in the main courtyard as she entered the gate. Thirteen years of pain, regret, and longing had separated them, and all she could do was stare.

"Fukumatsu! Fukumatsu-*chan*!" The sound of his childhood name jolted him into movement.

"*O-kasan*! Mother!" He strode toward her with long steps, stopping a few feet short of where she dismounted. For a moment, they just stood there, oblivious of everything around them. Matsu looked at him in wonder. The boy she had envisioned in her mind had become a man. A young man, lean and strong, with eyes that reminded her of her own father.

Matsu approached him slowly, as if in a trance, and reached out her hand, touching his hair as she did. "Fukumatsu-*chan*," she repeated softly, taking his hands. She could barely control the tears that welled up in her eyes. "My son!"

They were rudely interrupted by a stocky middle-aged woman who cleared her throat in announcement, a false smile on her face. More than half her teeth were missing.

"Welcome, welcome, milady!" the woman said loudly in slow Chinese, as if the language would be easier for her to understand that way. The spell was broken. Matsu released her son's hands in embarrassment, suddenly aware of the many curious onlookers who had gathered round.

"This is Housekeeper Liu, mother," Zheng Sen said. "She welcomes you and says she has heard many good things about you. You will understand that we had very little time for preparation, as your arrival was still unexpected. Your last letter arrived only recently." He took her by the arm. "Housekeeper Liu wants to show you to your rooms, but I will do this myself."

He turned to Liu and spoke to her with authority, to which Liu nodded obligingly. Matsu gave him a grateful look, pleased that he was in control. She had seen the fleeting, haughty glance Liu had thrown in her direction and had taken an instant dislike to the matronly housekeeper, whose humility toward her son was anything but sincere. She was well aware of the prejudices that were prevalent among the Chinese against the Japanese. Apart from that, she intuitively felt what kind of woman Liu was.

"Thank you, Housekeeper Liu," she said in more than passable Chinese, glad that she had made some effort at grasping the language over the years. "You are very kind, but my son wishes to show me to my room himself," she said in a tone that implied enough.

Liu flashed her false smile again, inclining her head in an irritating manner that reminded Matsu of a sly fox.

"Liu, see to it that the luggage is delivered to my mother's quarters," Zheng Sen said sharply, upon which Liu obeyed, somewhat vexed at being excluded from the scene. Matsu glanced sideways at her son, no longer a boy, yet not yet a man. Ah, she thought. He has already learned to use the tone of authority. He truly is the young master. She smiled, happier than she had been in many years.

She fell in step with Fukumatsu, two servants following them with her luggage. Zheng Sen brought her to her quarters, explaining that they were temporary until they could make other, more suitable arrangements. The rooms were spacious and clean but simply furnished. It was obvious that no one had expected her.

"Father is not here," he said. "He should be returning later this week. Grandmother – and Lady Yan, Father's second wife – would like to meet you in two hours. I will come back later so you can refresh yourself. I will have some food brought to you."

"Thank you." She looked at him fondly, still unable to believe that she had her boy back.

"You've become a man. A handsome man!"

Zheng Sen smiled, and then suddenly grew serious. "I've missed you, mother. It's good to have you here."

Matsu swallowed, surprised at the strength of her emotions. "And I have missed you. You will never know how much."

We finally meet," Lady Zheng said loudly as she scrutinized her daughter-in-law. Matsu had donned a modestly embroidered deep-turquoise silk Chinese tunic for the occasion. She knew the color suited her well.

"You were given permission to leave your country after all? I understand there were some travel restrictions in place."

Matsu met the older woman's gaze, a hint of a smile on her face. She tried to ignore the curious women and children who stood gawking at her.

"Yes, milady. It was difficult, but everything has its price. I found passage on board one of the Dutch merchant ships."

Zheng Sen sat comfortably as he interpreted for his mother. His Japanese was somewhat rusty, but still good enough to understand what she was saying.

The matriarch scoffed. "Hah. At least these yellow-haired barbarians are good for something. You know that you will have to learn Chinese if you are to live here."

"Yes, Lady Zheng. I will make every effort to learn it as soon as possible." She hesitated. "I speak a little Chinese, but it is not very good." she added in Chinese.

Lady Zheng gave a slow smile. "Ah. At least your pronunciation isn't bad. There is hope yet."

"What I know I learned from my son," she said, reverting to Japanese again.

"That is good. For no one here speaks Japanese," said Lady Zheng. "I understand that you have had to leave a child behind in Japan. That must have been difficult."

Matsu averted her eyes and nodded. She did not trust herself to speak.

"Good," Lady Zheng went on. "Let me introduce you to your new sister, Lady Yan. I do not believe you have met." She gestured to the heavily pregnant, rather prim-looking woman standing by her side. It was obvious she had made a special effort to look grand. Her hair was beautifully coiffed, her makeup meticulous, and her jewels stunning. Matsu thought she didn't look very friendly. She couldn't really blame her. Her arrival must have caused her at least some distress, always having been under the impression that she was Zhilong's first wife. For all these years she had been first in rank, above her husband's eight concubines. And now she faced her, his true first wife, and a Japanese one, at that.

Matsu bowed slightly, wondering how Lady Yan had felt when she had first learned of her existence. Especially when she heard that she might be joining the Zheng household. From the look of her, she imagined Lady Yan hadn't been very happy about it.

Lady Yan inclined her head. "Welcome, Lady Tagawa," she said formally. "These are my sons, Du and Shiyin." She gestured to two boys, still in their early teens, who merely stared at her with brooding eyes. "And perhaps…." She patted her extended stomach with a calculated smile.

"It is good to meet you, Lady Yan. I hope you are feeling well and that the pregnancy has not been too hard on you." Zheng Sen translated her words and Lady Yan nodded with a sour smile.

"Good," Lady Zheng interrupted the exchange, suddenly tiring of the introductory rituals. "I trust you two will get well acquainted now that you have a husband to share." The corner of her mouth lifted in a sardonic grin. The old lady then turned to Cuiying. "And this is Deng Cuiying, your daughter-in-law, and the mother of your grandsons, Jing and Xi." Cuiying stepped forward and smiled prettily at Matsu.

Matsu took in the delicate, expensive gowns and precious pearls glowing in her coiled, shiny hair, and saw the dissatisfied set of her mouth. Instinctively she knew what kind of a girl her son had married. Her son had not written much about her in his letters, hinting at the fact that he didn't find her very intriguing. Meeting her only confirmed her suspicions.

"I look forward to meeting my grandsons, Cuiying," Matsu replied. It occurred to her that it had probably been an advantage for Cuiying not to have had an interfering mother-in-law during the first years of her marriage.

"As for my son – your husband," Lady Zheng continued, "he is travelling. He should be returning sometime during the next few days. That should give you enough time to prettify yourself."

"I will see to it that you are fitted with a suitable wardrobe," Lady Yan volunteered. "You did not bring a great deal, I understand," she said sweetly, looking Matsu up and down with an air of disdain.

"No, Lady Yan. I could not bring much. Thank you for your kindness," Matsu replied with equal sweetness. She actually felt relieved to hear that Zhilong was away. It would give her time with her son to get to know what kind of man he had become. She glanced at him as he sat next to his grandmother on the other side of Lady Yan. He smiled at her, insensitive to the undercurrents that had been set in motion among the women in his life.

Matsu hardly recognized her husband when he returned from Nanking, where he had been to discuss military matters with a Ming royal. It had been many years since she had seen him. His face had hardened, it had become more angular. His left ear bore a scar from a knife wound, and she saw that he still had the roving eye of a virile young man, his eyes scanning over the curves of her still slim body with interest. It had made her heart quicken once. Now it only made her shiver.

Much to Lady Yan's fury, Zhilong visited Matsu on the first night of his return. Matsu had not been sure that he would. Her husband had numerous concubines, some of them young and lovely, and she had been uncertain as to whether Zhilong would be interested in claiming his conjugal rights after so many years, or whether he still desired her.

It turned out that he did. She found that there was little affection from his side when he bedded her that first night, just curiosity, a show of power and lust. Once they were left alone, he had pulled at her clothes impatiently and thrown himself upon her hungrily, his mouth on Matsu's pale neck. She had tried to hold him off for just a while longer, willing him to look her in the eye in the hope of finding some gentleness there, to rekindle the old bond between them. But he didn't even notice. With hardly any effort he flipped her over like a doll, drew her up against his loins, and entered her roughly from behind. He came with a low grunt, lay down next to her, and soon fell asleep.

Matsu got up, cleansed herself, and blew out the lanterns that lit the corners of the room. She returned to her bed, listening in the darkness to her husband's breathing, which gradually ascended to a snore. She thought that her physical reunion with her husband hadn't quite been what she had imagined in all those years of being alone.

Her husband had changed. He was so very different from the man who had pursued and married her when she was seventeen. It felt as if she had made love to a stranger. It didn't matter: she was no virginal maiden. It wasn't for this man that she had left her country behind. She had come to China for her son.

8

The Imperial Surname

THE peace and quiet in the courtyard came to an abrupt end as Zheng Sen and the members of the Black Guard entered the gate. Chickens scattered in all directions to evade the horses' hooves, cackling in alarm at the sudden intrusion. A steady stream of servants and stable boys emerged from the surrounding buildings, greeting the men loudly, relieved that they had returned from the battlefield unharmed.

Matsu always insisted that the servants notify her immediately once the Black Guard was spotted on the hill's crest. She quickly made her way to the courtyard, awaiting their long-expected arrival. She took her place next to housekeeper Liu. Liu had aged considerably over the past few years: she had lost her plumpness, but her face was as prim and unforgiving as ever. Her voice shrill, the old housekeeper lost no time in doling out instructions to her unfortunate subordinates.

Zheng Sen jumped down from his horse and greeted his wife and children.

Cuiying stepped forward. "Welcome home, husband," she said, flashing a smile for his benefit, holding Xi's hand. His fourteen-year-old son, Jing, looked as disinterested as ever.

"Welcome home, Master Zheng," Liu said, bowing respectfully.

Zheng Sen nodded, acknowledging her briefly, and then turned to Matsu, who stood waiting to greet him. Whenever he returned from a long absence, it felt as if she was seeing him as an adult for the first time.

Once again she felt a rush of pride and affection. He walked up to her, grinning broadly.

"Mother!"

"Fukumatsu," Matsu whispered, her eyes holding his. In their moments of privacy, she still called him by the Japanese name she had given him at birth.

The jumping toddler at her side tugged at Zheng Sen's sleeve insistently. He dropped to his knees so he was at eye level with the two-year-old child.

"Orchid! How is my little sister?"

"I am so glad you are back, *gege*, older brother." The child told him happily. "You've been away far too long. I have missed you."

Zheng Sen lifted his younger sister off her feet, giving her an affectionate squeeze. "I have missed you too, *meimei*, little sister. But you know I have to travel now that I work for Father's business. I wish it were otherwise." Zheng Sen smiled at his sister, who looked at him with a grin that displayed just two front teeth. He squeezed her affectionately, but when she became too active in his arms he put her down. She took a firm hold of her big brother's hand, not intending to let go for a while yet.

Within a year of her arrival, Matsu had given birth to a daughter. But the delivery had been complicated by a breech; even though the child was healthy, she would never be able to bear another child again. Orchid turned out to be a blessing and a joy to her and her brother, who never tired of playing with her during his rare moments of leisure.

Zheng Sen made his way through the inner courtyard, his mother falling in step beside him while Orchid skipped along. Matsu noticed that he had broadened, especially across the shoulders.

"You have grown again, Fukumatsu," she said, admiring the muscle tone of his arms. "You are truly a man now."

She knew this pleased him. His father had insisted that he continue training in the arts of the sword next to his studies and company duties, commissioning the boy's uncle Feng as his instructor. Feng made the youth train hard at his routine, and he had become stronger as a result.

Matsu had managed to settle in well in her husband's household since her arrival nearly three years ago. Most members of the family had accepted her by now, and there were quite a few with whom she had actually formed friendships. Even those who had been downright hostile toward her in the beginning she could now count among her friends.

The relationship between Matsu and Lady Yan, however, remained strained. Matsu made every effort to try and win her over, yet she soon found that Yan simply wasn't capable of seeing her as anything but a rival for her husband's affections and a threat to her position, as well as that of her young sons. Finally, she gave up on her efforts, accepting the situation for what it was. During larger family gatherings they were always civil to one another, although they never became close.

Zhilong's many concubines were pleasant toward Matsu. Some of them were intrigued by her foreign origins, and questioned her at length about the customs and way of life in Japan. Her stories were seen as a welcome break to the monotonous routine of life in the Zheng household. The others treated her with the respect that was her due as first wife but kept their distance, preferring to stay in their own safe worlds.

Matsu and Cuiying left each other well enough alone. The two women were very different in character and had little in common, and they both knew it. They rarely sought each other's company, and, on those occasions that required both of them to be present, they were no more than cordially polite. Matsu realized that she had not been involved in the selection of the girl as her son's bride, and she had been absent at the wedding. She had not been there to witness her son's journey into fatherhood, and had thereby missed an important part of her role as mother-in-law. She often thought that perhaps this was a good thing. Taking on the role as the traditional mother-in-law at such a late stage in her son's marriage did make it easier for her to keep her distance and resist the tendency to interfere in her son's married life.

Matsu mastered the local language within a year and even obtained a Chinese name. Zhilong employed one of the best swordsmiths in the entire province, a man by the name of Weng. The old widower, who did not have any children of his own, had taken an instant liking to her. The Tagawas had a long line of military history, and as a result Matsu had developed more than a passing interest in the art of sword forging. She, too had learned how to use one from a young age, and she had often parried with her sons for relaxation.

In order to escape the stifling atmosphere of rivalry and gossip among the women, Matsu took every opportunity to visit the swordsmith. The old man enjoyed her visits, during which she would often sit talking to him as she watched him work, fascinated by his craft. In turn, he treated her like a princess, jesting with her as he worked. He would often express his wonder about the fact that fate had provided Lord Zheng with such very different wives. She had to smile at this, thinking of the rather empty-headed Lady Yan, and took his remarks as a compliment.

One day he had playfully suggested that he would adopt her as his daughter, and he gave her the name Weng Shi. It was their private little joke, but before long the servants picked it up and they began to address her as Lady Weng, so the name stuck.

Her bond with Zheng Sen was remarkably strong considering they had been apart for so long. Whenever he faced a dilemma of some sort, he would turn to her for advice, considering her counsel wise. He had inherited his love of poetry from her; when time permitted, they would take turns writing verses, the results often pleasing to the ear.

When her son was away travelling, Matsu spent her days looking after Orchid, occasionally leaving her with Hua, her personal maid. From time to time she would visit old Lady Zheng in her quarters together with Lady Yan or one or two of the other women, just as the old matriarch dictated. Lady Zheng was becoming elderly and had developed a persistent dry cough that wore her out, at which point she would close her eyes and signal that their visit was over.

* * *

"I spoke to your father this morning," his mother told Zheng Sen one afternoon as she walked him back to his quarters after a martial arts session. "He wishes to see you when he returns."

"Thank you, Mother. I will see him this afternoon." He waited at the door for his mother to leave, not asking her to join him. Matsu understood: her son wished to be alone. He needed his privacy, and she respected that.

Zheng Sen replaced his training weapons in their frames on the wall, wondering what his father would require of him this time. He knew he had high expectations of him, and that he had plans for him. His father had shown himself to be a hard taskmaster, and he often had the feeling he made a conscious effort not to treat him any differently from the others under his employ. It didn't bother him. No doubt his father had his best interest at heart and wanted to prepare him both mentally and physically for what was to come.

As he prepared to remove his tunic, which was soaked with perspiration, a young, fresh-faced female servant he had noticed before entered his quarters to prepare his bath. He followed the girl with his eyes as she tended to her work, the gentle curve of her breasts straining against her tunic as she reached forward. Yes, it was good to be home, he thought.

After his bath, he cornered the girl, making sure the doors were shut so no one could come in. She looked at him coyly and made a play at trying to escape, her eyes wide with feigned shock at his amorous ploys. Giggling and struggling playfully, she allowed herself to be dragged to the futon, where Zheng Sen unclothed her, kissing her neck and breast as he did. He entered her urgently, the girl gasping beneath him as she allowed him to ride her, his need culminating until he came with a loud cry.

In the months to come, Zheng Sen spent increasing amounts of time with his father. His formal, theoretical education had prepared him for dealing with ledgers and the various official documents that were required, but his father taught him the practical aspects of the trade. He felt that he had learned more in that one year than during the four years he had spent at the academy. Zheng Sen accompanied his father on his trips to the Pescadores and Formosa, where he was introduced to the right people within the VOC. After the fateful battle at sea between his father's ships and the company's, the Dutch had been sobered, realizing that they could not bypass his father if they wished to trade with the merchants in China. In spite of the ceaseless efforts of the Dutch, the highly desired trading rights with China continued to elude them. Humbled, they had renegotiated a deal with his father, once again relying on him to trade on their behalf.

Zheng Sen always listened closely whenever his father dealt with the company officials, carefully observing the body language and mannerisms of the Dutchmen whose cheeks and big noses were almost invariably red from sunburn.

He soon learned which products the Dutch desired most. Silks in a myriad of colors and patterns were brought in from the Chinese mainland. Sandalwood, fragrant herbs, and spices were carried on their ships to the island, as well as porcelain and silver. These products were mostly re-exported by the Dutch for the European market. In return, Zheng's ships carried rice and sugar grown on Formosa back to China. Other local products such as dried venison, deer skins, and deer horns were brought to Japan or to China to be sold there.

Acting as intermediary for the Dutch was highly profitable for his father's business. Not only did he receive a fee for the commodities he brought in, he was also able to obtain reasonable prices with the merchants, many of whom he knew personally, providing him with an even better profit margin. In return for his patronage, the merchants rewarded him for bringing them the lucrative VOC business, willingly greasing his palm to ensure that he did not go to their competitors instead.

So far, the Zhengs had experienced no adverse effects from the war that was taking place north of the Yangtze. The Manchus had not yet reached the south and therefore conquered no harbor cities. Manchuria was no seafaring nation, so the Zhengs' area of trade had so far remained untouched. But the breath of war was upon them, and his father made sure that all the males in the Zheng family aged ten and over were well trained in the military arts. In particular, Zheng Sen and Cai were forced to train with their uncle and his lieutenants for two hours every day, with various experts hired to instruct them in the different disciplines.

Zheng Sen proved a far more apt pupil than any of the other boys.

His younger brothers Du and Shiyin lacked both speed and skill, and although his cousin Cai tried his best, he simply could not match him. Before long, Zheng Sen was well respected among his father's soldiers, who saw him as his father's son: a natural-born leader. It wasn't long before his officers agreed that he was ready to fight.

Zheng Sen was delighted, impatient to put his skills to good use, desperately wanting to get involved in the military expeditions. He would be able to fight the Manchus at last. His father's fierce loyalty to the Ming had long been instilled in him, only to be reinforced by the constant threat that Manchuria had posed to China during the twenty-odd years of his life. He believed that this was what he was born to do.

The exhilaration he had first felt at being able to join the fighting soon evaporated. Much to his frustration, he was always closely guarded by a regiment of the Black Guard, which was obviously instructed to keep him out of harm's way. It irked his pride, as he was eager to prove himself and didn't want to be watched over like a child.

As time went by, there were plenty of opportunities to show his worth, and his actions did not go unnoticed. Two senior officers commended Zheng Sen for his bravery and military skill. Fierce with pride, his father promoted him in rank.

Yet the enemy continued to advance. Manchu troops progressed further south toward the Ming capital of Peking, where the emperor's battle-weary and malnourished troops made a last but futile attempt to stem the tide. Many soldiers had deserted, some joining the Manchus in an effort to save their skins. Reports repeatedly reached Zheng Sen that the Ming was losing the towns in the north to the invaders. Then the news came of the emperor's death. After a reign of seventeen years, Emperor Zhu Youjian had hung himself in his landscaped gardens.

Zheng Sen had listened in shock as he heard the messenger's words. The Ming dynasty, the glorious dynasty that had reigned over China for almost three hundred years, actually seemed to be coming to an end.

South of the Yangtze River the Ming still lived on. Fujian and Guangdong were especially known as Ming-loyalist strongholds. The area harbored numerous Ming princes who were willing to fight to regain what had been lost, and with the aid of his father's armies, one prince gained the necessary support and backing to become Emperor Longwu. The emperor was dead; long live the new emperor. Subsequently the entire imperial court was moved to Nanking.

The people of the south seemed to derive strength from the newly established Ming court. While the population of the half-conquered, war-torn country struggled to survive, Zheng Zhilong publicly declared his undying loyalty to the Ming, rallying behind Emperor Longwu. Zheng Sen, too, was hopeful. He refused to believe that the Ming dynasty could possibly come to an end. Gratified by the Zhengs' loyalty, the emperor summoned Zheng Zhilong and Zheng Sen to his court, where he wished to honor them.

Dressed in their official robes, father and son were presented to the Son of Heaven. The emperor sat on his dragon throne in full regalia as if he still reigned from within the walls of the Forbidden City. The hall of the palace was filled with the emperor's many relatives and officials, both minor and high ranking.

Escorted by the imperial guard, Zheng Sen and his father were brought forward. The emperor nodded approvingly as the two men dropped to their knees and kowtowed their respect.

"Come forward," commanded the emperor, just recently a prince. The two men stood up, their eyes still lowered, only to drop to their knees again within yards of the throne.

"Zheng Zhilong," the emperor began.

His father grunted as he acknowledged the emperor's address without looking up, his brow creased with the gravity of the moment.

"You have done well in backing the Son of Heaven," Longwu continued. "Those loyal and brave enough to fight for my ancestors' great dynasty shall not go unrewarded."

Zheng Sen listened in awe, conscious of the many people that filled the hall, all of them dressed in the finery that boasted their status. With bated breath they hung onto every word the emperor said. Zheng Sen knew that without his father's support, the man on the throne would be just one of many princes and powerless in the face of the Manchus' advance. Emperor Longwu owed him favors, which served to make his father even more powerful.

"Zheng Zhilong, you will be promoted above your present rank of military commander of Fujian Province and are given the mandate to fight the enemies of the Ming." There was a pause. The clerks scribbled urgently with their brushes to record the emperor's utterances while a cacophony of whispers and gasps filled the hall.

Zhilong kowtowed once more to show his gratitude, pressing his forehead to the carpeted floor for at least ten seconds. Zheng Sen followed his example, humbled. But the emperor was not yet finished.

"The Son of Heaven has no daughter to give to you in marriage. If I had, your family would be forever linked to my name. Alas, I cannot repay you in that way. However, to further show our gratitude," the emperor continued slowly, pausing for full effect, "your eldest son Zheng Sen will be adopted by the Son of Heaven in name to symbolize the loyalty that you have proven to me and my ancestors."

His father gasped. A ripple of astonishment went through the hall, and Zheng Sen gaped at the emperor with open mouth. Realizing that he had broken the protocol, he quickly collected himself and faced the floor, completely taken by surprise. He had seen the emperor's eyes twinkle, obviously pleased with his newly invested powers that enabled him to carry out such rituals.

"Let it be known that from this day forward, you have permission to use the imperial surname of Zhu, and you will be given the name of Chenggong, to mark all that you have achieved for one so young. Your name will be Zheng Chenggong, lord of the imperial surname."

Zheng Sen muttered his thanks to his emperor, stunned at this turn of events. "The son of heaven bestows upon you the military rank of commander of the guard and the title of duke."

Father and son kowtowed their gratitude once more, stunned at the honor they had received.

"I believe a gift would be appropriate at this time," the emperor declared. At his signal, one of his servants rushed forward and handed Zheng Sen an ancient, fragile looking scroll. "These are poems, written by the first emperor of our dynasty, my glorious ancestor. These will be given to you to commemorate this day."

Zheng Sen took hold of the precious scrolls, awed, and held them reverently against his chest. When he left the palace that day with his father, it was as Koxinga, lord of the imperial surname.

It was a title that would lend him power and rank, and one he would carry for the rest of his life.

9

A Question of Loyalty

THE reports that reached the south were of growing concern. As more cities and towns fell into the hands of the Manchurians, firms engaged in foreign trade started to scale down their enterprises and kept a low profile, hoping to ride out the storm. The independent merchants took no risks and left the region for safer havens. Zheng Sen and his father noticed that the number of Portuguese in Macao dwindled as many merchants sent their families home rather than stay in a country at war. The Spanish also opted to stay away from the region, preferring to observe the developments from a distance in the Philippines. Trade suffered as a result.

Yet Zheng Sen found that the family business was hardly affected. The demand for Chinese goods in Europe seemed insatiable, and the deal that Zheng had made with the VOC proved to be even more lucrative than they had hoped. Chinese merchants increasingly turned to his father to sell their goods to the Dutch now that the trade with the Portuguese and Spanish had slackened.

In a strange paradox, the VOC seemed to benefit from the war, but only through his father's extensive contacts among the Chinese merchants. The company paid him handsomely for the large volume of goods that he brought to the island.

As the Zheng trade imperium grew, so did Zheng Sen's responsibilities. Du and Shiyin showed hardly any interest in the business; they kept themselves occupied gambling and playing board games. Their father had largely given up on trying to involve them. Zheng Sen did so well that his father delegated more and more tasks to him, in particular with regard to leading his military campaigns. Zheng Sen felt honored and took to his new tasks with enthusiasm. The role of commanding officer became him: he felt that it was his calling. He still remembered the words once uttered by the fortune-teller in Hirado: *You will be great leader one day.*

Yet he did notice that his father was gradually distancing himself from military matters, and he decided to confront him with this one day.

"Father, the emperor has informed us that he intends to undertake a land-based military expedition to attack the enemy. He expects that we will send our troops to support him."

Zhilong eyed his son thoughtfully. "A land-based attack?" he repeated, sucking air through his teeth in doubt. "A land-based operation would not be prudent under these circumstances." He turned his attention back to his clerk, who worked the large abacus with agile, practiced fingers. "We must remain realistic," Zhilong said. "A maritime strategy would be far wiser right now. Our fleet is at the emperor's disposal for naval expeditions. Sending our troops north to fight the Manchus on land would be of little use."

Zheng Sen was somewhat taken aback at his father's refusal. It had not been an imperial order: the emperor had simply assumed that they would back him in his operations without question. He had not expected his father to turn down the request.

"But Father," he blurted out. "The enemy has to be stopped, we must —"

His father rounded on him in anger, his eyes cold. "You dare question me? How dare you tell me what I must do! I will not tolerate this unfilial behavior from my own son!"

Zheng Sen's cheeks burned with indignation at the injustice of his father's words, but he still felt he had to pursue the matter. Lately he found that his father was more concerned with his own interests, particularly his personal wealth. Zheng Sen had slowly come to suspect that it had not all been earned in an ethical way. But now his father was neglecting military matters, and his outburst disturbed him.

He dropped to one knee to prove his piety, his eyes on the ground. "Father!" he almost shouted. "I apologize profoundly if I have caused offence to you in any way. However, I respectfully wish to remind you of our allegiance to our emperor and our duty to –"

"My duty?" Zhilong bellowed. "Get up!" Zheng Sen straightened and looked at his father, bewildered. The clerk, shocked at the sharp exchange of words between his employer and his son, took his cue and quickly left the room, closing the door behind him.

"Don't you dare tell me of my duty, son," Zhilong said, and then lowered his voice. "Think! Look around you! Emperor Longwu is no more than a pawn in a game of chess! The Ming has been weakening for decades. You have studied the annals of history. Dynasties have come to an end before. Haven't you seen the signs?" He hesitated before he went on. "I have been in contact with their generals," he whispered.

"Their generals…?" Zheng Sen asked.

"Yes. They are willing to make me viceroy of Fujian and Guangdong if I cooperate."

Zheng Sen stared at his father with an open mouth.

"No!" he shook his head. "You cannot mean this. I do not believe it."

"We've tried, Zheng Sen. Heaven knows we have tried," his father continued matter-of-factly. "But this time, there is no stopping the enemy."

His voice softened somewhat as he saw his son's expression. "There is no stopping destiny. It is only a matter of time. We have to think of ourselves, of our future, or we will lose everything. We have to be practical."

Zheng Sen stood rooted to the ground, unable to comprehend what his father had just said. So he had been talking to the enemy. His own father! Whatever happened to the man of high morals, who had sworn his undying loyalty to the emperor and had sworn to protect the dynasty until his death? In one horrifying moment, it dawned on him that he did not truly know his father. Had he been so deceived by his words of allegiance to the emperor? His whole life the importance of filial piety had been ingrained into his very being. Piety toward his father, but more so toward the Ming, and its emperor. For as long as he could remember, he had been taught to defend the dynasty at all cost, to hate the enemy that threatened its very existence, to fight it to the death.

"Father!" he blurted out the word in anguish. "I refuse to believe that you would even consider.... All that we believe in...." But he saw that his father's eyes were cold, empty, and resigned.

"What we believe in is no longer of any consequence. It is a matter of survival."

Zheng Sen's world came crashing down upon him. All that was important to him and what he stood for was suddenly coming undone. He took a step backward to regain his footing, the strength in his legs sapped. He opened his mouth to say something, but the words wouldn't come out. The situation was far worse than he could possibly have imagined. Not only did his father refuse to support Emperor Longwu in his hour of need, he was actually about to betray him. And all to save his own skin.

Trembling with shock, he saw his father as the man who had once removed him from his mother's side against his will. It was as if a veil had been removed from before his eyes. He now saw Zhilong's growing greed, and remembered the dark rumors that he had heard about him, the inconsistencies and lingering doubts that could never be dispelled. Somewhere, from deep within, he recalled the taunting remarks of fat Yoshi, who had called his father a pirate. And then he heard again those other words, which now echoed through his head, prophetic. *No. I no see father. Your yin, your aura too strong, too powerful.* And all that he could feel for him now was contempt. Contempt for everything that his father turned out to be, and all that he represented. Unable to stand there any longer, he turned around and left the building. He ran blindly, hardly knowing where he was headed. He didn't stop until he reached the beach, where he dropped to his knees and cried, oblivious to the curious stares of the fishermen hauling in their nets.

When he finally returned to the house that afternoon, he looked for Cuiying, to discover that she had gone to visit her family for the day. Confusing his mental anguish with lust, he roamed the compound in hunger, searching for a woman to fulfil his almost painful physical need. When he came across a scullery maid, he summoned her to his quarters, pulled the clothes from the reluctant girl's body and bedded her with a fury that left him spent. When he realized what he had done, he was disgusted. He felt disgusted with the girl, with himself, but most of all, with his father. He pushed the sobbing girl away from him, took his sword, and galloped away into the hills.

* * *

Matsu knew that something had happened between her son and her husband. Even from within the confines of her room she thought she had heard their voices raised in anger. She had looked through the window and seen a grim-faced Zheng Sen stride across the inner garden toward the stables. Several times she had left her quarters to see whether he had returned. But there was no sign of him, and no one could tell her where he had gone.

When he did return to her that evening, she gasped at the sight of him. His clothes were smeared and disheveled, his expression hard and bitter. The youth seemed to have aged years in a single day.

"Fukumatsu!" she rushed forward with a cry of compassion. He took her into his arms in a desperate embrace, sobbing hysterically. Frightened, she tried to pull back to look at his face, but he held her tight.

"Fukumatsu! What is it? Tell me, what...?"

"My father ... is not the man I thought he was," he stammered into her hair. Matsu managed to pull away from him, not understanding.

"He has made a deal with the enemy," he muttered. "He told me."

"What...?" Matsu dropped her arms to her side, shaking her head in denial, although an awfully familiar feeling of suspicion nagged at her, and it seemed as if some things were finally beginning to fall into place.

"Mother, my father, your husband," he laughed bitterly, "intends to betray his country."

"That cannot be. You are mistaken." She squeezed her son's arm.

"No, Mother. He told me he believes there is no more use in fighting." His tone and expression were hard. "He refuses to send troops to back the imperial forces. He will betray us, just as he is now betraying the emperor. And all to save his own skin!"

"No! Your father —"

"Is a coward and a traitor to his country!"

Matsu let go of him. She shook her head in disbelief. She had long known that her husband was a selfish man, and the years of their separation had made him even more so. Since her arrival in China, she had made her position to her husband quite clear. She could not deny him his visits to her bed, but she did not encourage them either, secretly hoping that he would turn to Lady Yan or his concubines instead. The love and affection that she had felt for him in her youth had evaporated, leaving only the bond of parenthood between them. But now she had the uncomfortable feeling that something else had changed. She had long suspected that he was not of such noble character as she thought when she married him, and often wondered at his increasing lack of ethics when doing business. How had he really earned his fortune? During the many years that had passed, his greed had won over his scruples – she knew that now. But this?

"Fukumatsu, he is your father," she tried, still unwilling to face the truth.

Zheng Sen took a deep breath as if he were about to submerge himself in deep water. She opened her mouth to say something, but he put his fingers against her lips.

"No," he muttered. "No." He gently pushed her away from him. "Goodbye, Mother. I will continue to fight our enemy, even if Father won't."

"Fukumatsu! You cannot leave, you...."

"You know I cannot stay here. My father has become the enemy. It is the worst thing...."

"No! Fukumatsu, no!" Her son shook his head and backed away from her, his hands holding her at bay, afraid that she might be able persuade him not to leave. Then he turned around and ran into the darkness, leaving Matsu behind, her arms despondently at her side.

* * *

That same night, Zheng Sen fled the family residence to be among his men. Shamed, he told no one of the bitter exchange he had had with his father. They must have sensed a change in him, as he saw the way they exchanged glances. He even made an effort to avoid Cai, who knew him better than anyone and who must have known that something was wrong.

"Everything all right?" his cousin inquired out of earshot from the others. Zheng Sen scowled, turning his back on him without saying a word. He could sense Cai lingering there, behind him, uncertain, the question hanging unspoken in the air. But he didn't want Cai to see him confused and upset like this.

"Just please go away. Leave me alone!" he snarled at him.

Cai fell back, stricken at being so shunned, and left him in his anguish.

The following day, Zheng Sen gathered his men and went to Zhangzhou to obtain supplies and troop reinforcements. In an attempt to forget his father and lose himself in his work, he set himself to the task with a passion that won many new recruits but puzzled his senior officers.

In Zhangzhou he received word that Emperor Longwu had proceeded with his intended land attack. It appeared that his generals had also counselled against it, just like his father had done, but the emperor's pride had proven stronger than his prudence.

Zheng Sen reacted bitterly at the news. They should have supported the emperor. He wondered how Longwu had reacted when he found out that his father had no intention of sending his army. His refusal to do so must have been a great loss of face. Had the emperor's vanity contributed to his stubborn decision to proceed with the attack? It now seemed that Longwu had taken his army north, in search of the ever-advancing army. It was a disturbing development. Just as his father and generals had done, he had also questioned the wisdom of the decision. A naval attack would have had a far better chance of success. He believed the emperor had seriously underestimated the situation, especially without his father's army. Only time would tell.

* * *

"Lord Zheng! Lord Zheng!" The calling in the courtyard was insistent. Zhilong made his way to the entrance to find a messenger in the doorway. The man was breathless and anxious yet undaunted by the guard's brusque handling to prevent him from entering his private quarters unannounced.

"Let him go," he ordered the guards when he recognized the man.

"Lord Zheng! The emperor is dead!" the messenger gushed. "The army has been annihilated. Emperor Longwu has been beheaded!" The man began to sob, finally allowing the contents of the message he had just delivered to sink in.

Zhilong's hand went to his goatee beard, stroking it. The far-superior Manchu armies had surrounded the imperial armies with ease, just as he had foreseen. Longwu had even been so guileless as to lead the army himself. And now he had been executed. He had reigned for little more than a year.

With some wonder, he realized that the news hardly affected him. He asked himself if this would have happened if he had aided his emperor as requested. It was too late now. He turned around and walked back to his private quarters without a word, lost in thought.

But when he reached his rooms, he found the door to be barred. Matsu stood there like a statue, her coal-black eyes large with dismay. How long had she been standing there? She approached him slowly, her tread cautious. Judging from her expression and pallor, she must have been listening in when the messenger had brought him the news.

He looked at her dispassionately. She was his first great love; she had always been loyal to him and supported him without question. She had left behind the country of her birth to be with him and their son. Yet he had turned out to be lowly and unscrupulous, while she had been nothing but noble. There was no doubt that she would judge him for this, and hold him in contempt for the treason he was about to commit. Yes, he had been avoiding her these past few days and had not dared to tell her of his plans. But the look on her face revealed that she knew. Zheng Sen had probably told her. He avoided her look, uncomfortable in his guilt.

"You should have gone to his aid," she said. Zhilong looked at her sharply. "Is it true?" Matsu's voice was a low whisper. "Is it true that you are considering going to their side? That you are talking to their generals? The enemy?" Slowly she approached him, ever closer, and he felt trapped by her look, accusing him, judging him.

"Tell me, Zhilong. Is it true what Zheng Sen says?"

He could no longer evade her. This woman, possibly the only woman for whom he had any respect, had finally discovered his true nature. He felt ashamed, and his shame made him feel vulnerable, naked. It was a sensation he had not known for a very long time, and one that unsettled him. Before he knew what he was doing, he lashed out at her for her impudence. She fell to the floor, nursing the burning bruise on her cheek. Then she looked up at him with loathing.

Zhilong glowered back at her. There was no question as to how she felt about him now. It made him feel like a child caught breaking the rules.

"Don't look at me like that," he said with a growl. Matsu remained where she was, her wide eyes still fixed upon him, as if paralyzed by a predator's glare.

"Get out!" he barked at her. He was beyond shame. Matsu blinked at the unaccustomed rebuke, the trance broken. But she dared not move, afraid of what he might do.

He advanced on her menacingly. "Get out, I said!"

She scrambled up and backed away from him, stumbling, then she caught herself and fled from the room.

From that moment on, their relationship changed entirely. He went out of his way to avoid her so as not to see the reproachful look in her eyes. He did not want to be reminded of the undisguised contempt that she felt for him now. So he was a lowly, mercenary pirate, in spite of everything. But he could not reverse what he had set in motion. Deep in his heart, he knew that it would only be a matter of time before the Qing troops would conquer the land south of the Yangtze. And that they would eventually reach Anhai. He was well aware that his influence and power as supreme military commander of southern China made him one of the key figures in the ongoing resistance to the Manchurians. If the south should fall to the enemy – a possibility that grew by the day – he himself would have a high price on his head, and that was an unpleasant thought.

But he had always been a clever, pragmatic man. He had to be in order to survive. The emperor was dead. He had anticipated this, ever since the Manchurian forces had reached Nanking. There was no longer any hope for the Ming, and he knew that he had to make his move now. His own trade imperium would be under serious threat if the enemy arrived in these parts. Many others had taken this path before him, and it appeared that the Manchus kept their word when it came to the deals they made with those who defected.

He had trusted no one when making his plans. Not even his son had had an inkling that he was about to betray them all. Through his spies and network of men of dubious character, he had sent secret messages to the Manchu generals. When the generals became aware of who he was, they soon recognized his usefulness as a powerful vassal and quickly entered negotiations. He knew that all the Zheng men, including his brothers and uncles, had each proven to be worthy foes for the Manchus. They had all been active in some military campaign against the Qing, and he was well aware that his defection could prove to be very valuable.

As he had expected, the negotiations had borne fruit, and the generals offered him the high posts of viceroy of Fujian and Guangdong provinces if he cooperated and foreswore his allegiance to the Ming. It was for this reason that he failed to send vital reinforcements at crucial times, thereby accelerating the emperor's demise.

Zhilong knew that his son, young and idealistic as he was, would never be able to understand his actions. Still, he had fought and worked hard for what he had built all his life: the titles, the respect, the power, and the wealth. He had no intention of watching it all fall apart just because the forces of history brought a dynasty to an end. One had to be pragmatic.

His son's angry reaction had shamed him, as had the look that his wife had given him when it dawned upon her what he was about to do. Yet there was no turning back. The machinations of his betrayal had begun and could no longer be stopped. He could focus on only one thing: saving his family, his residence, his wealth. And himself.

He wrote one last letter to Zheng Sen, confirming what his oldest son already knew. It simply stated his intention to cease his hostilities to the Manchurian enemy and to side with the inevitable victor. The Manchu generals had promised him titles and deeds in reward for his defection, and he did not want to wait any longer. He resigned himself to his decision, knowing that some things could never be explained.

* * *

In his anger, Zheng Sen felt a strong need to deny his paternal roots and with that, the Zheng surname. Having been adopted in name by the emperor, he embraced his title as Zheng Chenggong with a vengeance. He now insisted that all address him as Koxinga, lord of the imperial surname.

He rallied his troops and left Zhangzhou to return home to Anhai. Once home, he found the household in chaos, the servants nervous and tense at the imminent arrival of Qing troops. They all knew it would be a matter of only weeks.

The household was agog with rumors that his father was planning to defect to the enemy. Several principled servants had left in disgust, while others, such as housekeeper Liu, went to great pains to convince their master of their never-ending loyalty in an attempt to save themselves. And then there were those who no longer saw the point of waiting, and decided to disappear in the night to defect themselves.

Cuiying rushed up to him and clutched at his tunic, whining in a voice that was shrill with panic. He ignored her pleas and pushed her away, striding past her to find his mother, whom he found pacing the room in a highly agitated state.

"Fukumatsu! So it is true. Your father intends to join the enemy."

"I know, Mother. He has written to me," Koxinga said, his tone sharper than he intended. "He believes that what he is doing is right."

She threw herself at his feet. "Zheng Sen, you are his oldest son. You must try and stop him. It is a trap, I just know it. They will kill him!"

"He will not listen to me. All he thinks of is his power and his wealth," Koxinga said bitterly. "He is doing this in order to save himself. He is nothing but a coward."

"Zheng Sen, you must! It is your duty to your father. And your ancestors," she added, averting her eyes.

For a moment, he detested her for bringing his ancestors into the matter. He cursed under his breath. His mother knew he held his family history in high esteem. "All right. I will go to him. But I cannot promise that he will listen to me."

His mother nodded, her tears running freely down her face. "Thank you, Fukumatsu."

It was only then that he saw the bruise on her cheek. "Did he do this?" he asked, gently touching the coloration on her skin.

She turned her face away in shame. Koxinga bristled, scowling angrily as he strode out of the room, ignoring her cries of protest.

The courtyard and the area outside the gate bustled with activity. A regiment of the Black Guard waited outside the compound walls, the men as restless as the horses they tried to keep in check. As he neared the stables, he saw the horses readied for departure. Two stable boys busied themselves tying bundles of luggage to the saddles. His father's horse was among them, as was Lady Yan's, his grandmother's, and those of his two brothers.

"Where is Lord Zheng?" he demanded. The servants bowed to him humbly, wary of his tone.

"In his private quarters, milord," one of them said timidly. "He intends to leave soon."

Zheng Sen strode off toward his father's rooms and entered unannounced. Before he knew it, he found himself standing face to face with the man he had looked up to for so long but could now only loathe. Behind him was his stepmother, Lady Yan. She looked wan and unsure of herself. He did not bother with the usual ceremony of piety but confronted his father as an equal, boldly looking him in the eye. It was the first time they had seen each other since his father had informed him of his intended betrayal.

"Father, don't do this," he said simply. He expected his father to lash out at him for his lack of respect, but Zhilong merely looked at him, impassive, knowing that rebuking his son for his lack of ceremony would be of no use. The circumstances were beyond that now. Things had changed.

"You don't understand," Zhilong said wearily. "All is already lost. The enemy will be here soon. I'm doing this for you. You fight on, if you wish. I respect that. Lady Yan is coming with me, as is your grandmother and your brothers. They are scared of what might happen to them if they stay here."

Zheng Sen knew that there was nothing he could do or say to stop him. "What about my uncles?" he asked. "Are they like you, or are they still fighting?"

Zhilong dropped his eyes to the floor. "I don't know of their intentions. I suspect they will continue in their fight. Your Uncle Feng probably will. He always did have more honor than me." He laughed, but the sound was bitter. "I know he is your favorite uncle."

Zheng Sen did not answer. It was true that Uncle Feng was the only one of his father's many brothers he really trusted.

"Send your wife, mother, and the boys to the Pescadores," his father told him. "They will be safer there. I have chosen to take another path. Call it treason. Call it cowardice. But I no longer wish to fight for a lost cause. If I tried, all that I have worked for," he gestured with his hand, "will be lost. Then it will all have been for nothing. If I do this, I might be able to save some of it. One day, this could all be yours." He turned his back for a final check of his luggage.

"How do you know you can trust them? They might kill you if you go to them."

His father shook his head. "They won't. I'm too valuable to them." He looked his son in the eye. "Fight on if you must. If you know your path in life, then you must take it."

Zheng Sen could no longer contain himself. He had promised his mother he would try and stop him, but found that he could not. The frustration and helplessness he felt caused him to suddenly strike out at his father, glancing a hard blow at his face. Zhilong staggered back, nursing his jaw with his hand. Still, he remained where he was, expecting more, ready for more. It seemed as if he welcomed the blow, as if he knew that he deserved it.

Zheng Sen had drawn his dagger and stood firmly in the doorway. His heart raced. He couldn't believe what he had just done and lowered the weapon at his side. He simply could not do it. This was his father, and that was a bond that could not be denied.

Zhilong glowered at him, daring him to strike again, making no effort to defend himself. Then, when it became clear that his son had lost heart, he brushed past him contemptuously. Zheng Sen let him go. He didn't even turn around to see his father leave. He had failed to stop him, as he knew he would. During that awful, brief moment, he knew that he would never see him again.

His mother had refused to join her husband in his defection, spitting at his feet to emphasize how she felt. Now she refused to leave China for the Pescadores, in spite of Zheng Sen's attempts to relocate her to a safer haven. As his father had suggested, he did send Cuiying and their two young sons to take refuge on the islands, as his departure for the battleground would leave them too vulnerable in his ancestral town. Cuiying had quickly complied. While she was busy preparing herself and the boys for departure, Matsu was resolute about staying in Fujian, and would not give up Orchid to the care of Cuiying. She insisted that she stay with those who still had the heart to defy the enemy.

Unable to persuade her otherwise, Zheng Sen made arrangements for his mother and sister and what remained of his household to stay at the family fortress in Anhai, a place his family had always gone to in times of unrest. It would be easier to defend and they would be safer there. He set up a guard to defend the fort during his absence, and left.

Disillusioned, he headed back to Zhangzhou, where he continued to recruit soldiers and gather the necessary supplies and arms for his next expedition: fighting an enemy his father had chosen to embrace.

* * *

For more than a week Zheng Zhilong and his family rode in the direction of Fuzhou, the weather conditions terrible. He and his family were escorted by three hundred men from the Black Guard who had joined him in his defection. These men were mercenaries, after all: they did not care who paid their wages.

They finally reached the outskirts of Fuzhou, where his spies had set up a rendezvous with the Manchurian go-between. Once identified as the expected Chinese defecting commander, he was escorted to the military encampment of the Manchus, where the sight of thousands of well-armed troops sent a shiver down his spine. Even at rest, the squat, broad-faced warriors with their thick, oily queues dangling down their backs looked fierce. Zhilong knew of their reputation as highly skilled artillery men and archers whose weapons seldom missed their targets.

Hundreds of suspicious eyes followed their every movement as they rode, the Manchurian soldiers gawking at the women brazenly. His old mother seemed to shrink under their hostile scrutiny, while his wife trembled visibly. Du and Shiyin glanced around, their eyes skittish. But then the Manchus' attention turned to something exotic, something that they had never seen before: the dark-skinned African, Arab, and Moluccan soldiers of the Black Guard, who returned their stares stoically. The Manchurian troops closed together around the back of the Black Guard, keeping a wary eye on the men.

They finally reached a large reddish-brown tent, where one of the guards rudely gestured them to wait. Within a minute, a tall, broad-shouldered Manchu officer emerged from the tent, followed by a dwarf of a man still fussing over him with a barber's blade. On seeing the Chinese men and women on horseback, the tiny barber stopped in his tracks and gaped at Zheng Zhilong. His jaw dropped at the sight of the dark foreigners that escorted him.

The officer sent him away with a dismissive gesture of his hand, at which the barber scurried back into the tent.

With one hand caressing his jawline to test the smoothness of his shaven skin, the Manchurian officer regarded the newcomers coolly. He barked an order at one of the guards, who hurried forward and kneeled before him. The officer listened patiently as the guard spoke to him. Once satisfied with the information, he stepped forward, his stride exuding all the confidence in the world.

Zhilong observed him with interest, knowing that this must be a man of authority.

"So you are Zheng Zhilong, military commander of Fujian Province and mandarin of Quanzhou."

It wasn't a question but a statement. Zheng blinked, as surprised at the lightly accented yet fluent Mandarin as at the accuracy of his information. Recovering swiftly, he looked the man in the eye and nodded. It disgruntled him that the man knew exactly who he was, while he could only guess at the identity of the officer, whom he assumed to be of high rank. His tunic looked new and was richly embroidered, hinting at wealth and prominence. The man's manner was one of casual arrogance.

Zheng's horse moved restlessly beneath him, sensing her rider's tension, ill at ease at being surrounded by so many hostile strangers. The Manchu approached the handsome dark mare and laid a hand just across her nose, stroking her softly. The horse instantly relaxed and became still, its gentle eyes on her new-found friend.

"I am Bolo, prince of Manchuria." The man stated.

Zheng Zhilong started at the name, one that he had heard often during the past months. The prince had the reputation of a fierce warrior and a very capable military leader, and was both feared and respected by the Chinese military. The warrior still held his horse's head, while the mare continued to nuzzle his hand. It irritated Zhilong that his horse had taken to the stranger so soon.

"You are welcome in my camp," Bolo told him, pleased with the horse's reaction. "I will receive you with the honor that your station deserves: Alone."

"I have brought my family, your highness," Zhilong said.

"You will come alone," Bolo repeated, unimpressed. "I will see to it they are well taken care of." He barked some orders to a nearby officer, released the horse and strode back inside the tent.

The armed Manchu guard surrounded the Black Guard at once and gestured to the men to dismount. It was obvious that the Manchus were taking no chances, and the Black Guard had little choice but to obey.

Zhilong was unsure of the true meaning behind Prince Bolo's words: *The honor that your station deserves.* He wondered if he could be trusted, and more importantly, if Bolo trusted him.

Separated from his men, he was led to a tent, three armed guards taking their positions outside its entrance. They left him in no doubt that they would not let him out of their sight, or his men, for that matter. A servant brought him a leather sack of water and some salty broth, both of which he downed hungrily. He remained where he was, stretching his legs in order to ease his muscles, which had stiffened during the long ride. Then he waited, cross-legged on the bedding that was provided, with the assumption that he would soon be summoned.

An hour later, an officer appeared at the entrance of the tent and signaled for him to follow. He jumped up and followed his escort, his nerves rattled by the long wait, uncertain of what was to come.

Dusk was about to fall, and the camping grounds around him were alive with the flickering flames of torches and fires. Several soldiers stood laughing raucously by a fire. As they saw him, they fell silent and regarded him with suspicion. One of the men spat on the ground contemptuously as their eyes met. Once he passed them by, they turned back to the fire, laughing again at some comment the spitting man had made, most probably at his expense.

He was brought to Prince Bolo's tent surrounded by stony-faced guards, one of whom stopped him with his palm outward. Zhilong handed over his weapons and opened his arms wide to show them he was now unarmed. After a quick but thorough body search, the guard pushed the tent flap open to let him in. The inside of the tent was well lit with several torches; and it was surprisingly luxurious with colorful cushions and bedding rolls piled up in the corner. Bolo was lying on his side with his head propped up by his elbow, his queue dangling casually across his chest. A military officer of obvious high rank was seated next to him, eating what appeared to be some kind of nuts from a bowl in front of him.

With an amused expression, Bolo looked up at the newcomer and moved into a seated, cross-legged position in one easy motion, gesturing to Zhilong to join him on the cushions next to him. Zhilong sat down hesitantly, trying to face the tent entrance to keep an eye on the two guards. At this point he didn't trust anyone.

Prince Bolo snapped his fingers and gave an order, upon which one of the two guards disappeared through the tent flap.

"It appears you are a powerful and important man south of the Yangtze," Bolo began.

"Your reputation precedes you, your highness."

"Why have you come here?" Prince Bolo asked, chewing on a handful of nuts.

Bolo's fluent Mandarin unsettled Zhilong, as did the unaccustomed lack of ceremony and the prince's direct manner. He was momentarily at a loss.

"I ... I received a message that I was to meet with your generals in this valley," he stammered.

"As you may know, I have been in communication with them for some months now." A manservant returned with a tray of food, followed by someone else with tin cups filled with a sweet beverage. The men waited in silence while the food and cups were positioned between them.

"Yes, I am aware of that. I am also aware that you and your men have fought against our troops over the past years, killing scores of our men. You have your own navy. It has attacked our ships on numerous occasions. Caused us quite a headache."

Zhilong nearly shrugged his shoulders. "War is war," he managed to say. "I am a soldier, just as you are. You know that."

"And mandarin. And merchant. And pirate."

Zhilong blinked. Not even his own son knew this. His days of piracy had long been a thing of the past; it was something that he had tried hard to wipe from everyone's memory, including his own. There were few men who dared call him a pirate to his face, and those who had were no longer alive. He decided to ignore the provocation.

"But you are now an important man, it seems. You helped put Prince Tang on the Dragon throne. Emperor Longwu, I think you call him. Or should I say, 'called'," he said with a sly grin. The officer seated next to him chuckled.

Zhilong wondered if they had tortured the emperor before they killed him. His adversary was well informed, and he felt strongly at a disadvantage. Bolo reached forward and popped a lump of meat into his mouth. Zhilong followed his example, chewing what tasted like mutton.

"You were fighting for the emperor. That makes you a loyalist. So I will ask you again. What brings you here?"

"I am a practical man, your highness. I know when fighting becomes futile, when we should admit defeat." He paused for dramatic effect. "The Ming dynasty has been waning for some time now. The country is in a state of economic collapse, and there is discontent among the people. You will know that rebellions against the authorities are a regular occurrence in many parts of the country these days." Prince Bolo continued to eat from the tray as he listened. "What I have built up, I have worked for all my life," Zhilong said, his back straightening with pride. "And I wish to protect my family, my sons. I have extensive business enterprises and many excellent contacts, and a great deal of influence of which you shall have much use. That is, of course, if you are interested," he hastened to add, anxious to get to the point.

"You mean if we reward you," Bolo said with his mouth full. Zhilong said nothing at the barb. "Yes, you could be of some use to us, you are right. Eat, eat," Bolo insisted, his hand motioning to the tray of food. Although he found it difficult to eat in the circumstances, Zhilong took another mouthful of the meats on offer.

"This is what I propose. You will cooperate with us, control your armies, and keep us informed of the movement of the imperial troops through your spies. Do this and we will name you viceroy of Fujian and Guangdong." He grinned. "Of course, once we have conquered those parts as well, which we will, in time."

Zhilong swallowed. He was about to sell his soul and he knew it. For a brief moment, he hesitated.

"Of course you will be able to continue with your business, and, as viceroy, you will run the administration in the two provinces under your jurisdiction," Bolo continued.

"Yes. I can agree to that," Zhilong said. It sounded reasonable. There was now no turning back.

"You brought your whole family? Everyone is here?" Bolo leaned forward. He and his general stared at him, unmoving, waiting for the answer. Zhilong suddenly felt uneasy.

"I have brought my family, yes. My wife is here, as is my old mother and my two sons."

Bolo abruptly stopped chewing, and he and his general exchanged glances. "What about the others? Your brothers, Bao, Feng, and the other two?"

"Eh, no. They are not here," Zhilong began to perspire in spite of the evening's coolness. Bolo narrowed his eyes and spat out a small bone. "What about your oldest son? The one they call Koxinga, the lord of the imperial surname? I assume he is here?"

"No," Zhilong muttered.

"Will he be joining us?"

"N-no." He felt queasy as the reasons for these questions began to dawn on him.

"I cannot hear you. Speak louder."

"No. He did not come with me," Zhilong said, louder this time. He now knew that his coming had been a mistake.

Bolo squinted again, his eyes no more than slits. "So it's true. I had heard the rumors that he does not share your ... sentiments." His general sprayed a mouthful of the beverage in front of him as he choked with laughter.

Zhilong's unease increased. It was obvious that the general was well informed and that he was probably the one who had told the prince of Koxinga's continued fight. Prince Bolo, however, seemed far from amused.

"Koxinga. Lord of the imperial surname. Some title," he snorted. "Still loyal to the Ming. So unlike his father. That is admirable. But not exactly filial, is it?" he prodded cruelly. Zhilong looked away, unable to meet the prince's eye for the shame of it. Then Bolo's tone turned cold.

"You say he is not here. But you must control him. That is part of the deal."

"I ... I cannot," Zhilong stammered. "He does not.... I no longer have any influence over him.

"He is a grown man. He has chosen his own path." His face had gone quite red.

"What about your brothers? Will we be able to expect them to join us?"

Zhilong remained silent. His brothers had their own armies, their own agendas. They did not listen to him. Only Bao had hesitated when asked to join him in his capitulation, but he had eventually sided with the emperor.

"I asked you a question." Still, Zhilong said nothing. Bolo motioned to his general, who leaned over to press a blade against his throat.

"You will answer the question," the man said, his foul breath on Zhilong's face.

"No!" he said, aghast. "I cannot speak for them. It is true that I am here just for myself."

There was an uncomfortable silence. This was obviously not what the prince wanted to hear. Bolo stared into his tin cup for a moment, then he got up and hurled it in the corner of the tent, swearing and cursing in his mother tongue. It made Zhilong jump.

"What use do I have for a couple of old women and pampered children?" Bolo shouted.

"Without your oldest son and those brothers of yours, who continue to harass my troops, your defection is useless! You have been wasting my time. Is this some kind of trick to let your son and brothers slip away from me?"

"No!" Zhilong shouted. "Please believe me, I —"

"The deal is off. We will be taking you and your females to Peking."

"Peking?" Zhilong's eyes went wide. "Peking?" He repeated. He had not expected his. "What about my appointment as viceroy in Fujian and Guangdong? We agreed —"

"Be silent!" Bolo shouted. "What were you thinking? We agreed that you would bring your entire family. What good is your defection without your oldest son and your brothers? They will continue to harass us! The deal is off. You are going to Peking."

Zhilong looked at Bolo in dismay. "You are taking us all prisoner?!"

"Call it what you like. I see it more as having you as our 'honored guests.' "

"You mean you will hold us hostage."

"Ah. You are beginning to understand. Perhaps when you are in Peking with us, your oldest son will rediscover his filial feelings for you."

"You cannot do this!" Zhilong cried out. "I told you, I no longer have any influence over him. Or my brothers, for that matter. You would be wasting your time."

"No, you are wasting mine. You are betraying your emperor and country by being here. Your emperor trusted you. So why should we trust you now? I still say this is a trick!" Bolo no longer made any effort to hide his contempt. Zhilong felt the blood drain from his face.

"Don't worry. You will be handsomely rewarded for your cooperation. You will have your viceroy's post as agreed, and you will be able to carry on your business, but in Peking, where we can keep an eye on you."

Unable to restrain himself any longer, Zhilong jumped up and made an awkward attempt to lurch for the warrior prince, but the general had seen the warning signs and was ready for him.

He caught Zhilong by the arm and held the blade of a dagger against his throat.

"Let him go," Bolo said with disgust. After giving Zhilong a last threatening look, the general shoved him back to the floor.

"What about the rest of my family?" Zhilong tried. "My other wife and family who remained in Anhai...."

"I'm sorry," Bolo said coldly. "My troops already headed in that direction early this morning. It is too late. There is nothing I can do about that. They shall be at the mercy of my men."

Zhilong stared at him, horrified. Bolo motioned to two soldiers, who came forward and lifted him bodily to his feet. Still stunned, he allowed himself to be led out of the tent. But once outside, he suddenly dug in his heels and turned to Bolo, who stood in the tent opening.

"This is not what we agreed. You have betrayed me!"

"As you are betraying your country and emperor," Bolo retorted. "Do you know what we do with people like you in Manchuria?" The two men eyed each other, the air charged with tension, the question left unanswered. "Take Lord Zheng to his tent. Take them all prisoner!" the prince ordered.

"Guards! Guards!" Zhilong screamed. "We have been betrayed! They are taking us prisoner!"

The members of the Black Guard reacted as one. They must have instinctively sensed the danger, as they instantly assumed their battle positions. The metallic clamor of a hundred swords being drawn at once sounded across the valley. Lady Zheng and Lady Yan screamed in alarm, but their thin voices were lost in the din of the fight. The foreign warriors, their eyes bright with the lust of the fight, let out bloodcurdling cries as they smashed their swords onto the skulls of the Manchus that circled them.

Prince Bolo remained standing at the tent's entrance, unperturbed as he watched the battle unfold in front of him. The strength of the black soldiers impressed him. The whole camp had come alive as thousands of Manchu soldiers came down the hill to surround them. The bodies of the dead and dying quickly piled up as the Black Guard fought hard against impossible odds. For every Manchurian it took down, two others would take his place.

The prince had finally seen enough. He yelled an order at one of his officers. Within seconds, Zhilong, his arms still pinioned behind him, gasped as he saw his mother, wife and two terrified young sons dragged before him. They each had a dagger at their throat.

"Call off your dogs or they die," Bolo hissed at him.

Zhilong hesitated for only an instant. "Cease fighting!" he yelled at his commander.

"Cease fighting!" he repeated hoarsely. "Surrender! They have my family!" Three more lives were lost by the time the fighting finally ceased. It was over. Zhilong looked at his family. Shiyin had fainted with fear. Lady Yan was sobbing quietly, her body trembling like a reed, the dagger still at her throat. He could see drops of blood seeping from where the blade had scratched her skin. His old mother stared ahead, her eyes big, a tell-tale dark stain marking the crotch of her emerald-green travelling robe. He could smell the acid of her urine, mixed with the cold sweat of the unwashed men around him.

"You fool!" Bolo growled at Zhilong. "Did you honestly think you had a chance? Here, in my own camp?" Zhilong said nothing, his nostrils flaring with every painful breath that he took. Bolo slapped him hard in the face, livid at the unnecessary loss of lives among his troops in the skirmish. "Take them away! All of them!" And with that, he strode back to his tent.

The following day, Zhilong was taken with his family under heavy guard to Peking. As he left the valley for the long journey to the north, he thought to himself that his son had been right, as had Matsu. His betrayal had been a mistake. He would have to pay the price: he would probably never see his home again.

* * *

Zheng Sen turned around at the sound of horses' hooves approaching fast.

"Lord Koxinga!" The captain of arms looked pale and drawn as he pulled up his horse alongside his own.

"What is it, captain?"

"Lord Koxinga, my scouts have just reported seeing a large enemy regiment moving across the border of Quanzhou."

Zheng Sen reined in his horse, turning to the captain with a frown. "When was this?" He cursed his mother for stubbornly refusing to evacuate to the Pescadores. She was still in Anhai, together with Orchid.

The captain hesitated, unhappy at being the bearer of bad news. "More than a day ago, my lord."

"Was it moving toward the coast?"

"Yes, milord," the man said, evading his eyes as his sweating horse pattered its hooves nervously on the mud. Zheng Sen knew what this meant. The family fortress in Anhai would be right in their path.

"How large?" he asked.

"Large," the captain confirmed. "The scout I spoke to estimated their numbers at a couple of thousand."

Zheng Sen felt his blood freeze. The regiment he had left at Anhai to defend the fortress would never be enough in the face of such numbers. And if the regiment had been seen moving at the border two days again, then that would mean.... He nodded as if to himself, acknowledging the news without a word. Then he looked away, gazing at the horizon as if in search for answers. Deep inside, he felt a fear building up, a fear that he had not known before. Fear for the safety of his mother and sister, fear for the loss that he might have to bear. But there was nothing that he could do. They were too far away, and there was no way on earth that his army would be able to intercept the enemy in time. He felt utterly helpless. He turned to the messenger, who had kept his eyes lowered to the ground, waiting, obviously uncomfortable with the emotional potency of the news he had just brought. In a fit of impotent rage and without warning, Zheng Sen lashed out, hitting the captain hard across the face. The man tried not to flinch as he struggled to stay in the saddle.

When he realized what he had done, he turned away, breathing hard, trying to control his unreasonable anger. Then he saw Cai, who was never far from his side since he had appointed him as one of his closest lieutenants. The look on his face jolted him. Quickly he looked away, ashamed at what he had just done. This wasn't the first time that he had attacked one of his own officers for being the bearer of bad news. Yes, he did feel the need to be hard on his men for insubordination, or to punish those who dared speak their minds against him. That was simply necessary; but this was different. Yet it could not be undone. It had happened, and to show remorse for his action would only be a sign of weakness. It did disturb him, just as it had on those other two occasions. It seemed as if he was no longer in control of his emotions, as if his fury was stronger than himself. His father's act of betrayal had changed him, and that was something of which he was painfully aware.

He spurred on his horse to escape his cousin's accusing looks. He gathered his troops and made his way southward, hoping to stop the Manchu troops before they reached Anhai. The horses shone with perspiration in their effort to get their riders to the coast ahead of their enemy, the clods of earth flying from their hooves. His heart clenched with anxiety, Zheng Sen prayed to the goddess of the sea that they get there on time.

* * *

Matsu felt a cold shiver run down her spine as she realized that the approaching army was not that of her son. From a distance she had tried to make out the banner wearing the Zheng crest, the familiar Chinese style of clothing and armor, the characteristic way her son always carried himself on his horse, riding at the front, as usual. But it wasn't them. The enemy had come. The fact that they had managed to get this far south could only mean one thing: Zheng Sen's army must have faced it on its way north and been unable to stop them. Had he been defeated? Horrified, she thought of his being dead, or wounded, dying still. Then all would be lost. The regiment he had left at the fort would not be able to stand a chance against such numbers.

Bells of alarm clamored urgently, the sound carrying far across the valley below.

The soldiers left to protect the fortress tried desperately to prepare for the unexpected attack. The first flaming arrows heralded the enemy's arrival, many of them finding flammable material upon which they fed hungrily, in spite of the persistent drizzle of rain. Matsu watched in dismay as the attackers gained entrance to the walled compound in a matter of seconds, easily slaying any who tried to stop them. Within minutes, the place was littered with the guards' bodies.

Orchid! She had to get to her daughter, who she had left in the care of Hua, near the kitchens. Her heart racing, she pressed herself against the walls of the stables, her dagger clasped in her hand.

Having spent their fury on the sentries stationed to defend the residence, the Manchu soldiers turned on the fleeing servants. A stable boy was stopped in his tracks as an arrow embedded itself in his neck, his head held at an odd angle as a fountain of blood splattered the ground. From where she stood Matsu saw one Manchurian soldier shout with glee as he set off in hot pursuit of a female servant, who stumbled, screaming with fright. Before she had the chance to recover, the soldier stood over her, grabbed her by the hair, lifted her head and cut her throat.

Enemy soldiers roamed the courtyard, holding their burning torches to the wooden buildings. Fires sprang up everywhere, spreading greedily along the dry timber roofs, crackling and hissing, filling the air with smoke.

Matsu decided not to wait any longer and dashed across the courtyard, toward the kitchens. There she spotted a looting soldier, and she dove for cover behind a pillar, hoping that she hadn't been seen. From where she stood, she could see how Housekeeper Liu was dragged outside, screaming like a banshee. Liu had implored Zhilong to take her with him as part of his entourage in his defection, but her husband had commanded her to stay in Anhai to serve her and Orchid. She watched with horror as the life of the elderly woman was cut short, a dagger in her chest. Her murderer held on to her tunic and coolly watched her die before he finally dropped her body to the ground.

With the soldier's back turned to her, Matsu hurled herself into the nearest building, desperate to find a way around. But there she froze. Standing in the doorway to the servants' sleeping quarters stood a Manchu soldier whose shaven pate glistened with sweat. He stopped dead in his tracks at the sight her. Seeing her fierce look of determination, his mouth formed a twisted, scornful smile. Then he lurched forward. She gripped the dagger firmly and struck out. But she was no match for the trained, hardened soldier, and in a fraction of a second, she was disarmed, her arms pinned behind her back in a painful grip, his breath reeking of rotting meat. She struggled violently to escape his clutch, but he held her fast.

"Ah, you want to play? We'll play," he grinned, and threw her to the ground.

Before Matsu had a chance to scramble for her dagger, he was on top of her, his weight pinning her down. With one free arm, she lashed out at his face, drawing blood with her nails. He winced, but caught her arm before she could hit him again. Angered, he fumbled with the layers of her clothing. Matsu cried out, the tears of her desperation and distress streaking her face. He briefly struggled with his trousers, but then he was inside her, the accumulated lust from months without a woman culminating in that one moment. He pushed away into the soft female flesh beneath him, her resistance to him adding to the urgency of his need. He closed his eyes when he exploded inside her, oblivious to all around him.

"Hoo-ge!" A thundering voice called them both back to reality. The soldier quickly rolled off her and hurried to pull up his trousers, as his superior spat out angry abuse at him. In a reflex, the soldier drew his dagger, half lifting Matsu off the ground, about to end her life. Her breath rasping with sobs, she closed her eyes and waited, certain that death would come.

Again she heard the booming voice at the doorway.

"No! Leave her be!" The officer shouted.

Hoo-ge stopped and looked down at the woman on whom he had just spent his seed. He tossed her back to the floor, leaving her in a heap before he made his way past his superior officer, who cuffed him hard on the head as he passed. Neither man saw Matsu reach for her dagger and quickly hide it inside the sleeve of her garment.

With Hoo-ge gone, the officer approached her with interest. Trembling, she averted her face, but not before she had seen the way he looked at her. His eyes were fixed on the pale, exposed flesh of her thighs. Aroused by the sexual act he had just witnessed, he strode over, rolled her on her back and straddled her limpid form, repeating the act that his subordinate had just performed. He was about to climax when a searing pain struck him. His hands groped for his neck, where he found the long sharp blade of Matsu's dagger deeply embedded. In quaint surprise he looked down at the woman lying underneath him and saw his own blood splattering across her cheeks.

With the strength that was left to her, she pushed him off her. She kicked fiercely at the body of the man, bleeding fast, dying. Her body trembling all over, she covered herself, feeling sullied and foul. After she ensured that he was truly dead, she retrieved the bloodied knife from his neck and held it in her rigid hands, ready should any other man dare come near her. In a state of shock, she stayed where she was, huddled against the wall at the far end of the room, where she curled herself up in the fetal position, gently rocking her body to and fro.

Less than half an hour after the band of soldiers had begun their raid, an unnatural silence descended on the compound, save for the sound of the rain that now fell heavily. Voices speaking in an unfamiliar tongue could be heard somewhere in the distance. Matsu stumbled into the courtyard, a throbbing pain between her legs where the two men had violated her. She had no idea how long she had sat in the corner of the room, floating in and out of consciousness to escape the horrors of her ordeal. She had to find Orchid. Orchid! The thought of her daughter coming to harm filled her with dread.

As she emerged from the building, the signs that the fortress had fallen were everywhere. The enemy had spread out across the complex in search of food, liquor, and women. Manchurian sentries had already taken their positions on the fortress walls, tossing the bodies of the dead down below. Careful not to be seen by the invaders, she ran from building to building, searching, ignoring the fires that raged around her.

She started as she came across the body of one of her servants lying face down in a pool of blood. "Orchid!" she screamed at the top of her lungs. "Hua!"

A pitiful whimper emerged from the kitchen's storerooms. Matsu rushed over to find Hua on all fours. Hua started to wail at the sight of her, one arm reaching out for her. From the way her clothing was torn it was clear that she had suffered the same fate as herself.

"No! Don't go in. Don't go in," the woman sobbed. The plea had the opposite effect on Matsu, who looked at her in horrified understanding. She let go of Hua's hand and walked into the store room. Inside the doorway she stopped, standing like a statue as she stared at the scene in front of her. The body of one of the servants lay sprawled across what looked like a bundle of cloth. The bloody dagger in her hand clattered to the floor. In morbid fascination, she walked up close, only to find that the bundle of cloth was her daughter, Orchid. With a low, unearthly scream she pushed the corpse of the servant aside. It appeared that the man had tried to protect her daughter and had died in the attempt, his hands clutching at the weapon in his throat.

She stared down at the lifeless, half-nude body of her child. The girl had no wounds, and her eyes were wide open, staring. Her otherwise rosy cheeks were drained of color, the skin possessed of a strange bluish sheen.

In what seemed like a nightmare, Matsu kneeled and touched her daughter's cheek with a trembling hand. It was stone cold. With a cry of anguish Matsu ran out of the storeroom, ignoring Hua, who was still wailing piteously. Her legs numb with shock, she ran, her arms flailing to catch her from falling, her face expressionless like a doll's, the sash of purple silk at her waist trailing behind her like a rivulet. Two Manchu soldiers walking across the courtyard laughed as she fled before them, one of them making a half-hearted attempt to grab her. Matsu darted away like a hunted sika deer, a long, high-pitched sound escaping her throat.

When she could run no longer, she collapsed onto the dirt near a gnarled tree in the oldest part of the garden. There was no one around. The Manchus obviously hadn't yet bothered to explore the outer reaches of the fortress. Still panting, her cheeks smeared with mud, she looked up and saw the tree in front of her. Zheng Sen had once told her that he and Cai had climbed it when they were young, placing their bare feet on the stumps along the trunk where its branches had been sawed off during centuries past. She looked up at the larger overhanging branches and raised a hand to protect her eyes from the incessant rain.

With an enormous effort, she got up and approached the tree. She began to climb it as she imagined her son must have done as a boy. She gasped as she nearly lost her footing on the slimy bark; but she stubbornly continued, slowly making her way up the trunk. There she sat, perched on the thick, gnarled branch, taking in the bodies of the dead, the numerous fires, and the dark plumes of smoke as if in a dream. Her daughter was dead. Her husband had gone and had betrayed not only his country and emperor but her as well. The enemy had succeeded in coming this far south, and had taken the family fort. Her oldest son was probably dead. It was over. Carefully she removed the silk sash at her waist, tied it securely to the branch, and wound the other loop around her neck. Then she jumped.

* * *

Zheng Sen and his army were confronted by the trail of death and destruction that the raiding Manchu army had left in its path long before they reached Anhai. By the time he came to the hillcrest overlooking the valley, the tell-tale sign of black smoke rising from his hometown confirmed his worst fears: they had come too late.

Fires raged everywhere. A few survivors were making futile efforts to douse the flames, while others stood by dumbly, the fire reflected in their dull eyes. Zheng Sen charged down the hill at full speed, his heart beating wildly. Gone were the familiar sentries he had commissioned to guard the fortress. They had been replaced by the enemy, by men whose foreheads were shaven and who wore their hair in queues. His stomach lurched as he realized the fortress had fallen.

He and Cai were among the first to arrive at the gate. The Manchurian sentries had seen them coming and aimed their deadly bows at the horsemen. This time the arrows missed their mark. His men fought hard, furious that their enemy had attacked the Zheng fortress, the very core of what was left of the Ming resistance.

The small Manchu regiment that was left stationed at the fortress was no match for Koxinga's vengeful army. Within half an hour of their arrival, every single Manchu officer and soldier was dead.

As Zheng Sen and Cai caught their breath to take in the once-familiar surroundings, they saw death and devastation wherever they looked. Zheng Sen ran from building to building, Cai following right behind him.

"Mother! Orchid!" The sound of his own cries pierced the eerie quiet that had fallen. He found the body of his younger sister first. By the time he came across his mother dangling from the tree, he was unable to utter another sound.

The bodies of his mother and sister were buried the next day, close to the graves of his ancestors. With war waging all around them, there was little time to perform the full funeral rites, but he still took pains to ensure that his mother had a burial that honored her.

Wrought with sorrow, he allowed the priest who attended to the burials to convince him to visit the Confucian temple.

"This is a time to pray to your ancestors. Honor them, and their spirits will guide you," the old man said.

Zheng Sen came to his feet swiftly, reacting as if stung by a bee. He charged at the priest, only just keeping himself from harming him. When he realized what he had been about to do, he looked at the man in anguish, still unable to believe the enormity of his loss. He dropped to his knees, sobbing, heedless of the priest who watched him with compassion. The old man nodded in understanding and let him be.

Zheng Sen sat in the graveyard for two hours, barely moving, simply staring at his mother's grave. Cai remained close by, his expression full of grief, feeling the loss of Matsu and Orchid as keenly as he did.

Later that afternoon, a sudden mood change took hold of him. As if possessed, he ran back to the ravaged stronghold where he searched blindly until he found what he was looking for: his scholarly robes. With the cloth bundle tucked under his arm, he rode back to the Confucian temple, Cai never leaving his side. Once there, he jumped from his horse, took one of the torches that lit the darkness of the shrine's interior, and set the bundle of robes alight in the center of the courtyard. He stood watching the flames devour the cloth, the reflection of the fire glittering in his bloodshot eyes. Out of the shadows the temple priest emerged, his face impassive.

"Burning one's scholarly robes is a symbol of turning your back on knowledge and wisdom. But also on your past," the man said kindly. "Is that what you wish to do?"

Zheng Sen turned on the man, his eyes swimming with tears. "What choice do I have?" he shouted, at no one in particular. He had become vaguely aware that Cai and his senior officers had followed him and that they were watching him from a respectful distance, the concern on their faces clear to see. "I have been educated a scholar. I have been a good

Confucian all my life!" His voice had become hoarse with emotion. "I have always honored my ancestors. My true emperor is dead. My mother and sister are dead. Raped and murdered by the enemy. And my father —" his nostrils lifted in contempt, "has deserted me. He betrayed me." He dropped to his knees, his body now racking with sobs. "I am an orphan without an emperor," Zheng Sen went on, as if to himself. "My family is gone. I have no country. I have no home."

Cai stepped forward, wishing to comfort him, just as distraught as he was. He laid a gentle hand on his shoulder. Zheng Sen recoiled at his touch, horrified that Cai and his officers had been witness to his emotional tirade. This is not how he wanted them to see him, weeping and weak, like a woman. He pushed Cai away furiously, upon which Cai lost his balance and fell hard on his backside. Bewildered, Cai got to his feet, hurt by his cousin's violent reaction. He blinked at him, completely at a loss. Then he mounted his horse and galloped away, the other officers in tow.

Zheng Sen hardly noticed. He stood up, wiped angrily at his tears and made his way unsteadily to the shrine, where he stood, his hands reaching out to support himself on the wooden altar table. Seven fragrant incense sticks were already burning there, the smoke curling like the soft contours of a graceful female dancer. The scent filled his nostrils, intoxicating him, reminding him of days long gone.

With an unsteady, trembling hand, he picked up an incense stick and held it against the red-hot glow of one already lit, and placed it carefully in the pot, its end burning brightly.

"I have sworn to fight the Qing army to the end," he said. "But my own father has betrayed us. He has forsaken us for the enemy, so I have no choice but to be an unfilial son. It goes against all that I have learned, against everything I have always believed in." The grief overpowered him, and he cried unashamedly. He felt the priest's comforting hand on his back, but this time he ignored it. "Please forgive me," he whispered to the spirits. "Forgive me."

"There is nothing to forgive," the priest said, his scraggly white beard moving as he spoke. "You must do what you have to do. We are all given a choice of paths in life. Take the path that you have chosen."

Zheng Sen turned to stare at the man's wise, serene face. "My father used those exact same words," he said.

"Perhaps your father is not as bad a man as you think. We cannot all be heroes." He shrugged his shoulders. "But perhaps you can," he added with a hint of a smile in his eyes.

Zheng Sen stared ahead in silence, mesmerized by the dancing trails of fragrant smoke. Then he turned to the old man, feeling utterly lost, desperate for something to believe in.

"I am a soldier now. Just a soldier who has sworn allegiance to his emperor." He gathered himself, taking a deep breath. "And one who vows to avenge the death of his family."

The priest closed his eyes and nodded. Koxinga bowed to him in gratitude. Then he got on his horse and was gone.

Later that evening, in the dim light of torches and candles, the priest prepared his ink, took up his calligraphy brush, and with practiced, smooth strokes, recorded the events of the day.

* * *

As word of Zheng Zhilong's defection and captivity in Peking spread, most of his allies rallied to back Zheng Sen. They were powerful and wealthy men, still believing in the Ming cause and willing to back the latest Ming prince, stubborn in their conviction that they could still resist the invading army. They sent their families to Formosa, where they would be safer. Those who left for the island themselves continued to support them from there, nurturing the hope that they might return to the mainland one day.

But the next claimant to the throne was no more than a weak figurehead who relied heavily on Zheng Sen's army. The newest emperor vested in Zheng Sen all the powers that he deemed necessary to continue the struggle against the Manchus. All remaining hope rested on his shoulders.

With his mother and sister dead and his father in captivity, the young man who had been born Fukumatsu and grown up as Zheng Sen was no more. He had become the head of the formidable Zheng clan, and by now everyone addressed and referred to him as Lord Koxinga. His reputation as a born leader grew, as did his capacity to incite fierce loyalty in his men. And so Koxinga, lord of the imperial surname, became the most powerful of all military leaders of the Ming and, in essence, the true leader of southeast China.

PART TWO

10

Leaseholders, Merchants, and Missionaries

FORMOSA, 1650

ANTONIUS HAMBROEK descended the path along the rice paddies, Frederic Coyett at his side. He watched the great ox pulling the plough below them, impressed by its vigor. He could see the vapors rising from the animal's dark, glistening back against the early morning light, the muscles laboring heavily. What had previously taken so many farmhands to do was now done quickly and efficiently since these strong beasts of burden had been brought to the island.

"Daniel!" he shouted, and waved.

The young missionary looked up at the sound of his booming voice and waved back with a grin.

Together the two men made their way toward him, Antonius' two young daughters skipping happily behind them. As he reached Daniel Gravius he shook his hand firmly in congratulation.

"You must be proud of yourself. And rightly so. You've done well," Frederic Coyett said in the slight sing-song accent that betrayed his Swedish origin.

"Reverend Hambroek, Mr. Coyett. Good morning, Miss Cornelia, Miss Johanna." He bowed his head gallantly toward each of the girls, both of whom giggled prettily at his exaggerated antics, their coppery locks of hair peeping out from under their smocked white bonnets. The sound of their cheerful titters caused the workers in the fields to lift their heads and peer at the children from underneath their conical hats. The girls had inherited their father's ruddy, freckled complexion, which attracted a good deal of attention from the local populace.

Daniel held out his hand toward Coyett. "And may I congratulate you on the birth of your son?"

Coyett beamed at him. "Thank you," he said.

"We've already seen the baby," the six-year-old Cornelia told Daniel importantly. "His name is Balthasar, and I was allowed to hold him. Johanna wasn't, because she is still too young," she jeered, and stuck her tongue out at Johanna provocatively, giving her a small shove. Her sister took the bait and gave chase, at which Johanna dashed off, emitting an ear-splitting screech of satisfaction, her sister in hot pursuit.

"Sisterly love," said Antonius drily, upon which the three men looked at the girls with amusement.

Daniel turned to Coyett. "The birth went well?" he asked. "Your wife is in good health?

"Yes, very much so, thank you. And Balthasar is of good, robust size – a strong boy, I'm happy to say."

Antonius nodded knowingly. It had been five years since Chief Merchant Coyett had married Susanna Boudaen, a strikingly handsome woman from a good family, yet they had not been blessed with children until now: Balthasar was their first child. From his wife, Anna, who got on well with Susanna and who saw her regularly, he had learned that Coyett's wife had been pregnant on a number of occasions, but none of those pregnancies had ever come full term. So Balthasar was a great blessing for the couple. Antonius had been moved when he had held the infant in his huge hands during the baptism. He had grown close to Frederic over the years, especially as they had arrived on Formosa on the same ship.

The three men stood to watch the stately movements of the laboring beast, whose massive, horned head bobbed up and down with every step it took. Daniel stood beaming with pride, and rightly so. The young missionary had petitioned persistently that the company bring oxen to the island, but the council had been unwilling to invest in the venture. In the end it had been Frederic Coyett who had suggested that the VOC give Daniel a loan to execute his plans. Eventually the members of the council agreed, admitting it might be a worthwhile experiment, as long as the company did not have to carry the financial risk.

Under Daniel's personal supervision, the yield from the harvest increased manifold. The venture had proven so successful that the council was already talking about appointing officials in charge of raising the cattle on the island. The oxen provided great physical relief to the field workers, who soon treated Daniel with gratitude and respect for providing them with the sturdy beasts that had been used for this purpose in China for centuries. They treated him like a hero. His standing among the Chinese had grown to such an extent that they even turned to him with their grievances.

The farmhands working the field had begun to squabble about who was allowed to handle the ox next, the novelty of which still hadn't worn off. The man presently driving the ox ignored them, making his way to the side of the field where they were standing. He recognized Daniel with a grin and waved. Daniel returned the gesture good-naturedly.

"You're a popular man," Antonius observed, brushing his fingers through his hair, the tight curls stuck against his forehead from the humidity. He had arrived on Formosa nearly two years ago with his wife and three daughters, his wife pregnant with a fourth at the time. Since then he had gradually grown used to the climate. "The Lord knows you deserve it," he added.

"Governor Overwater was a reasonable man," Daniel said. "I wish I could say the same of our present governor."

Antonius agreed with him. He noticed that Coyett remained silent, and he felt slightly sorry for the chief merchant. He was aware that Coyett, like himself, did not like the new governor, but he still had to work closely with him. He still could not fathom why the council in Batavia had appointed Nicolaes Verburgh as governor in the first place. Unlike Verburgh, Overwater had recognized the importance of the missionaries' work on the island, so he had been compliant when they had asked for more men. The mission had since grown considerably, and they now had a chain of moderately successful schools to thank for it. Some of the schools in the more populated villages had as many as several hundred students. Without being immodest, Antonius felt that the missionaries had contributed to the island in a very significant way. They had devised a way to write the native language with the Roman alphabet, and the number of baptized Christians on the island had grown to nearly seven thousand.

But Verburgh hardly cared. As soon as he had taken up his post, he had made it clear that he did not see the added value of the mission. Its work and accomplishments didn't interest him in the slightest, and he often made derogatory remarks about it, even to Antonius' face. He let it be known to all that he found it preposterous that there were as many as five reverends on the island. Verburgh even went so far by announcing he was prepared to pay one thousand guilders to any school who managed to produce "individuals worthy of being admitted to Christian society."

Antonius had to admit that many of the natives simply learned the texts of the catechisms by heart without ever understanding the contents. Most of the conversions to Christianity were only undergone by the locals for practical reasons, while still practicing their own beliefs. Even as a man of God he could understand that.

Yet both he and Daniel had taken an instant dislike to Verburgh from the moment he set foot on the island just under a year ago. From the start, the new governor had taken a hard line toward the local people and the Chinese migrants, and completely failed to win them over. The same could be said about quite a few of his officers, Hambroek thought to himself wryly. In his ambition, all Verburgh seemed to be concerned about was to control the island and the people on it, and this he did with a hard hand. Understandably, Nicolaes Verburgh was a man with enemies.

Antonius knew that Governor Verburgh harbored animosity toward Daniel, envious of the respect with which they spoke of him in Batavia after his oxen exploits. The new governor must have known of the influence Daniel had with both the local people and the company council. One thing had been clear to Hambroek from the start: Verburgh was a very jealous man.

"Any further developments regarding the printing press?" Daniel asked Antonius. Antonius smirked without humor when he was reminded of his early morning meeting with Verburgh. They had petitioned on numerous occasions for a printing press, something that had become an urgent necessity if they were to produce enough books for the schools. The number of mission schools had become far too large to copy the revised translations of the Bibles by hand.

"'Perhaps next year.' That was his answer. He said there was no budget for such 'extravagant' items right now," he said with a scowl. "I wish it were an extravagance." He saw that his daughters had become weary of watching the workers in the field and they were now playing a kind of skipping game on the dirt track behind them. Cornelia was bossing her younger sister around, as usual.

"The man is insufferable," Daniel said.

"I wish I could be of assistance, Daniel, but I can't," Coyett said. "You know that I've raised the matter with him many times. I personally believe it would be a praiseworthy venture, you know that."

Antonius nodded, frowning in thought. He knew that Verburgh felt somewhat daunted by Coyett. All the reasonable suggestions that Coyett had raised on making improvements on the island, Verburgh had struck from the agenda as if to make a point. Antonius had already warned his Swedish friend that Verburgh saw him as a rival, and that as long as the man was governor he would have to sit back and bide his time, however difficult that might be.

Coyett had been on the island for two years. Prior to that he had been stationed in Deshima, where he had been governor. Overwater had actually recommended him to the Batavian council as candidate for the same post on Formosa, but they had had other ideas and sent Nicolaes Verburgh instead.

"There is more, unfortunately," Antonius said. "And you're not going to like it. Remember we put in a request for additional schoolmasters from Patria to further the mission's cause?"

"Of course." After Daniel had a serious clash with Verburgh over some issue a few months back, he and Antonius had thought it might be better if Antonius met with the governor to represent them on mission matters.

Daniel had readily agreed, as he didn't care for the man one bit, a fact he found increasingly hard to hide.

Antonius took a deep breath before he made the announcement, knowing the reaction that must follow. "The governor wishes to assign soldiers to do the job."

"Soldiers?" Daniel cried in indignation, ignoring the fieldworkers' looks as they reacted to his raised tone of voice. "Those lowbred, mercenary ruffians? God knows that most of them cannot even read and write in their own language, let alone teach these children."

"He insists that some are suitable," Antonius countered, "Admittedly, some of them have been here long enough to speak their language."

"This is ludicrous! He is doing this just to insult us. After all the work that has been done. After all our predecessors have accomplished over the past two decades. Soldiers?" He shook his head in dismay.

"And, as expected, no increase in our wages," Antonius added.

"Well, there's a revelation," Daniel said. Hambroek sighed. However much they might have accomplished on the island, their wages were still low, their housing barely adequate.

The sound of people shouting drew their attention, causing them to look up. A Chinese man carrying a child on his back and a frail-looking woman holding a bundled baby had been making their way up the hill when they were stopped by a Dutch company official. Two company soldiers trailed behind him with apparent indifference.

"Your *hoofdbrief*! You must show me your hoofdbrief!" the official barked at them. A Chinese interpreter, a meek little man of low rank, translated the order. Timidly, the husband withdrew a document from his clothing and handed it over, his wife's skittish eyes on the ground. She looked wan and was as thin as a reed.

"This has already expired," the official said with satisfaction. "You should have paid for the renewal days ago!" The interpreter's words were barely audible as he translated.

"My wife was taken ill," the Chinese man explained, keeping his eyes down. "She needed my care. I did not dare leave her to make the journey to the fort. Please, sir, let us pass."

LEASEHOLDERS, MERCHANTS, AND MISSIONARIES

The official threw a cursory glance at the woman, who had to lean against her husband to remain upright. "That does not exempt you," he said. "You will have to pay a levy for having an expired *hoofdbrief*. Either that, or we will take you to the fort jail."

But the man was not intimidated. "I have no money to pay the levy because I haven't received my wages yet. I am on my way now to collect the money. Like I said, my wife has been ill. I have been unable to leave my house before today. Please, I beg you to show some understanding...."

"Then you will be taken to jail, Jan!" He called to one of the soldiers, who ambled over reluctantly.

Antonius, Daniel and Coyett had all listened to the exchange with growing outrage. Daniel was the first to respond, cursing beneath his breath as he strode up the hill.

"Let these people be," he commanded. "I know this man and I can attest that what he says is true. His wife has been seriously ill and he has been absent from his work for three days in order to care for her. Give the poor man a chance to collect his wages. He will pay his dues in time. Let them go."

"You are interfering with official company business," the official retorted.

"I told you to let these people be. You heard why the *hoofdbrief* expired. Show these people some clemency. It's wretched scum such as yourself who give us Hollanders a bad name." He scrutinized the official, positioning himself between the inspector and the Chinese farmer. "Where is your official insignia? I don't see it," he asked. "Are you authorized to stop these people for inspection?"

In the meantime, the escorting soldiers had spotted Antonius and Chief Merchant Coyett witnessing the exchange with interest. They must have realized that he and Coyett would side with Daniel. Uncertain, the soldiers stepped back. The interpreter merely stood there, at a loss on what to do.

Antonius suppressed a smile. All those acquainted with Daniel knew that the young reverend could be a hothead who rarely lost an argument, and people preferred not to cross him.

The official's face had turned red, his bravado gone now that the soldiers had fallen back. He realized that he was on his own, and stammered something to the effect that he had left his insignia in his office.

"Well, you know the procedure. No official insignia, no inspections. Be gone with you, for the love of God!" Daniel bellowed.

"You will live to regret this!" the official shouted over his shoulder. "The governor will hear of your interference in legitimate company business."

"Do give the esteemed governor my regards, while you're at it," Daniel shouted after him with unconcealed sarcasm. The moment they were gone the Chinese man thanked Daniel, apologizing for the trouble he had caused, grabbing his hand to express his gratitude. His wife mimicked his gestures weakly.

"*Beh iau kin.* It's nothing," he assured the man. Daniel returned to join Antonius and Frederic, who both greeted him with a grin.

"Making yourself popular with the governor again, eh Daniel?" Coyett said, laughing as he laid an amicable hand on his shoulder.

"May the Lord protect you from his wrath!" Antonius hollered.

* * *

It irked Frederic Coyett that Verburgh, like some of the members of the council of Formosa, was so ill -informed of the developments that were taking place in China. He felt that they simply could not afford to remain ignorant, especially with everything that was going on there.

Verburgh was not a thinker for the long term, which was unfortunate considering the circumstances. Who knows what the consequences might be for Formosa. While he was posted on Deshima he had had various dealings with the Zhengs, who dominated all trade in the region, and he had watched their imperium grow with interest. But for some reason they had recently lost sight of their trade intermediary. However, his son Koxinga was increasingly in the picture. It even seemed this Koxinga had taken his father's position as head of the Zhengs. Apart from that, he also appeared to be a man of some military importance. Frederic had informed Verburgh of this, but the governor wasn't interested.

"It looks as if Koxinga has taken over in his father's absence. He plays an increasingly significant role in the China trade. We can no longer afford to ignore him if we are to obtain trade in greater volumes."

"Ah, yes. The pirate's son. What's his story again?" Verburgh asked, looking at General Isaaks. The general deferred the question to Frederic. "I think that Mr. Coyett would be more able to fill you in on this, sir."

Frederic nodded his appreciation toward the general, who had only recently replaced Peter Boenck as the first in command of the military presence on Formosa. Frederic had already asked him for his support in counselling the governor on the issue, as Verburgh was unwilling to take anything from him. So often the man had interrupted, even patronized him in front of others. He was beginning to lose his patience with Verburgh, and often wondered how long he would be able to stand working with the man.

"It is true that some call him a pirate. But the man does have a substantial fleet to his name, and at this moment he is one of the most influential and powerful people in southern China," Frederic explained, warming to the subject. "The Ming loyalists have put some prince on the throne as their emperor, but this man is no more than a figurehead." Much to his irritation, Verburgh had begun to scribble some notes in the ledger in front of him, already distracted. "The Chinese on Formosa hold him in high esteem. Apart from that, he plays a growing role in our trade with China. His father is Zheng Zhilong, also known to Westerners by his baptized name Nicholas Iquan."

Verburgh looked up at this. "The mandarin merchant? He has been our trading partner for years."

Frederic nodded. "Yes," he said, exasperated at how badly Verburgh listened. He had told him this before. "We were under the impression that he had been killed by the Qing army, but evidently he is still alive. Some say he has defected to the Manchus, but rumor has it that they are holding him captive in Peking. We do not know what to believe at this point."

Verburgh was thoughtful for a while, his hand rubbing his chin. "That might justify the drop in the silk trade. We're not getting much in these days," he grumbled. "So this Koxinga – his name sounds almost Friesian – he is some kind of admiral, you're saying?"

"It would be wise to regard him that way, sir," General Isaaks said. "His ships – and those of his father – have brought many Chinese families to the island. Wealthy, influential families. He is a respected man among the people here. I hear he even has a fort up in the north of Formosa."

"He doesn't seem to be a nuisance to us. So why the concern?"

"It appears he has a substantial part of his fleet stationed close by in the Pescadores. His navy has so far managed to keep the Manchurian army away from the coastal provinces, but eventually...." The general left his sentence unfinished.

"Eventually what?"

"With his navy and the size of his following in the vicinity, he could become a threat to us here, sir."

"I seriously question that. He's too busy fighting those Tartars, Manchus, whatever they are. Wouldn't worry about it for now," he said dismissively, moving on to other matters.

Frederic exchanged glances with Isaaks. He sincerely hoped that Verburgh was right, but somehow he didn't think so.

The fact that Batavia wasn't forthcoming with funds to improve Formosa's infrastructure was part of the reason Verburgh had decided to assign eleven soldiers – whose prowess in the arts of war were sadly lacking – as teachers for the schools.

Frederic and Antonius were appalled at the decision. Frederic seriously questioned it during council meetings, which had done nothing to make him popular with Verburgh. He argued that the soldiers were not qualified to teach, but Verburgh was unrelenting and had pushed it through with determination.

Without batting an eyelid, he then went on to say that with the soldiers taking up their positions of teachers, there was no longer any need for five reverends, and suggested recalling two who had been on the island the longest.

Frederic knew exactly whom he was thinking of, and Daniel Gravius was one of them. He had always known that it would only be a matter of time before Verburgh and Daniel would come to a clash. Verburgh's jealousy of Daniel's popularity and success was well known, Verburgh would need only the smallest pretext to get rid of him. He even had the gall to say that what they saved on their earnings could be used to improve their housing or on the printing press that the mission wanted.

The others in the council were non-committal on the subject, their looks evasive. But Frederic had to speak his mind.

"I beg to differ. The mission and its schools have never prospered as much as now. Besides, relations between Daniel and the locals are excellent. The man still has many good years in him. Why remove him, of all people?"

Verburgh pursed his lips. He shifted in his chair, shaking his head in a manner that suggested that Frederic was a complete idiot.

"You know the answer. Because we have been told to save costs. Do I have to keep repeating myself?"

"But why Reverend Gravius? He has achieved a great deal and...."

"Like I said, he has been on the island the longest," he said, glaring at him with barely suppressed anger. "I do believe I make the decisions here, Mr. Coyett. I will write to Batavia on the matter. We shall await their answer. Enough said on the subject for now. Let us move on."

* * *

The following Monday Daniel was summoned to the fort. Annoyed at being disturbed during a lesson, Daniel told the errand boy that he had to wait, insisting that he finish his class first. Forty minutes later, he appeared at the governor's office, where he found Verburgh fuming at being kept waiting.

"*Mijnheer* Gravius, so good of you to grace us with your presence," Verburgh said. "Perhaps you could make an effort next time to come to me straight away when summoned."

"I was in the middle of a class," Daniel said, unimpressed.

"May I remind you that you are in the employ of the VOC, and that you answer to me as the company's governor of this island?"

"I am a servant of God, as you well know."

"Perhaps so. But it's the company that pays your wages, in case you have overlooked that fact."

"I have not. However, delivering these souls from eternal damnation is more than enough reward for me," Daniel said innocently.

Verburgh's face turned quite red. "I am warning you," he said, his hands firmly planted on his desk as he stood. "Do not interfere with company business. You teach your heathen, native brats, and translate your Bible for all I care. But do not interfere with the work of the inspectors!"

"They are not brats," Daniel said, trying not to lose his temper. "These people and their ancestors have been here for thousands of years. This is their homeland."

"May I remind you that this island was annexed by the VOC on authority of the government of the United Seven Provinces more than twenty-five years ago? Watch your step. Your words ring of treason." Verburgh was now no longer in control of his emotions. "There is more. You do not have the mandate to receive the village heads. If they have a complaint or wish to discuss any matters involving the company, then they should come to me."

"Oh. Is that what this is all about?" Daniel asked. He noticed that the veins at Verburgh's temples stood out threateningly. "I cannot stop them from coming to talk to me if they so wish. They regard me as their friend, and I regard them as mine."

Daniel suspected that if the large oak desk hadn't been between them, Verburgh would have launched himself at his throat.

"You *Godverdomde* bastard."

"How dare you!" Daniel growled, angered at both the blasphemy as well as the personal insult that questioned his parentage. "I hope for your sake that the Lord will forgive you, because I most certainly will not!" He stormed out of the office, his face as red as Verburgh's.

"I will have you removed from your station!" Verburgh shouted. Daniel turned around and glowered at him, ignoring the curious clerks that had emerged from their offices to witness the exchange.

"You do as you please," he retorted, and was gone.

The animosity between Daniel and the governor was no longer a secret in the fort, or outside of it, for that matter. Verburgh had uttered the words in front of members of his staff, and Daniel knew that in order not to lose face or credibility he would be forced to take measures.

Jacobus Vertrecht, who had arrived in Formosa on the same ship as Daniel four years previously, accompanied Daniel to see Verburgh.

"No prizes for guessing why we've been summoned by the governor," Daniel said to his colleague as the two men strode up the hill.

"You think our time here has come to an end?" Jacobus asked. He and Daniel worked closely together and there were few secrets between them.

"I do, indeed. You know how eager the governor is to get me off this island. He's probably finally received word from Batavia on how to proceed."

"Hmm," Jacobus muttered. "To tell you the truth, I wouldn't be terribly unhappy at the prospect of leaving. I do hate the humidity and find many of the tasks the governor assigns us both tedious and thankless."

Daniel said nothing. He, too, had long ago discovered that many of the "Christians" had converted for the privileges that came with the conversions, and not out of religious conviction. He enjoyed teaching, but the attendance of the aboriginals was so inconsistent that it frustrated him. He couldn't blame Jacobus for feeling the way he did.

"I wonder where we'll end up next," Jacobus said.

"Batavia, no doubt. At least I will finally be able to get married. I have kept my betrothed waiting long enough as it is. Not that I particularly want to leave Formosa. I have a certain fondness for the people here. Their mentality appeals to me. Besides, there is still so much to be done on the island, in particular with these former soldiers assigned as teachers. They'll need intensive training."

Jacobus nodded, allowing Daniel to climb the steps toward the fort ahead of him.

"Ah, gentlemen. Come in," the governor said, obviously in a good mood. He didn't bother standing up. The two men muttered their good mornings civilly but without warmth.

"I have good news and, alas, also bad. Please sit down." Verburgh motioned to the leather chairs. The men took their seats warily, expecting the worst.

The governor pointedly touched a letter on his desk with all the fingertips of his right hand, glancing at it as if to remind himself of its contents.

"You will be gratified to learn that your request for a printing press has been approved by the council. Please would you also convey this information to your colleagues Hambroek, Hapartius and ..." he consulted his notes, "Reverend Johannes Cruyf. I would be pleased to arrange for the order if you so wish."

Daniel said nothing: he thought it was about time. He and Antonius Hambroek and their predecessors had been lobbying for a printing press for years.

"Unfortunately," Verburgh said, not making any attempt to hide the fact that he didn't find whatever he was about to say unfortunate at all, "Batavia has sent notice that there is a surplus of reverends on the island. There are the costs to consider. With the new teachers taking up their positions soon, it will no longer be necessary for all five of you to remain on Formosa. Budgetary reasons, as I'm sure you will understand." He tried to look contrite.

Jacobus shifted in his seat, Verburgh cleared his throat theatrically.

"I'm going to have to release the both of you from your posts." He gave them his saddest expression possible, but Daniel saw right through him: Verburgh wasn't much of an actor.

Neither he nor Jacobus reacted. They had both seen this coming for some time.

"Very well," said Daniel. "I suspect that we will leave after the training of these new *teachers*" he sneered at the word, "has been accomplished?"

Verburgh was momentarily at a loss. Obviously he hadn't considered the matter carefully.

"It would not be very reasonable to expect Reverend Hambroek to train the soldiers all by himself," Daniel pressed on, knowing that Verburgh would only be too pleased to put him on the very next ship. "Mr. Cruyf and Mr. Hapartius have just recently arrived. They are still far too inexperienced. Besides, they haven't mastered the native language yet."

Verburgh's mouth twitched. "One month should be adequate," he acceded. "Then you will sail for Batavia. I shall inform the council when to expect you back in the East Indies. Perhaps they can make some other arrangements for you in the meantime. Do you have any questions?" he asked, disappointed by their lack of response.

"No, no questions," Daniel said. "We all know what this is truly about. This is personal. Obviously you are not able enough to not let it get the better of your judgment. Our paths will cross again, and I shall not forget this." He looked at Verburgh coldly to emphasize his point. The governor returned the look, but said nothing.

Daniel and Jacobus left Fort Zeelandia for the last time. Neither of them would have any reason to return there.

Once Daniel knew that he would have to leave, he started making plans, believing that he was young enough to make something of his life elsewhere. Above all he looked forward to being reunited with his fiancée in Batavia. She was a vibrant young woman to whom he was introduced before he had sailed for Formosa, and with whom he had conducted extensive correspondence during the years that had followed. It so happened that her father was a senior official at the VOC regional headquarters in Batavia, and even though the man had been averse to the idea of his daughter marrying a modest minister, he had been quickly won over by Daniel's enthusiasm and business instincts. The success Daniel had achieved with the cattle import to Formosa, along with his infectious, boundless energy had led his fiancée's father to change his opinion in Daniel's favor.

When word arrived in Batavia that he would be leaving for the East Indies, it wasn't long before a suitable position was found for him. He landed a respectable post in the Education Department, where he was given the supervision of all Christian schools in the colony. For Daniel, who had been reluctant to leave Formosa, it was a positive development, and he was married within months of his arrival.

Daniel lobbied for Jacobus Vertrecht and found him a suitable teaching post at one of the schools on Java. From Antonius Hambroek he regularly received letters that the schools on Formosa suffered under the changes that Verburgh had imposed. Not surprisingly, the training of the former soldiers to become schoolteachers had turned into a complete fiasco. During the first month, most seemed enthusiastic and keen to learn, but after his and Vertrecht's forced departure, there wasn't enough supervision. Soon it became apparent that the majority of the men had seen the teaching profession as a means to escape their dreary military duties. Daniel knew that a soldier's regimental life at the forts was hard. Teaching the locals was far less demanding. Hambroek wrote that many of the soldier-schoolteachers had proved to be ruthless opportunists who preferred to spend their service time in the villages where they were assigned to teach, and were given a lot more freedom than they had at the fort. Some of them turned to unscrupulous extracurricular activities to supplement their wages, abusing the status of their new careers to intimidate and bully the locals into providing them with goods and services. Hambroek lamented that the new teachers often failed to show up at the schoolhouses; and when it became obvious that the majority were totally inadequate for the job, a growing number of students stopped coming to the schools altogether. As they had foreseen, Hambroek and Johannes Cruyf soon found that they were spending most of their time sorting out the various problems that had arisen from the employment of the unmotivated, unqualified men.

Hambroek wrote with relish that he, Frederic Coyett, and the two other remaining reverends had gone to the governor to inform him of the deteriorating situation at the mission schools. They had urgently requested that the governor reconsider matters and replace the two missionaries that had departed. But Verburgh wasn't inclined to admit he had made a mistake, especially to Coyett. Instead, he had demanded what business it was of Coyett's to interfere, upon which Coyett had reminded the governor none too subtly that it was his business, as he was a member of the council.

While reading Hambroek's letter, it occurred to Daniel that the opportunity to get even with Verburgh was within his reach, and he lost no time in notifying certain gentlemen of the council in Batavia about the mission's predicament on Formosa. Quoting the relevant contents of Hambroek's letter, he too conveyed his concerns to the council. With no small amount of drama, he explained to the council that if the VOC wished to maintain control over the future generations on the island, then it was vital that the company invest in education. He suggested that it would be in their interest to educate the children properly, and that with the growth of the population, it simply didn't make sense to reduce the number of qualified personnel at the schools. On the contrary, he recommended an increase.

Encouraged by his influential father-in-law, and due to the regard with which he was held as head of the Education Department of Batavia, his concerns and recommendations were taken seriously. Many members of the council became convinced that the governor of Formosa had sent him away on a pretext in order to settle a personal score. They had previously dismissed the rumors about the conflict between Daniel and Verburgh; but in view of Hambroek's letter, Daniel's arguments seemed relevant.

* * *

While Verburgh was travelling to the island's interior, Frederic was discreetly shown a letter by Verburgh's private secretary that contained information that the governor would most definitely have preferred to keep to himself.

It was from Governor-General Reijnierszoon, the first in command of the VOC at its Asian headquarters in Batavia. The letter was addressed to Verburgh. The gloating secretary – who rather disliked Verburgh and felt sympathy for poor Mr. Coyett, whom he suspected must surely be frustrated – felt it was something he might like to see.

Indeed, Frederic read it with interest. The message in the letter was painfully clear. The governor-general reprimanded Verburgh, stating that the Batavian council had more important things on its mind than a surplus missionary or two. Moreover, it had only recently received reports with the figures of the seven thousand baptized local and Chinese Christians on Formosa, and that a chain of some thirty schools was up and running successfully.

Frederic chuckled. He knew that Reijnierszoon had a penchant for reports and figures. The governor-general went on to write that they had so far heard only good things about the mission's work on Formosa. "It has come to our attention that the previous removal of two reverends as recommended by your person from the island of Formosa was an error in judgment, with no consideration for the growing numbers of families arriving on Formosa. Furthermore, we would like to remind the governor that education forms a fundamental part of the company's policy in order to safeguard our future interests."

He informed Verburgh that he was to expect Mr. Rutger Tesschemaker and Mr. Johannes Ludgens before the end of the year 1651, both appointed to the mission schools.

Gratified, Frederic returned the letter to the secretary, who, grinning with mischief at his indiscretion, told him that Verburgh had been livid when he received the dispatch. Frederic could just picture it. He was in no doubt that somehow Daniel had a hand in the matter. Revenge could be so very sweet at times.

The rebuke and corrective measures taken by the governor-general not only undermined Verburgh's authority, it had also caused him to lose serious face. Verburgh would have to tread carefully from now on. Frederic thanked the secretary for showing him the letter and returned to his work, smiling with satisfaction.

* * *

The three aboriginal men looked grim and determined as they addressed the Formosan council. Frederic knew them well: they were the elders from the three main villages that shouldered the Bay of Tayouan. Their dress was an odd array of clothing: one was clad in colorful textiles, another was wearing a faded Chinese gown, and the third was dressed in faded breeches that must once have belonged to a Dutch soldier. On top of that the elder wore a tunic of the same colorful material as the first was wearing.

Governor Verburgh looked at the threesome with feigned concern. He had dark circles under his eyes from lack of sleep, as one of his children had taken ill the previous day and had kept him and his wife up most of the night.

"Gentlemen," he began with a weary voice. "In what way can I be of assistance? Ting-bin!" He beckoned toward the ever-present He Ting-bin, one of the company's most capable interpreters. Ting-bin went through the preliminaries while a clerk made a note of the names of the three men and the villages they represented. The men briefly exchanged glances, uncertain as to who should speak first.

"Excellency," the man in the soldier's breeches began, "We thank you for receiving us so soon."

Frederic pursed his lips, knowing that the men had in fact waited six weeks before Verburgh had finally agreed to see them, in spite of the urgency of the matter.

"Please be informed that our people are finding it increasingly difficult to make a living. The wealthy Chinese leaseholders, those who have the exclusive rights to trade in our villages, are setting the prices for their goods at too high a price." The village elder glanced uncomfortably at Ting-bin, who was a fair representation of the type of wealthy Chinese merchants he spoke of. Ting-bin was far more than an interpreter: he was also a company tax collector, village head, leaseholder, and a successful businessman who had his connections, both on Formosa and in China. He spoke Chinese, Dutch, and a smattering of Portuguese, which made him invaluable to the company. In fact, he personified all that the aboriginal islanders had come to despise.

"You see, excellency, the number of deer has been falling at an alarming rate. As you know, trading deer products is our only means to survive, but more villages are forced to share the same hunting fields. And if this goes on...." The man paused trying to find the right words. "The Chinese merchants, they set unfairly low prices for buying our produce; we have no choice but to accept. They are making it impossible for many of our people to get by." The elder sighed. "We humbly ask you to look into the situation. We should also warn you that relations between our people and the Chinese are not very good right now." Once again the man glanced uneasily at Ting-bin, probably wishing that the governor had assigned another interpreter to translate for them that day. But Ting-bin continued to translate the aboriginal's words, hardly blinking.

"Many of our people feel cheated by the merchant leaseholders. Incidents have already taken place. You know this, excellency, as we told you this last month." The man's face hardened at the reminder, his tone taking on a sharper, more desperate edge.

Frederic knew that the trade leases were causing problems. The wealthy merchants monopolized their trades and were taking advantage by buying goods at ridiculously low rates, then increasing the prices manifold when offering the goods to the VOC and the traders in China. Although the leases had worked well initially, the situation had gotten out of hand. The matter had been discussed before; it had even been brought to the attention of the governor-general in Batavia, but to no effect. The high revenues from the annual lease auctions now formed such a substantial part of the company's income on the island that the Batavian council was reluctant to abolish the practice.

Verburgh nodded his understanding at the three men upon hearing their grievances. But Frederic wondered if he had truly listened. As usual, the governor promised he would look into the matter and told the three men to return in six weeks' time.

Verburgh's procrastination vexed him. Frederic thought that if he had been governor, he would have dealt with the situation differently.

The three aboriginals left the fort, their shoulders sagging despondently at the governor's reaction, which hardly differed from what he had told them the month before.

* * *

It was Antonius who brought the growing discontent among the native islanders to Frederic's attention. Before Daniel's departure, he and Antonius had tried to persuade Verburgh to take the necessary measures to curb the Chinese merchants' power and protect the villagers from their greed. The two missionaries stood far closer to the aboriginal community than any other company employee, and they knew firsthand what kind of impact the trade leases had on their lives. They could see up close how unfair the monopolies created by the leasehold system were for the aboriginals, who were left with no other alternative than to sell their goods to the Chinese merchants at the low prices they were offered. Antonius also told Frederic that the system was causing a growing rift between the natives and the Chinese, and went as far as to warn Verburgh that the hated system might one day even turn the aboriginal population against the company, something which Verburgh immediately dismissed as nonsense.

In Batavia, it appeared that Governor-General Reijnierszoon also had his misgivings about the system, in the belief that they should better look after the natives' interests. He agreed to write to his superiors in the Netherlands, recommending that they abolish the system altogether.

But the *Heren Seventien* wouldn't hear of it. They found the exclusive leasehold system far too lucrative to simply do away with. Besides, the gentlemen argued, the system had also been set up to regulate the trade between the aboriginals and the many Chinese arriving on the island, not just to raise money. This way, they could keep better track of the commercial activities of the Chinese. If they abolished the system, the company would have to come up with an alternative to regulate trade between the two population groups.

Their decision did nothing to solve the problem on Formosa, where they all were of the opinion that something had to be done in order to prevent the growing unrest that the leasehold system had caused.

At Frederic's urging, Verburgh finally called a meeting with the island's seven major leaseholders, among them village headman Guo Wen-bao. Verburgh suggested to the Chinese that they set the same prices for their goods across the island, explaining that the inflation that they were imposing on the islanders was becoming a source of discontent.

"But your excellency," Guo replied smoothly, "this is a large island, with the mountains and gorges making many parts of it almost inaccessible. The transport to some of these parts is much more costly. It would not be reasonable to buy products for the same price across the island."

Frederic knew that Guo had a point. If the company insisted on having set prices, they would have to do so per region, and then they would have to adjust the administrative regulations. Setting prices for different regions would lead to highly complicated administrative processes, and they didn't have the necessary manpower – or funds – to implement them.

Verburgh scowled, as they appeared to be back at square one. "Gentlemen, I'm going to have to ask you to agree among yourselves to keep your prices at a level the villagers can afford. In the meantime I would like to inform you that the council has discussed the possibility of free market days." The Chinese merchants exchanged glances, not understanding.

"Let me enlighten you," Verburgh said. "Free market days are the future. They have been held in the East Indies for quite some time now, and with considerable success. My superiors in Batavia propose that we start holding them here on Formosa on an experimental basis. Starting next month, we will be holding free markets in Saccam on Fridays.

"The local tradesmen from the other surrounding villages will also be invited to come and sell their wares," Verburgh went on. "They will be permitted to offer their produce for the price that they want, to any willing buyer. Your exclusive trading rights as leaseholders will not be valid on these days."

The Chinese leaseholders looked at him in dismay. This measure would make a serious dent in their profits.

"Your excellency, that is an excellent idea," Guo offered, the quiver in his voice only just betraying how he truly felt on the matter. "I am sure that my colleagues and I," he gestured toward the men at his side, "will also be able to do good business on these market days."

Verburgh looked relieved. He must have thought that this had gone well. But Frederic frowned, doubting very much that this was the case. He warned Verburgh that the lease-holding merchants would most certainly not take this lying down. Particularly Guo Wen-bao, whom he knew well. The man was as greedy and sly as a fox, and he suspected that his mind was already brooding on some plan to circumvent the market days. Time will tell, he told himself.

Frederic followed the developments with interest. During the first weeks, the market days were a great success, especially for the aboriginals. The markets attracted more tradesmen than ever before, both native and Chinese. Native tradesmen came in from different parts of the island, bringing their wares to sell at the markets at more favorable prices than before.

While the aboriginal villagers in remoter areas still faced high monopoly prices, the trading conditions in the villages near Zeelandia and Saccam improved, as did the lives of the aboriginals. Before long they learned to wait until the Friday markets before offering their goods, getting much better deals and selling their goods at better prices. The free markets were lively and vibrant, and everyone seemed happy. Except the Chinese leaseholders, who suddenly had to compete among themselves for their business. They felt the crunch in their purse now that the aboriginals refused to trade with them during the week, preferring to wait for the Friday markets.

Just as Frederic had foreseen, some leaseholders tried to evade the system. Shrewd as they were, they employed men of dubious character to await aboriginal tradesmen entering the village boundaries before the markets began, bullying them into selling their goods at low prices.

Soon enough, someone complained about this harassment. The following market day, Verburgh gave orders for edicts to be posted, forbidding any Chinese from trading goods anywhere but at the markets. In order to ensure that the irregularities were not repeated, soldiers were stationed at the access roads, and all seemed well.

But after six months of free markets, the seven merchant leaseholders demanded another audience with the governor. The men glided into the audience hall, an air of arrogant confidence about them. Once the greetings and pleasantries had been translated, Guo quickly came to the point. He said that he and his fellow merchants had seen their income from the Zeelandia and Saccam area dwindle drastically. They had tried to correct the imbalance by selling their goods in the remoter villages, but with the higher transport costs and administrative fees they could not make up for their losses. The men felt downright cheated.

"The free markets are having a serious impact on our businesses, your excellency," Guo said primly.

"That was to be expected," said Verburgh, his patience running thin. "Free market days have been the order of the day for years, and not just here on Formosa. These markets were organized to give everyone an honest opportunity at trade, something you refused to do with your uncivil prices. We already spoke of this." Frederic was surprised to find himself fully agreeing with Verburgh for once. The only thing that mattered to these men was money.

"Ah," Guo replied, obviously the spokesperson for the group. "That might be true. But your excellency is forgetting something. We paid a lot of money for our trading leases, but with these markets, they have become worthless. We have come to claim compensation. We would like to have the money returned to us that we paid at the annual auction." He smiled complacently.

"That simply isn't possible," Verburgh said, shocked.

"Well in that case, I am sure your excellency will understand that none of us will be renewing our leases at the coming auction in two months' time," Guo said calmly, bringing his point home. "Your excellency." He bowed, signaling that as far as he was concerned, the meeting was over. He left the hall, the other six men following in his path.

* * *

The council of Formosa now had a problem. The money that they raised annually from the leasehold auctions from these men alone was about half of what they raised at the auctions across the entire island. If these seven men carried out their threats, the loss in income would be considerable. It was a decision Verburgh wasn't prepared to make by himself.

It turned out that he didn't have to. The general consensus in Formosa, Batavia and finally in Amsterdam, was that the scale of the trade on the island, and the income it generated, had become too big to ignore. In addition, trade between the Chinese and the aboriginals was a natural process that could not be stopped, so it had to be regulated. It was finally decided to maintain the leasehold system. The free markets days, which had initially proven to be so attractive for the aboriginal tradesmen, gradually became more and more regulated in favor of the Chinese leaseholders. Before long they lost their point entirely and eventually ceased to take place.

When the time came for the annual leaseholds to be renewed, things started to go wrong. Once it became apparent to the Chinese merchants that the leaseholds would become lucrative once more, there was a mad rush for them. The auction prices of the leaseholds shot up to astronomical amounts, far surpassing their worth. Not surprisingly, many leaseholders were unable to pay the second instalments of the leases, forcing them into debt.

The VOC was lenient to the leaseholders at first, but as the number of debtors and the amounts owed to the company increased, it had to take measures to prevent the situation from spiraling out of control. The company announced that those who still had not paid their debts from previous years would no longer be allowed to join the auctions. Strict measures were taken against those who were unable to clear their debts, forcing many into bankruptcy. Even the wealthier leaseholders suffered, and resentment among the Chinese grew.

Life for the aboriginals deteriorated as well. The unfavorable conditions under which they were forced to sell their wares had returned, and worsened when the price of deer products, which were their main trading staple, dropped even further. Tough times lay ahead for Chinese and aboriginals alike.

In the meantime, the company filled its coffers with the money raised from the leasehold auctions, collected *hoofdbrief* taxes, hunting licenses, fishing licenses, and sales taxes on everyday essentials. Long gone were the days when migrant farmers had been given tax breaks and even subsidies to lure them to the island. Now the livelihoods of the farmers were at the mercy of their Dutch creditors and tax collectors. Added to this were the corrupt soldier-schoolteachers and other low-ranking company officials who posed as inspectors and squeezed money from the people to add to their wages.

Formosa's economy also began to suffer from the war in China. And then there were the fickle moods of Mother Nature to deal with, in the form of the weather.

11

The Uprising

GUO WEN-BAO had always believed that fortune had smiled upon him. He had been a wealthy man, perhaps one of the wealthiest Chinese on the island, and not without influence. No one was surprised when he was elected headman to represent Zeelandia's Chinese community with the Dutch authorities. His father had been Guo Jinbao, who had emigrated to Formosa in the early days of the colony. He, too, had been a village headman then. Longfei, his mother, had at first been critical of her husband at what she regarded as his meek submission to the Dutch colonists. According to his older brother, there had once been an incident in which the Dutch had humiliated her, and that was something she had neither forgiven nor forgotten. But when his father had been asked if he would take on the position of village head, she had appeared as flexible as bamboo. She was shrewd enough to realize the advantages of such a position. His father had hesitated before taking the job, but it was his mother who had persuaded him to accept.

Since then, the company had rewarded him well for his new-found loyalty, and the money and goods he received for his services he invested wisely in various ventures that had generated a small fortune. Their days of hard labor were behind them, and Longfei had the luxury of staying at home as the wife of the village headman.

As their wealth increased due to his clever investments, they built a new home and were able to take on servants. His mother had given birth to another son, whom they called Huai-yi. Longfei coddled both her sons, but especially her youngest boy. She made no secret of the fact that he was her favorite.

Just like their father, who had become a successful entrepreneur and creative in ways to make money, Wen-bao and Huai-yi turned out to be smart, practical and enterprising of nature. When their father died, he left a sizeable sum of money to them both.

By the time their mother passed away, the Guo family name had become synonymous among the Chinese on Formosa with influence and wealth. After Wen-bao took charge of the family business, he soon discovered the dubious but profitable business of moneylending.

He finally settled in the town of Zeelandia, close to the fort and the governor's residence, an area that had always attracted rich Chinese migrants. When the VOC started the auctions for the trade leases, he and his brother Huai-yi were among the first to purchase the more lucrative ones.

In spite of the increased competition from the arrival of other affluent Chinese migrants, Wen-bao continued to make handsome profits, and the number of people on his payroll grew as the years went by. He was smart enough to make sure he paid tribute to the Dutch officials, regularly sending gifts to the governor's residence and often inviting him to his home. Some of the previous governors had occasionally visited his house out of courtesy – and curiosity – but Governor Verburgh always declined his invitations. This didn't matter to him ... as long as he had the Dutch on his side. It was, after all, pragmatic to maintain good relations with the authorities, especially if they upheld a system that made people like him rich.

Wen-bao and his brother looked down on the aboriginal people, regarding them as coarse and uncivilized. He had absolutely no qualms about taking advantage of the system. It was the Dutch that had imposed it upon the island's economy, after all. Instead, he felt that it was his right to ask whatever prices for his goods that he pleased, considering he had paid good money for the annual leases. Moreover, he had a living to make, and the other major leaseholders were doing exactly the same.

Now all that had changed. Due to the flasco surrounding the leasehold auctions, he was one of the many people who had run into serious debt. Just like his brother, he had a small army of agricultural laborers working the plots of land that he leased, for which he paid a mere pittance. With the exorbitant prices that they had paid for the leases at the last auction and yet another poor harvest in September, he found himself unable to repay the instalments he owed the company. Those loans dated back two years, and things were beginning to look bleak. It appeared that the company not only ruled over the island, it was also in control of what had once been his fortune. And that stung.

But tonight Wen-bao didn't want to think about all that. By manner of distraction from his troubles, he had arranged for his latest acquisition to be brought to his bedchamber. This is what he had done it all for. The girl was the oldest daughter of one of the farmers who was in his debt, given to him by means of repaying him. The girl was his now, and he could do with her as he pleased. He shivered with pleasure as the young girl allowed the silk jacket to fall from her shoulders, just as he told her to. Her small breasts were firm and pert, so different from his wife's, which had the curious tendency to both shrink and sag. He beckoned the girl to come closer. She was his second concubine, not yet fifteen, still shy and not yet deflowered. Quite delicious.

He reached out to her, beckoning her to come to him.

"Come closer, little flower," Wen-bao whispered, his hand now taking her by the arm, pulling her toward her. "You lie down now. I won't hurt you," he said hoarsely, his excitement mounting at seeing her naked breasts, her skirts still held up by the sash at her waist. The girl swallowed, and reluctantly lowered herself next to him. His naked, soft white belly protruded above his pantaloons. She closed her eyes in shock as a hand closed onto one of her breasts, first stroking her gently, then squeezing and finally pinching her nipple until she cried out in pain, the tears springing from her eyes. Wen-bao smiled. The power he had over her thrilled him. He was going to enjoy deflowering her.

The hardness of his manhood seemed to have a life of its own, throbbing so insistently that it almost ached. He got up from the bed and dropped the rest of his clothes, the girl eyeing his genitals with a mixture of curiosity and alarm. Grinning lustfully, he slowly untied the sash at her waist and pulled the skirts down to observe the triangle of her pubic hair. The girl tensed.

"Now don't be afraid, little one," He considered asking her to toy with his manhood, but the novelty of her youth and virginity made his need urgent, impatient to get inside of her. He straddled her, his floppy belly flattening across hers as he pried her legs apart with his one hand, searching. He felt her go rigid, resisting. "Come on now, let me in," he told her, his patience wearing thin. He would go easy on her, his appetite for more eccentric sexual games would have to wait until he had weaned her from her innocence. When he found her warm wetness, he wriggled his bottom and forced his way inside her. The child beneath him whimpered as he penetrated her fully, the rhythm of his need taking over. He looked askance at his warped image in the polished bronze mirror that he had placed strategically by the bedside. Seeing the reflection of his coupling made him come with a shudder, the pockmarks on his cheeks emphasized against the pink flush of his orgasm. He rolled away from her, spent and sweating, and fell asleep almost immediately. The girl curled up on her side, her back toward the man who now owned her, and cried herself to sleep.

The following morning he received word that Huai-yi wished to see him. Joining forces with several others who faced the same grim future of bankruptcy, his brother had asked him to come to discuss their future. Wen-bao decided that he had little left to lose and went to his brother's house, where Huai-yi had dismissed his servants for the evening so that no one could overhear them talk. The men gathered in his house, where they sat cross-legged around a low table dotted with chinaware tea cups.

"Things are getting bad," Huai-yi began, making sure he had every man's attention. They leaned forward, thrilled by the air of conspiracy. "We cannot allow this to go on any longer. We have to take the future of this island into our own hands. We must grasp the power from these red-headed barbarians. The time has come for us to act."

The men nodded, muttering their agreement.

"I have thought of a plan," Huai-yi continued. "We could invite the Dutch governor and all his senior officials to a large banquet to celebrate the coming Moon Festival."

One of the men's eyes lit up with understanding. "Yes!" the man said with enthusiasm. "Once they are drunk with their filthy liquor, we can catch them off guard. They would be at their most vulnerable. We could kill them all." The others nodded eagerly, prodding Huai-yi to continue.

"Exactly. At the same time, we will gather ourselves an army in Saccam and spread the word among our fellow countrymen. They will join us in our cause, of that I am sure. While we slaughter these barbarian pigs at Zeelandia, we attack the fort at Saccam. That way they will not be able to send for help. This is our only chance for success." As the idea began to take shape, the men voiced their thoughts in excited whispers, careful not to be heard.

But this was not at all what Wen-bao had in mind. "It is a good plan, *sio-ti*, younger brother, and it may just succeed," he said in a honeyed voice. "But perhaps the time is not yet right for this. I would think it would be better to wait." His expression was pained. The truth was that his brother's plan might hurt his own interests. As a resident of Zeelandia and one of the headmen reporting to the Dutch, he enjoyed the privileges and respect that the authorities gave him, and he had no intention of giving these up. Moreover, he had other sources of income, sources the Dutch authorities didn't know about and of which they – or his principled younger brother – would probably not approve. If the VOC were to fall, much of his income would be lost. And what if things went wrong and the company found out about his involvement? He had far more to lose than his brother. But he would have to be cautious. His brother trusted him. He secretly hated his younger brother, jealous of his charismatic presence and good looks. Wen-bao had neither. Huai-yi had been his parents' favorite, however much they had tried to hide the fact. And that had always gnawed at him.

"Besides, we have heard nothing from Lord Koxinga," he continued. "We do not know if he can support us at this time. If we start this, the

Dutch will summon their troops from the other military forts to protect themselves. Believe me, the time is not yet right."

"We can wait no longer," his younger brother said, vexed by his brother's negative attitude. "We must strike now. If we do not, the peasants will just continue with their small, ineffective riots. The Dutch will easily crush those, just as they have done in the past. And that would only put them on their guard. No, we have to do this now, and surprise them. We must take action now."

"He is right," one of the other men said, his eyebrows set in a constant, worrying frown. "We must do something." The man had just given them a boring, detailed account of his financial situation, saying that he had no choice but to fire most of his house servants. His wife was furious with him for denying her the luxuries that she had grown used to over the years.

Wen-bao had listened to the man's complaints with increasing impatience.

"We must inform Lord Koxinga, so that he is aware of our intentions. Perhaps he can assist us in ousting the ugly foreigners," someone else suggested. The others nodded.

"But what if we fail?" Wen-bao tried. "If the Hollanders discover our plot, what shall become of us then? Not only shall we suffer, thousands of our innocent countrymen who know nothing of our plans will be at the mercy of the company troops." His expression was grave and full of concern, the long shadows of the candlelight highlighting the pockmarks on his cheeks.

The others looked at him but said nothing.

"*A-hia*, older brother, I am surprised at your words," said Huai-yi, "It seems that I have misjudged you. The seeds of rebellion have been sown, our decision has been made. If it is your own skin for which you are afraid, then feel free to leave. Go home to your latest concubine." One of the men snickered maliciously.

"We will be able to solve this," said Huai-yi, his tone confident. The others remained silent and looked ahead impassively. It was obvious that they were siding with Huai-yi.

Wen-bao turned red, furious that his brother had caused him to lose face in front of the others. None of the men supported him in his restraint, and his younger brother had actually accused him of being a coward. Painfully aware that Huai-yi's words were close to the truth, he could bear it no longer. His soft belly hampering him, he got to his feet clumsily, a look of feigned indignation on his face.

"I hope you are right about this. For all our sakes," he said, and left in a huff. Fuming, he strode to his home, but then he calmed somewhat as he realized that in time he would surely find other like-minded individuals such as himself. And when he did, he would talk to them, and they would eventually listen to him, and not his brother.

* * *

It was right after sunset, in the abrupt darkness of the subtropics, when the sentries at the fort were surprised at the men's sudden appearance. The three Chinese men hastened toward the gate, glancing around them nervously, the drizzle of rain steadily soaking their outer garments, their dark shapes silhouetted against the receding light. Captain Danker, who was on his evening shift to supervise the guards, observed them with suspicion. He was even more taken aback as he recognized the men as some of the most prominent Chinese residents of Zeelandia. One man in particular was very familiar to him: this man often visited the governor. Normally he was accompanied by an entourage of servants and clerks. That these men were out here in this weather, at this hour on the night of the Moon Festival, was unusual.

"I wish to put a matter before the governor. I would like to see him," the portly man with a pockmarked face said, his tone full of authority.

"Not now, friend," the captain told him in rudimentary Chinese. "If you need talk business, come back tomorrow. The governor is at his home now, getting dressed for banquet this evening. Now is not good time."

"It is an important matter," the man insisted.

"That's what they all say. Sorry, no. You come back tomorrow," said Danker, annoyed that the man was so persistent. Two of his sentries stepped closer, their muskets held at the ready to help him bring his point across.

But the man remained where he was, unperturbed. His two companions did likewise.

"It's an emergency. It would also be in your own interest to let us see the governor, my friend."

"What's the nature of this emergency?" one of the sentries wanted to know.

"We have come to warn him. It will be for the company's good, and yours," the man added. The ominous way in which he said this made Danker think twice. He exchanged glances with the sentries uncertainly. This was highly unusual. Yet he was the responsible officer on duty, so it was his call. He was reluctant to disturb the governor, but there was something about the manner of the three men that irked him. He allowed them to enter, but insisted that they stay where they were while he went out to notify the governor.

The rain had stopped by the time he knocked on the door of the governor's residence. The sound of thonged feet shuffling across the floor came gradually closer before the door was opened by an elderly dark-skinned slave. She had probably been tending to her mistress's dress for the evening banquet.

"I must see the governor," Danker told the woman, who did not look pleased at being disturbed. "Hurry up!" he snapped, seeing the stubborn look on her face. "There are some men here who wish to see him. They say it is urgent."

The woman relented, muttering curses under her breath as she let him in, gesturing toward the governor's study on the first floor. She obviously had no intention of disturbing her master herself. The governor's wife appeared at the top of the staircase, startled at the sight of the captain inside her house. As yet, she was dressed in only her undergarments.

"My word, captain! Whatever is the trouble?" she asked, alarmed, as she modestly held a hand to her chest in spite of the more than adequate coverage of her underdress.

"*Mevrouw*, forgive me for disturbing you at this hour, but there are some Chinamen wishing to see the governor. They say it's urgent," he added. "Some of the men are merchants; one of them appears to be the village headman."

"Nicolaes! You'd better come here!" she called over her shoulder. Her husband emerged from the study, dressed in his official attire without his jacket, the top of his shirt as yet unbuttoned.

He frowned at seeing his semi-clad wife in conversation with his captain. "Captain Danker, what on earth is going on?" he demanded.

"Please come with me, sir. Something seems to be amiss; there are some Chinese gentlemen who wish to see you." He stopped at seeing the governor's look of irritation. "It seemed important, sir," he added apologetically. "They said they have come to warn you about some peril or other."

"Right," Verburgh muttered. "Get me my shoes, woman," he told the slave hovering in the background. She hurried into action to do as she was told. "Where is he?"

"In the courtyard, sir. I asked him to wait for you there."

"Get General Isaaks and Mr. Coyett, just in case," he told Danker. "And get Ting-bin. We will need him to interpret."

Wen-bao had been waiting for some time when He Ting-bin arrived on the scene, looking quite pleased with himself. Wen-bao greeted him sourly. Ting-bin was, just like him, a wealthy and influential merchant with excellent connections within the VOC. But it was his function as interpreter of the highest rank that he envied. Ting-bin was in a position to know firsthand all that went on in the highest echelons of the VOC on Formosa.

It was true that they shared a common interest in that the company was responsible for their wealth and status, but he wondered if he could trust him. It was a well-known fact that Ting-bin did frequent business with the Zhengs, probably with Lord Koxinga himself. It was more than likely that Ting-bin played both sides: these days it was impossible to know where one's loyalties lay. He thought the Hollanders were such fools for appointing the man as their first interpreter.

"There had better be a good reason for this," Verburgh growled as he approached them.

"I assure you, there is, your excellency," Wen-bao said, glancing through the gate of the fort as if anxious that no one see them. Verburgh understood, and gestured for them to go inside where they would not be seen from outside the fortress walls. General Isaaks hurried his way across, and they were soon joined by Frederic Coyett. Both men were wearing the full military uniform required for the evening's formal event. The two of them threw the Chinese men questioning looks.

"Your excellency, we have come to warn you of a grave situation," Wen-bao said dramatically. "Tonight you and all your officers are invited to celebrate the Moon Festival with the Chinese people at the village of Saccam at an official banquet."

"I'm well aware of it," Verburgh said scathingly. "What of it?"

Wen-bao allowed himself a small smile. The Moon Festival had been used for years for elaborate gatherings of the Dutch authorities and prominent Chinese residents. He knew that the governor found such events tedious and merely attended them as part of his official duties. The Chinese delicacies were wasted on him, and it was rare for him to stay longer than half an hour. Only the governor's wife seemed to enjoy them, giving her an opportunity to pretty herself up and show off her latest expensive gowns to all the other Dutch women.

"Your excellency, the banquet is a plot to attack you and your men," his voice dropped to a whisper. "They plan to ply you with wine and food, so that they can kill you in a most cowardly manner in order to take the fort."

Verburgh's eyes narrowed and looked at Wen-bao with suspicion.

Coyett was the first to react. "Is this some kind of foolish jest? If so, I find it in very bad taste."

"No jest, Chief Merchant Coyett. This is indeed very serious," the other two men nodded emphatically, parroting Wen-bao's words to bring their message across.

"But there is more," continued Wen-bao. "A large peasant army is being formed in Saccam as we speak. While the villagers of Zeelandia plan to attack you when you eat and drink your fill, this peasant army will attack your settlement across the bay in Saccam." Ting-bin translated obligingly into Dutch, his tone one of excitement.

"How do you know all this?" Verburgh demanded.

"There is a farmer by the name of Guo Huai-yi." Wen-bao grimaced as he realized he was about to betray his very own brother. He knew that if Huai-yi should ever find out about his betrayal, he would most probably kill him. He continued nonetheless; there was no turning back now.

"Apparently he ran into some debt," Wen-bao looked contrite, "and now he is blaming your revered company for his personal misfortune. The wretched man has gathered an army of peasants. An attack on your countrymen is imminent, good sir."

Verburgh paled. "I thought you Chinese were of the peace-loving kind!" he exclaimed. Ting-bin dutifully translated the remark for the benefit of Wen-bao, who feigned a pained expression.

"Take these gentlemen inside," Verburgh ordered to his officers. "And seal off the fort! See to it that no one will know what's going on inside its walls. I don't want anyone to know that we have been warned."

It surprised Wen-bao how quickly the fort was brought to the highest state of military alert. Within half an hour, the place was swarming with soldiers. As darkness set in, a curfew was imposed: no one was permitted to leave the village of Zeelandia for fear that the rebels in Saccam be put on alert. The governor gave orders for the houses of Chinese households in the immediate vicinity of Zeelandia to be searched for weapons, but none were found.

"Captain Danker!" Isaaks called. The captain was at his side immediately. "Have someone cross the Narrows and ride to Saccam fast as he can to send warning and tell the colonists to take refuge at the company stables. They'll be safest there until we can get to them. And take some of your men to find out what's going on and report back to me at once. Make sure no one sees you."

Within minutes, two horsemen set off southward along Pineapple Isle to wade across the shallows in order to warn the settlers in Saccam of what lay ahead. Dankers, by now well familiar with the lay of the land, mounted his horse and disappeared with a couple of his men into the darkness. When they had rounded the bay and reached the main island, the three of them dismounted and climbed the dunes to obtain a good view of the rice fields on the other side. What they saw made their skins crawl.

On one of the largest rice fields of Saccam, thousands of peasants had gathered, some with torches. Others were armed with sharpened bamboo spears and farm tools that could easily double as weapons.

For a minute, Danker and his men lay pressed against the dune, assessing the numbers and the threat that the motley army of peasants posed. Then they stealthily made their way down back to the beach.

In their retreat, one of the men disturbed a nest of birds of prey. Startled, one of the adult birds took off in fright, its peculiar cry of alarm ringing across the bay.

Down in the field below, a farmhand squinted his eyes into the darkness to discern the origin of the sound. Then his eyes grew wide. He pointed at the hillside.

"*Angmo-lang*! Hollanders!"

From the mob's reaction, Dankers knew they had been spotted.

"Quick! The horses!" He didn't wait another second, stumbling down the hill toward the bay where the horses waited, and galloped off at full speed, the others close behind, back to Zeelandia.

* * *

Guo Huai-yi and his collaborators eagerly awaited the guests to arrive at the Moon Festival banquet. More than half an hour had passed after the set time of the venue, yet not one single colonist had turned up.

Huai-yi knew they had been betrayed. And he instinctively knew by whom. His face dark with rage, he swore that he would have his vengeance. But he had no time to linger on such thoughts now. His plan had been compromised, so he had to think fast. He and his men hurried to the fields of Saccam, where the peasants were gathering. They had no choice. They had to attack the foreigners now, or all suffer the consequences of a brutal crackdown from company troops. But they had still had no word from Lord Koxinga, and somehow he doubted if they would.

When Huai-yi arrived at the fields of Saccam, the news that they had failed their attack on the Dutch spread like wildfire. The thousands of Chinese that had gathered in the fields were nervous and agitated. He could almost feel the tension of the crowd. Quickly assessing the situation, Huai-yi lost no time and addressed the people.

"Yes, it's true that the first part of our plan has failed!" he said as loudly as his voice would carry. "The Dutch officials never showed up at the banquet. Someone has warned them, we have been betrayed." There was a restless murmur. "But it doesn't matter anymore. The time has come to take action! We have to rise against the Dutch now! These foreigners have taken land that doesn't belong to them!" he shouted, his voice carrying far across the fields. "They came here with their company to make profits for their king from our toil!" The people roared in agreement, their torches and weapons raised high above their heads.

"We toil in their fields to grow their rice and their sugar. For this, we are paid next to nothing! And when we buy the rice and sugar at the markets, we pay taxes for what we ourselves have planted and harvested. With our very own sweat and blood!" He paused for his words to take effect. "Lord Koxinga, the great lord of the imperial surname, fights with his troops in China against our enemy, the Manchus. He has instructed us to fight our foreign enemies here, on Formosa. It is our duty!" He paused again as the crowd roared in approval "The Hollander soldiers and officials harass and abuse us. They take from us the last of our money in their greed and corruption. They have cleverly pushed many of us into debt so that they can control us, like slaves. We can no longer accept this! We've had enough! Enough!"

"*Khoa beh loe*! *Khoa beh loe*! Enough! Enough!" they repeated, a thousand voices concurring in the evening air. Sharpened bamboo sticks and harvesting tools bobbed up and down in staccato rhythm, their cries in unison. The sound gradually subsided as Huai-yi signaled that he wished to continue. At that very moment, the alarmed cry of a kite rang out over the valley. The unexpected, piercing sound brought instant silence. Everyone knew that these birds of prey normally didn't venture out in the dark of night, and that made the sound all the more ominous.

"The barbarians! *Angmo-lang*! Hollanders! Over there!"

It took a moment for a thousand pairs of eyes to fix itself upon the hillside, its lush subtropical foliage many shades of black. Half hidden by the larger plants, the pale face of a man in the uniform of a Dutch officer flashed in the light of the torches before it quickly disappeared again.

Those who had spotted the Dutchman rushed at the hillside to give chase, their yells of anger reverberating across the fields. It was enough to set the mob in motion.

"To Saccam! To Saccam!" ordered Huai-yi. The call was taken up, and the crowd headed en masse to the Dutch settlement, where several company warehouses and horse stables were located. And where many of the hated Dutch lived.

"*Thai*! Death to all the Dutch dogs! Kill them all!"

In the village of Saccam, the eight-year-old son of one of the stable stewards had sneaked out of the house, wandering toward the rice fields in search of frogs among the paddies. When he thought he heard the sound of voices, his curiosity got the better of him and he hid behind a shed.

There, hidden from view, the boy froze. What he saw were thousands of people gathered in the fields, their faces angry and fierce in the flickering torchlight, their voices loud and belligerent. Never before had he seen so many Chinese people in one place. This wasn't even allowed, he knew from his father. Mesmerized, he listened to the man speak, and saw how the crowd reacted. The people listened, shouted in unison, brandishing their weapons. He had heard and seen enough: his instincts told him there would be trouble. Making sure no one saw him, he ran back to the village as fast as he could.

* * *

The rains had stopped, the sky had momentarily opened up, the clouds moving to the west. Antonius and Anna Hambroek felt it was a perfect moment for an evening stroll to get a taste of the festivities. A clear, full moon showed itself high above their heads, shedding light on the festival for which it was named.

Yet there was something odd about this particular evening. The teahouses in the village, usually filled with people, were deserted. After spending so many years among the Chinese, he knew that the Moon Festival was a happy occasion, a time where all families were out on the streets in their finery on their way to have picnics to share their sweet, sticky moon cakes. But, save for the occasional old woman and a few mangy, scrounging dogs, the streets were empty. He tried not to dwell on it for long, but the lack of the festive mood that normally prevailed on this traditional holiday did puzzle him. He called out to two Chinese farmers coming down the street from the opposite direction and waved, but the men's reaction was muted, at best, and they averted their eyes as they continued on their way.

This intrigued him. He knew those men: they usually greeted him enthusiastically whenever they met. Perturbed by their uncharacteristic behavior, Antonius walked on, his wife's arm linked in his own. Something wasn't quite right.

Anna let out a startled cry when they were nearly knocked off their feet by Hans Smit, the stable steward's eight-year-old son. The boy had come rounding the corner as if chased by the devil himself, bouncing off Antonius' considerable girth.

Hambroek caught the breathless boy, grabbing him by the sleeve. It was clear that child had been scared witless.

"Hey, Hans, what's the hurry, boy?" he asked the child. "Is something wrong?" Hans tried to catch his breath, fearfully glancing over his shoulder.

"Angry people, Reverend," the boy managed between gasps. "Many angry people in the fields. They've got weapons. I think they mean to harm us."

Antonius' blood ran cold. "Chinese?" he asked, even though he already knew the answer. Hans nodded.

Antonius wasn't in the least bit surprised. They should have known this was coming. He had known that it would; he had warned the governor about this often enough.

"Should I get the children?" his wife asked in alarm.

"Yes, Anna, get the children. Soldier!" he yelled at a Dutch soldier on the other side of the road. The man looked up, surprised at the missionary's urgent tone. "Evenin', Reverend. What can I do for ya?"

"Looks like we have a problem on our hands," he said, his voice muted. "All the Chinese have disappeared. Young Hans Smit just came back from the Amsterdam polder. He tells me there is a large gathering of people there. They seem to have armed themselves. Doesn't sound good at all."

The soldier's eyes went wide. "You're positive about this?"

"Yes, I am," Antonius said, seeing the expression on Hans' face. The boy looked absolutely terrified.

The soldier turned in a half-run. "The company stables," he called over his shoulder. "It's the strongest building we have at our disposal. Tell everyone to head there."

Antonius knew what he had to do. "Hans, go to your father. Tell him what you saw and take your family to the stables. Now!" The boy didn't need to be told twice and was gone.

Antonius and the soldier ran through the street, where they banged on the doors and shouted their warnings to the Dutch settlers. Pale, bewildered women and men women appeared at the doorsteps, herding their children and servants in the direction of the stables as fast as they could. News of what was happening spread quickly among the colonists, and, within minutes, all were alerted to the danger that awaited them. The tension and confusion had mounted palpably.

"What's going on?" one man asked.

"It's the Chinese," Antonius said. "They appear to have formed an army, and they are coming this way." He tried to remain calm, but his own heart was beating wildly, and not just from the effort of running.

"Hans, Smit's son, he saw them in the fields," someone shouted.

"And they've got weapons!" a woman shrieked. For an instant, the stables were silent. Then many voices spoke at once, and confusion reigned once more.

"Silence!" An officer had entered with four soldiers. He looked with contempt at the frightened, babbling colonists. The last voices faded away as he took charge of the situation. "I have sent word to the fort that we are expecting an attack. So help will be on its way, but we have to be patient. In the meantime, we have to defend ourselves as best we can."

"Listen!" a woman hissed. "You hear that?" Everyone grew quiet. For a brief moment, they could hear nothing, except for one of the horses that whinnied uneasily, sensing the distress of the humans that had crowded inside their stables. But then they all heard it. In the distance, a low gurgling. The sound grew louder, its source closer. It was the unmistakable cacophony of thousands of enraged people on the move, coming right in their direction.

"Bar the doors! Quickly!" the officer shouted. "Get the women and children to the middle!" The women grabbed their children and backed away from the entrance. Antonius rushed forward to help lower the two heavy wooden beams in place to bar the doors. The system had been put in place years ago in case of just such an eventuality. Antonius saw his wife, her children pressed against her, their faces a ghostly white. Their eyes met, and he knew that she, too, was thinking of only one thing: the safety of their children. Outside, the eerie, troubling sound reached a terrifying crescendo. Twelve settler families huddled together while the men prepared to defend the entrance and vulnerable parts of the building. They were as ready as they could be at such short notice. Antonius breathed a small prayer of thanks for the steward's son. He shuddered to think what would have happened if Hans hadn't warned them.

Not everyone managed to reach the safety of the stables in time. The mob came across a native aboriginal, dressed in the garb of the Dutch. He was an elderly gardener in the service of the VOC. He never had a chance. Almost deaf, he had not heard the shouted warnings. Bewildered, he watched as the mob descended upon him with their torches and knives. Frustrated at not finding any Dutch, the Chinese punished him for his misplaced loyalties. Two minutes later, he was lying in a pool of blood, his face and crotch mutilated.

There were more people who had not been alerted in time. An aboriginal villager, also dressed in the clothes of the hated colonists, had been in the outhouse, cramped up with dysentery during the commotion, too focused on his troubled bowel movements to know what was taking place outside. When he emerged, he was fair game for the rioters who thirsted for blood. Frightened, he broke into a run, but his body was weakened by the disease that plagued him. An angry peasant overtook him and pushed him to the ground. While on all fours trying to get up, a harvest knife, its blade sharpened only that afternoon, swung down, severing his head cleanly from his body. The peasant executioner laughed at his success, retrieved the head and placed the gruesome item on a bamboo stave, parading it around for all to see. The sight of the severed head made his companions whoop with delight.

Two other aboriginals dressed in Dutch attire had the misfortune of returning to Saccam from a neighboring village. The timing of their return could not have been worse. The peasants rounded on them, not satisfied until their quarries had both lost consciousness. One of them was long dead before they cut off his nose and genitals, and finally, his head. His companion suffered the same fate, his bloodied head placed on a stave to add to their grisly parade.

* * *

Once the news of the impending attack had spread, all officers and soldiers had reported for duty. Fort Zeelandia soon filled with people. Women and children came seeking refuge within its walls, taking their most prized possessions with them.

Captain Danker was the first to return to the fort, and he leapt from his horse, leaving it untethered. He bounded up the steps, where he nearly collided with Coyett, who stood talking to General Isaaks.

"General! It's true, sir. Thousands of Chinese, armed and preparing for war," he exclaimed.

"Where?" demanded Frederic.

"In the Amsterdam Polder, Mr. Coyett," he said, referring to the most fertile valley in Saccam. "I'm afraid they saw us, sir," he told the general.

His commander cursed under his breath, scowling. "God's wounds! That means we have no time to lose."

Verburgh appeared and hurried in their direction. Isaaks quickly briefed him on the latest developments, while Danker stood by, awaiting his orders.

"It's true, Mr. Verburgh. The captain has seen it with his own eyes," Isaaks said. "Danker reports thousands of armed peasants in the Amsterdam Polder. Unfortunately they saw him. Which means that they're probably attacking Saccam as we speak."

"Let us hope that they received a timely warning," Verburgh muttered. Isaaks and Coyett remained silent, their faces somber.

They all looked up at the sound of horse's hooves slamming into the packed earth of the square. It was one of the sentries stationed in Saccam. The man didn't bother to dismount, such was his urgency.

"General, sir! Saccam is under attack! Chinese rebels have gathered...."

"We know," Isaaks interrupted him. "We sent warning. Didn't our messenger reach you to tell you this?"

"No, sir! 'Twas the steward's son who alerted us. He spotted them in the fields, with their weapons an' all. If it weren't for him...." He didn't finish his sentence.

"Did our people get to safety on time?"

"Most were able to take refuge at the company's stables, sir. Strongest structure in the village."

"So it is," said Frederic. "But they will never last long against those numbers. General Isaaks, we have to act fast if we are to save these people from an undue fate."

Before Isaaks could say a word, Captain Danker stepped forward, waiting to voice his thoughts. "If I may, sir?" he began. His superior commander nodded his assent.

"If I might make a suggestion, sir. We could launch an attack by boat. If the settlers have taken their refuge in the stables, the rioters are bound to head for them. The stables are within view of the beach. If we send a company of musketeers by boat across the bay, we might be able to surprise them from the water. Especially as it's dark."

The governor considered the suggestion. He turned to Isaaks. "General, what's your opinion?"

Isaaks looked up at the sky. It was overcast, the clear full moon that had earlier lit Zeelandia bay was nowhere to be seen. "We might be able to pull it off."

"Then do it," Verburgh ordered.

While the captain proceeded to put his plan in operation, Verburgh gave orders for messages to be sent to the larger aboriginal territories in both the north and the south. He told them that if their warriors were willing to fight the Chinese rebels alongside the Dutch, they would be rewarded with the colored Indian cloth that they so valued.

"You intend to bribe the aboriginal tribes to get them to fight for us?" Frederic asked, incredulous. "They hate the Chinese as it is. And vice versa. This will only worsen matters."

Verburgh glared at him. "I do believe that I make the decisions here, Mr. Coyett," he said coldly.

Frederic knew better than to go against him, but he couldn't help it. He expected the native tribes to side with them in their fight against the Chinese rebels, knowing how much they hated the Chinese for their superior airs and ruthless exploitation. Of course they were more than willing to fight, especially for a reward.

In the meantime, one hundred and twenty troops armed with muskets boarded several longboats, which were launched across the Bay of Tayouan. The boats skimmed the water's surface as inconspicuously as they could. Luck was on their side: heavy cloud obscured what would have been a perfect full moon. As they approached the beach, they found the stables surrounded by several thousand rebels.

The many burning torches threw long shadows near the stables. The Chinese rioters encircled the building menacingly, seeking out weaknesses and possible ways of getting in, but there were none. Made of stone, the stable walls could not be set alight. Even Huai-yi didn't quite know what to do.

One of the farmers squatted against a small shed facing the bay, disappointed that the Dutch colonists had escaped, bored with non-action. Then he thought he saw something on the water that was strangely out of place, as if he had seen the reflection of fire upon steel. Puzzled, he peered into the darkness, but whatever it was seemed to have gone. All at once, he was able to make out the contours of two longboats approaching them from the darkness. It was a perhaps one thousand feet offshore, close enough to see the men seated low in their boats.

He jumped up, alarmed. "Boats!" he shouted. "There are boats coming! The Hollanders are coming!" He had to yell at the top of his lungs to be heard above the many men, talking, shouting. They turned toward the bay, where they, too, saw the boats come in across the water. The shouting and laughter suddenly ceased. They all sensed that something was about to happen, and they reacted on instinct. Like ants they poured down the beach to prevent the troops from landing.

But they were too late. The Dutch longboats had run aground on the sandbanks that had been exposed by the low tide, but the boats were quickly pulled free by the men who had jumped overboard. The oars ploughed through the water once more, upon which the vessels sped through the water toward the beach before they were stranded one final time. The one hundred and twenty musketeers lowered themselves into the knee-high water, and waded the last dozen feet, their muskets aimed at the mass of irate figures lit by the light of the torches.

The Dutch soldiers at the forefront winced as the first daggers and improvised javelins flew through the air, most of them missing their mark to land harmlessly in the water.

Huai-yi looked on with horror as he realized that he could not control the undisciplined army of rabble he had formed. "Let them come!" he yelled at his men. "Let them come! We will kill them here! On the land! Then we can give them what they deserve!"

His deputy turned to him, not understanding. "No! What are you doing? We mustn't let them get this far! We should kill these motherfuckers while we can. Don't let them reach the beach!" he growled, and turned to run down toward the surf. But Huai-yi grabbed him roughly by the arm. "No! Let them come. We shall slaughter them here!"

His deputy saw the dark look on Huai-yi's face, and hesitated. Then, not willing to take the responsibility, he repeated Huai-yi's orders loudly to all who were near. Huai-yi stayed where he was, halfway between his men and the advancing Dutch. The Dutch soldiers continued to advance, wading their way closer toward the shore, their guns at the ready, waiting for the command to fire.

Not all had heard Huai-yi's orders, others simply ignored them. Some did as they were told and retreated back onto the beach, their feet sinking deep into the soft sand. But most of the rioters kept rushing forward, until hundreds stood pushing and jostling each other in the shallow water.

But they had underestimated their enemy. Once they were within range, Captain Danker gave the command. "Fire!" The first salvo rang out, followed by shouts of alarm and screams of pain. The bodies of several Chinese disappeared beneath the surface, to be sucked back to sea by the receding tide. Those wounded during the first salvo turned and limped their way back to the beach, only to be hit in the back by the second salvo. In tight formation the Dutch troops pushed on, ignoring the blood-curdling yells of rage.

Those Chinese who fell on the beach were replaced by scores of others, desperate to stop the advancing company of soldiers from coming ashore. Some of the soldiers went down, vulnerable as they were at having to wade through water against the sandbanks at low tide, hit by arrows, knives, and whatever else the Chinese hurled at them. But even with their greater numbers, the Chinese peasants were no match for professionally trained soldiers with firearms. The troops reached dry land, still shooting, their discipline undiminished. Only then did it begin to dawn on the rebels that the odds were very much against them.

Horrified at the turn of events, Huai-yi stood transfixed, not knowing where to run. His hesitancy proved fatal. He saw a blast of gunpowder sprayed brightly at him from the darkness, followed by a sharp searing pain at the base of his neck. He clasped his hands to his wound, but the blood found its way out and seeped between his fingers. Huai-yi gargled something, then fell face forward onto the sand. His deputy stared at him, rooted to the ground, his eyes wide with horror at the loss of their commander. Then he bolted for the woods like a frightened rabbit.

When the rebels saw their leader down, the chaos was complete. In a panic, the peasants tried to turn and flee from their attackers, only to run into a fresh wave of rioters who forced them back into the line of fire. Those who weren't shot fell into the water to be trampled upon, drowning in the shallow waters as they struggled to get up. The survivors scattered into the darkness, fleeing in all directions as the musket pellets found their mark, thudding into human flesh.

By the time the Dutch troops had taken the beach, the Chinese were gone. Apart from the cries of the wounded, an eerie, unnatural silence had descended on the bay. Inside the stables, all the colonists of Saccam were found huddled together, terrified but safe. When they emerged from the stables, they discovered the mutilated bodies of the four Christian aboriginals, their body parts scattered across the village.

* * *

When the ghastly details of the murders of the Christian aboriginals became known, Verburgh cracked down hard. He gave orders for every last Chinese rebel to be found. The uprising had to be suppressed at all cost, its ringleaders to be caught and punished.

The aboriginal warriors, hunters skilled with bow and arrow and an array of weapons, had been quick to side with the Dutch to fight the Chinese migrants they despised, fired by the promise of the woven fabrics they valued so much. They eagerly joined the Dutch in their hunt for the fugitive rebels, many of whom had hidden themselves in the sugarcane fields. There the Chinese were slaughtered without mercy.

Armed only with their harvesting knives and wooden spears, another group of rebels that had managed to flee had gathered in a bay. They never had a chance. The ill-equipped rioters were no match for the company troops, their guns, or the pent-up fury of the aboriginals. Those who managed to escape the onslaught fled to the south, only to run into large bands of tribal warriors, who captured and killed them with relish. One tribe captured Guo Huai-yi's deputy and handed him to the VOC authorities, who burned him alive and severed his head, which was then displayed on a stake for all to see. It was their revenge for the killings of the converted Christians and served as a warning that there would be no mercy for any who dared defy the Dutch.

The riot lasted for two weeks and resulted in the deaths of more than four thousand Chinese, women and children among them. The incident had a tremendous impact on everyone on the island. Because the aboriginals had allied themselves with the Dutch, the tensions between the Chinese and the native islanders worsened. For fear of reprisals, the two population groups lived more segregated from each other than ever before, and trade between them came to a complete halt.

While the relationship between the Dutch colonists and the Chinese settlers deteriorated to one of mutual fear and distrust, the company council suppressed any form of dissent for months to come. In the face of increased Dutch military presence, the Chinese decided to keep a low profile.

The rift between the Chinese peasant farmers and the wealthy headmen living in the village of Zeelandia also widened. Ordinary Chinese people, who already despised the village headmen for their corruption and abuse of power, became suspicious of the role they had played in the uprising.

The village was agog with rumors of who had betrayed Guo Huai-yi and his rebels.

Not surprisingly, Wen-bao worried that the truth might come out and became paranoid about his safety, fearing for his life. He rarely ventured out without a bodyguard.

At the end of the year Coyett was sent back to Japan as governor of Deshima, the small artificial island in the port of Nagasaki to which the Dutch had been restricted for their trade with Japan. The posting was for just the one year, as the Japanese did not want the VOC governors to become too cozy with the local authorities. It was a difficult posting, especially since the Japanese had banned Dutch women and children from the island. There was very little for the men to do during the long months of waiting for the merchant ships to arrive. With their freedom restricted, most men found their stays on Deshima oppressive. Some even likened it to a prison.

While Coyett was away, his place as chief merchant was taken by Thomas van Iperen, who also took up Coyett's position on the Formosan council. The news of the uprising on Formosa dealt another blow to Verburgh's reputation in Batavia. The loss of so many lives among the Chinese settlers appalled the governor-general, as well as the *Heren Seventien* in the Netherlands. More than anything, they had been shocked that the Chinese had risen against them.

An investigation followed, questions were asked. Surely the grievances of the Chinese were not as grave at all that? Didn't the Dutch treat them well enough? What had led the Chinese to undertake such drastic steps against the company? Hadn't Verburgh seen this coming? Had this severe loss of lives truly been unavoidable? And had it really been necessary to involve the aboriginals in suppressing the rebels, compromising the already strained relations between the two population groups?

Serious doubts were cast in their minds on the competence of Verburgh as governor of the island. Although the VOC council acceded that it was a commercial enterprise and that it had to protect its territories, it stressed that the company was highly reliant on Chinese migrants on Formosa. The *Heren Seventien* were of the conviction that the Chinese were a peaceful, non-violent people, so they demanded that Verburgh justify the brutal, suppressive measures he had taken. They conveniently forgot that they had decided to continue with the hated leasehold system that had been the root of discontent.

Governor-General Reijnierszoon became increasingly critical of Verburgh, who in turn became unsure of his position. It made him irritable, and his family and those who worked for him suffered the consequences. Verburgh knew he had made numerous enemies over the years, both in Formosa and Batavia. Quite a few of those men would be more than happy to search their memories for his past mistakes.

Daniel wasn't surprised when the Batavian council consulted him in the course of the investigation. After all, he had spent four years on Formosa before the rebellion. Perhaps he could shed some more light on what could have led the Chinese people to take up arms against the company?

Man of God he might be, Daniel detested Verburgh and was still bitter about his forced departure from the island. While hiding his personal dislike of Verburgh, he was more than happy to give his views on the events that had taken place.

"Of course I came to know the Chinese quite well in the course of my work as a schoolmaster," he told the council. "Naturally the governor could not always make the time to get to know them, and I do understand that." Governor-General Reijnierszoon nodded as the clerk's quill hovered over his book to record Daniel's comments. Daniel continued, taking his time.

"I am certain that Governor Verburgh is an excellent administrator and that he is very capable of looking after the company's commercial interests. But it is my humble opinion that he kept himself at too great a distance from the people. I speak not only of the Chinese and the aboriginal natives, but also of his fellow Dutchmen." He paused for a moment as if recalling an incident.

"Therefore he could not know what it was the people desired, or what grieved them the most. Either that, or he chose to ignore it. Whatever the case, he took no steps to alleviate the problems that have caused friction over the years. If you asked my opinion, I would say that these grievances contributed considerably to this sad event."

"Of what nature are these grievances you are referring to?" Reijnierszoon asked, pressing a handkerchief to his forehead to stem the perspiration.

"With all due respect, sir. I speak of the *hoofdbrief* tax. For one thing, Verburgh did very little to constrain the soldiers and prevent them from harassing the Chinese for their *hoofdbrief* money. Unfortunately, some of our own countrymen have succumbed to the temptation of corruption. They take advantage of their status to squeeze money and goods from the locals." The feather on the clerk's quill now quivered furiously. "You should know that some of our soldiers – and others, I'm afraid to say – have no scruples or conscience. Some of these *rascals*," he emphasized the word with suppressed anger, "raid the Chinese homes at night under the pretext of *hoofdbrief* inspections. They blackmail these poor people, taking their money and livestock."

"Undoubtedly Governor Verburgh should be able to deal with this. Does he not punish those guilty of these crimes?" Reijnierszoon asked irritably, surprised that this was still an issue.

"Not while I was there, sir," Daniel responded. "And from the letters I receive from my esteemed colleague, Reverend Hambroek, these practices still continue. Oh, the governor gives the occasional reprimand to the culprits, makes a public show of it, hands out a levy once in a while, but then he becomes lax again. He seems reluctant to tackle the problem structurally." Daniel took a sip of water. The council waited patiently as he drank.

"Alas, there is more, sir. As you may know, many of the farmers who leased land for farming have run into debt. Serious debt. When I was out there, the auction prices were pushed up to exorbitant levels. Not even a good harvest would have been enough to make ends meet to pay those kinds of instalments, and we all know how poor the last two harvests have been. I've seen many families bankrupted by the system. Their misery must have pushed them to turn against us."

The governor-general rubbed his forehead wearily as Daniel paused to allow the clerk to catch up with him. Daniel took another sip of water and briefly enjoyed the relief of the cool air fanned in his direction by a Javanese boy, whose burnished skin shone with sweat.

"Governor Verburgh has taken a very harsh attitude against those who are unable to repay their debts," Daniel went on. "He punishes them, penalizes them for something for which they cannot be held liable. He could have shown more charity and compassion toward these people under the circumstances."

Reijnierszoon grunted gruffly. Daniel realized that the subject of the leasehold system in Formosa must have kept the governor-general busy throughout his posting. No wonder it wearied him. He had heard it said that Reijnierszoon had voted against the system, but that he had been heavily outvoted.

"Quite so. You are aware that Governor Verburgh enlisted the help of the native aboriginals to suppress the uprising?" Reijnierszoon asked, changing the subject.

"Yes, sir, so I've heard," Daniel fell silent for a moment, thinking about the native islanders he had known and taught for years. He found it difficult to believe that the people he thought he knew so well could have become so violent, even against the Chinese, who had exploited them to the bone. "Am I correct in understanding that the governor bribed the local tribes to fight the Chinese?" Daniel asked. Reijnierszoon gave him a look that made clear that he didn't care to answer the question. For Daniel, that meant enough.

"So," he said with a sigh. "We have now managed to turn them against each other. It will be worse than before. May God forgive us," he muttered, almost to himself. Then a thought struck him. "The governor was warned, was he not?"

"Indeed he was," said Reijnierszoon. "It appears that he was approached by some Chinese living in Zeelandia. Affluent merchants, I believe they were. However, we do know now that it was in these men's interest to do so. They all seem to have strong links to the company. Even so, we should thank the Lord our God that they did warn us. Things could have turned out quite differently if they had not."

Daniel nodded, his eyes staring into space as the faces and names of the merchants living in Zeelandia sprang to mind. Most of those who worked closely with the company were clever bastards, and quite a few he knew to be downright untrustworthy. He knew that at least several of them would not be above such betrayals if it was to their benefit. The red, pockmarked face of Guo Wen-bao was foremost in his mind. His intuition told him that Wen-bao must have been responsible for the betrayal.

"I shall pray for those who lost their lives," Daniel said before he left the building. Outside, the hot sun greeted him, and he smelled the sweet scent of cloves mingled with the bougainvillea rustling gently in the wind. But his thoughts were back on Formosa.

* * *

Frederic was delighted when he returned to Formosa at the end of 1653. Not only was he happy to be reunited with his wife Susanna and Balthasar, he thoroughly enjoyed the freedom that had been denied him on Deshima, where the endless days of waiting for the merchant ships were dull and monotonous.

Balthasar was now a healthy, active toddler. However, Frederic did worry about his wife's appearance. In his absence, Susanna had suffered a late miscarriage, and Dr. Beyer told him that she had not yet fully recovered from this. Susanna herself had dismissed his concern with a wave of her hand, and smiled, just as she always did.

He had first met her when he had only just started practicing law, and he was quickly charmed by her beauty, her wit, and her strong-willed, adventurous spirit. She belonged to the nobility, born to the Boudaen family of the southern provinces. Frederic had known from the very beginning that her reason for leaving the Netherlands had been due to a romantic liaison she had once had. Her reputation blemished, she had left for Batavia to be with her sister, whose husband happened to be the trade director there. Frederic had never paid heed to the gossip that surrounded Susanna, nor did he care if any of it was true. Within a year, he had married her. He would have been the first to admit that he owed a great deal to her, and that her family connections within the company had been beneficial to his career. But more than anything, he loved her, and he wanted her to get well.

Upon his return from Japan he found that a fair amount of his work was in some way related to the rebellion that had taken place the year before. Verburgh, who had given him the posting of administrator in Saccam upon his return, still had Chinese peasants brought in for questioning on a regular basis, which invariably meant that they were tortured. Frederic abhorred the practice and tried not to get involved, but he had to admit that they had gained a better picture of how the uprising had started and who had played a part in it. The number of Chinese in prison was considerable, and executions were a frequent occurrence. The Dutch didn't trust the Chinese, and vice versa. He seriously wondered if that would ever change.

The death threats Guo Wen-bao received against himself and his family never ceased. It became so serious that Wen-bao had approached him and requested military protection. The Chinese within the community must have somehow discovered that he had been the one who had betrayed the rebels.

Frederic put the request to Verburgh. Even though they both despised Wen-bao, they agreed to give him and his family protection, if only for the fact that they probably owed their lives to him. It was to no avail, as less than a year later, Wen-bao was found dead in his bed one morning with a dagger in his throat. Everything indicated that the killer was a member of his very own household; but the authorities failed to identify who it was. None of the servants had seen or heard anything that night. Or so they said.

For the first time, the Formosan council received word from Batavia that they were concerned that "the pirate's son" Koxinga might pose a threat to Formosa. They had received new intelligence from Martinus Martini, an Italian Jesuit who had been on a Portuguese ship captured by the VOC.

Apart from being a missionary, Martini was a skilled cartographer who had been in China for many years and who spoke various Chinese languages. Governor-General Reijnierszoon had been most interested to hear about the latest developments in China, and he had questioned the man at length.

Martini was convinced that Koxinga must eventually lose his battle against the Qing, and the Jesuit had witnessed firsthand a steady stream of refugees crossing the strait for Formosa. According to him, Koxinga had lost yet another hopeless battle against the superior Manchurian troops and had retreated to the Pescadores to lick his wounds. They all knew that the islands fell under Chinese sovereignty, which meant that they ran the risk of being attacked by the Manchu navy. Strong rumors suggested that this was about to happen, and if it did, Koxinga would have nowhere to go except Formosa. And then the Dutch colony would be in jeopardy.

For Frederic, this was nothing new. On Formosa they were far nearer to the source, and he had followed the disturbing developments in China for years. Previously Verburgh had dismissed the various reports as of no consequence, but even he had been convinced that they had to be wary. Besides, there were increasing indications that Koxinga's men had played an active role in inciting the rebellion.

In his dispatch, Reijnierszoon felt obliged to mention that not everyone in the Batavian council believed that Koxinga posed a threat. Some simply refused to believe that Koxinga would be foolish enough to attack a major naval force such as theirs, or a fortress as formidable as Zeelandia. Nevertheless, he had taken the Jesuit's warning seriously, and therefore sent a request to the Netherlands for more troops on Formosa. He also recommended Verburgh to take the necessary precautions in the event that Koxinga should attack.

Frederic was relieved that Batavia had finally acknowledged that the colony might be in danger. Verburgh took the recommendations to heart. He ordered the construction of Fort Provintia, a new fort to be built in Saccam, just across Tayouan Bay from Fort Zeelandia on the main island's shore to better protect the Dutch colonists there. Against Frederic's counsel — and that of his engineers — he rushed the construction so that it would be completed as soon as possible. The reverse happened. During the first week, reports came in that the building activities were being sabotaged. The work that had been done by day was being undone during the night, by persons as yet unknown, and Verburgh was forced to order round-the-clock security on the site.

It became gradually clear to Frederic that the Batavian council had lost faith in Verburgh. He was unsure as to whether this was due to the accumulation of events under his command or because of the seed of doubt that Daniel Gravius had possibly sown. He wasn't at all surprised when Verburgh was finally dismissed from his post.

Verburgh returned to Batavia an embittered man under a shadow of disgrace from his failure. In Java he was given a commercial post of no real significance. Frederic knew that Verburgh, angry as he was, would continue to try and blacken his name from there, but he was relieved that he would not have to work with the man any longer.

Verburgh was replaced by Cornelis Caesar, an experienced administrator in his late forties who had been with the company for twenty-four years and who had held several previous postings on Formosa. Frederic was appointed deputy governor, a function he performed from Fort Provintia. Caesar's appointment coincided with the retirement of Governor-General Reijnierszoon, which meant a changing of the guards in both Batavia and Formosa. Personally, Frederic questioned the wisdom of such a move.

When Caesar took up his post as governor of Formosa, he had to deal with the legacy of ten governors and almost thirty years of cononization. Since the Dutch had settled on the island, Formosa had changed from a conquered land of savages to a complex society of different peoples and beliefs, where distrust and wariness of one another were the order of the day. The number of aboriginals had grown considerably, while the Chinese population was ten times what it had once been. New forts had arisen, as had numerous warehouses. The skyline across the coastline was dotted with numerous houses and buildings and had changed dramatically since Caesar's days as a junior officer. The company had firm control over the ever-increasing population and had extended its power across the island. The colonization of Formosa seemed to have reached its peak.

Yet the rebellion led by Guo Huai-yi had left its mark, and it was no easy task to undo the damage that had been done. In the meantime the Dutch discovered that the uprising had been far better organized than they originally thought, and they were painfully aware of what the consequences might have been if there had been no warning.

After taking all this into consideration, Cornelis Caesar had no choice but to rule with a firm hand, applying discipline where necessary. But it seemed that the gods were against him. Shortly upon his arrival, Formosa suffered a spate of natural disasters. A huge swarm of locusts caused untold damage to the crops. Powerful earthquakes rocked the area, leaving many buildings devastated and numerous dead. If that were not enough, a severe typhoon lashed the island, leaving damaged buildings and ships and destroyed crops in its wake. To make matters worse, a highly contagious disease descended on the colony, killing indiscriminately among the Chinese, Dutch, and aboriginals alike. And then there was the man they called Koxinga.

Koxinga's increased presence in the Formosa Strait, his growing power and the way he dominated – and often hampered – their trade bothered Caesar immensely. Relations between the VOC and Koxinga had so far been cordial and polite, but Caesar's rigid attitude toward the man and his activities caused this to change. Rumors that Koxinga and his men had a role in inciting the 1652 rebellion persisted, and Caesar did not trust him one bit. Relations between Koxinga and the VOC deteriorated as a result.

12

The Physician

"But, sire, a Dutch physician?" Wang asked, stunned. Koxinga could practically hear the man thinking of how this would affect his reputation. It was true that Wang had been his physician for nearly eighteen years, tending to his ailments, of which, he had to admit, there had been many. He realized that this would mean a loss of face for the doctor, but so be it. He had made up his mind.

"Yes, doctor. You haven't been able to cure me of this thing, whatever it is. Perhaps the big-noses can. I have heard that their physicians are very learned. However, you will have a supervisory role. Make sure they don't poison me or something. And besides," he grinned, "we may as well make the best of the situation. This will help gain their trust. If I ask for medical assistance, it will give them great face, and they might get the impression that we trust them. It will certainly help improve relations," he explained, as he examined the painful lumps on the skin of his left arm. He had the impression his condition had become even worse after Wang had administered his foul-smelling potions. The itch was driving him wild.

"But, sire, will we be able to trust the Dutch? What if—"

"You can leave that for me to decide," interrupted Koxinga. The truth was that he didn't trust the Dutch one bit. But because of all the years that he and his father had worked with these foreigners, he now knew how to deal with them. In recent months he had repeatedly made compromises toward this Caesar, the new governor who seemed intent on making his life difficult. No doubt this request would be regarded with suspicion. But he had no choice. Wang and his team had tried all kinds of treatments, but his symptoms were only getting worse.

"What if they refuse?" his physician asked, pained at the very suggestion that he might be replaced by some foreigner. Koxinga regarded the man with amusement. Wang had the reputation of being one of the best physicians money could buy in southern China, and the man was arrogant enough to believe it. He had offended Wang, and he knew it. But he hardly cared. All he wanted was to be cured.

"They will not refuse. As my chief physician you are responsible for my health, so see to it. Have a letter with the request sent to their governor. The sooner someone relieves me of this wretched affliction, the better."

"Very well, my lord."

Koxinga watched as Wang made a praiseworthy effort to hide his feelings. He dismissed him, whereupon the physician left his patient's quarters, his eyes carefully averted. Koxinga sighed, almost feeling sorry for the man. He knew that he had never been an easy patient, and that Wang had had to suffer his moods for years. How many times had he thrown his foul-tasting herbal infusions to the ground, stubbornly refusing to follow his advice or take the medication that Wang prescribed him?

His mood lightened as he saw the pretty servant girl waiting to attend to him by the door. He dismissed the older woman at her side with a toss of his head. The woman pursed her lips in prim disapproval as she exited, closing the door behind her.

Knowing what to expect, the girl smiled at him coyly, and sidled up behind him, rubbing his back through the cloth of his robe to alleviate the incessant itch. He closed his eyes, enjoying the relief that her gentle massage offered. After five minutes, he reached behind him and grabbed her arm, pulling her forward to deftly catch her on his lap. She smiled up at him as he put his hand inside her tunic, in search of her breast.

* * *

"This is an unusual request," Governor Caesar said, Ting-bin's translation of the letter still in his hand. Frederic noted that even Ting-bin seemed surprised, as they all were. And he was the last person to show his emotions, if ever.

Caesar looked at Frederic expectantly. "Frederic, what do you think?"

"I must admit this takes me by surprise as well," he said honestly. He would never have expected that the great lord of the imperial surname would even consider asking the Dutch for any kind of assistance. "But I suppose it wouldn't do any harm to comply."

Secretary Van Doorn nodded emphatically, sharing his sentiments.

"Ting-bin. What are your thoughts on this?" Frederic asked the interpreter, curious of his opinion.

"Ah, Mr. Coyett. I would not be the right person to advise you on this," he said, inclining his head in a show of humility. "But," he cocked his head pensively, "this means that the lord of the imperial surname trusts you. He gives you great face. Our Chinese men of medicine are held in high esteem, sir. To come to you for help for a Dutch physician, well, that certainly signifies something. This would provide an excellent opportunity to establish closer relations, to gain his trust. Would it not?"

Frederic was inclined to agree. Koxinga, the de facto ruler of southern China, had requested a Dutch physician to treat him for his ailment. He watched Caesar preen with gratification. No doubt the man was already asking himself what possibilities this might bring. Idly, Frederic wondered what malady Koxinga had that his own physicians could not cure. Or was this just a ruse? Still, it seemed as if they had little to lose.

* * *

Christian Beyer was working in his apothecary, busily sorting his newly arrived supplies of pharmaceutical ingredients when the junior clerk came to summon him. He felt somewhat annoyed at being interrupted, especially when the clerk told him that no, the governor was not ill and no, he had no idea why he had to go and see him.

On his way to the governor's office he noticed a Chinese junk in the harbor bearing the flag with the insignia of the Zhengs. Apparently there was an envoy at the fort, but he didn't think anything of it. Koxinga's envoys came and went to the island to communicate on all sorts of matters, and he had no interest in the politics of it. He had heard various tall tales about the son of the pirate turned mandarin. Skeptical by nature, he had taken them all with a pinch of salt.

"Doctor Beyer," Caesar cordially received him. "Please sit down."

Beyer took his seat warily. Indeed, the governor appeared in good health and once again the doctor wondered why he had been summoned. Frederic Coyett, who stood leaning against the governor's desk, did not seem sickly either.

"How can I be of service to you, governor? Someone in your family feeling poorly?" He had, after all, plenty to do with the drastic shortage of qualified doctors on the island, especially with the wide range of exotic diseases that so often struck the colonists.

Caesar rose from his chair stiffly, hampered by the arthritis Beyer knew had afflicted him since his arrival on Formosa. His thin frame paced the room as he spoke. "We have had a rather unusual request, doctor. I assume you are acquainted with the name Koxinga?"

Beyer sat up a little straighter, the governor had his attention now. "Why, yes. Of course. What of him?"

"This morning we received a dispatch requesting medical assistance for his person."

Beyer raised his eyebrows. "This is quite out of the ordinary. Any details on what ails him?" He didn't like where this was going.

"Not at this stage. However, it provides us with a very good opportunity to ease the tension between the two sides in these times of evil rumors, as I'm sure you'll understand." He stopped pacing the room and looked Beyer directly in the eye. "He is asking us to send a physician to Amoy to tend to him there."

Beyer felt stunned as he realized what Caesar was about to request of him. "You are asking me to go to Amoy to treat him?" he asked.

"Yes. He has specifically asked for you, not by name, but by description. It certainly fits you."

Caesar tried to suppress a smile, while Frederic coughed into his fist to hide his grin. In a reflex, Beyer's hands went to his ears. He didn't have to ponder long on how the Chinese might have described him.

"He has requested the best physician we have. Your reputation precedes you, doctor."

"You are sending me off to Amoy?" he asked again. "What about my undertakings here? We have more physicians. Cannot one of the other doctors go? I am getting far too old to partake in so bold and daring a venture such as this."

"It is imperative that you do take on this venture, Christian," Caesar reverted to the doctor's first name, making it personal. "We find ourselves in a predicament. There is a great deal at stake. He has asked us for the most qualified physician that we have at our disposal. I'm going to have to ask you to do this. And what's more, this way we can keep an eye on what he's up to. You can spy on him a little for us."

Beyer was momentarily at a loss for words. The fact that Caesar was suddenly using his given name was not lost on him. "But ... I don't even know what ails the man. How can I know what medication to bring? And what if his affliction is severe, and he dies under my care?" Beyer asked, exasperated. "Have you considered what would befall me then?"

"I do not believe he suffers from a life-threatening disease, or we would have heard about it," Caesar reassured him. "There seems to be no real sense of urgency."

"And what if they keep me hostage? You never know with these people."

"We have been assured that you will be treated well and with due respect to your profession. We shall just have to take their word for it. I must prevail upon you to do this, Christian."

Beyer clasped and unclasped his hands in agitation, his eyes blinking rapidly.

"For how long?" He thought of his family, whom he was loath to leave behind.

"We do not know. Do your utmost and cure the man, if at all possible. That is all I ask."

"Will I be provided with an assistant? An interpreter?"

"No. They were quite clear on this. But they will give you every possible assistance that you may deem necessary."

Beyer shook his head, frowning. He liked to be in charge of a situation, or at least to know what he was up against. There were too many uncertain factors to his liking. "You are asking a great deal of me, Cornelis," he muttered.

"I am aware of that," Caesar acceded, but his expression was unrelenting.

"I will need to prepare a full travel apothecary. I have no notion of what I will be requiring, after all. And I will be expecting some kind of additional reward upon my return for this ... rather questionable undertaking."

"I think that can be arranged," the governor said. "You will sail early tomorrow morning and travel on the envoy's junk, it will take you to him. I will let you go to make the necessary arrangements. I am indebted to you, Christian." He shook hands with the reluctant doctor, who made his way back to the apothecary, still muttering and shaking his head in dismay.

When Christian Beyer finally arrived in Amoy, it took a team of six coolies to carry the boxes of instruments, medicine, herbs, and ingredients from the junk to the quarters that he was assigned. In his concern that they might wander off with his precious load, he was adamant that he personally supervise them, unwilling to let them go ahead without him. In particular the opium – which he used as a painkiller – had a tendency to disappear from his cabinets.

It wasn't until late in the afternoon that he was to be taken to his patient. This only confirmed to Beyer that his charge was not seriously ill and this irked him, leading him to wonder again what he was doing there. It did, however, give him the opportunity to settle in and explore the area.

Two young street urchins, their faces smeared with grime, followed him along the beach, staring with unabashed curiosity. He tolerated their presence as he walked around, but shooed them away half-heartedly when they started gesturing and laughing at his ears. When it became clear that the boys had no intention of leaving, he decided to ignore them.

He gazed with some awe across the narrow channel at the mountainous mainland only a mile away. He had heard exotic tales of the extensive land of China and its ancient culture, and he wondered if the art of Chinese medicine was worthy of investigation. Perhaps that was the only positive thing about his predicament: he might have the chance to learn something from his Chinese colleagues while here.

He passed the time skipping pebbles on the water, gaining childish satisfaction from the way they bounced off the surface. He was about to throw another one when he saw a party of men walk in his direction. Lowering his arm, his heart skipped a beat. The time had come: his patient had summoned him. Judging from the size of the entourage, it seemed as if he was being summoned by Koxinga's personal physician himself. Beyer could well imagine how the Chinese doctor must feel, losing face due to being replaced by a foreigner to treat Koxinga.

Beyer looked at the man, feeling hesitant. A youngster with a thick lock of jet-black hair dangling in front of his face stepped forward.

"Please, sir, this is Doctor Wang," he said in halting Dutch. "He is personal physician to the lord of the imperial surname. Please, sir, you come with us." The accent was so strong that Beyer could barely discern the language spoken as his own. Wang greeted him courteously, but the fixed smile was so false that Beyer almost felt sorry for him. He stepped forward trying to look more confident than he felt, inclining his head slightly toward the Chinese physician in respect.

"Pleased to make your acquaintance," he said formally, articulating his words with exaggeration for the interpreter's benefit. "I am Doctor Christian Beyer, chief surgeon for the VOC on Formosa." He tried a smile, but his nerves merely allowed him what looked more like a grimace. He waited for the interpreter to finish translating, upon which Wang gestured to him that he should follow. The party left the beach, a trail of curious, laughing children trailing behind.

When they arrived at Koxinga's residence, the physician Wang went ahead of him. They made their way across several single-rise buildings that had been linked by courtyards and corridors until they finally arrived in Koxinga's private quarters.

The quarters were more modest than Beyer had expected. He had thought that the great military commander whose reputation had reached mythical proportions would live in far more grandeur. The quarters were sparely furnished as if they were only of a temporary nature.

Wang cleared his throat loudly as he entered. "My Lord Koxinga."

A man half-reclined on his futon, naked from the waist up, his back resting against a pile of cushions, his eyes closed. Wang waited for his employer to acknowledge him.

The man sighed before he opened his eyes. "He is here?" he asked, not bothering to get up.

"Yes, sire." He beckoned to Beyer with his hand to enter the room. "*Jinlai, jinlai.* Come in, Come in." The interpreter stayed outside by the doorway, just within earshot.

Koxinga sat up and looked at Beyer with interest. He said something that was left untranslated, upon which the others laughed. Beyer tried a smile, not sure how to react. Then Koxinga stood up in an easy motion that showed off his lean, muscled torso. Beyer observed him with a professional eye. So here he was: southern China's great military leader of whom the Dutch on Formosa had heard so much, and who increasingly gave them the jitters. Somehow, Beyer had expected him to be taller and broader. However, the face of the man did reflect his reputation: his eyes were shrewd, the expression hard and uncompromising, and something else, something disturbing that Beyer could not quite place.

Koxinga walked up to him, lifted his hands to his ears and pulled forward, grinning. The room filled with raucous laughter, which ceased just as suddenly, all eyes focused on him, awaiting his reaction.

My goodness, Beyer thought to himself with a sigh. It really is the same everywhere. He saw the expectant faces, and finally grabbed his own ears, which he pulled forward to maximum effect, and bellowed with laughter himself. They all stared at him in stunned silence. Then they all burst out laughing again, the shrill tone of their glee betraying the tension that had filled the room only moments before.

Still smiling, Koxinga beckoned him to come forward, which he did with caution. Koxinga pointed to his left arm.

"*Ni kan ba.* Look." he said. The interpreter translated. Beyer's training and professionalism took over; he was glad that he could finally be of use. He rolled up his sleeves and peered closely at the red irritated lumps that rose from the skin on his patient's arm. Then he examined the rest of

Koxinga's body with scrutiny, upon which Koxinga got up and dropped his trousers without any sense of shame. Beyer took his time inspecting his buttocks and crotch, where he thought he could make out a similar kind of rash that was even more intense. He was fully aware of Wang looking on with a prim expression, the corners of his mouth drawn down with resentment at having another doctor – and a foreign barbarian at that – examine his patient. Beyer ignored him.

"It itches?" he inquired, while simulating a scratching movement on his own bare arm. Wang began to speak on his patient's behalf, but Koxinga held up his hand imperiously, giving the Chinese physician a warning look. Wang pursed his lips and stepped back.

Koxinga nodded at Beyer. "It is the cold wind that has caused this," he said. Beyer listened to the interpreter's elaborate translation, but again he said nothing, continuing his physical examination, meticulously examining his eyelids and the soles of his feet. Wang, the interpreter and two personal attendants looked on with interest. Finally, Beyer straightened up, surprised at the number of people surrounding his patient. He had almost forgotten they were there.

"I have brought ingredients for medicine," he told the interpreter. "I will have to brew a concoction so that I can administer it this evening."

The youth translated the message haltingly, whereupon Koxinga said something to Wang, gesturing to Beyer and then himself, at which he laughed. The others joined him in the laughter, all except for Wang, who now looked positively sour. Beyer didn't have to think too hard to imagine what the exchange had been about. He knew that Wang was probably being instructed to watch him to make sure that he would not poison or harm Koxinga in any way. That Wang did not relish being demoted to some kind of bodyguard was evident.

Early that evening, with the aid of the instruments that he had brought, Beyer examined Koxinga more thoroughly, consulting from time to time one of the two heavy, tattered medical books that he had brought along. Reclining against the futon, Koxinga watched him as he worked in silence, inspecting the assorted bottles of prepared medications, occasionally muttering to himself as he pored over the yellowing pages of his book.

Wang took his job seriously, smelling with suspicion each of the different bottles of medicine, the mixing of which he had witnessed in the makeshift apothecary earlier that afternoon. He stood up close as Beyer used the various instruments to carry out some tests. Beyer had shrugged at the Chinese doctor's exaggerated curiosity, but now he looked up irritably as Wang got in his way yet again, gesturing that he give him some more room.

Wang protested that he was only doing his job, but Koxinga silenced him harshly. Scowling like a child, the Chinese physician retreated to survey Beyer's work at arm's length.

Beyer had difficulty forming an immediate diagnosis, wavering between different ailments.

The curious lumps that had formed on his patient's left arm were definitely not the result of cold, wind, or any other external influence. The origin of the lumps had an internal cause, and although the skin lesions did not appear to make Koxinga ill apart from the irritation and itching, the doctor was unable to say if the affliction was serious.

He began treatment by applying ointments and creams to the lesions, allowing several days to see if they had any effect. Apart from the immediate relief from the itching that the application provided, they didn't. The treatment plan he then set up was a combination of diet, daily baths in lukewarm water, and adjusted ointments that he himself had prepared.

During the next few days it became apparent what kind of a patient Koxinga was. If he did not feel like being treated, or if it cost him too much effort on his part, he refused to cooperate. The diet that Beyer prescribed excluded pork and hot spices, but Koxinga shrugged off the advice and stubbornly continued to enjoy his favorite dish of the forbidden, fierily spiced meat. He often refused the herbal preparations that were given him, complaining that they were foul-tasting, spitting out the contents on the spot. The oil-infused baths that Beyer recommended were taken sporadically, and then only if he had the patience and inclination for them.

Beyer continued to treat Koxinga with resolve, in spite of his patient's lack of cooperation. With the intensive treatment of his patient and the great amount of time he spent with him, Beyer came to know Koxinga as an inquisitive, intelligent man who was interested in the world beyond China's borders. When he worked on his skin, meticulously rubbing in the ointments or mixing his infusions, Koxinga would ask him many questions, which the interpreter translated for him.

"You are married?" he inquired one day.

"Yes, sir, I am. I have four children...."

"Sons?" Koxinga asked again.

"No. Just daughters," Beyer said. Koxinga frowned in sympathy. Beyer smiled. He had long since learned that the Chinese favored boys over girls. He also knew it was so ingrained in their culture that he thought it wiser not to pass comment.

"I have two sons by my first wife," Koxinga volunteered proudly. "She recently gave birth to a daughter, but the child was still-born," he said matter-of-factly. "I have six more children by my other two wives. And more on the way."

"Your family resides here, on Amoy?" Beyer inquired.

Koxinga regarded him for a moment, probably wondering if he could be trusted. "No. They are on Penghu, in the Pescadores. It is safer for them there."

Beyer nodded wisely as he finished massaging the ointment on his back, and began to gather his things to return to his quarters.

"Do not leave yet." It was more an order than a plea. "I wish to know more about you. Sit."

The interpreter looked at the military commander, startled at the more personal nature the conversation had taken between the great commander and the foreign doctor. He translated nonetheless. Beyer laid his things back on the table and took his seat across Koxinga, who turned to lie on his side, supporting his head on his elbow.

"Your parents. Are they still alive?" Koxinga asked him.

"No, they both expired some time ago, God bless their souls."

"Tell me. In your country, do men take more than one wife?"

"No, sir. Our God has instructed us to love but one spouse. Dutch women are too proud. Besides," he grinned, "my wife would never tolerate such a thing. She would surely drive me out of the house!"

Koxinga chuckled before the interpreter could complete his sentence, shaking his head in wonder. "We Chinese honor more than one god. But I particularly revere Matsu, goddess of the sea. My mother...." He paused for a moment, looking away. "My mother was Japanese."

Beyer looked up, surprised at the revelation.

"She was a proud woman. She was also a strong and honorable woman. She accepted my father's having more than one wife, even concubines."

"She no longer lives?" Beyer asked.

"No." A look of pain took hold of Koxinga's expression, followed by one of fierce anger.

"She died ten years ago. They raped her," he said vehemently. "The Manchurian soldiers, they raped her. Then she hung herself, from the very tree I used to climb as a boy. I found her."

Beyer watched Koxinga's eyes go black as he dwelt on the memory.

"They attacked our fortress when I was only several *li* away. By the time we came back, it was too late. They also killed my sister. She was only three years old." He stared ahead dully.

Beyer was shocked into silence; he did not know what to say. "And your father? Is he still alive?" he said after a while.

The interpreter tensed, hesitating as he looked from the commander to the physician, and back again at Koxinga, who got up into a seated position. His eyes were on the interpreter, expectant. The pale youth still did not speak, not quite knowing what to do. Beyer now knew that he had asked the wrong question. He nearly jumped when Koxinga bellowed at the poor boy, upon which the interpreter reluctantly obliged, throwing out the Chinese words rapidly, as if to be done with it.

When Koxinga heard what Beyer had asked of him, he went rigid. He got to his feet, startling him. He grabbed his tunic and slipped it on, turning his face away from him.

"My father," he said, his voice ominously low. "Is dead to me. He has betrayed his emperor and his country, and I do not care whether he is dead or alive." Then he walked out of the room, leaving Beyer and the interpreter in stunned silence.

After several weeks, Koxinga's symptoms still hadn't improved. As the novelty of Beyer's presence had begun to wear off, Koxinga seemed to tire of having him around and often sent him away if Beyer became too insistent on treating him. Only if the itching became unbearable would he summon him for the application of the ointments. Wang would hang over them, watching, with a smug expression on his face that Beyer could not fail to notice.

In his spare time, Beyer wandered around the island. Often he would come across regiments training in hand-to-hand combat, swordplay, or archery. Discreetly he would observe the military exercises, if only out of sheer fascination. Koxinga's officers noticed his presence but tolerated it, probably with the purpose of impressing upon him the prowess of their men. From a safe distance he would watch as twenty men lifted their bows on cue, their bows released as one, their arrows rarely missing their mark. From what he saw, any illusions that Koxinga's army consisted of undisciplined rabble were dispelled from his mind. He was daunted by what he had seen. In fact, he was so awed that it made his skin crawl.

* * *

Koxinga enjoyed the conversations he had with the Dutch physician. He was fascinated by the world Beyer came from and wanted to know everything about Western culture. In spite of all that he had learned from his father about the Dutch, there was still so much to know. He was curious to find out what had led them to sail across the vast oceans in their tall ships in search of countries like his own. How did the Dutch think? What was their philosophy of life, and how had it come to be that they regarded women so differently than his people did? Every chance he got he questioned Beyer in detail, even on mundane matters. From time to time, he would read the poems written by his own hand to the Dutchman, and Beyer would listen to the translations, occasionally passing comment.

He was also eager to know what type of man Governor Caesar was, and often asked questions about him, which the doctor answered willingly. Now and again he asked him about life on Formosa, to which Beyer gave measured answers. Once, when he innocently asked how many Dutch troops there were on the island, Beyer had smiled at him and answered,

"Oh, I really would not know anything about that. I am just a humble doctor," at which Koxinga had laughed, knowing that Beyer was no fool.

Ever since Koxinga had reacted so strongly to Beyer's questions about his father, he found that the Dutchman had become more cautious when asking his questions. This disappointed him, but he could not blame the man. There were just some things that he did not want to talk about.

Nonetheless, he found their conversations refreshing. It had taken a while before Beyer had dared to speak to him freely, but now he was one of the very few who was totally frank with him, and he needed that. Even Cai, whom he had known since childhood and in whose company he had always felt so comfortable, had become more distant of late, more wary of him. It was something he couldn't understand; it wounded him. Had he really changed so much? Perhaps his mother's death and his father's act of betrayal had affected him more than he realized.

As the weeks passed, it was only natural that Beyer would get to know Koxinga's darker side. But Koxinga didn't care: his reputation in the eyes of his men as a strong military leader must be maintained at all cost. Besides, he had little choice. Their enemy had become more aggressive, and it was crucial that they regain the territories that were lost to them. That meant that if his officers returned from the battlefield and dared not look him in the eye to tell him that they had been defeated, they would have to be punished. Those men had to be made an example of. Better that they die on the battlefield than return to tell him they had failed. Corporal punishment was effective in such cases. It kept his men sharp.

Even so, he was aware that his uncontrollable fits of anger were occurring more frequently. Such fits were usually provoked by his officers' reports of defeat. Then his sight would become blurred, he would see a red haze, and he would be unable to stop himself from lashing out at them, irrespective of who they were. Often he would not even know what he was doing.

He would find out only afterward, when he asked why someone's lip was bleeding, or upon inquiring how someone had broken the fingers he was nursing. San-ge, his general, would later inform him in private that it had been his own doing. He would also see it in the frightened faces of the men around him and realize that he had performed yet another act of cruelty. At first, such incidents disturbed him, but then he would shrug his shoulders and continue with whatever it was he was doing. After all, sometimes one had to be cruel in order to prevail.

On occasion, he would have these fits in the presence of the Dutch doctor. That was simply unavoidable, as Beyer was with him often for the treatments he required. Koxinga had made a habit of conferring with his officers while he was being treated. Whenever he had given someone a thorough beating, the doctor would pale and become uncommunicative.

One morning Beyer had accidentally witnessed the execution of a junior officer. Koxinga had caught sight of the Dutchman, who had been on one of his early morning beach walks. Beyer had just stood there, rooted to the ground as the executioner had cut the man's throat, and stared at the mutilated body as the blood stained the sand dark red. Koxinga had met his look, unconcerned, before returning inside. The rest of the day Beyer had remained silent and morose, speaking only when questioned.

Several days later, Koxinga was in a good mood, having just enjoyed the intimacy of a pretty young maid. The girl was still in his room, her face and neck still flushed from intercourse. Koxinga was lying on his front while Beyer carefully rubbed ointment onto his neck and shoulders. Wang jealously hovered around him, vigilant as always. The interpreter remained close, available to them should they require his services.

His mood buoyed by sexual release and the relief that Beyer's ointments provided from his constant itch, Koxinga felt like talking. He asked Beyer who ruled the country of his birth, and was astonished to hear that the Netherlands had neither king nor emperor, but that it was in fact a united republic that was governed by several regents. To him, the concept was hard to fathom.

"Might I be so bold as to inquire why you had that officer killed two days ago?" Beyer asked as he was working the skin around Koxinga's armpit. Wang winced at the boldness of the question, but Koxinga merely smiled. After all, he had been expecting the question for some time.

"He gave me wrong counsel. And then he questioned my judgment in front of my men."

Beyer's hands fell still. He walked over to the table where he had laid out his instruments and medications, his back turned to him. For a long moment, there was nothing but silence between them. Then, still standing with his back to him, he spoke again, choosing his words with care.

"If I question your judgment, in that it compromises your health by refusing to heed my advice and not accept my treatment, would you have me killed also?"

On the other side of the room, Wang let out a small gasp as his words were interpreted. But Koxinga did not seem to mind.

"No. You are a physician, not a soldier. It is your job to insist on treating me, whether I choose to cooperate or not. If one of my soldiers or officers questions my judgment, then I lose face in front of my men. I cannot let that happen."

"So losing face would be reason enough to have someone killed?"

He turned on his side to face Beyer, his expression hard. "Yes. If you command an army like the one I command, yes. If you want men to respect you and you want them to obey your orders, even if doing so might go against their beliefs, yes. Can you understand that?"

Beyer returned his gaze, nodding wordlessly. Koxinga lowered himself into a prone position once more, pleased at having brought his point across.

As the weeks passed, it became clear that Beyer's various treatments were not going to cure his affliction. Once he realized that even the Dutch physician's medical knowledge would not be able to help him regain full health, he became less inclined to cooperate. He would leave for days at a time – sometimes more than a week – without giving the doctor any prior notice, and without taking with him the medicine that he was prescribed. When he returned he would be reprimanded by Beyer, who insisted that Koxinga himself was to blame if his condition deteriorated.

Of course he was right. The symptoms only worsened whenever he was away. He would come back ill-tempered through lack of sleep, his itch more intense than it had been before.

One day, as Beyer was treating him, they were disturbed by two officers who had just returned from the mainland. The men appeared uneasy, on edge, and Koxinga gestured in no uncertain terms to Beyer to step back and let him be.

One of the officers, his hands fidgeting restlessly on his lap, reported that while on their mission to obtain food from the coastal villages on the mainland, they had been ambushed by Qing troops. They had been forced back to their boats, losing men in the process. With a voice that was barely audible, the man added that they had not managed to bring back the necessary supplies that they had set out to obtain.

Koxinga had listened to the officer in silence, his expression growing darker by the minute. He had counted on these men. The food on Amoy had become more and more scarce, and they had come to depend on the supplies coming from the mainland. That would only become worse. Yet giving up wasn't an option: they had to bring in food from the Chinese coast. It was vital that all his officers understood this well.

"You! Translate!" he ordered the interpreter. Startled, the youth translated what the officer had just told him.

Beyer blinked, unsure why the officer's story had to be translated for his benefit.

The tension in the room was almost tangible.

Koxinga regarded the officer intently, whereupon the man dropped his eyes to the floor, his hands trembling.

"So you have failed in your mission," Koxinga said in an ominously soft tone. The other officer's eyes darted in their sockets as he saw the change that had come over his commander.

Koxinga got to his feet. "Outside," he ordered. The officer on his knees looked up, not understanding, while the other man backed out of the door in panic.

"Outside! Now!" Koxinga shouted. The kneeling officer scrambled clumsily to his feet, bowing and groveling to him as he did. Once in the courtyard, Koxinga called his sentries.

"Hold him," Koxinga ordered the men, pointing to the second officer, who made a desperate attempt to flee. The sentries quickly complied, pinioning the man's arms behind his back. Koxinga lunged at the first officer, breaking his nose in one fluid movement of his fist. The man wailed, his hands flying to his face in a reflex of pain. Immediately, Koxinga kicked him in his crotch, which was now vulnerable and exposed. The man bent over and fell to his knees, wailing as he nursed his privates. Another kick landed on his skull, sending him sprawling backward.

Then it happened, as it had happened several times before. A rush of adrenaline coursed through his veins, that same red haze blurred his sight. Unable to stop the overpowering rage that had suddenly taken hold of him, he kicked the man hard in the face, his chest, his groin, again and again. He didn't stop until his victim no longer fended off his kicks and ceased to move altogether.

The other officer stared at the unconscious man in shock. Before the officer knew what was happening, Koxinga drew his dagger and in a split second slit the man's throat. The victim's eyes were still wide with disbelief as his body dropped to the earth, the dark blood snaking from underneath him.

Koxinga looked up to see Beyer staring at him, his mouth agape.

"That was for failing in your mission." He spat the words at the two lifeless bodies, for the benefit of the soldiers and officers who had witnessed the killings. Everyone stood frozen in place, their eyes averted. Koxinga turned and stopped as he passed Beyer in the entrance, only inches between them.

"They failed me," he said, still breathing hard from the effort. "We needed those food supplies."

* * *

Beyer fled to the relative sanctuary of his private quarters, still trembling at the horror of what he had just seen. What offence had those two men been guilty of, to warrant such a cruel end? They had been Koxinga's own men! What unsettled him most of all was the look in Koxinga's eyes. It had been fanatical, manic, without the slightest hint of empathy or regret. He had not cared that two of his best officers had just been put to death for being unable to do what had most probably been impossible anyway. The look Beyer had seen in those eyes was that of a madman. And this seriously disturbed him.

The doctor had thought he could become accustomed to Koxinga's erratic temper, but now he was no longer sure. The bouts of rage were becoming more and more frequent. One moment he was the civilized, humorous mandarin reading his elegantly written poetry, then cruel and psychotic the next. Most of all, he was utterly unpredictable, and that made him all the more dangerous. It felt like watching a predatory cat about to pounce on its unsuspecting prey, without knowing when or how it was going to happen.

Beyer became increasingly tense around Koxinga and no longer slept well. It had been six weeks since he had arrived in Amoy, and he yearned to return to Formosa. He missed his family, he missed being among his own people. He was now also convinced that whatever ailed the military commander, it was unlikely that he would be able to heal him.

He finally sent a message to Governor Caesar, in which he stated that he had not yet come up with a cure, but that he requested permission to return nonetheless. Permission was refused: Caesar insisted that he continue with the treatment until Koxinga was well again, as this was in the interest of all concerned. Depressed and unmotivated, Beyer started to drown his sorrows in the local brew in the evenings, if only to help him sleep.

A week later, while Beyer was working in his apothecary, he was startled by a woman screaming, the sound joined by the pleading cries of a man. Disturbed by the commotion, he went outside to see what was happening. Reaching one of the courtyards, he pushed his way through the crowd of gathered soldiers. On her knees, her arms held cruelly high behind her back, was a young woman. Beyer recognized her at once as one of the attractive female servants who regularly frequented Koxinga's quarters and shared his bed. Between sobs her breathing sounded far too rapid: she was hyperventilating from fright. Kneeling next to her was one of Koxinga's officers, a grimace of pain on his handsome face as blood poured from a wound on his forehead. Behind them stood General San-ge. Koxinga himself was nowhere in sight.

Without warning and before Beyer could even move, General San-ge drew his sword and swung it down hard at the man on his knees, severing his head cleanly. Blood splattered the woman, who retched miserably, her eyes staring as she went into shock. San-ge walked round the man's body, pulled up a loosened strand of the woman's hair and jerked her head backward.

Beyer instinctively threw himself forward in a desperate effort to intervene, but the soldiers barred his way. His eyes sought San-ge, who met his gaze head-on, his lips twitching into a cruel smile, as if he wanted him to see this. San-ge lifted his sword and swung down at the woman's pale neck. Beyer uttered a cry of utter dismay as he saw the head roll away, a tangled mess of long, shiny black hair and blood. The headless body slumped lifelessly to the ground. Feeling the bile rise in his throat Beyer turned away to vomit convulsively onto the sand.

"Why in the name of God did you have her killed?" Beyer blurted out as he dragged the interpreter by the arm into Koxinga's quarters, his fury and sense of injustice too strong to care for his own safety. "Why did she have to die?"

Koxinga looked up from his ledgers and frowned at the sudden intrusion. Then he resumed his work, ignoring him. Beyer walked up and slapped the palm of his hand hard on the open page of the book.

"Why, you poxy bastard? Tell me why!" Beyer demanded.

Koxinga sighed wearily and looked at him coldly. "They were lovers." The interpreter stammered the translation of the words, scared witless.

"What?! That young officer you killed – I was acquainted to him. I have spoken to him on numerous occasions. He worshipped you. He would have given his life for you. He cannot have betrayed you. I do not believe it."

"I saw how they looked at each other. It was unacceptable," he said, scratching his neck.

"You saw how they looked...." Beyer stopped midsentence. Much to his astonishment, he saw tears running down the military commander's cheeks.

"If you think your tears will absolve you...." Beyer said, staring at him with disgust.

"This does not concern you," Koxinga told him, his voice low.

"Yes, it does. Oh yes, it most certainly does." And with that, he was gone.

Beyer felt utterly sickened by what he had seen, and he had had enough. The more he thought about it, the more afraid he became for his own safety. Nine long weeks he had been on Amoy, and now he wished to leave, whether he had the governor's permission or not. He waited for an opportunity to present itself when Koxinga appeared to be in a more reasonable mood.

"Sir," he began quietly, breaking the silence. Koxinga grunted, raising an eyebrow at him in question. There was no other way but to ask the question bluntly.

"Sir, I respectfully ask that you allow me passage to return to my people on Formosa."

Koxinga looked up at him, his expression cold. "Why do you wish to leave?"

"I have done all that I can for you," Beyer said. "You are the most willful patient I have ever encountered, and even if you did listen to me and permitted me to give you the proper treatment you require, I am not convinced that I can cure you of your ailment."

The Chinese military leader looked him in the eye, blinking only once.

"Furthermore, I have been here now for more than two months. I wish to return to my own people, my wife, and my children. There are many sick people on Formosa who need my expertise far more urgently than you do. I beseech you to allow me to leave Amoy. Doctor Wang is a good, capable physician. I have instructed him. He can help alleviate the symptoms with the medicine I will leave behind."

Koxinga remained silent as he continued to hold his gaze. Even after nine weeks of intensive interaction, Beyer still found it difficult to read the man's mind.

Koxinga lay back down again. "You have my permission to leave," he said simply. "As long as you will see to it that I am provided with all the medicine that I might need in the future."

Beyer gawked at him. He had never thought it would be that easy. "Of course, Lord Koxinga," he stammered, trying hard not to betray the immense relief that he felt.

Wang did his best to look inscrutable but failed miserably in the attempt. The Chinese physician was practically glowing with self-satisfaction. Beyer could tell what he was thinking: the foreign doctor with the ears of an elephant had not been able to find a cure for the commander either. It would be better for Wang if he left. Then he would no longer have to suffer the terrible loss of face and would once again enjoy the respect that was his due as Koxinga's personal physician.

"Doctor Beyer?" Koxinga called after him as he was about to take his leave.

"Yes, Lord Koxinga?" His heart missed a beat. For one ghastly moment, he thought that Koxinga was playing him, that he had changed his mind, and that he would not be given permission to leave after all.

"Do you believe in fate?" Koxinga asked. "That all is determined beforehand, and that there are those who are able to predict this?"

The unexpected question threw Beyer completely off balance. What did he believe? He believed in God. He believed that God would determine his fate. But was he genuinely free of all superstition? The truth be told, he knew that he wasn't, even if he were a man of science. Didn't he hold a fascination, attraction even, for mystics and fortunetellers and all that one could not comprehend or explain? Didn't all men, when it came down to it?

"My religion bids me to believe in our one and almighty God, but perhaps his truth is not the only one. There may be those who have the gift of seeing into the future." He frowned at hearing himself voice his thoughts aloud, thoughts that surprised even himself. "Yes," he acceded, defeated somehow. "Yes, I do believe that in some way, our fates are determined, that we are destined. Why do you ask this of me?"

Koxinga's eyes were glazed; they seemed to look past him, at nothing in particular.

"It is written that a large island, not so far from here, shall one day be mine to rule. That the fate of this island will be entwined with my own. It was predicted. I believe this island to be Formosa." The words were spoken calmly, as if they were a simple matter of fact, and utter conviction.

Beyer peered at him, uneasy. What was this man saying? Was this a threat? Should he believe this nonsense?

"Forgive me, I don't.... If I understand correctly, you are saying that you believe that Formosa will one day be yours?"

"Yes. This was predicted a long time ago, in the days of my youth."

Beyer held up his hands in a helpless gesture. For a moment, he did not know how to respond. "I ... I fear this is beyond my comprehension, Lord Koxinga. I really would not know," he stammered. "Now, if you will please allow me to take my leave?"

Koxinga nodded absentmindedly, whereupon Beyer backed out of the room, seriously troubled by what he had just heard.

Two days later he was brought back to Formosa on one of Koxinga's own junks. When he arrived, Caesar wasted little time to summon him and subject him to interrogation.

"Ah, Christian!" the governor said amicably, rising up from his chair to shake the doctor's hand. "Good to have you back. You have made our Chinese friend well again?" It was a rhetorical question, and exactly the one that Beyer had expected.

"Well, no. Not quite," he said, unconcerned.

"Then I presume he is well on the road to an expedient recovery?" Caesar asked, still standing, smiling.

"No, sir, he is not." He met the governor's gaze, almost defiantly. Caesar's expression changed, the friendliness he had just displayed gone.

"What?" Caesar shouted. "I had specifically given you orders to stay until...."

"Mr. Caesar!" Beyer bellowed, his face turning red with pent-up anger. "I have followed your bloody orders and I went to Amoy to treat your Chinaman, and not of my own volition, as you may recall." His tone was cold. He had too much self-respect to allow anyone to talk to him in that way after all that he had been through over the past two months. Not even the governor.

Governor Caesar looked up, startled at Beyer's uncharacteristic explosion of anger.

"As long as you are employed by the company...."

"You don't have to tell me what my duties are," Beyer interrupted him. "I am painfully aware what is expected of me. For nine weeks, nine bloody weeks I have tended to this man, who you would be wise to regard with great prudence. It was hell out there. I risked my life out there every day.

The man isn't sane!" He forced himself to take a deep breath, surprised at his own outburst. "And anyway, I could not help him. In that sense, I have failed miserably."

Caesar sat back in his chair. "Sit down, Christian. Tell me what has transpired."

"I tried, Cornelis. Really, I did," Beyer said apologetically, calmer now. "But the man wouldn't cooperate and, the truth be told, I don't think I could have cured him of his disease if he had."

"So you took it upon yourself to decide you could leave? Even against my specific orders?"

"I was afraid for my own life, Cornelis. I no longer felt safe. I perceive him to be highly intelligent, well educated, and learned. Both his adversaries and allies regard him as a brilliant military leader. I am told he knows Sun Tzu's *The Art of War* by heart. But he is also a madman. He is cruel to his own people, his soldiers, and his servants. Even his women." He fell silent as the image of the woman's blood-soaked tresses of hair came flooding back. "What I saw there...." He shook his head, closing his eyes to shut out the vivid images. Then he lifted his head and looked the governor right in the eye.

"Cornelis, you would be wise to listen to me. Koxinga is unpredictable of temper, susceptible to severe mood swings, and a very difficult man to read," Beyer said. "His madness is almost certainly caused by whatever ails him."

"You describe him as a madman. Then he is probably incapable or leading an army for an invasion, and we should not worry ourselves about his endeavors, and all these rumors are just spread to frighten us."

"No, Cornelis. On the contrary, we should be very concerned. He has everything firmly in hand. His organization is more than praiseworthy. I was quite impressed. I have seen his armies. His officers and soldiers are well trained, and I have rarely seen such discipline, even among our own troops. I have watched them practice for battle. This is an army to be reckoned with. And he is a man we should not underestimate by any means. But there is something else you should know."

He winced, unwilling to repeat what was no more than nonsensical superstition. Yet he felt he had no choice. "The man believes in some divine prophecy that was made at the time of his youth. It appears that some kind of fortune-teller has told him something about his providence. That his destiny is here, on this island. He is of the conviction that Formosa shall one day be his to rule." The governor frowned and looked at Beyer as if he had lost his mind. Beyer could hardly blame him. Why on earth had he told the governor this? He must be mad.

Caesar shrugged his shoulders. "So the man is superstitious. But what do you think ails him? Did you manage at least to get a diagnosis?"

"Hard to say. Could have been various things, with all the exotic diseases in these parts. At first I suspected swamp disease; but there was no fever. The symptoms don't tally." He cocked an eyebrow, his professionalism returning, "Some diseases are too intricately challenging to diagnose, as their symptoms could apply to various ailments. 'The Great Imitator,' for one. That would also explain the unpredictable, even violent behavior, the sudden mood swings."

"The Great Imitator?" the governor asked.

"Yes, Cornelis. I'm not certain, but it's possible that he has syphilis."

13

A Lack of Trade

For the coastal provinces there was no more escaping the war that had already had the rest of the Chinese empire in its grasp for years. On Formosa everyone was affected, as trade was nearly non-existent and the VOC suffered a serious drop in profits. Governor Caesar wrote to the council in Batavia, stating that they had to wait until the war between the Ming loyalists and the invading Manchus was over.

Koxinga's growing power and influence did concern Caesar. It was reported that he had an estimated three hundred thousand men and three thousand junks at his disposal at Amoy and the Pescadores. Rumor had it that he was gathering his fleet and troops, an indication that he was planning a major attack on the mainland, while everyone knew that the Qing generals had already gained firm control of the south.

Caesar decided not to take any chances and wrote to Batavia requesting more ships and troop reinforcements, as well as permission to increase the number of military forts along the coast. Measures were taken to reinforce Zeelandia, while spies were sent to the Pescadores and Amoy to investigate what Koxinga was up to. They returned to report that they had not encountered anything out of the ordinary such as increased naval activity. They did, however, learn that in order to raise money for his troops in his ongoing battle with the Qing, Koxinga had intensified his foreign trade with other ports in Southeast Asia This explained the serious drop in company sales in those ports.

The fact that trade between China and the VOC had slackened because of the war was something the company had come to accept. But for Koxinga to compete with them for trade in other parts of Asia – that the council found highly objectionable. In a courteous letter accompanied by lavish gifts, Johan Maetsuijcker, the company's newly appointed governor-general in Batavia, informed Koxinga that they could not permit trading activities in these waters. After all, the company had trading privileges in those foreign ports, so he asked him politely but firmly to cease trading there. To emphasize their point, they sent a small fleet to Sumatra, where they intercepted two of Koxinga's junks and confiscated his cargoes of prized pepper.

A few months later, the first of a series of disturbing communiqués began to arrive on Formosa, addressed to the governor, and it appeared to have been written by Lord Koxinga himself.

"This is outrageous!" Caesar bellowed on reading the letter. "The man has issued an edict in which he forbids all Chinese to sail to the Philippines. 'The penalty for disobeying this edict will be death.' The man has taken leave of his senses! Who does he think he is?" He handed the translation of the edict to Frederic, who quickly read its contents. Frederic found that Koxinga's normally courteous, articulate style of writing to which the VOC officials had grown accustomed had changed. The tone was hostile, the wording of the letter disturbing.

"He demands that the edict is announced on this island, and that we enforce it," he said, shaking his head in wonder. "'Furthermore, I must complain about the treatment that my people suffer from the Dutch.' His people?" He raised an eyebrow. "He talks about the Chinese on Formosa as if they are his subjects."

"Yes. Apparently he deems himself the king of Formosa. The impudence of the man!" Caesar exclaimed, red-faced. "He speaks of his subjects, and has the nerve to issue his edicts on us, and is brazen enough to ask us to enforce them!" he raved as he paced up and down.

"Seems a bit out of character, especially considering the previous correspondence we've had with the man," Frederic put in, equally surprised.

"Very strange. I honestly don't know what he is up to, but if he thinks he has any sovereignty over this island, or any of the people living here, then he is badly mistaken! We shall have to make this quite clear to him. The arrogance of the man!" He sniffed indignantly.

Once Caesar's anger had subsided and they had held their counsel, Caesar ordered a letter to be written. In the first draft the wording was far too direct and uncompromising, at which Frederic subtly counselled him to adjust it to include the courteousness that Koxinga had come to expect. "After some deliberation, we regret that the council of the VOC has decided that it must decline your most interesting request in order to preserve the sovereignty of the VOC on Formosa." The message the letter was putting across was clear enough: provoking Koxinga any further would not benefit anyone.

For a while, Koxinga did not respond. Several months later, however, a group of influential Chinese merchants living on Formosa urgently requested a meeting with the governor and his council.

"We have received a dispatch from Lord Koxinga, the contents of which cause us great concern," their spokesman said. "Lord Koxinga writes that the Dutch have captured his junks, harassed his crews and confiscated his wares. He even states that the VOC intends to put a trade embargo in place to stop him from trading in Southeast Asia."

Frederic and Caesar exchanged glances. What the man had just said wasn't the exact truth, but it was close enough.

"What's worse, excellency, is that he has ordered us Chinese merchants to cease all trade with your honored company with immediate effect," the man continued, "Unless, that is, we manage to persuade you to allow his junks safe passage in Southeast Asia and to stop harassing his crews. Excellency, Lord Koxinga has warned us in no uncertain terms that if we do not cooperate he will issue an edict forbidding all traders in China to do any further business with us."

This was an unexpected turn of events, and Frederic could imagine that the men were horrified. A large part of their income came from trading with the VOC. If they stopped their trade with the company as Koxinga had ordered, their livelihoods would be seriously threatened. But if they refused then Koxinga might carry out his threat and bar the merchants' trade with China, which would result in the same. It seemed as if they were caught between two fires.

Shocked at Koxinga's deviousness, Caesar, Frederic, and Chief Merchant van Iperen withdrew to hold counsel while the Chinese merchants waited. After more than an hour, they returned to the men, their faces anxious. The governor cleared his throat.

"Gentlemen, with all due respect to Lord Koxinga, he seems to be ill informed. Koxinga's poor opinion of the Dutch people is, as you well know, unfounded and based on false rumor. The VOC is an honorable company. It would never subject any of Koxinga's – or any other Chinese ships' crews to such ill abuse as he suggests. Any incidents that may have occurred in the past were unfortunate skirmishes at sea. Fear of piracy, self-defense, that sort of thing. This is all no more than an unfortunate misunderstanding." He smiled at them reassuringly.

"Will you be enforcing the edict that he has issued, your excellency?" One of the merchants inquired.

"Most certainly not. I can assure you that we will not enforce any edicts issued by anyone other than the VOC, which has sole sovereignty over Formosa. Rest assured, gentlemen, that you can ignore any edicts issued by Lord Koxinga, as they are simply not valid on Formosa. He has no authority here whatsoever."

The men left the fortress, but Frederic thought they didn't look very convinced.

"I have heard that there have indeed been incidents involving Koxinga's ships, Cornelis," he said once the Chinese merchants had left. "The company did seize two of his junks with cargoes of pepper. The crews were given quite a hard time, from what I've been told."

"Yes, I am well aware of the incidents in South Sumatra, Frederic. May those poxy councilmen in Batavia be damned. This doesn't make things any easier for us. I had better send a dispatch to Batavia about this. I just lied through my teeth to these merchants, but I can't keep that up for long. On that point Koxinga is quite right, of course. Unfortunately, Governor-General Maetsuijker has instructed me to pretend ignorance of the matter. Maetsuijker seems to believe that if we keep up this farce, Koxinga will stop harassing us. Personally, I don't think for one minute that he will let this rest."

Frederic nodded gravely: he could not agree more.

A few days later a letter was sent to Koxinga to let him know that the Dutch had absolutely no intention of propagating or enforcing his edicts in any way. Within a month, the same Chinese merchants were back with Koxinga's response.

Frederic took it upon himself to read the translation to the others. "'After learning about your refusal to put my previous edict into effect, my initial reaction was to put an embargo in place for all trade with Formosa. However, in the interest of my people living on the island, some of whom might have been travelling and who did not receive news of my edict on time, I will allow one hundred days for Chinese vessels to travel between China and Formosa. Henceforth, the only goods that may be traded are local products, such as venison, fish products and Formosa-grown sugar. Any junk holding products in its holds that were originally from anywhere but Formosa will have its crew executed and its cargo confiscated. That means that no pepper, cloves, tin, or other such goods may be traded. I will have inspectors in place to examine all vessels landing on the Chinese coasts. Also, those who defy my edict and intend to receive the forbidden goods will be executed. This is my word and my mandate, which will be as permanent as writing engraved in stone.'" Frederic returned the document back to Caesar in silence.

"Merciful God," the governor breathed, "the man is serious. Not only is he attacking the company, he is also striking at his competitors." He faced the troubled Chinese merchants, his hands trembling as he tried to control his rising temper. "I must warn you, on pain of death, that if any of you spread notices to the effect of this edict anywhere on the island or even breathe a word about this to anyone, you will be severely punished." He crumpled the paper furiously in his hand, his knuckles turning white. "This," he said as he held it in front of their faces menacingly, "will be destroyed."

The merchants' faces had become a sickly green. Frederic felt sympathy for them, as he knew they were now caught between the will of the company and the wrath of Koxinga's displeasure.

In spite of the fact that the merchants had agreed to hold their tongues, word of the edict spread, and the damage was done. All tradesmen on the Pescadores were suddenly reluctant to sell their provisions, for fear of what Koxinga might do to them. One could not blame them: the isles were crawling with junks carrying Koxinga's banners, under the pretext of collecting taxes.

Everyone knew that they were in fact carrying the feared inspectors dispatched to make sure that all Chinese merchant vessels complied with his edict. No one dared load their junks with any product that was on Koxinga's list of forbidden goods. With their livelihoods depending on the company's foreign wares and frightened by Koxinga's threats, many of them left, taking their families with them. An exodus had begun.

Then word reached the Formosan council that a Chinese junk had been detained by Koxinga's men in Amoy. Upon close inspection, a cleverly hidden cargo of pepper was revealed. Not being a Formosan product, it fell under Koxinga's category of forbidden products. The junk's captain was immediately executed, and all the crew members had their right hands cut off. All those who still had any doubts on whether Koxinga meant to carry out his threats were left with no illusions.

The news of the incident spread fast. Merchants and tradesmen panicked, and many aborted their trade plans, turning around mid-voyage to unload their pepper, spices, and tin in the warehouses of Zeelandia.

In an effort to stem the panic among the merchants upon whom the VOC had come to depend, Caesar decided to proclaim an edict of his own. In it, he forbade anyone to bring or make public on Formosa any edicts other than those issued by the company. Any person found to be in the possession of documents that might compromise the interests of the colony was to face severe corporal punishment.

Then one day, soldiers brought a Chinese man to the governor's office, dressed in the robes of a minor official.

"Sir. This man has been caught performing unlawful inspections on Chinese vessels. He was found to be carrying official papers. It's more than likely that they come from Koxinga himself."

In fear for his life, the captured official spilled all that they wanted to know. As suspected, the man's instructions came from Koxinga himself. The man had been ordered to inspect all departing vessels, and to bring Koxinga a list of the names of all ships and merchants on Formosa who still continued to carry pepper and other foreign goods on their ships. Once those defiant merchant ships arrived in the ports of China, the ships were to be earmarked for inspection, their captains and crews to be killed. For his efforts, the inspector would be rewarded with half of the confiscated cargoes.

"We also found these on his person, sir," the arresting officer said. "It appears that this also comes from Koxinga."

Caesar snatched the papers from his hand and peered at the official with suspicion. "Fetch Ting-bin," he snapped at his secretary.

Once Ting-bin had translated the document, of which there were many copies, it turned out to be an edict, obviously meant to be circulated on the island.

"To all my loyal subjects," Caesar read. "I strongly recommend that any of my subjects who have settled on Formosa in the course of the years return to the Empire of China with some haste, so that they can live here in peace."

Caesar turned purple. "'My subjects.'" he snorted. "Again, he talks about the Chinese on Formosa as *his* subjects. Who the bloody hell does he think he is?"

He strode across his office, the paper crumpled in his hand. He waved it in the face of the frightened official.

"You may convey to your employer that he does not have the privilege to intimidate or threaten our subjects, Chinese or other. And tell him, that he would not stand for it if we were to issue edicts in areas under his rule. Tell him that we can only conclude that he seeks to damage the good relations that we have built up over the years."

* * *

Word of Koxinga's edicts spread across Formosa in no time. The Chinese merchants, convinced that Koxinga had the means to carry out his threats, panicked. They loaded their junks with venison and fish products to sell in China before the one hundred days elapsed. The sudden surplus caused prices of the local goods to drop drastically, which tempted the village leaseholders to buy large amounts of deer meat and many hides cheaply.

Within weeks, an oversupply of Formosan goods ensued everywhere. Warehouses on both sides of the strait filled to excess, and prices dropped even further. The leaseholders who had renewed their leases on credit soon found they were unable to repay their debts. A credit crisis loomed.

Trade with China was now badly affected. Months would go by before another trading junk sailed into Formosa, but it would bring only rice or other daily commodities and not the precious silk, gold, and silver that the company so desperately needed to sustain itself. Goods such as fabrics, tobacco, and ceramics became increasingly scarce and therefore expensive.

To make matters worse, the Manchurian court in Peking had issued an edict forbidding any traders in China to do business with Koxinga's people. The penalty for disobeying the edict was death. The effect of the Peking edict was devastating. The small amount of trade that remained between China and Formosa now came to a complete standstill. Goods that were once prized had become worthless. The shelves in the stores selling day-to-day commodities ran empty, and many Chinese could scarcely feed themselves. Everyone on the island suffered.

In order to counter Koxinga's growing dominance in the region, the VOC made an effort to form an alliance with his enemies. An envoy was dispatched to Peking, offering military support to the Qing in their fight against Koxinga. The Dutch believed that if they negotiated with the Manchurian court and did them the favor of obstructing Koxinga along the sea coasts, relations with the Qing court would improve. Perhaps they might even be able to strike a deal to open trade with China under the new, foreign dynasty, and establish a trading enclave such as the Portuguese had.

The mission failed. The envoys were cordially received, but the court officials were no fools. They had become weary of the numerous, persistent requests for trading rights from the Western powers, in particular from the Dutch. The newly installed Manchu emperor wanted to gain full control over the Chinese empire, and he already perceived the presence of the Portuguese on Macao as an affront. He had absolutely no intention of letting the Dutch gain even a foothold on Chinese soil, not even in return for their allegiance in their fight against Koxinga.

With his extensive network of informants and spies, Koxinga was aware of the Dutch envoys and their business in Peking, but he was too preoccupied to act on the provocation. Encouraged by a number of military successes, his troops finally launched a massive attack on the city of Nanking and succeeded in its capture. Koxinga entered into lengthy negotiations with the Qing generals for their surrender. What he did not know was that the enemy was only procrastinating, waiting for reinforcements they had secretly sent for. Koxinga waited. It was his one mistake: he waited too long.

Qing troop reinforcements arrived in large numbers, surrounding Nanking. Koxinga's men did not have a chance against the overwhelming odds, and all they could do was flee. His army was practically annihilated, his military organization shattered. Many of his senior officers met their death under the executioner's sword, and thousands of his soldiers were killed. What remained of his army made their way back to Amoy, where Koxinga and his men retreated to count their losses.

His defeat was compounded by a betrayal more terrible than Koxinga could have imagined. In order to protect his own interests, one of his senior trading partners had chosen to defect to the Manchus, taking with him valuable, detailed knowledge of Koxinga's secret trading network. At a time when the mainland Chinese were forbidden to have any dealings with Koxinga on pain of death, the man's treachery was lethal. Armed with a fresh list of Koxinga's trading partners, the Manchus mercilessly persecuted those who had for years done business with Koxinga and his father before him. They paid for their loyalty with their lives.

14

Merchant, Interpreter, Intermediary

FREDERIC knew that Caesar was under enormous pressure from Batavia to break the crippling trade embargo. Caesar was renowned for his uncompromising nature, which appeared to get worse over the years. The tone that Koxinga had struck in his letters to Caesar had done nothing to improve matters. Caesar refused to make any concessions toward Koxinga, which led to a stalemate that showed no sign of relenting. For almost two years, Koxinga held the company – and the Formosan economy – in a stranglehold. The whole population suffered, many families hardly able to feed themselves. Following Frederic's advice, Caesar finally agreed to lower the tolls and taxes, but it made little difference. As long as the trade embargo was in place, matters could not improve.

The council in Batavia finally lost its patience with Caesar's ineffectual methods, deciding that he was incapable of dealing with "the Koxinga issue." After three years of governorship, they replaced him, and appointed Frederic in his stead, in the hope that he would be able to deal with the problem.

It would have been surprising if they had not appointed Frederic, considering his experience and his many years on Formosa. After all, he had been on the island since 1648 – give or take a year or so when he was intermittently governor on Deshima – and there were few men who knew the place and its people, in all its complexities, as he did. It was Caesar himself who had suggested that they appoint Frederic, having worked closely with him for three years.

To the VOC, the fact that Frederic was not Dutch but a Swede mattered little. The company employed many foreigners, even in its upper echelons. And Coyett had grown up in Holland. Frederic's family had arrived there at a time when the country had only just recovered from the war with Spain, which had lasted a staggering eighty years. Almost four generations had been subjected to relentless and persistent religious persecution from the Catholics, and this had left its mark on the people. Yet the ending of the war had its consequences: the new peace that now reigned had given way to fierce competition among the European powers for maritime trade.

The regents of the Seventeen United Provinces of the Netherlands realized that if they wished to achieve anything in the spheres of world trade, they would have to tolerate the presence of foreigners within their borders. The harbor city of Amsterdam had become home to the VOC's headquarters; and with its established, powerful stock exchange, it attracted businessmen and traders from Europe and beyond, creating a cosmopolitan hub of a city in which many a language could be heard. As a result, the country's economy thrived.

Frederic's father had been working in Stockholm as a goldsmith when he was recruited as master of the mint in Amsterdam. The family moved to the liberally minded Dutch city, where they settled in well.

Having left Sweden at an early age, Frederic barely remembered the country of his birth. Looking back now, he would be the first to admit that his aristocratic antecedents and the connections that came with them had benefited his career. Nonetheless, he had proven his own worth long ago. It seemed that travelling was in his blood. His oldest brother grew up to become a diplomat, while his other brother moved to Moscow, where he owned a glassblowing factory.

Frederic had been the first Swede to visit both China and Japan, where the VOC had discovered his talents in dealing with their Asian trade partners. Where so many of his Western colleagues failed in the face of the numerous cultural differences, Frederic seemed to have an uncanny ability to know the minds of his Asian counterparts. The company had recognized his value, and before long he had managed to make himself indispensable.

Frederic did nothing in haste when he took up his new post. He allowed himself to be counselled by his members of staff, including Chief Merchant Van Iperen. He regularly consulted Antonius Hambroek and the chief surgeon, Christian Beyer, who, like him, had been on Formosa for years, and with whom he had formed a firm friendship. Apart from that, Beyer was the only one who knew Koxinga personally. Frederic used Beyer's knowledge to his advantage, questioning him in detail in order to get to know as much about him as possible.

He started a careful correspondence with his superiors in Batavia and the *Heren Seventien* in Holland, breathing life into an idea that had previously been rejected as preposterous and unacceptable: that they reopen trade negotiations with Koxinga through a Chinese intermediary.

Frederic was well aware that his predecessors had regarded Koxinga as a rebel, a pirate, and a downright nuisance. They had all stubbornly refused to see him for what he had become: the de facto ruler of southern China. The company had become so accustomed to using force in its pursuit of trade that its officers had almost forgotten their diplomatic skills. In their arrogance – and ignorance – they had neglected to approach him in that capacity, and he felt that it was time that they did.

The idea was adamantly rejected at first. But after considering his arguments, Batavia finally agreed. They left it up to him to find a suitable candidate to appoint an intermediary to smoothen relations between the VOC and Koxinga. They had little to lose: it might be the only way to break the embargo that threatened to cripple the company. And besides, an intermediary would be able to inform them of Koxinga's activities.

Frederic soon discovered that it was no small feat to find the right man for the job. The candidate would, after all, have to meet quite a number of qualifications. He would have to be a Chinese resident of Formosa, someone who was very familiar with the company, who had influence and connections with both the local merchants as well as with the powerful Zheng family, and be eloquent and persuasive enough to act as envoy for the company. And it had to be someone they could trust.

That last requisite for the job proved to be the biggest stumbling block of all. Frederic did not trust the Chinese merchants, many of whom he thought were deceitful. The company had had trouble with double-dealing Chinese intermediaries from the moment they had set foot on Formosa.

After considering his options, Frederic appointed the prominent merchant and leaseholder He Ting-bin, who had interpreted for the company for years. The man spoke their language, was familiar with the workings of the VOC, and, most important, he was well connected with the Zhengs. Still Frederic hesitated, as he did not fully trust Ting-bin. The man had the reputation of a greedy opportunist, of someone who always acted in his own interest, and, mostly, of a man without scruples. It was a delicate decision, but in the circumstances he was left with no alternative: Ting-bin appeared to be the best man for the job. It was a calculated risk he was willing to take.

"Governor Coyett, this is an unexpected request," Ting-bin said, affecting a puzzled frown. "You wish for me to meet with Lord Koxinga to negotiate with him on behalf of the company?"

"Yes, Ting-bin, that is exactly what we are asking of you." Ting-bin's solemn expression did not fool Frederic. He knew Ting-bin well enough to know that he was delighted by the proposition that had just been put to him.

"That will be a difficult undertaking, Mr. Coyett. From what I understand, Lord Koxinga is away often on his fighting expeditions. He is a busy man."

"You can start by negotiating with his family. I hear that his uncles often deal on his behalf."

"Indeed, the Zhengs are very powerful, Mr. Coyett. But do you believe, considering the incidents in recent months," he cocked his head, coughing apologetically, "that they will agree to allow your company to trade again freely?"

"It will take considerable effort, I'm aware of that. But I am of the opinion that we should try, Ting-bin. The question is, will you do it?"

"Excellency, I am most honored that you have come to me with this request, as I am only a simple merchant of humble means."

Frederic smiled at the statement coming from someone so full of self-importance.

"You understand that you ask a great deal of me," Ting-bin said. "You may have heard the rumors that Lord Koxinga is not a man known for his reasonable character. Some would even describe him as ... dangerous." He uttered the word with drama.

Frederic narrowed his eyes at him. "We both know that you had extensive business contacts with the Zhengs prior to this, so he cannot be as dangerous as all that. And besides, you will be duly rewarded should you succeed." He let the words hang for a while, counting on the man's avarice.

Ting-bin tried to look inscrutable, but Frederic saw the glint in his eyes. "You will allow me a day to consider your proposal, excellency?"

"Of course," he said, upon which Ting-bin bowed and took his leave. Frederic leaned back in his chair, his hands behind his head, and sighed. So far Ting-bin had reacted just as he had predicted. Not for the first time, he wondered to what extent he could be trusted.

* * *

Following two days of sharp negotiations on his reward, Ting-bin agreed to act as the company's trade envoy. After the governor had briefed him extensively and believed him to be ready to the task, Ting-bin finally sailed for Amoy.

Ting-bin had not told the governor that his thoughts on the mission differed somewhat, and that he had a strategy of his own. Knowing the mind of Lord Koxinga far better than Coyett, he believed he would never get anywhere with mere talks. He would have to do it the Chinese way if he wished to succeed at such a diplomatically sensitive mission. Just as his people had done for millennia among themselves in order to get things done, Ting-bin planned to pay tribute to the Zhengs. He would have to bring lavish gifts and letters of flattery as well as the promise of money if he wished to achieve anything.

Yet Ting-bin knew the company policy on the payment of tribute. The Dutch found it a feudal and dubious, if not costly, practice. And even if they did allow the payment of tribute, it was only done toward kings and emperors of nations that held the promise of lucrative commercial contracts. And this was where the Dutch were making a serious mistake. Lord Koxinga may be no king or emperor, but he was powerful and influential nonetheless, and believed himself worthy of tribute. He knew he would demand tribute for even entering into negotiations with the VOC in the first place.

The governor would never have agreed to what he was about to do. But Ting-bin felt he had no choice: if he wanted to achieve anything at all, then tribute there would be, and he planned to do this on behalf of the VOC, even if no one at the company had any knowledge of it. The only problem was that he did not yet know how.

When the yacht carrying Ting-bin sailed into harbor at Amoy, he was received cordially but with suspicion. He was well known to the Zhengs, with whom he had had commercial relations for years. It was the fact that he arrived on a vessel bearing the flag with the VOC crest that confused them. He knew he would have some explaining to do.

Initially he was received by Koxinga's uncle Feng, who regularly did business with him on Koxinga's behalf. Later he was taken to Lord Koxinga himself, surrounded by an entourage of family members, Feng and his cousin Cai included. They regarded him with interest as he went through the rituals of greeting and subservience, bowing reverently.

"My lord, you are in good health?"

Koxinga grunted with a brief nod of his head. "Did the Dutch doctor Bei'er provide you with ingredients for my medicine?"

"Indeed he did, my lord. I have also brought you letters and gifts from the Dutch governor...."

"That big-nosed turtle egg!" Koxinga snorted, his eyes blazing. "This man Caesar, he insults me. He makes a mockery of me. Who does he think he is?" He spat onto the floor venomously.

Ting-bin merely blinked: Koxinga's reaction hardly surprised him. He was aware of the way Caesar had responded to Koxinga's edicts and demands.

"Sire, the governor Caesar has gone. He has recently been succeeded by a new man, by the name of Coyett. Frederic Coyett. A Swede by birth."

Koxinga narrowed his eyes at him. "You are telling me this Caesar is no longer governor of Formosa?"

"Yes, sire. The new governor, Mr. Coyett, is a just and reasonable man, and of far superior intellect than Caesar. He has been in Formosa for many years. The man is well respected, both by the Chinese merchants and the Dutch. His superiors as well his subordinates are full of praise for him. You will find it far more agreeable dealing with this man."

"Dealing with this man? Is that why you come here under his banner? Did he send you?"

"Nothing misses your quick eye, my lord," Ting-bin said. "It is true that he has asked me to act as intermediary. The company – and the island's economy – is suffering. The strong control your lordship holds over their trading activities is crippling their company, and the new governor has recognized this fact. He wishes to pay his respects to you in our own traditional way." He gestured to one of his men, who handed him a leather folio containing the letter. Cai stepped forward and took it from him, retrieving the document from its interior.

"Read it please, cousin," Koxinga said. Cai obliged willingly. The letter had been carefully worded, laced with the necessary terms of respect. Coyett had gone to considerable effort in writing the letter, consulting Ting-bin on the terms of flattery and was not satisfied until the fourth draft. Ting-bin had been suitably impressed. In the letter, Coyett introduced himself and let it be known that he hoped for a long, pleasant, and fruitful relationship. He stated that he trusted that his lordship would accept the gifts that Ting-bin had brought with him and concluded with the humble request that the lord of the imperial surname consider reopening trade so that both sides would once again come to prosper.

"After all their arrogant behavior?" Koxinga asked, suspicious. "After the way they have treated my people? Harassed our ships, stole my pepper? Forced my sailors to labor on their ships like slaves? No. I won't even think of it." He snorted with contempt at the idea.

Ting-bin had to think fast. If he failed in his mission, he would lose great face in front of the new governor. And in front of Lord Koxinga, who would simply dismiss him and send him back to Formosa.

"I agree with you, my lord, that these atrocities are unacceptable. But you could use this to your own advantage. You can decide the terms. And besides," he paused momentarily before telling the lie, "the Hollanders are willing to pay for the privilege. They would agree to pay an annual tax, in the form of money or goods, as you may wish." He knew that the governor and his staff were likely to twitch in convulsions of anger if they knew what he was up to.

"There is no mention of this in his letter," Koxinga noted.

"No, sire, this was done purposefully to see if you would be willing to negotiate trade without the annual tribute," Ting-bin said quickly. "The governor has asked me to convey that part of the message orally."

"Unusual," Koxinga grunted.

"They are but ignorant barbarians, my lord. They do not know our civilized ways, even though, I must say, this new governor makes an effort worthy of some praise."

He saw Koxinga exchange glances with his uncle Feng. Ting-bin knew that the VOC had products in their warehouses that the Zhengs would love to get their hands on. Materials for weapons, for one. An annual cash payment would also be more than welcome. He could fund his expensive military campaigns with the money.

"Very well," Koxinga said. "I will need a few days. I want to discuss with my counsellors whether it would be in our interest to reopen trade with the Dutch. Indeed, we shall set the conditions. And if I agree, we will determine the amount of goods and taxes to be paid, which will not be negotiable."

Ting-bin smiled pleasantly. He had won a small victory, even if it meant that Koxinga only agreed to consider the request. Yet his stomach churned. He had started the lie; now he would have to see it through. The question remained, how? But he trusted that the answer would come to him in time. It always did.

After two days of deliberation, Koxinga agreed to reopen trade with the company, with Ting-bin as intermediary. He had an official letter drafted that set out the payment and conditions. First of all, the company was to pay him an annual tax of 5,000 silver taels. Secondly, the Dutch were to supply him annually with 100,000 lead arrow shafts as well as one ton of sulfur. And finally, the company was to cease its harassment of his ships and people with immediate effect.

Ting-bin boarded his junk to Formosa, his mission successful. On the first evening of the sea journey, when he was alone for the first time, he removed Koxinga's letter from the leather pouch and read it through carefully. Koxinga had just accepted a fictitious offer that the VOC had never actually made. He knew that Coyett would not agree to Koxinga's conditions. He held the letter to the candle and watched as the flame eagerly lapped at the paper, the blackness devouring the elegant characters hungrily. Then he dropped it onto the tin tray, where the fire extinguished itself to leave nothing but soot and ashes. He had plans of his own.

* * *

Frederic was delighted when Ting-bin reported that Koxinga had agreed to reopen trade.

"You have the documents upon your person?" Van Iperen asked excitedly.

"No, Mr. Van Iperen. I do not bring documents. Lord Koxinga insisted that I convey his message to you orally."

Frederic raised an eyebrow. "Most odd." He shrugged his shoulders and turned to his secretary.

"Van Doorn, are you up to this momentous task?"

"Yes, sir! Of course, sir!" Van Doorn eagerly sat down at the corner desk and took up his quill, ready to begin. Frederic nodded at Ting-bin, who cleared his throat to formally deliver his official message.

"Lord Koxinga, Zheng Chenggong, lord of the imperial surname and supreme military commander as appointed by the son of heaven, wishes to express his gratitude for the gifts and complimentary letter that your excellency has provided him with. He was quite pleased with your gracious letter, and most gratified that your excellency has been appointed governor. He was under the impression that your predecessor, Cornelis Caesar, was still in office. At first he was most irate, sir, that I came to talk on behalf of the VOC. Even the mention of Governor Caesar angered him."

"I understand he and my predecessor were not on very good terms. It is understandable. Mr. Caesar was merely trying to do his job."

"Of course, sir. I explained that you, sir, as the new governor, are a man of honor, reason, and great intellect, and that you are more willing to listen to someone as humble as myself."

Frederic had to smile at Ting-bin's exaggerated flattery. They waited while Ting-bin reached for the cup of tea that had been placed in front of him, and sipped from it at leisure.

"After several days of discussing the matter with his council, Lord Koxinga agreed to end the restrictions that are hampering your trading activities. However, he has set four conditions. First of all, his lordship must insist that you write to your superiors in Batavia to make sure that the company stops attacking his ships and ill-treating his crews throughout Southeast Asia." He waited patiently for Van Doorn to take it all down. Ting-bin once again reached for the porcelain cup and took his time to drink.

"Second, Lord Koxinga complains about the long delays that are caused by the toll inspections on goods leaving Formosa. He says that with the newly added tolls your honorable predecessor has imposed, the inspection time has become too long. This causes losses of perishable goods and loss of revenue for the Chinese merchants. His lordship requests that the situation is reviewed and the inspection time shortened."

Frederic nodded, taking it all in as he paced the floor in front of him.

"Also, his lordship complains that the Chinese merchants experience long delays in the payment for their deliveries. He insists that payments are made promptly and that receipts are issued upon the arrival of goods at the warehouse." Secretary Van Doorn scribbled furiously, the feathers on his quill taking on a life of their own.

"Finally, his lordship has one more grievance. Your honorable predecessor forced the Chinese merchants to sell their building materials such as timber and roof tiles at low prices, under the pretext that they would be used for company buildings. However, it has come to his attention that your predecessor used the materials for his own private housing. This he finds quite unacceptable. Of course, he trusts that your excellency would never resort to such practices and that he will pay fair prices for these commodities in future."

Frederic listened attentively to the various conditions that Koxinga had set as a prerequisite to resuming trade. But he was no fool. Somehow, he suspected that Ting-bin had not told him the full story, and that he could well have added things to further his own interest, especially those last three points. That was the problem with having nothing in writing: Ting-bin would have the freedom to make up things as he went along. Yet he only had his story on which to base his decision.

Following several heated discussions, the council of Formosa accepted Koxinga's proposal as relayed by Ting-bin, which seemed reasonable enough. Frederic sent Ting-bing back to Amoy with gifts and a letter of response, expressing their pleasure in the reopening of trade.

"Your decision greatly pleases us, as it will result in improving the well-being of your people as well as our subjects on Formosa," Frederic wrote, determined to be clear on the sovereignty the VOC had over the Chinese people on Formosa. "We will make every effort to ensure that the Chinese merchants of Formosa will enjoy better treatment and that the abuses carried out under Mr. Caesar's administration will be a thing of the past."

Eight days later, Ting-bin returned to Formosa with the news that Lord Koxinga was gratified to learn that the VOC had agreed to his terms. Koxinga had ordered that declarations were to be put up in Amoy and the Pescadores to inform his subjects that they were once again free to trade with the Dutch on Formosa. Trading junks sailed out once more, and commerce gradually picked up, much to everyone's relief.

But Frederic found that he did not have everything in hand. In spite of his assurances toward Lord Koxinga that Batavia had agreed to the conditions he had set, it appeared that the company had captured yet another of Koxinga's junks fully laden with goods, bringing it to Formosa as its prize.

According to Ting-bin, Koxinga had been livid when word reached him of the incident, and he had summoned him straight away.

"Lord Koxinga was quite upset, excellency," Ting-bin told him. "He threatened to have the trade declaration notices torn down and to block trade once again. I had to use all my skills to placate him."

The incident infuriated Frederic just as much. Frustrated, he tried to control the damage.

"This must have been an isolated incident, however unfortunate. It's likely that not all Dutch captains were fully informed of the newly reached agreement."

Ting-bin nodded in agreement, saying he had used words to that extent to Koxinga. Then he handed a letter to Frederic, written, Ting-bin said, by Lord Koxinga's own hand.

Frederic read the letter closely. "I plan to once again enter into battle with our enemy, the Manchus, to the end of liberating my country," it read. "Your company possesses certain goods which are produced on Formosa and that I require for this purpose. These goods are whitewood, feathers, and fish intestines for the purpose of making arrows. I trust that you will provide these goods as a token of your trust and cooperation."

Frederic frowned upon reading the letter. There were several things that struck him as odd. This was the first time that there was any mention of payment or a request of goods. Koxinga's previous correspondence had not contained any such reference. If Koxinga had truly expected that they provide him with such supplies, then why had he not stated this before? Moreover, the tone of the letter was different from any of the others he had read. The wording was brusque and direct, and did not even come close to the rather flourishing style that was his custom. He noticed another thing too. Koxinga now spoke of "your rule" while he had always spoken of "his" subjects, or "his" people. Something wasn't quite right.

In spite of his misgivings, Frederic had to admit that Ting-bin had succeeded in getting what he wanted. Trade had resumed, and the island's economy had picked up almost immediately. Prized goods such as gold, silk, and pepper once again reached the shores of Formosa, and revenues went up steadily. Everyday goods once again filled the shelves and became available at reasonable prices, and the general mood on the island became one of optimism.

The company started to do so well, in fact, that its revenues in 1658 were higher than ever before. Everyone praised Frederic for his vision and the results that he had achieved, especially as he was only just into his second year as governor of Formosa.

"You have my utmost praise, sir," his aged secretary said once the figures were known. "It has truly been an excellent year. We made a neat profit, unexpectedly so, considering the circumstances. My compliments, indeed."

"I cannot take all the praise for myself, Van Doorn," he said. "I didn't do it all on my own."

Van Doorn couldn't help but smile. "It is my humble opinion that you are doing a splendid job, sir," he said sincerely.

"There are those who would be at odds with you on that," Frederic said with a humorous twinkle in his grey-blue eyes. "Nicolaes Verburgh, for one."

His secretary chuckled. "Ah, yes. A very jealous man, that Mr. Verburgh." He opened his mouth to say more but thought the better of it. More likely than not he didn't think it wise to criticize his superiors, even if they were no longer around.

Coyett saw him hesitate, and smiled. "Verburgh is a bitter man," he conceded, a frown creasing his brow, knowing that a bitter man could be dangerous. They both knew that Verburgh had been trying to discredit his successors ever since he returned to Batavia.

Van Doorn nodded, obviously relieved that the governor shared the sentiments he had voiced.

"Let us gossip about my predecessors no more, Van Doorn," he said good-naturedly. "We might have made record profits according to these ledgers, but we still have to keep Koxinga at bay ... and off the island, if at all possible."

Van Doorn's face sobered. They had all had heard the rumors, which were gathering in frequency and strength. But whether they should believe them or not, no one could say for sure. One thing was certain: they now knew they had to be wary of Koxinga. He was not, however, the only person they had to keep an eye on. Ting-bin was another.

As a precaution, Frederic had given instructions to his customs inspectors to keep a close eye on Ting-bin whenever he returned from Amoy or the Pescadores. His caution proved to be justified when one day one of his administrators brought an indignant Ting-bin before him. One of Ting-bin's junks was found to be filled with official edict notices from no other than Lord Koxinga himself.

Frederic summoned another interpreter to have the notices translated straight away. It took the lesser qualified man a while before he had finally completed the task, and Frederic was disturbed by the message the notices conveyed. Ting-bin insisted that the notices were circulated on the Pescadores and Amoy just to inform the tradesmen that trade with the Dutch was once again permitted. This wouldn't have been a problem, if it hadn't been for the tone of voice: "In the course of time, I have come to acknowledge that my people on Formosa have suffered as a direct result of the embargo that I set in place. I feel I must aid them in these troubled times and it is for these reasons that I reopen trade, so that merchants, tradesmen, and all my other subjects are able to earn their living as before."

"God's wounds," Frederic cursed, scowling. "This man keeps proclaiming that he has sovereignty over Formosa. Again, he speaks of 'his' subjects." It only confirmed his doubts on the authenticity of some of Koxinga's letters. He walked toward Ting-bin, his face only inches removed from his face. Ting-bin's expression froze.

"You should know," he said, his voice low. "Pray tell me what the meaning is of this declaration? Precisely what does Lord Koxinga hope to achieve with this? Is it merely intended to provoke us, or were these duplicates meant to be circulated here, on Formosa? You had better explain."

Ting-bin blinked. "Don't worry, your excellency," he hastened to say. "These notices have only been put up in Amoy and the Pescadores. They are not meant for Formosa."

"Then for what reason did you bring them here, if they are not meant for Formosa?"

Ting-bin blinked again, forced to take a step backward, intimidated by Frederic's sudden proximity.

"This declaration, your excellency, has been brought to you with the intention that you should approve it, and only upon your approval, would it be put up for the people of Formosa to see. It is different from the one that has been put up in Amoy and the Pescadores," he added.

Frederic looked at Ting-bin intently, still within inches of the man's face. "You just told me that this edict was only meant for Amoy and the Pescadores," he said with a deceptively soft voice. "Now you are saying that there are two versions. That one is meant for Formosa, upon my approval."

"Ah, yes, your excellency," Ting-bin said, paling. "That is correct. Only upon your approval, of course."

Frederic looked at him, narrowing his eyes with suspicion. Had Ting-bin just changed his story to placate him? What else had he been lying about? He remained where he was, his eyes boring into the Chinese merchant's. Ting-bin had no choice but to meet his gaze.

"Out of the question," Frederic snapped. "Permission refused. Van Doorn, have all these destroyed," he ordered with a gesture of his hand. His secretary came forward immediately, taking hold of the stack of notices with disdain.

"That will be all, Ting-bin," he said, dismissing him.

Ting-bin, who had managed to remain fairly inscrutable during the interrogation, now seemed at a loss at the meeting's abrupt ending. He remained where he was, wavering.

Frederic tried to hide his amusement. His ploy had worked. "Is there anything else I should know?" he asked. It was clear that Ting-bin had expected more. Further questioning on his inconsistency, a reprimand, an accusation perhaps?

"N-no, your excellency." The goatee beard on his chin bobbed up and down as he spoke.

"Very well. Let us both get back to our duties, Ting-bin. You must have plenty to do."

Ting-bin hastened toward the door, threw him a hesitant look as if to be certain that the conversation was truly over, and was gone.

Frederic sat back in his chair and rubbed his chin thoughtfully. He now knew for a fact that the letter from Koxinga in which he had asked for the military supplies had been a forgery. He was also convinced that Ting-bin could not be trusted. Yet he had to be cautious. The council in Batavia had expressed that they were most pleased with his efforts, and the *Heren Seventien* were delighted that he had managed to break the embargo.

Profits were up, and the general mood on the island had changed for the positive now that the people were able to buy the goods that had been previously been scarce. And they had Ting-bin's mediation to thank for it. Still, Ting-bin had lied to him. But why? He was hiding something. It simply didn't make sense.

Within a year of Frederic's appointment as governor, Susanna fell ill with severe dysentery, so the comings and goings of his trade intermediary became unimportant. Together with Balthasar he stood at his wife's deathbed, watching in agony as her dehydrated body breathed her last.

Deep in his heart he had always known that she would not be blessed with a long life. Ever since his return from Deshima she had been of ill health, losing weight at an alarming rate. During the past months Christian Beyer had warned him repeatedly that she would be highly susceptible to the many infections that were rife among the Dutch colonists. If it had been up to him, he would have locked her up inside their house; but Susanna would have none of it. Beyer had tried everything to save her, but it was a battle that he could not win.

During the last hours of her life, she had insisted that he remarry, if only for Balthasar's sake. He had remained strong for her and given his assurance that he would, but now that she was dead he felt completely lost. He had so much to thank her for, and now that he was governor, he needed her more than ever.

Susanna was buried at the cemetery on Pineapple Island, not far from Fort Zeelandia. Frederic tried to contain himself for Balthasar's sake, but upon seeing the stricken look on his son's face, he no longer had any control of his emotions. After the church service, Antonius and Anna had embraced him, both their faces awash with tears.

Life without Susanna continued, however unbearable at first. Frederic arranged for a governess to take care of young Balthasar, and he threw himself onto his duties by way of distraction in order to obliterate his grief.

Now that trade had picked up and life on the island took on more normal patterns, he had more time for matters that needed attending to, such as the Christian mission. By this time, there were ten reverends on the island. His predecessor Verburgh had often been in conflict with the men and had taken a hard line against them, but Frederic was a God-fearing Christian who had a great deal of respect for what the missionary men were doing for the native villagers of Formosa. He did realize that there were exceptions among them: some were unscrupulous rogues without a conscience and who abused their station, but generally speaking they were gentle men of God who had proven their worth. He believed in giving them free rein in performing their duties, and would often listen to their various grievances. But some of the missionaries could be a bit too zealous for his taste, even quite meddlesome. And there had to be limits.

Antonius Hambroek, now head of the mission on the island, had become a good friend of his during the years that they had spent on Formosa. He and his wife were a tremendous support for him after Susanna's death, and they truly went out of their way to make sure he and Balthasar were well. Yet Antonius could be headstrong and principled, like many of the others.

Having enjoyed a proper education in Dutch seminaries, the missionaries were often put to work for other purposes, simply for the reason that they were better educated than the majority of the colonists. One of Antonius' predecessors had even led a battalion, after which he had become known as "the fighting reverend." But like so many of his predecessors before him, Antonius had difficulty reconciling commercial profits with the work of the missionary, which was to spread and teach the word of God. And he was not alone in this.

Frederic frequently received Antonius in his office, together with Reverend Johannes Cruyf and Reverend Petrus Mus. They would complain to him about the company's "exploitation" and "mistreatment" of the locals and Chinese, often pleading for tolerance on debts on their behalf. Frederic admired them for their loyalty and dedication, even if their views conflicted with the interests of the VOC, as the reverends couldn't always see it from the company's perspective. Moreover, in their work as teachers of young, impressionable aboriginals, many of the reverends were unaccustomed to having to answer to superiors, especially if they were stationed in more remote areas. Only God stood above them, or so they liked to believe. And that attitude often led to conflicts, as they were, after all, employees of the VOC.

What troubled the reverends most was that many aboriginals, even if they had converted to Christianity, continued in their idolatry, still worshipping their old gods and symbols on a large scale. Petrus Mus had voiced his concern about this before, and Frederic guessed that this would once again be on the agenda for this morning's meeting.

"Sir?" Frederic looked up from his ledgers to find Van Doorn peering at him over the brim of his spectacles. "The Reverends Hambroek, Mus, and Markus Masius are here to see you, sir."

"Ah, yes. Please have them come in," Frederic said. "And Van Doorn? Would you join us to register the meeting, please?"

"Naturally, sir," said the old man, who fetched his things and took his seat at the corner desk.

"Gentlemen, do be seated," Frederic motioned to the three men.

Markus sat slumped forward in his chair, both his hands clutching the armrests and looking much older than his actual thirty years. Antonius settled into his, totally at ease. Petrus Mus, severe and unsmiling as always, leaned forward, eager to speak.

Frederic took a deep breath. He disliked Mus. He thought of him as an overly zealous, irritating man who loved the sound of his own voice too much. He was invariably the first to speak at these meetings.

"Your excellency, I believe you will remember that I told you that our native Christians converts are continuing in their idolatry."

Frederic regarded him without comment and folded his hands in front of him.

"We regularly catch them at their old pagan rituals, Mr. Coyett." Mus licked his lips with relish.

"We have discussed this among ourselves and agreed that this is not acceptable. The matter has traversed across a certain boundary, Mr. Coyett. Something has to be done to remedy the situation."

"Surely this is not too much of a problem?" Frederic countered. "These people have had their habits and rituals for thousands of years. We should not expect them to adapt to our ways entirely. This was their land before we came here."

"Mr. Coyett, you don't understand!" Mus rose to the occasion with passion. "They worship their old pagan gods. We cannot accept that they worship other gods. These people should be punished. They should be made an example of in that there is but one God. Once they have accepted our true faith, they should turn their backs on their *heathen ways*." He slapped his armrest to emphasize the last two words.

Frederic sighed and turned to his friend, the older and more experienced of the three.

"Antonius? What are your thoughts?"

Antonius uncrossed his legs in a relaxed manner, straightening in his chair.

"Well, truth be told, many of our converts do retain their old ways. They believe that they can practice two religions, just in case, in a manner of speaking," he said.

Mus inched forward to the edge of his chair.

"Sir, it is my opinion that many of these ... that these unfortunate brethren of ours have converted simply to satisfy the authorities and for the benefits that their conversion brings. They are deceiving us. They are deceiving God with their heinous sins!"

"What would you do in their place?" Frederic asked. "You are forgetting that the Hollanders have just fought a long war against the Spanish over the issue of faith, among other things. For as long as I can recollect, the Dutch have been pressured, no, persecuted if their beliefs deviated from that of the pope."

Mus was silent, sulking.

"Reverend Mus, we know firsthand what it's like to be bullied into adopting a faith that is not truly our own. If you insist on this path, then we would be no better than the Spanish Catholics." He paused, standing up and resting one buttock on the heavy oak desk. "Pray tell me, Reverend Mus. If the Catholics had offered to feed your starving family, would you not convert to the Catholic faith or would you let them starve?"

Mus turned red at the analogy. "Mr. Coyett! You do not understand. If we don't act, we will undermine God's authority. They must be taught sincerity if they are to call themselves Christian." His eyes gleamed as he brought his point home. "What's more, it will undermine the company's authority. These heathens are making a mockery of us this way." He took out his handkerchief with a flourish, making a show of mopping his brow as if the converts were responsible for his discomfort.

"You should not take their actions so personally, Reverend Mus," Frederic said.

"With due respect, sir," Mus said primly. "If I am not mistaken, you have taken upon yourself the governorship of this island and sworn to do your duty to God and country. Is it not our duty to ensure that all those living on the island are brought the knowledge and faith of Christ, and to save these blind and miserable worshippers of Satan from the jaws of that infernal wolf?" The man was standing now, raving.

"Sit down, Mr. Mus! You forget your place. I have no need for your castigating sermons here, or to be reminded of my duties. Be warned," he said, his irritation with the man growing by the minute.

Mus sat down again and fell silent, mopping his brow with a wronged expression on his face. The much quieter Markus Masius still sat hunched in his chair, avoiding the governor's eye. Antonius sat up, compelled to try and save the situation as he had done so many times since Mus had arrived three years ago.

"I think what my esteemed colleague here is trying to convey to us," he said with measured tones, "is that the situation is indeed beyond our grasp. We cannot allow them to make a mockery of Christ and God as openly as they are doing. Reverend Mus' words ring true. We cannot condone how the locals are conducting themselves. They are actually gathering in public places, in broad daylight for all to see, to perform their old pagan rituals." He looked down at his large hands, folded on his lap in front of him. "The point is," Antonius continued, "that what's happening is profoundly demotivating for all the missionaries working in the company's service. Many are threatening to leave for other work if the company doesn't take corrective measures. They believe they are being made fools of and feel that they are losing face, if you'll forgive the use of the Chinese expression. Frederic, if they turn their back on their duties, and the good Lord knows we need all of them for the schools, then we will find ourselves in a situation."

Frederic regarded the three men as he leaned against his desk, his arms folded in contemplation. "I see. Reverend Masius, is there anything you would care to add?"

The soft-spoken Masius shook his head. "No, sir. Not really, sir. I think Reverend Hambroek is right."

"Very well, gentlemen. I have listened to your arguments and I now see that this is a practical problem that needs to be addressed. As senior minister, Reverend Hambroek and I will further discuss what will need to be done. You will be given due notice of my decision. I am grateful for your time."

The reaction of Mus and Masius could not have been more different. Masius, who had barely uttered a word and sat through the meeting shifting in his chair, shot up from his chair, eager for it to done with. Mus sat frozen in his chair, obviously struggling with the dismissal and frustrated at being excluded from further discussions. He twitched his head and finally got up, his pride hurt. Antonius pressed his lips together to hide a smile.

After discussing the matter with Antonius, Frederic realized that he had to do something. He decided to make a proclamation, as a warning to those who actively engaged in blatant, open idolatry. He did this with some reluctance, as doing so was not without risk. Besides, he and Antonius both knew that the effect would only be superficial: the old rituals would continue, but the converts would now be more careful about performing them openly. The proclamation was no more than a compromise: its intention was to stop the public idolatry that so offended the missionaries, while it would placate the mutinous men of God. This way, Frederic attempted to save face for everyone.

Once a month the proclamation was to be read in public; and it was affixed to public places such as the doors of churches and schools, translated into all the languages of the island so that no one could pretend ignorance of the matter. Idolatry in the first degree was to be punished with whipping and banishment, while lesser sins would be punished accordingly.

The light mutiny that had begun among the reverends gradually subsided, and the men of God returned to their duties once more. Just as he expected, the locals continued to worship their old gods, but they did so more discreetly, at least making sure that the Dutch authorities would not catch them at it. Those who were careless enough to be caught doing so openly were made an example of, but the few punishments Frederic had to mete out were generally light.

Then, however, the very thing happened that had made Frederic reluctant to make the proclamation in the first place. News of the edict travelled along the Southeast Asian trade routes and reached the Japanese port of Nagasaki. The Shogunate, caught in a mood of extreme xenophobia, suspected that the Dutch had similar plans for Christian converts on Japanese soil. It flexed its muscles in warning.

In the Netherlands, the reaction of the *Heren Seventien* was one of alarm. This was something that the VOC could well do without: it could not afford to alienate the Shogunate and risk losing their trading privileges with Japan. Frederic soon received a letter from the supreme council saying that the restrictions on religion were "not in the spirit of the Hollanders," and demanded that the proclamation not to be put in effect. After all, they said, the United Netherlands were still recovering from the religious persecution suffered under the Spanish, and they all felt it was wrong to pursue the path he had taken.

Secretly, Frederic was relieved. He quickly saw to it that the readings of the proclamation ceased and that the punishments stopped. To placate certain missionaries, the affixed notices were left up, but they were not replaced when they became torn, faded, or illegible – or disappeared altogether.

At the urging of his family and friends and with the mediation of his sister-in-law, he decided to marry again. Two years after Susanna's death he married Helena de Sterke, a young, childless widow who personified in every way the meaning of her Dutch surname: strength. She was a comely woman of good character, who was more than happy to be able to care for young Balthasar. She may not have possessed Susana's exquisite porcelain looks, but Frederic enjoyed her company for her wit and down-to-earth nature. Apart from that he was delighted that Helena got on well with his son, who readily accepted her as his stepmother.

Meanwhile, he continued to keep a close eye on Ting-bin. Now that Frederic knew Ting-bin could not be trusted, the merchant interpreter was no longer given any information of significance and was seldom invited to join meetings of any importance. Frederic was aware that Ting-bin had enough knowledge on their military situation to harm them, should he decide to provide Koxinga with such information. He would have to try and control the damage as much as possible.

Soon, the company clerks reported discrepancies in Ting-bin's payments, finding them far higher than necessary. Coyett had Ting-bin brought in for questioning, but Ting-bin seemed to be prepared.

"Excellency, as you question my expenses, perhaps I should bring to your attention that I have saved your honored company a considerable amount of money."

"I don't know what you mean. Exactly what are you trying to say?" Frederic asked.

"Well, your excellency, the father of Lord Koxinga, Zheng Zhilong – I believe you know him as Nicholas Iquan – used to receive several thousands of taels from the VOC for the privilege of trading with him." He sniffed, extracting a silk handkerchief with which he wiped at his nose before continuing. "Since his father was taken captive by the Manchus, these payments stopped. However, Lord Koxinga finds that the company still owes him for the years that the payments did not take place."

"That's preposterous," Van Iperen snorted. "We don't owe him anything of the sort!"

Ting-bin pretended not to hear the chief merchant's outburst. "Excellency, Lord Koxinga has calculated that the company owes him one hundred and thirty thousand taels of silver."

"What? That can't be! The company –"

"Excellency, pray let me continue," Ting-bin went on sweetly, again ignoring van Iperen. "I suggested to Lord Koxinga that he must be mistaken, for according to my knowledge – and you know I have my sources – the company never paid his father such payments, and certainly not on a yearly basis. I mentioned that there might be some confusion, as the company did pay tribute to his esteemed father and his mandarins in the form of gifts on several occasions. This was during the early trade negotiations when your fellow countrymen first came to Formosa."

Van Iperen scowled. "This cannot be," he said. "The company doesn't pay tribute. It never has. And, anyway, how could you know this. You would only have been a child then. This is utter nonsense!"

"Well, perhaps you might wish to look into the records from that time, Mr. van Iperen. The Hollanders have always been so meticulous in keeping their *dagregisters*, and you will find that this matter was recorded. I have seen this with my own eyes."

"Very well, Ting-bin, we will examine the registers and we will let the matter of your expenses rest for now," Frederic said, realizing how craftily Ting-bin had distracted the conversation away from the accusations that faced him by throwing this piece of information at them. He was frustrated that he was not informed of any of this, and he would have to look into it. As if he didn't have enough on his mind as it was.

Before long he discovered that Ting-bin seemed to be exporting large numbers of lead arrow shafts and a sizeable cargo of sulfur, which was primarily used for the production of firearms. When confronted on this, Ting-bin informed him that Koxinga had commissioned him to buy the necessary war supplies, explaining that these goods were unobtainable on the mainland. Frederic, who was used to Ting-bin's entrepreneurial ways, could see no reason to object, as he did not seem to be doing anything illegal. The company was still too dependent on the man for his diplomacy and he didn't want to risk damaging relations at this stage. But it did make him wonder.

Then he started getting numerous complaints from the local merchants that Ting-bin was making them pay additional taxes on the export of local products.

"We simply cannot afford to pay export tolls to both the company and Merchant He Ting-bin," one of the merchants said. "He won't let our boats leave until we have paid him the taxes he requires. I have been forced to reduce the number of trips across the strait. It is proving too costly with the double taxes."

Frederic had Ting-bin summoned once more. "A number of individuals have complained to us that you are harassing them, forcing them to pay tolls for their trade junks to leave the island. You know very well that this is not permitted. What do you think you are doing?"

Ting-bin looked offended, shaking his head as if the whole idea was too ridiculous for words.

"These are but malicious rumors that come from those who wish me ill," Ting-bin responded. "There is no truth in this, your excellency, I guarantee you."

"Somehow I would have expected a riot on our hands if this were true. Right now, I'll have to take your word for it. I must warn you, however, that you should not even entertain the thought of collecting such tolls. Only the VOC has that right."

"Your excellency, I know this. And I would never do such a thing," Ting-bin said with a pained expression.

In spite of such warnings, Ting-bin continued his dubious activities of pressuring tradesmen to pay him additional taxes. Those who were not able to pay him were given credit at exorbitant interest rates. Other Chinese, who had caught wind of what he was doing and saw that he got away with it, had begun to do the same. Frederic was left no choice but to act.

After a formal charge, Ting-bin was dismissed from his job as company interpreter, fined, and his position as village headman was dissolved. He had been lucky that his punishment was relatively mild, and only because of the role that he had played in reopening trade.

The following day, Ting-bin was gone. Apparently he hadn't taken any chances and had fled the island, probably, thought Frederic wryly, with far more on his conscience. By disappearing, he left behind him a stream of heavy debt. Debts owed to the company, but also to moneylenders, both Chinese and Dutch, from whom he appeared to have borrowed. They all complained woefully to Frederic that they had lost their money, and that they had been ruined.

One thing Frederic could not understand was how Ting-bin had managed to get into such debt. What had he needed the money for? His spending patterns and lifestyle over the past months had remained the same; Frederic could not find the answers there.

Ting-bin's disappearance concerned him, especially as he had been privy to rather sensitive information. He knew, for instance, how many troops were stationed on Formosa. He knew the number of marine ships that lay anchored along its shores, and he might even have detailed information on the arsenal. He did not want to take the risk, and decided to warn Batavia of the dangers. In his letter to the governor-general, he warned that a former Chinese company employee, who had been fired, had disappeared. He suspected that the man might provide Koxinga with sensitive military information on the island, and he ended the letter with an official request for more troops.

It took several months for the council in Batavia to respond, and even then, the answer from Governor-General Maetsuijker was courteous but non-committal. "We advise you to be continuously on your guard against Koxinga's schemes, in that they may not harm our interests in any way, and we fully rely on your wise precautionary measures to deal with the situation. However, we find it unnecessary at this stage to send more troops, as we have every faith that you will be able to manage with the resources already at your disposal." And with that, Maetsuijker placed the responsibility firmly back on Frederic's shoulders.

15

His Father's Fleet

KOXINGA's hands trembled with suppressed anger as he read his father's letter. It had been eight years since he had last heard from him. And now, with the threat of violence hanging over his head, Zhilong had complied and finally written to him. Eight years! In his indignation, Koxinga was almost unable to take in the contents as he read.

His father wrote that the Manchus wished to negotiate a truce with him, promising him high stations and grand titles if he ceased his fight against them. It was clear that his father had written the letter under duress, and this is what hurt him the most.

Koxinga had known for some time that the Qing generals were growing frustrated that they still had not succeeded in neutralizing him. On every occasion, his armies had managed to elude them. The Qing court had even turned to diplomacy, trying to lure him with promises of great wealth, his father's freedom, and the grand title of duke if he capitulated.

He had refused, time and time again.

But this was different. Now the Qing had resorted to stronger measures. It seemed as if the Manchus had calculated that his sense of filial piety would be enough to make him listen to his father, especially with the thinly veiled threat that his family would be in danger of their lives if he did not comply.

Koxinga felt resentful at the hypocrisy of his father's pleas for filial piety and family loyalty, considering the fact that he had not communicated with him in all those years. In an emotional state, he wrote back, knowing that the letter would be intercepted and read by the Qing officials. His answer was brief and bitter. He wrote that he would never be like his father, that he would never be able to betray his country and emperor as he had done. Besides, he did not intend to make the same mistake his father had made by trusting the Manchus, and concluded by stating that he intended never to give up his fight.

A month later, he learned that the circumstances of the house arrest that his family were held in had deteriorated markedly, the threat of execution coming closer every day. He now knew for certain that they must have intercepted his letter. They had indeed counted on his filial piety, but they found that they had made an error in judgement. Frustrated in their attempts to neutralize Koxinga by threatening his captive family, the generals had probably begun to wonder what use the Zheng hostages still were to them.

Koxinga kept himself busy, throwing himself into his campaigns with a passion in an attempt to shut out the feelings of guilt that had taken hold of him like a rampant weed.

Several weeks later his lieutenant informed him that his half-brothers had arrived and had requested an audience. Koxinga was so astounded by the news that he immediately agreed to see them. He dismissed all of his men, even Cai.

"*Gege*! Older brother!" Du dropped at his older brother's feet, blubbering with relief upon seeing him after their perilous journey. Shiyin just stood there listlessly, looking wan and exhausted.

Koxinga recoiled at the sight of them. He had not seen them for more than eight years. If he had run into them on the streets, he would not have recognized them. This was a mistake. At that very moment, he knew that he should have refused to see them. This was exactly what he had wished to avoid. He had closed his heart to his father many years ago, and now his half-brothers had come to rekindle the emotions that he had thought banished from his heart. But now those feelings had reared their ugly heads and they were as painful as they had ever been. There was now no turning back.

His brothers treated him with reverence, formally even. He was their oldest brother after all, and they had been separated for years. Under normal circumstances they would have greeted him in a more familiar way, but it was clear that they held him in awe. To them he was the lord of the imperial surname, the warlord who still resisted the generals of the Qing, and little more than a stranger to them.

They told him everything. They spoke of their situation as hostages in Peking, which had become so unbearable that they decided to come to see him. With the assistance of a few loyal members of the defected Black Guard, the two of them had managed to slip away unseen to make their way south to meet him.

Koxinga snorted, immediately suspicious. "They sent you. Where father's letters failed, they now think that the sight of my brothers, my own flesh and blood, might inspire in me what loyalty I have left for him."

"No, *dage*, older brother. Please listen to me," Du pleaded. "We have come to you to ask you to reconsider your position. Our father admires your undying loyalty to the Ming emperor, as do we. But now you are putting us all in great danger. You must reconsider. Help us. He is your father. We are your family. If you come with us to capitulate, they will set us free. Is it not your filial duty to your family to —"

Koxinga nostrils flared in anger. "Don't you dare lecture me on my filial duties. Father turned his back on us all when he defected. He is a fool. Does he not see that this is a trap? The Black Guard is as corrupt as anything. Those men are willing to work for anyone who would pay them well. Should I walk into the same trap he did back then? I am not the fool he is."

"*Gege*," Du sobbed, desperate. "You have changed. You don't even remember your family anymore. You don't understand. Please. They will kill us all if you take this path."

"They killed my mother, after raping her first," Koxinga growled, finding it hard to control the intensity of the emotions that came flooding back at the memory. "They also killed my little sister. They are my enemy! I could never go to their side," he said, gnashing his teeth. Then he turned his face away from his half-brothers. "You think I have forgotten my own father. I have not. I could never. I wish I could forgive him, but I cannot. Do you think this is easy for me? Do you?"

Du was silent, his shoulders heaving as he wept.

"Uncle Bao is coming with us," the younger Shiyin blurted out.

Koxinga stared at him, slowly shaking his head in an attempt to deny what he had just heard.

"Uncle Bao? He is going back with you? He is surrendering?"

Shiyin nodded, not trusting himself to speak. "They will probably kill us if we return without you. It is you they want, *dage*," he tried. "If you come with us...."

"No!" He was still shaking his head in denial. "Stop it. Stop it! I cannot. I made my decision years ago. I cannot do what you ask of me." He looked at the two youths, their faces already marked by the hardships that they had faced. "When Father took you with him when he defected, you were only children. This has nothing to do with you. That is what makes it so sad." He covered his face with his hands, overwhelmed by doubt and remorse. He grimaced, tried to harden his resolve. "I regret that I cannot. Please go now. Leave me. I will write a letter to father for you to take back."

His two brothers stared in disbelief.

Unable to look them in the eye he turned his back on them, shamed. Their shoulders drooping, Du and Shiyin left him, deflated by his decision. They had barely left the building when he rushed at the writing desk in front of him, upturning it with a roar of anguish. The delicate wooden top splintered as it smashed onto the stone floor, while the porcelain drinking cup that had sat upon it broke into a thousand fragments. Then he picked up a chair and threw it at the door through which his brothers had just disappeared.

* * *

Two days later, Du and Shiyin started on their return journey to Peking, their mission a failure. They considered fleeing, but found that their older brother was right: the members of the Black Guard who had escorted them to Amoy had been paid to bring them back to Peking; their loyalty was bought with cold, hard cash. Just as Koxinga had suspected, the court officials had been aware of their secret mission all along, the success of which would only be in their interest.

With them, Du and Shiyin carried a letter for their father by their oldest brother's hand. It was cryptically worded in the knowledge that it would be censored by his jailers. When the two brothers arrived back in Peking with their uncle Bao, they were immediately made to join their family under house arrest. Now that it was clear that Zhilong's eldest son held no feelings of piety or loyalty for his family, the Zhengs found their privileges of luxury removed and their limited freedom further restricted.

Zhilong read his son's letter with a stabbing pain in his heart. Between the eloquent lines, he could read of his son's bitterness and disillusion at his betrayal. His son even called him a hypocrite for the fact that he had never written to him in all those years. And now that he had, it had been under duress, only to plead with him to capitulate in order to save his skin.

The words of accusation cut Zhilong like a knife. He made himself read the letter over and over, again and again. He welcomed the pain, knowing that he deserved it, allowing it to wash over him like salt water into an open wound. His son, his firstborn, had been right all along. What he had done was wrong.

He knew what he had to do. Whenever there was no one around, he took up his brush and wrote to him. He no longer pleaded for Koxinga to surrender or side with them, or to think of his family. Instead, he wrote of the gut-wrenching remorse he had felt when he had read his letter. He wrote of the mistakes he had made in his life, and of the lies that he had believed coming from the mouth of their enemy. He implored Koxinga never to believe a word the Manchus might say. He informed him of all that he knew about the Manchu military operations. Finally, he told his oldest son to fight his enemy to the end.

With the help of his family and servants, Zhilong made every effort to have the letter spirited away, well hidden from the eyes of the ever-watchful sentries and sharp-eyed censors who normally read every single stroke he put on paper. The letter made it out of Peking. It even made its way out as far south as Fuzhou. There, carefully folded and tucked away in the seams of a garment, it was finally discovered, its contents revealed to the Qing authorities.

When word of the smuggled letter got back to court, the Manchu generals were livid. They stripped Zhilong of all his titles and rank. Next, the house arrest imposed on his family was changed to imprisonment. Frustrated and angry that their ploy hadn't worked and that Zhilong had even attempted to incite his son against them, they spared no effort in humiliating him. They also made sure that none of the Zhengs would ever be able to escape.

The Zhengs' new prison comprised of less pleasant quarters than they had so far been used to. Zhilong was taken from his family and placed in isolation. He would remain in his prison cell – which was damp and moldy in summer and icy cold in winter – chained like a common criminal as he awaited his death sentence. The generals made sure that the news of Zheng Zhilong's imprisonment and death warrant were circulated widely. It was a cruel, calculated move to get at Koxinga as best they could.

But even with his family held hostage in the most terrible conditions, the Qing could still not subdue Koxinga. To the outside world, he became known as a bitter, battle-hardened commanding officer, a man without weaknesses. Not even the threat of killing off his entire family seemed to have any effect on him. But it did nonetheless.

* * *

Koxinga had listened to the news of his family's imprisonment in silence. He knew that the Manchus wanted to provoke him to react, but he did nothing. He forged an allegiance with yet another descendant from the House of Zhu, which strengthened his position considerably. He now had a large army at his disposal, as well as a substantial fleet, awaiting his orders. For a while, he decided to keep a low profile, and things appeared to quieten down. Lulled by the interlude, the Qing generals were under the impression that they may finally have subdued Ming resistance in southern China. They were wrong.

While the Ming prince moved west with his army, Koxinga ventured south to launch a major attack, using the element of surprise. His men fared well and held their ground; but the prince's troops were less fortunate.

Outnumbered by enemy forces, the prince fled, finally making his way to Burma. This was a poor choice. Betrayed by his own men, he was captured and taken back to China, where he was beheaded with ceremony to symbolize victory and the death of yet another Ming royal.

Koxinga's army suddenly found itself without backup. Qing troops were advancing on him from both the north and the west, forcing him to retreat to the coast. Now that his army had been trapped, he had no alternative but to flee the mainland and head for Kulangsu, a small island near Amoy.

Early one morning, on a misty day in March 1661, Koxinga's breakfast was rudely interrupted by one of his officers, who entered unannounced, ignoring his manservant's protests.

"Lord Koxinga," the man gushed, pushing his way forward to kneel in front of him, his eyes averted. Koxinga continued to eat, slightly vexed. It occurred to him that few men dared enter his quarters in such a manner these days. They got away with this only when matters were truly urgent.

"Sire, a messenger has come from the mainland with important tidings," the officer said. Koxinga scooped the remains of his rice into his mouth and lowered the bowl. There was something about the way the man spoke that caught his attention, but he could not quite place it. Something had happened, something big. He could feel it in his bones.

"Well, let the man in."

A lean, scrawny-looking man was ushered into his quarters.

"My lord," the man began breathlessly as he dropped to his knees, his eyes to the floor. Koxinga frowned as he recognized him as one of his spies.

"I hear that you bring news of some importance."

"Yes, sire, I do, I do. The man hesitated under Koxinga's glare." My lord, I have some unsettling news. Grave news. News of your father. He.... Word has reached us that your father has died." The messenger waited for the reaction that he knew must come. "He died over a month ago."

Koxinga's eyes stared at him as if in wonder. Delicately, he set down the rice bowl and laid the chopsticks on its brim.

"I see," Koxinga said, looking down, trying to deal with the emotional turmoil that had suddenly taken hold of him. "How did he die?" he whispered hoarsely. The question made the man cringe visibly. He stayed silent for a moment too long.

"How did he die?" Koxinga yelled.

The man cringed. "They cut him."

"Did they torture him?"

"Yes."

"Tell me what they did to him," Koxinga insisted, his voice a low rumble. The man shook his head slowly. "They cut him," he repeated.

"Show me the edict. Bring it to me!" Koxinga ordered.

The messenger looked at him, aghast. Seeing the look on Koxinga's face, he quickly backed out of the building, to return minutes later. With shaky hands he handed over the edict that detailed Zheng Zhilong's execution.

Koxinga snatched it from him, forcing himself to read it without understanding the reason. He learned that the circumstances of his father's death were even more gruesome than he could have imagined, and far crueler than anything he had ever ordered done to his own enemies.

His father had been subjected to the slicing method, an excruciatingly slow and painful death that was performed by slicing the flesh from the victim's arms, legs and genitals. Those cuts were then cauterized, closing the blood vessels but burning the flesh, only to add to the pain. In his final moments of life, before he had lost consciousness, they had performed the same horrific rituals upon his two sons, in full view of the dying man. Uncle Bao suffered the same fate. The women, his grandmother Lady Zheng and Lady Yan, had been more fortunate: they had simply been beheaded.

Koxinga dropped the edict upon reading it. As if in a trance, he stood up, picked up his bowl of rice in the palm of his hand and lifted it up to his eyes, studying the intricate patterns that lay beneath its glazing. Without warning, he hurled it against the opposite wall, the remaining rice spraying as the porcelain shattered. The sudden, sharp sound of the breaking porcelain made everyone jump. Slowly he got up, his eyes glazed over.

"My father died a long time ago," he muttered, his voice raw with emotion. "To me, my father died when he betrayed us, turned his back on us. He was an opportunist and no more than a common, cowardly pirate. I have not since been able to feel the piety that a son should feel for his father." He was breathing heavily now, almost hyperventilating as the sobs shook his frame.

"My brothers. He had no right to take my brothers with him to his death. They were boys. Just boys!"

Grief stricken, he looked at Cai and the officers standing next to him, as if imploring them to help him in his distress. They all stood rooted to the ground.

The messenger coughed softly. "His men are here now," he said with a timid voice.

"His men? I don't understand. What...?" Koxinga stared at him through a haze of tears, his hand held against his rapidly moving chest.

The messenger straightened and backed away respectfully toward the doorway, and beckoned to someone outside to enter.

Two elderly ship's captains stepped into the room, inspecting his face minutely. Then one of them uttered a cry of recognition and dropped to his knees.

"Lord of the imperial surname, chief commander! We come to you in the name of your revered father."

Koxinga flinched. In the name of his father? What nerve.... "What is it that you know of my father? Who are you?" he demanded, his face flushing with confusion. He felt his head glow with heat, and then shivered. Hot, cold, hot, cold.

"We are but two humble officers who worked for your father," one of the men answered with calm authority. "We were given instructions by your father that in the event of his death, we were to report to you to await your orders."

Koxinga gaped at him, completely baffled.

"My lord, perhaps you had better come outside and see for yourself," one of the captains said. "There is something you should see."

Koxinga followed in a daze, his thoughts no longer in control. He walked out of the building through the courtyard and rounded the corner toward the beach, facing the strait of Formosa.

What he saw left him frozen. Against the glare of the early morning sun, hundreds of war junks and trading vessels lay anchored along the shore.

"Your father's ships, my Lord Koxinga," the captain said.

"We are at your orders, my lord," said the other.

"He could not do anything while he was still alive," the captain explained. "His captors never trusted him, so he had to keep his fleet under control, for his family's sake. So his captains and their crews kept a low profile, just trading as your father bade them. He wrote you a letter. But that was intercepted...." The man's face turned somber. "But now that he's dead.... He was very clear on that, sire. We were to go to you and offer you our allegiance after his death. It was his wish. And besides, all these men are eager to finally be able to fight alongside you against those Manchu bastards. They all know that they betrayed your father."

Koxinga still stared at the sight of the junks edging their way toward the shore. The countless masts were alive with sailors tying up the sails. There were so many vessels that he could hardly make out the horizon.

"These are all my father's ships?" Koxinga repeated in awe, thinking he had not heard properly.

"Well, not all, sire. Many vessels joined us along the way. Loyalists, refugees – they all wish to fight under your banner."

"How many?"

"Five, perhaps six hundred."

He took several steps, staggering as he felt his strength drain away. He dropped onto both knees and stared at the spectacular fleet in front of him. The news of the execution of his father, whose very existence he had bitterly tried to deny for more than a decade, struck harder than he believed possible. His younger brothers and uncle Bao were dead. For a while, he had held their fates in his hands, but he had chosen to let it happen. That thought taunted him and gnawed at his conscience. Here, in front of him, was his father's naval fleet. While he had lived, his father had betrayed his trust, turned his back on him, deserted him. In his death, he had unexpectedly come to him in his hour of need. His shoulders shook as he lamented the loss of a father whom he had never truly known, and was filled with remorse for his family's death, which he had had the power to prevent.

He did not sleep that night. Images of his frail grandmother's and Lady Yan's headless bodies filled his mind. He pictured the cruel execution of his father, the details of which he had insisted on knowing. Guilt overwhelmed him when he remembered the oaths that he had made, calling for his father's death in his moments of rage. For so many years he had tried to block out his feelings concerning his father that he had convinced himself that he had succeeded. Now that he was actually dead, he knew that those feelings had just been hidden away, lying dormant in the depth of his soul, waiting to resurface.

Just before dawn, after a tortuous night and the realization that he would now never be able to reconcile with his father, he broke down and cried like a child. The following day, he issued an edict for public mourning.

With the report of his father's death came the sobering news that a seemingly endless supply of Qing troops swept further southward, eliminating the last remaining Ming strongholds. The few surviving Ming royals had finally defected, been killed, or had fled the empire.

With his father's fleet added to his own, Koxinga had more than three thousand war junks and vessels under his command. His army and navy now formed the last force of any real significance against the Qing. If he could not withstand them, no one could. It was a good thing that the Manchus did not have a proper navy. They were from the northern steppes, their strengths were their skills in horsemanship, hand-to-hand combat, and archery. Theirs was not a seafaring nation. Its people were lacking in naval experience, whereas the Chinese had sailed the seas and oceans since the beginning of the Song dynasty. They would be safe on the island of Kulangsu, if only for the time being.

While on Kulangsu, Koxinga felt strengthened by the thought that his father had come to his aid from the beyond. Once again he felt hope of being able to plan an assault on the mainland. Before the falling of darkness, he called together his council of war. He summoned his men and ships to rendezvous in the bay of Amoy, where he observed the fleet with awe. Surrounding the small island on all sides, a myriad number of masts bobbed up and down on the gentle swell of the sea. Never before had he seen a more powerful and mighty fleet in the waters of the Chinese empire, and it fell under his personal command.

16

An Unreasonable Admiral

FREDERIC read the dispatch with growing concern. It was the third dispatch he had received in less than ten days that warned of increased naval activity in the area. One ship's captain arriving from Japan had reported seeing large fleet movements along the coast. Another of the company's ships had limped in from Cambodia, its captain telling him that they had come under attack from Koxinga's "pirates." The crew told of being harassed, their attackers boasting that they would soon expel the Dutch barbarians from Formosa. He had grown used to such threats over the years: usually they were idle boasts, and not to be taken seriously.

He reread the message, and once again he could feel the hair rise on the back of his neck. Events that had occurred during the past weeks justified his sense of disquiet. He was aware that the Chinese on Formosa were getting restless. Rumors of an invasion by Koxinga grew by the day, and a growing number of Chinese had begun to sell their possessions, sending their money to relatives still in China. Many of the wealthy Chinese merchants sent their families back to China, setting an example for a growing number of Chinese laborers, even at the risk of running into Manchu troops.

The loss of valuable human resources was keenly felt by the company, but it was not what troubled Frederic most. It was the departure of the more prominent, rich Chinese that made him uneasy. It meant that they knew something he did not.

To Helen he had suggested that she and Balthasar leave for Batavia, where they might be safer. But Helen had been adamant and refused to leave, arguing that she had not become his wife to leave him at the first sign of unrest. Besides, she did not believe that it would be a good idea to remove Balthasar from his father: the boy had been through enough as it was since he lost his mother. Frederic had not pressed her any further, secretly relieved about her refusal and had embraced her warmly.

In March 1660, he was approached by one of the village headmen, who pleaded for safe haven within the walls of Fort Zeelandia. At Frederic's urging, the frightened man had hurriedly told him and Thomas van Iperen what he had learned.

"They say that Lord Koxinga intends to come to Formosa, your excellency," the man said in a subdued voice as he glanced around, anxious that no one should hear.

"We're aware of the rumors. Tell us what you know," Van Iperen said.

"I heard only yesterday, your excellency. I did not sleep. Oh, oh, my dear mother, my wife, and my brother's wife — they all wailed, all night long, out of fright."

"Yes, yes, we understand. What did you hear?" Van Iperen pressed again.

"I have no exact information as to what Lord Koxinga's plans might be, but my colleagues tell me they hear the invasion is to take place on the night of the next full moon, when the winds will change."

Frederic frowned. "Who is your source? How do I know this isn't just another rumor to unsettle us?"

"No rumor, Excellency. I ... cannot tell you more than this. Please allow me to take my leave now. My family is waiting. They are worried."

"Yes. Yes, of course," he muttered. They are not the only ones, he thought to himself.

Frederic called an urgent meeting with his staff, taking this newest warning seriously. He gave immediate orders for improvements and reinforcements to be made to Fort Zeelandia, putting the fort in a state of high alert. Messengers were sent out to the colonists in Saccam and all other Dutch settlements to warn the people there to do the same. Then he sent inspectors to examine the bastion of Fort Utrecht facing Zeelandia and cancelled all the soldiers' leave.

Under the heightened state of alert, he also gave orders to search and interrogate all Chinese still coming to the island. He even condoned torture, which was unusual for him and something he normally kept to a minimum.

Quite a few migrants were found to be in the possession of letters, in which friends and family were told to stand by for Koxinga's planned attack.

Frederic found he had no choice but to force the Chinese merchants to hand over all their grain and venison reserves, moving the supplies to the warehouses inside Fort Zeelandia. The company confiscated all horses, taking them to the company stables at Saccam. He even considered placing troops near the fields to guard their precious crops, but realized that he did not have the manpower and decided to focus on protecting the fortresses instead.

He wondered where the native population would stand in case of an invasion. Most probably they will join the side that proves strongest, he thought cynically.

For the third time in six months, he sent out a fast yacht with a dispatch to Batavia, urging the council to once again consider sending additional troops to Formosa, which he described in no uncertain terms to be in imminent danger of attack. Then he took measures for which he normally needed permission from his superiors in Batavia. He was not going to wait any longer for an approval that might never materialize. Or for one that would come too late.

* * *

Governor-General Maetsuijker had a strong sense of déjà vu when the matter was raised once more. His predecessors had also been made to consider it on numerous occasions: the inexorable need to capture Macao. The gentlemen of the VOC were still obsessed with the idea of taking possession of the foreign trade enclave, determined to oust the Portuguese and take their place as China's trading partner. They had already tried this more than once, and they had failed every single time. Yet now Maetsuijker felt that he had no choice. Due to the heightened military activity in the Formosa Strait, trade was almost non-existent and their profits had dropped to unprecedented levels. Macao still beckoned seductively, and the *Heren Seventien* had become convinced that capturing it was the only key to opening free trade with China.

All three men who now faced him had voted for the attack on Macao: Admiral Jan van der Laan, Hermanus Klenk van Odessa, and the former governor of Formosa, Nicolaes Verburgh, who had become a wealthy merchant in his own right. A skinny clerk with long tapering fingers sat at a separate desk, a quill hovering over his books to record the minutes for the *dagregister*.

The door to the meeting room opened unannounced and a young, hesitant male secretary approached the governor-general.

"*Ja*, yes, what is it, boy?" Maetsuijker muttered with some annoyance.

"An urgent dispatch from Formosa, sir. It is from Governor Coyett," the secretary said.

Maetsuijker held out his hand impatiently as the youth handed over the dispatch. He adjusted his eyeglasses, frowning as he read. "Yet another request from our governor in Formosa for troop reinforcements," he summarized.

Verburgh sniggered slightly and exchanged glances with Van der Laan. Maetsuijker's forehead creased in concentration as he read. "'... as we have received numerous signs of an imminent attack on the island. For the safety of the people and in the interest of the company I must repeat my urgent request for additional troops....'" Maetsuijker read aloud, then again silently to himself. "'I would also wish to inform you that I have taken the initiative to proceed with the reinforcement of the Fortress Zeelandia....'" He removed his glasses and rubbed his eyes. Maetsuijker had come to the East Indies as a lawyer a quarter of a century ago and had since watched the VOC transform from a commercial to a more territorial, military power under Jan Pieterszoon Coen. He, too, had played a significant role in that development. He felt tired, weary of the constant pressure the *Heren Seventien* were putting on him.

"Sir, if you will allow me?" Verburgh tried, grasping the opportunity.

The governor-general looked up at him and nodded. "Go ahead, Verburgh."

"You may remember that I was governor of Formosa for four years. I know the island and people well. I have always been of the opinion that the Chinese people are coolies and farmers, not fighters."

"Go on," Maetsuijker muttered.

"As for this man Koxinga, Governor Coyett exaggerates greatly. People speak of him as if he is a great menace, but in truth he is nothing but the son of a Japanese whore, fathered by a Chinese pirate. Likewise, the man is far too preoccupied fighting the Manchus. From my understanding, he has no genuine interest in Formosa. The troops already at Coyett's disposal should be more than adequate to withstand any attack from these pirates, even in the remote possibility that they will. I fail to comprehend why Governor Coyett is so concerned. Unless, of course," he paused again, "our governor has an inclination toward cowardliness." He said the words as if the mere possibility pained him.

The governor-general looked up at him over the top of his spectacles. "I will have you know that Mr. Frederic Coyett has an excellent track record and has so far proven himself to be a very capable governor. Might I remind you that he is the one who succeeded in reopening trade with China, something which his predecessors could not, Mr. Verburgh," he said tartly. Verburgh fell silent at the rebuke, a less than subtle reference to his own governorship.

Maetsuijker looked at his hands with a surly expression. "I do not believe that he is cowardly, and perhaps we would be wise to listen to his judgment."

Admiral van der Laan sat forward. "Sir, if I may?" he asked. Maetsuijker nodded, his spectacles bouncing on the bridge of his nose as he did.

"Allow me to investigate, sir. With your permission, I could take twelve ships to Formosa to see for ourselves if there is indeed any threat. I could even send a dispatch to Koxinga from there, and ask him of his intentions, assure him of our goodwill."

"Would you trust the word of a pirate's son?" Maetsuijker asked. "From any Chinaman, for that matter?" he asked, chuckling without humor.

"Sir," Verburgh interceded, "we should not dismiss the admiral's idea too hastily. If indeed there is a threat, something on which I seriously have my misgivings, we can stay on and defend the island. And if there is not, and this is just faint-heartedness on the part of Governor Coyett, then perhaps we could sail on and seize Macao from the Portuguese once and for all."

Verburgh and Van der Laan exchanged glances. Meanwhile, Klenk van Odessa listened to the exchange with interest, without saying a word.

Maetsuijker peered at the three men in earnest, carefully considering the proposition they had just put forward. That something needed to be done was certain. The *Heren Seventien* wanted Macao. He sighed, acceding that they had nothing to lose. Indeed, Van der Laan could evaluate the threat that Koxinga posed, and if it were a false alarm, he could proceed to Macao.

"So be it, gentlemen. Admiral, I bid you to prepare your fleet of twelve ships, as you suggest, and you will sail for Formosa, where you will evaluate the circumstances and provide assistance, where required. From there you will contact this man Koxinga and — out of courtesy and our goodwill — determine what his intentions are. Although I very much doubt whether or not this Chinaman will tell us the truth," he muttered, almost to himself. The clerk in the corner penned away furiously. "In the event that the situation is found to be secure, however, you will request additional troops from Governor Coyett to accompany you to Macao, where you will launch an attack on the Portuguese to capture the settlement.

"However," Maetsuijker continued with a frown. "Additional troops from Coyett may be obtained only upon his express permission. That will be entirely at his discretion, as governor of Formosa." He looked at the men intently. "I trust I am making myself clear?"

"Very clear, sir," Van der Laan conceded.

"As you will, gentlemen. I believe we all need a break after this. I certainly do. Van der Laan, I trust you will be busying yourself during the next few days with the necessary arrangements. You may go. You may all go." He got up and quickly ambled toward the exit, as he badly needed to urinate.

During the days that followed, the harbor of Batavia teemed with life as the fleet prepared for departure. Javanese coolies, their bare backs gleaming with sweat, formed a line to pass on the barrels of drinking water, the crates of fresh fruit, vegetables, weapons, and gunpowder to be loaded onto the warships. Naval officers shouted their instructions in Dutch with a smattering of Javanese.

Not far from where the ships were being supplied with provisions, two Chinese men, dressed in the garb of the common tradesman, silently observed the activities as they scooped noodles into their mouths and drank their fill of local brew. They had been there for the past days, chatting easily with the ships' crews in taverns, casually inquiring after the fleet's destination. They joked with the Javanese coolies in the port, throwing the odd glance at the boxes and crates to determine their contents. They soon learned everything they needed to know.

When they were satisfied, one of them paid the vendor and nodded toward his companion. They proceeded to their vessel, its papers and cargo of traded wares in good order should the Dutch authorities inspect it, and gave the final orders to depart. An hour later, two days before the Dutch fleet set sail, the lone junk sailed from Batavia in the direction of the Chinese coastal island of Kulangsu.

* * *

When Frederic was told the news by an excited sentry, he felt immensely relieved. He jumped up from his chair and hastened to the window facing west. There he saw them, still far on the horizon, twelve majestic warships silhouetted against the sun. The fleet must have narrowly escaped the wrath of the typhoon that had lashed the area a few days earlier. The seas had only just calmed again, the sky swept a clear blue.

His heart beating fast, he watched as the ships slowed before entering the bay. His heart beat faster still as he watched the spectacle unfold as the mighty ships came floating in, their masts crawling with sailors. The heavy flags of red, white, and blue, marked with the black VOC insignia, whipped proudly in the wind.

"*Dank u*, God." He breathed a small prayer of thanks in the language that he had long since made his own, and hastened down to the harbor to meet the admiral in long, eager strides.

The bay had come alive with activity as the twelve great ships bore down on the coast. Laborers were ordered into action to receive the ships while the first anchors were lowered, their chains whirring until the weights found their final depths. Chinese women and children stood in awe as they watched the admiral's flagship sidle along the quay, stepping back hastily as an officer barked at them to get out of their way. The air filled with shouted orders as the great ship finally came to rest and the gangplank was lowered. Two lithe young deckhands jumped across the gap to secure the ship's lines even before the plank was in place.

Frederic had already spotted Van der Laan, dressed in the officers' formal black robes of the VOC, his thick brown hair brushing his white collar according to the latest fashion. He saw that the man had taken pains to shave, as his face, with the exception of his rather scrawny moustache, was comparatively free of facial hair compared to those of his crew.

The admiral stepped briskly from the plank and headed straight for Frederic as he stood waiting, flanked by his officers Lieutenant Gerrit and Captain Van Aeldorp.

"Welcome, admiral. I hope you had a good journey and that the typhoon did not hamper you too much."

"Thank you, Mr. Coyett. It is excellent to be welcomed in such a warm and eager manner. No, no, the typhoon gave us a day's delay, no more." He flicked some invisible dust of his jacket with a slightly effeminate gesture.

"I am glad to see that the council in Batavia has finally come to realize our urgent need for military assistance," Frederic began as they walked together in the direction of the fort.

Van der Laan stopped and gave him a look of patronizing amusement. "Oh, but it remains to be seen whether our assistance is truly required. But we will discuss this later." He glanced around, his hands on his hips while taking in the surroundings. He ignored Frederic, who raised an eyebrow at his lieutenant.

"Perhaps you would be so good as to show me to my quarters," Van der Laan said, walking on. Frederic increased his stride to catch up with the admiral, the lieutenant and captain following right behind to stay within earshot.

"I can assure you, admiral," Frederic said, "that there is no question of whether or not the island requires military reinforcements for its defense.

And I believe that it is a matter of urgency that we have this discussion sooner rather than later. You may command your ships at sea, but may I remind you that while you are on Formosa, you answer to me. Is that clear?"

Van der Laan stopped again and inclined his head theatrically. "Of course, Mr. Coyett."

Frederic ignored the jibe and gestured to Gerrit.

"Lieutenant Gerrit will take you to your quarters, where you may wish to freshen up. Someone will fetch you for a meeting at my office within the hour." With that he turned on his heel and left the admiral in the hands of his lieutenant.

Frederic was still frustrated when he was back in his office, finding it difficult to concentrate on the paperwork in front of him, and he threw down his quill in irritation. The elation and relief he had felt earlier that morning at the sight of the Dutch war fleet had been short-lived now that he knew it might not stay to defend the island. He walked again to the window, which provided a stunning view of the harbor. The majestic Dutch warships seemed oddly out of place against the lush subtropical vegetation that lined the other side of the bay.

He narrowed his eyes and peered critically at the bay's entrance. From studying older maps, he had discovered that the entrance to the natural harbor had become decidedly smaller over the years, the currents having deposited sediments near its mouth. They had to keep a close eye on this development: another year and the company's larger ships would no longer be able to enter.

He returned back to his desk, racking his brain over what Van der Laan's intentions could be, let alone his instructions from Batavia. He knew the admiral: he had met the man ten years ago when he had fought the Chinese during the first rebellion on Formosa. He didn't like him then, and he liked him even less now. The man rarely listened to counsel, had too high an opinion of himself, and would never miss an opportunity to take credit where it was someone else's due. He had heard that he was brave enough, for sure, and had proven that bravery on numerous occasions, winning battles when the odds were heavily stacked against him. But his reputation was that of a commander who fought for the sake of fighting, and not for the cause. That made him the type of officer who liked to take chances, often risking the lives of his men. Rumor even had it that his orders had been disobeyed by subordinate officers in at least two battle incidents in the East Indies, as they believed that following those orders would prove fatal. By doing so, it seemed that they had avoided unnecessary loss of life. It was said that Van der Laan had taken the credit for himself and was later honored as a hero.

But why would Batavia send him with a large fleet of warships if they weren't convinced that it was vital? And why did Van der Laan seem so excited, almost happy? That wasn't like him at all. Usually he only behaved that way when a sea battle was imminent. He wondered, not for the first time, if Batavia had received all the intelligence that he had sent on Koxinga's movements over the past six months. He took a deep breath and berated himself for nearly having lost his temper with the admiral this morning. It wasn't a good start at all. Not if he was to convince him to keep his fleet at Formosa.

When the lieutenant arrived with Van der Laan, Frederic pretended to be busy and looked up, surprised, as if he had forgotten about his appointment with the admiral.

"Ah, admiral. Do sit down." He gestured from his chair pleasantly, without getting up. After witnessing the arrogance that Van der Laan had shown that morning, he wanted to make it clear who was in charge on Formosa.

Van der Laan took his time getting comfortable, crossing his arms defensively as he faced Frederic. Lieutenant Gerrit remained standing, placing one buttock on the ledge of the overfilled oak bookcase behind him. Captain van Aeldorp joined them and took his seat next to the admiral.

A Chinese woman came in to place a tray of teacups on the sideboard. Van der Laan's eyes followed her movements until she finally left the office. "They can barely be distinguished from the Javanese, don't you agree? Can't tell the difference. All look the same to me."

Frederic didn't respond. He thought there was a marked difference. It seemed to him that Van der Laan had never bothered to observe the Chinese and Javanese closely enough to see this.

"Van Doorn!" Frederic called out. Within seconds, the elderly secretary appeared, an eager look on his face as he took his seat at the corner desk.

"For the record, my secretary Mr. van Doorn will be taking notes of the proceedings." He looked at the admiral pointedly. "I will speak plainly with you, admiral," he said, leaning forward, his elbows on the desk in front of him. "Pray tell me what your business is here, and precisely what are your instructions from Batavia?"

"My instructions, Mr. Coyett, are to evaluate if the Dutch colony of Formosa is in any peril." He leaned back and crossed his legs. "I will have you know that as we sailed past the Pescadores, where this man Koxinga has a naval base, we could perceive no unusual activity. Some small trade vessels were lying at anchor, fishing boats offloading their catch, and perhaps a lone war junk or two, but nothing out of the ordinary." He gave Frederic a cold sneer. "Our orders are to remain here if indeed there is a threat to the island. And if not, which I seriously doubt, I am to proceed to Macao, where the company's interests are far more significant."

Frederic was stunned. "You have orders to attack the Portuguese at Macao? Now?" He almost whispered, the truth dawning on him.

Van Doorn's quill fell still, while Lieutenant Gerrit nearly lost his balance, forced to reposition his buttock on the ledge. Frederic knew that the company was desperate for the trade that the Portuguese had; this was not the first time they had attempted to take Macao. But he was perplexed at the timing. Was the Batavian council so oblivious of what was going on in the South China Sea? Was it truly prepared to dismiss the carefully obtained intelligence reports that he had been sending them?

"Yes, Mr. Coyett," Van der Laan said with nonchalance. "Those are indeed my orders. But, as I said, we have to assess if there is a threat to Formosa. First things first."

Frederic bristled at this. "The council in Batavia has seen the intelligence reports. Koxinga presides over an expansive network of spies on the island, and the greater part of the Chinese migrants are on his side. What's more, we've recently taken possession of letters from mainland Chinese that confirm what we already know. Many of the wealthier residents are relocating their families back to China. Others are selling their belongings and assets. These people are aware of something we're not. These are no longer rumors, admiral. Koxinga is still fighting a war against the Manchus in China; but more likely than not, he will lose. The Manchus are invading his country and then where will he go? Everything signifies that he will turn to this island for his refuge. Formosa falls beyond Chinese territory, and it's the nearest place for him to go. I tell you, it's more than likely that he will come here. The man has a powerful army and a large fleet at his disposal. We cannot ignore this."

Van der Laan shook his head. "Mr. Coyett, I do believe you are becoming obsessed. We scouted the area on both sides of the strait. There was no sign of preparations of war whatsoever, just some pirate ships, nothing of importance."

"But don't you see?" Frederic countered. "They must have known you were coming. Koxinga's people are all over the place: Japan, Siam, even Java. Even if your fleet's preparations for departure were discreet, he would have found out that you were coming here."

"You are not a military man, governor. I will have to presume that you do not have the experience to judge what it takes to defend an island such as Formosa. You have fifteen hundred troops at your disposal! That should more than suffice!"

"More than two hundred of them are sick," Captain van Aeldorp interjected. "They have been weakened by swamp fever, and Lord knows what other maladies are doing the rounds on this godforsaken island."

The admiral rounded on the captain, his subordinate an easy target. "Come off it, Captain. Those men are bound to recover. You have more than sufficient troops to defend this poxy island. They are trained, hardened soldiers, while these people," he gestured with his hand toward the window "are nothing but farmers, laborers. We have dealt with them in the past. They have no notion on how to fight. I think we have proven that by now. Only ten years ago, several hundred of our soldiers battled more than seven thousand armed Chinese, and we beat them in the blink of an eye." He chuckled dismissively at the memory.

"That was ten years ago," Lieutenant Gerrit countered. "Things are different now. The enemy we now face is far more dangerous. They are greater in numbers, far better trained, and battle-hardened from their ongoing war against the Manchus."

Van der Laan leaned forward, his hands balled into fists as they rested on the armrests.

"No, lieutenant, they are not different. Twenty-five Chinese are not even a match for one Dutch soldier. They are all the same: cowards with no backbone. Your own troops should be more than adequate to resist these Chinese dogs. They're not soldiers, they're a bunch of effeminate men."

Frederic stared at Van der Laan, utterly speechless. It was clear to him that the admiral was intent on sailing from Formosa, spoiling for a fight with the Portuguese instead of staying on to defend the colony.

"And what's more, I intend to write a letter to this Chinese pirate ... what's his name again?"

"Zheng Chenggong, lord of the imperial surname," Van Aeldorp said obligingly. "We know him as Koxinga. He's not a pirate, sir. He's the supreme commander of the Ming naval forces."

Van der Laan gestured dismissively. "As you will. To me, he is just the leader of a pack of dogs. I shall write him a letter. If he is as noble as you suggest, then perhaps he has the decency to reply to let us know what his intentions are. Show our goodwill. Let him know that we're keeping a perusing eye on him. That should put him off."

Frederic was beginning to lose his patience. "Don't you think that's what we've been doing these past few years?" Frederic retorted. "His father used to work for the company, he spoke our language for God's sake. Koxinga himself dealt with us for years. He knows how the company works, he knows more about us than any other Chinaman. And what's more, until recently we had a well-placed spy among our ranks who is now briefing him fully on our military state of affairs. Wake up, admiral. These waters are his territory. He is no fool; he's a clever bastard and we shouldn't underestimate him. He will never reveal his plans to us."

"I will write this letter," Van der Laan said stubbornly. "You!" he shouted, pointing a finger at a startled Van Doorn. "Come with me to my quarters and I will dictate the letter."

"You'll be requiring a translator," Frederic added helpfully, and arranged for one to be summoned. "I would not have too high an expectation of this, admiral," he said, trying to control his temper. Van der Laan whisked his cape from the back of the chair and was gone, Van Doorn trailing doubtfully behind.

* * *

Koxinga read the letter from the Dutch admiral with detached amusement. He had received several communiques from the Dutch in the past months: some were from the governor-general in Batavia, others from Governor Coyett in Formosa, and now from this visiting admiral. What intrigued him most was the fact that they were not consistent in what they were saying. Their policies regarding him didn't seem to be at all aligned. The VOC was beginning to show its weaknesses, like the finest of cracks in a porcelain cup, a prelude to worse things to come. This could be of advantage to him.

The letter was full of assumptions, some of them quite close to the truth, he had to admit, but so full of arrogance and bravado that it nearly made him laugh. It was a letter written to provoke, even threaten, but he had no intention of taking the bait. These Hollanders were such fools, he thought. Did they honestly think for one moment that he did not know what was going on? He had rewarded the two spies handsomely when they had sailed from Batavia to inform him of the large fleet of Dutch warships about to set sail for Formosa. He had immediately given orders for his own ships to lie low and stay well out of sight.

"Write a letter!" he ordered. Koxinga watched patiently as his clerk carefully poured the thick, jet-black ink onto the stone. The dark liquid ran down the stone's gradient, slowly forming a pool. He selected a brush from the selection dangling in front of him and with a practiced hand, he immersed the brush head sideways onto the stone and rolled it until it was completely saturated with ink.

"Honored and esteemed Admiral van der Laan," Koxinga began, as he paced the room alongside the clerk's desk, whose brush moved with every syllable he spoke. "We hereby express our particular goodwill and affection for the Dutch nation. Your letter was received in due course. However, we clearly see that your honor has heard many false reports and appears to have accepted them as the truth, much to my regret." He paused, looking over the clerk's shoulder and watching the characters rapidly appear on the paper. He glanced again at Van der Laan's letter and pondered for a moment on how to proceed.

"You say that you are aware of my ill intentions toward Formosa. But how can one know my hidden thoughts and tell what my actual intentions are, which have been revealed to nobody? Rest assured that we have no plans to take what is not ours to take, and that your enemy is our enemy. Our cause is the glorious restoration of the great Ming empire and to return it to its rightful people, the Chinese. For this purpose I have received the mandate of heaven."

He paused again, admiring the clerk's calligraphy, the characters emanating both strength and grace.

"You might understand that I am too busy with our campaigns against the Manchus to concern myself with a small island that produces nothing but grass. If such rumors are found to be circulating, then it may well be for the purpose of deceiving my enemies." He chuckled. "Signed, Zheng Chenggong, lord of the imperial surname, supreme naval commander of China."

He read what had been written, and nodded his approval. "Have it returned to the Dutch ship at once, so that the admiral may have his answer soon," he ordered. "It should please him," he added. He made his way to the harbor where the Dutch ship dispatched by Van der Laan lay anchored. For a while he just stood there, observing the foreign ship as it waited for his response. He scratched at the persistent itch on his left arm as he lifted his gaze to the horizon, in the direction of Formosa. Again, he imagined hearing those heavily accented words spoken to him, so long ago, in the harbor of Hirado. *I see island. Big island, not here, far away, foreign place. I see strangers, gaijin? Yes, gaijin. They not belong. Your fate, your fate is on island.* He shuddered, and tried to rid himself of the sensation that had suddenly taken hold of him.

* * *

While they waited for an answer from Koxinga, Frederic and Van der Laan avoided each other whenever they could. Any new intelligence, usually obtained by harsh interrogations of any Chinese migrant that Dutch officials deemed suspicious, was presented to Van der Laan, whose job it was to assess the information and act upon it. Much to Frederic's chagrin, he dismissed most of it as insignificant. He suspected that Van der Laan's mind was already made up, and that his thoughts were already somewhere in the waters of Macao. The admiral could often be found in his quarters poring over detailed sea charts of Macao with his senior officers, discussing possible naval strategies.

Van der Laan made a huge show of sending out ships to scout the coastline, where his men merely harassed fisherman and frightened small-time merchants making their way along the coast. He sent out scouting troops into the coastal villages to look for any signs of unrest, but the men invariably reported that they had not seen anything unusual.

Frederic was highly skeptical of how the admiral set to work. The sailors on Van der Laan's ships were tough brutes, most of them illiterate men who had nothing to lose. He held no illusion about the sort of men that they were. None of them knew Formosa. Hardly any of them were familiar with the Chinese and their ways, and he doubted if they could pick up any signs of unrest or subordination if there were any.

Antonius Hambroek, possibly closer to the native population than any of them, had told him that both the Chinese and aboriginals felt quite intimidated by the sudden, overwhelming military presence on the island. He had no doubt that any Chinese who helped Koxinga in any way would be wise enough to lie low under the circumstances.

For two months, Van der Laan and Coyett continued to argue their cases heatedly, without coming to an agreement. This led to a charged atmosphere in the offices of Fort Zeelandia. At home, Frederic let off steam in Helena's presence. Helena patiently listened to his elegy of complaints as he ranted on about Van der Laan's stubborn, inflexible stance. One day, after he had come home, she asked him how his day had been.

"And how did it go today with our Jan the Unreasonable?"

He laughed at that, and picked up on the nickname from that moment on. Others caught on, and within no time Van der Laan's troops all referred to him as "Jan the Unreasonable" behind his back.

When they received Koxinga's response to the admiral's letter, Van der Laan gloated openly. But to Frederic, who was by now well familiar with the Chinese commander's style of writing, the contents of the letter were exactly what he had predicted: non-committal, conciliatory, and vague, written in the flowery prose of the learned Chinese mandarin. To him, the letter had no value whatsoever. He asked the Formosan council for a vote, which resulted in an almost unanimous decision against the intended expedition to Macao, suggesting that they delay it until the following year.

Van der Laan was furious. He kept repeating what he so wished to believe: Koxinga's reassurance that all was well and that he wasn't in the least interested in Formosa. When Van der Laan announced that he wanted to leave Formosa to set sail for Macao with his fleet, it came as no surprise to anyone.

"I am of the belief that Formosa is in no danger of attack. I intend to focus my energy on more important company matters."

"You are making a serious error in judgement, admiral," Frederic warned him. "To leave now would be a dangerous mistake."

"In that, we obviously differ in opinion, governor, but I have my orders from Batavia. I must request an additional six hundred of your men for the purpose of taking Macao."

Frederic slowly got up from his chair and turned red, his eyes blazing as he approached the admiral. He stopped just inches away from his face.

"Six hundred of my men...." He swallowed hard, took a deep breath and recovered himself. "I do believe you are forgetting something, admiral," he said coldly. "You forget that as governor of Formosa, all troops now on this island fall under *my* command, including yours. The council has voted, and I refuse your request."

"You refuse —" Van der Laan started, but Frederic cut him off.

"I happen to be of the opinion that we will soon need all the troops we can get." He paused, trying to regain control of his temper and to give more weight to what he was about to say next.

"As governor of Formosa, it is *I* who will commission three of *your* ships and two hundred of *your* men to remain in Formosa for its protection, for as long as I deem necessary!"

Van der Laan looked aghast. "You cannot do that!" he shouted. "You do not have that authority."

"Truly not? Just watch me. I will give orders to withhold all supplies to your ships. I assure you, admiral, you won't get very far without fresh water and food supplies."

Van der Laan was fuming now. "You bastard. You cowardly bastard," he muttered under his breath.

"You had better watch your tongue, admiral," Frederic growled. For a long moment the two men glared at each other. Gerrit and Van Aeldorp exchanged glances, their expressions grim. Frederic was in no doubt that they would protect him if they thought it necessary.

Van der Laan took a swipe at a lock of hair that was now hanging in front of his blazing eyes. "As you will. Have it your way. But I swear to God you will come to regret this!" he spluttered, trembling with anger. "You're just a spineless fool!"

"Be gone with you. Get out of my sight!" Frederic spat at him.

Van der Laan gave him a despising look and left, his entourage of bewildered officers falling in behind.

"Captain van Aeldorp."

"Yes, Mr. Coyett?"

"Commission three of Van der Laan's ships. Make sure that the ships are well guarded with sufficient troops to ensure that they do not depart."

* * *

Van der Laan's significantly reduced fleet sailed out that evening in a north-western direction. At first the admiral had thought that Coyett was bluffing. He had not believed that the governor would have it in him to really take any of his ships. But his captains had returned to him to report that three of his ships had been confiscated and that access to them had been barred. So the governor's threat had been in earnest.

It had never occurred to him that this would happen. He decided not to go to Macao, as he knew that he would not stand a reasonable chance of taking the Portuguese enclave with his fleet and troops so diminished. He set out for a destination yet unknown, his entire crew suffering under his foul temper. Heavily frustrated at not getting what he wanted and still seething that he had to part with three of his ships at the governor's demand, he kept mostly to his quarters, where he continued to fume over his standoff with Coyett. The worst part was that he had lost face in front of his men. His vanity would never allow him to forgive Coyett for that.

Unsure of what to do, he remained in the area to consider his options. He knew it wasn't going to look good to sail into Batavia prematurely, with nine ships instead of twelve, and without having even come close to Macao. He realized he would have some serious explaining to do.

When his fleet did arrive in the waters of Batavia, word quickly reached the governor-general. Van der Laan was told to report to Maetsuijker within the hour. Expecting to be summoned, he had taken pains to make himself as presentable as possible during the last leg of the journey, his chin shaved and the brown locks of his hair combed back behind his ears.

He entered Maetsuijker's grand office with a practiced look of regret. Hermanus Klenk van Odessa sat facing the governor-general, his legs comfortably crossed.

"Admiral, you have returned," Maetsuijker said drily, peering up at him over the rim of his spectacles. Klenk van Odessa got to his feet, nodding at Van der Laan courteously.

"Sit yourself down, Van der Laan." The older man closed a heavily leather-bound book with a thud and pushed it away from him. It was clear to the admiral that Maetsuijker intended to hear him out at length.

"Your excellency. Mr. Klenk van Odessa," Van der Laan politely inclined his head toward the others.

"Fetch Verburgh, if you please," the governor-general told his clerk, who hurriedly exited the room to return within seconds with the former governor of Formosa. Verburgh greeted Van der Laan with a brief nod of the head and took his seat next to Klenk. Only then did Maetsuijker turn his full attention to Van der Laan.

"We did not expect you back quite so soon."

"Your excellency —" he began, but Maetsuijker cut him off brusquely.

"I take it you did not capture Macao, as you so confidently said you would."

"No, sir, I did not."

"Your explicit orders were to stay and defend Formosa or otherwise attempt to take Macao, as I recall."

"Yes, that is correct, excellency," Van der Laan replied, his tone more subdued.

"Yet you have returned to us, and it seems to me that you have done neither." With his elbows resting on the desk, he pressed the tips of his fingers together in displeasure. "It has also been brought to my attention that three of your ships have not returned. Would you care to tell me where are they?"

It was the opening Van der Laan had been waiting for, and his heartbeat quickened.

"They have been commissioned by Governor Coyett, sir. He ordered them to remain for the defense of the island."

"Yet you did not stay in aid of this defense." His superior's eyes narrowed. "I thought my orders were clear on this. Why did you return?"

"Excellency, you ordered me to make an assessment of whether or not Formosa was in any danger of attack. I have carried out those orders. My men have scouted the island's coast countless times. They scoured the island's interior for any sign of unrest, but there seems to be no sign of military threat. The only problem was that Governor Coyett seemed to be of a different opinion."

Klenk van Odessa and Verburgh exchanged glances, but said nothing. Maetsuijker threw up his hands in annoyance.

"Governor Coyett tells us in his many letters that the unrest taking place in China could result in these rebels turning on Formosa. I have seen various intelligence reports on the matter. This is why I sent you to aid him. I expect a damned good explanation as to why you have disregarded my orders. I don't believe I have to explain to you that this was an expensive expedition, admiral. And you have given us nothing for it in return."

"Your excellency, I am sorry that things went the way they did. But you must understand that matters were taken out of my hands by Mr. Coyett. You said yourself that he would have the right to deny me troops if I were to request them, but he actually commissioned three of my ships, plus two hundred troops. With the limited resources at my disposal it would have been futile attacking Macao. I am therefore not to blame for not being able to carry out those orders."

"I simply cannot imagine that Mr. Coyett has so seriously misjudged the situation."

"Alas, he is not a military man, excellency. During my stay on Formosa I have become convinced that he simply isn't capable of judging such matters. I believe he is becoming overly anxious. He surrounds himself with old, frightened men without any military experience. The governor truly overestimates the military prowess of these Chinese rebels. They are a disorganized, ill-equipped rabble that would be no match against us. You may remember that we managed to quell riots among these people in the past without too much effort. I am still of the opinion that Governor Coyett lacks the courage to deal with the situation."

Maetsuijker removed his glasses and rubbed his eyes wearily. Van der Laan quickly exchanged glances with Verburgh, who listened intently.

"As I was saying, excellency," Van der Laan went on, emboldened. "The governor sees threats where there are none. Further troops are entirely unnecessary. What's more, he has reinforced Fort Zeelandia and put the island in a state of military readiness months ago. For no real reason, as we established. As you will most likely understand, this is not without peril."

Verburgh seized the opportunity to jump in at this point. "Your excellency, if I may?"

Maetsuijker nodded, the corners of his mouth pulling downward grimly.

"You may recollect that you specifically denied Governor Coyett the funds and permission he requested to have reinforcements done to the fort. It appears he has directly disobeyed your orders."

Maetsuijker looked at Verburgh, and then up at the ceiling to his left as if trying to retrieve that particular piece of information from his memory.

"You are quite convinced you saw no unusual activity along the Formosan coast or in the Pescadores? No warships, no military activity whatsoever?" he asked, unwilling to believe that Coyett could be so wrong.

"No, sir, not one. Fishing vessels, a few merchant ships — nothing more. Not a single sign of preparation of war, not even along the Chinese coastline. We sent a communiqué to this Chinaman Koxinga the governor is so fretful about. He responded in a very courteous manner and informs us that he has absolutely no intention of attacking Formosa and has assured us of his goodwill. I have a duplicate of the translation on me." He retrieved a folded document from his jacket and handed it to the governor-general, having come well prepared.

Maetsuijker peered at it dubiously. Van der Laan threw another conspiratorial glance at Verburgh.

"Also," Van der Laan went on, "I have letters from our Chinese employees for your excellency. They wish to share their grievances with you about Governor Coyett. They complain about his harsh treatment of the Chinese settlers – even the merchants. Our governor has a tendency to arrest them on a whim, and his methods of questioning are," he shuddered dramatically, "despicable. Apparently he is so obsessed with this supposed threat from Koxinga, that he feels that such actions are justified." He handed the letters to Maetsuijker, who took them rather reluctantly, as if afraid of their contents. Van der Laan told the governor-general nothing of the intelligence reports that Coyett had shown him over the past two months, which indicated that Koxinga might indeed pose a risk.

"Many Chinese settlers are leaving the island, sir, due to the panic that Mr. Coyett has caused. The company cannot afford this. We need those people," Van der Laan said, his expression grave.

"We must also face the fact that Governor Coyett had no influence over this Chinaman he appointed as trade intermediary. Not only did the man disappear, there is also the likelihood that he has defected to Koxinga with information that might compromise us. If this is the case, then Mr. Coyett has caused us more damage than good. He shouldn't have trusted the man; he should have had him locked up while he still could."

"I'm afraid Admiral Van der Laan may be right," Verburgh said. "With regard to this intermediary, I don't think he handled things well at all."

"If I may be so bold, sir," Van der Laan added, taking up his cue. "I have always questioned Mr. Coyett's appointment as governor to Formosa. The man is not even a Hollander but a Swede. One never knows for certain where one's loyalties lie, as a foreigner."

The governor-general bristled at this. "I will have you know that Mr. Coyett's family has an immaculate reputation and is well connected with various houses of nobility in Europe. I would not have recommended that he get the job if I had been in any way undecided as to where his loyalties lie."

Van der Laan inclined his head in a gesture of admission. "I stand corrected, sir," he apologized. "Nonetheless, these rumors, they are no more than that. We have been hearing them for years, and nothing has ever come of them. They have been spread by ill-meaning Chinese to further their own interests. You know how devious these people can be."

"What about the vice governor, Jacobus Valentijn? How does he think on the matter?"

"He is much influenced by Mr. Coyett, I am afraid, sir."

"Do you think he would be up to the task of governor?"

Van der Laan shook his head and looked doubtful. "Not in my opinion. With all due respect for Mr. Valentijn, he does excellent work in Saccam. But he has no real leadership qualities," he said, remembering how strongly Valentijn had sided with Coyett. That was something he would not forget.

Maetsuijker sighed and tossed the letters onto his desk. "Perhaps you are right that Mr. Coyett was mistaken. Whatever the case, this has been a very costly and disappointing expedition. I am not at all happy at this turn of events, and will have to answer to the *Heren Seventien* on this. They will most certainly want to know why we wasted precious company resources on this nonsense." He got up and looked down at the globe by his desk.

"Very well. This situation requires remedying, we have to do something. As you well know the *Heren Seventien* wish to see results. I have explained the problems to them many times, but they will not listen. We have no option other than to take Macao from the Portuguese by force. And in order to achieve this, we will need those three ships. We simply cannot afford to leave them idle in Formosa." He slapped at a fly that was bothering him, coming too close to his face for his liking. Discouraged, the offending insect finally gave up and landed on the globe instead, somewhere in the middle of the Indian Ocean.

He walked toward the window and heaved a sigh. "It has every appearance that Governor Coyett cannot function without the constant reassurance of additional ships and troops. Perhaps we shall have to relieve him from his post and appoint someone who can." He took his seat once more, daunted by the number of letters that lay scattered on his desk.

Van der Laan coughed into his fist to hide his delight, glancing at Verburgh. What he saw on his face was a barely suppressed malicious smirk. The former governor of Formosa seemed to be firmly on his side. Either that, or he just hated Coyett's guts.

With bated breath the three waited for the governor-general to speak. Klenk van Odessa had listened to the discussion with growing interest in silence, and sat unmoving, expectant. Klenk van Odessa had been a senior member of the Batavian council for some years. Van der Laan knew him to be a man of ambition. If Coyett were to be removed from his post, the new vacancy might just be a logical next step in his career.

Maetsuijker turned to him, his mind apparently made up. "At this moment I believe that Hermanus Klenk van Odessa is the most suitably qualified officer for the function. I propose that you be appointed to the post of governor to Formosa, if only temporarily. I expect you will wish to prepare yourself for the journey."

17

Crossing the Strait

KOXINGA carefully weighed the information that his spies had provided him with. He now knew that the Dutch naval fleet had sailed back to Batavia, with the exception of the three warships that had remained at Formosa. Due to the vigilance of his spies, his own fleet had had enough time to scatter and lie low before their arrival, and the Dutch had left without them being any wiser.

His spies had done excellent work, especially He Ting-bin, first under the guise of company interpreter and later as trade intermediary. The intelligence that Ting-bin had provided on the military situation on Formosa was invaluable. Ting-bin had informed him of the number of troops on the island, the number of cannons, and especially how large the grain reserves were that were stored within the warehouses of Fort Zeelandia. He had been well worth his reward.

He wondered again at the stupidity of the Hollanders, who were so gullible and easily assured. He had not even had to lie in his letter to their self-important admiral. The truth of the matter was that he had no fight with the Dutch. He felt no particular ill will toward them. On the contrary, they had provided him, and his father before him, with lucrative business. The Dutch were of no real consequence to him; but now they were in his way. Moreover, they had colonized Formosa by force. If he needed Formosa as his base from which to launch his attacks on the mainland, then he would seize it from them.

Of course they would have to leave. He would, however, give them the chance to leave the island in peace, unless, of course, they refused to depart. Only then would it mean war, but he doubted that it would come to that. And even if it did, the Chinese people on Formosa would support him. Over the past ten years he had made sure an effective underground network had been set in place in order to undermine the Dutch colonists, so that his people could aid him in his hour of need. Still, he felt confident that this wouldn't be necessary. He recalled the prophecy made so many years ago. *The strangers will leave, one day. Then island your destiny.*

Now that the Dutch fleet had left the area, the threat it posed had gone. Yet the danger on the mainland was growing with every passing day. Bands of marauding Manchus had raided and captured the towns and villages of southern China, and the coastal area of Fujian was lost to them. Time was running out fast.

The outlook for the few remaining Ming strongholds had become increasingly grim. Even though they were not a naval force of significance, the Qing were learning quickly. Their navy was rapidly recruiting sailors and mercenaries from various parts of Asia, including Chinese, their loyalties as lissome as bamboo, shifting to the side of the victorious Manchus. They had already begun attacking his ships that were harbored at Amoy and Kulangsu, which had been their refuge. Those islands were no longer safe. Apart from that, Amoy was small, mountainous, and unsuitable for farming, and therefore unable to sustain his army for any length of time. That meant they were reliant on food supplies from the mainland, and that also posed a problem, as it was becoming more and more difficult to obtain the day-to-day essentials.

Whole villages in Fujian, loyal to his cause, had been a constant source of rice, vegetables, cooking oil, and poultry. Koxinga had always paid the farmers well for these items; but now the Qing troops were cracking down on anyone who dared supply his armies. Night curfews had been set up around the villages, and troops regularly patrolled along the coast in an attempt to stop supplies reaching the rebels on Amoy.

It would be a matter of time before they would encircle the island and then the standoff would begin, inevitably to end in the starvation of his men. He had no choice: they would have to retreat to the Pescadores while they still could.

He knew that the Pescadores would be able to offer them only a temporary haven. The isles had always fallen under the sovereignty of China, and the Qing would stop at nothing to drive them away. Formosa would be their last refuge, and he knew it.

Yet he still delayed their departure from Amoy and Kulangsu, as if leaving those islands was akin to admitting defeat, and the end of his dream. He refused to give up hope that he and his men would one day return to the mainland to restore the Ming.

He often thought back to the day that the emperor had given him his mandate to defend the dynasty. That memory still burned brightly in his mind, and it was something that had fired his spirit for many years. He had once sworn to defend his country to the death, and he intended to do so.

He had already held several secret meetings with his officers on the possibility of heading for Formosa. Some of his advisors who knew the island were reluctant to go there, counselling Koxinga that the place was full of swamp fever and other diseases, and that the *feng shui* was unfavorable. But he had already made up his mind, painfully aware that there was no alternative. Moreover, Ting-bin had provided him with valuable information on Formosa, describing it as a vast island with fertile fields that would bring rich yields and great opportunities.

Once the food supplies on Amoy became critical, he called his officers to hold counsel once more. "If we take Formosa, we could build our ships and manufacture our weapons there, and make it our base," he argued, looking hard at his men to bring his point home. "I realize that Formosa has been occupied by the Hollanders, but they have no more than a thousand soldiers in their forts. There is no shortage of food on Formosa. The fields are abundant with rice and vegetables, and we would be able to feed ourselves to become strong once again. Only then can we focus on the enemy possessing our homeland."

"What about the Hollanders' guns?" one of his generals asked, bold enough to question him. "They say that their forts are defended by powerful guns that can rip open a man's gut from several *li* away."

Koxinga looked at him, hard. "Don't be a fool," he retorted. "Even if they were in the possession of such guns, they are vastly outnumbered by our army. Besides, our people living on the island will help us. If the Dutch are fool enough not to surrender upon our arrival, it will only be a matter of days before their forts fall. The Dutch fleet has left the area, so it is vital that we cross the strait now, before the coming of the monsoon."

His officers put the issue to the vote, and the majority voted for taking Formosa.

Koxinga thus addressed his officers. They stood waiting for him in the courtyard of the old office building that his father had constructed so many years before. They looked at him, their expressions grave. They all knew that they had to face the truth, a truth that they had so far been unwilling to accept. Sobered by the reality of the situation but proud and straight-backed, he faced the hardened, grim-faced men who had stood by him for so long.

"We are here because we have been driven from our land by our enemy," he began. He saw their despondent faces, and realized that leaving China would be as hard for them as it was for him. "You also know that we cannot stay here. Our enemy has surrounded us and will not stop until they have driven us out. We can do nothing if we remain here."

The men nodded in unison. This kind of rhetoric they understood.

"Tomorrow, we shall sail for the Pescadores to regroup with our many allies. But you all know that we will not be able to remain there either. The Pescadores, however beautiful, fall under Chinese sovereignty and we will not be safe from our enemies even there." He paused to look at his men one by one, choosing his next words with care. "From there, we will eventually sail for Formosa. But we will not be sailing to Formosa as exiles." He lowered his voice to a growl as he paced in front of them, his hands behind his back. "Our homes and graves of our ancestors are there," he pointed in the direction of the mainland, "in China, for it is our country! We shall return!" The men nodded, loudly echoing his last words.

"But we must first take Formosa. To do that, we will have to drive away the foreign devils, these Hollanders. For Formosa, by right, is ours!" He paused dramatically for his words to have effect.

One of his officers picked up the cue, raised his fist and shouted in passionate agreement, his call taken up by all the others. "It is ours! It is ours! It is ours!"

"It is ours!" Koxinga repeated fiercely, and their voices subsided. "And we will make it our base. From there we can continue our struggle against our enemy, the northern invaders now in possession of our homeland!" He paused again with deliberation. "Tomorrow we leave for the Pescadores. My son," he motioned to his oldest son. Jing, now a young man in his early twenties, quickly dropped down on one knee in front of him.

"Jing, you are to remain here in Amoy with your men and ships to hold off the enemy for as long as you can. You will be responsible for the food supplies for our troops."

"Yes, Father," the youth said without hesitation. Koxinga nodded, pleased. He had no doubt that Jing would give his all to defend Amoy, just as he had always defended the Ming. All his life he had dedicated himself to this cause, and he expected no different from his oldest son. Little else mattered.

On a cold, rainy February morning in the year 1661, Koxinga's ships left Amoy and sailed for the Pescadores, thirty-one miles west of Formosa. As he had predicted, Jing's men had been forced to land along the Fujian coast in an attempt to obtain food supplies, a mission which was not without peril.

At great risk to themselves, many Fujianese farmers and villagers loyal to Koxinga continued to supply his men with food. This usually happened under the cover of darkness, at secret rendezvous in deserted places. They regularly ran the risk of running into bands of Manchus, often at the cost of lives. The Qing troops were without mercy: anyone found to be helping Koxinga's men was severely punished. Whole villages would be burned to the ground, their families slaughtered if there was even the slightest suspicion that they were aiding his men.

And still the farmers' support continued. Their loyalty often filled Jing with awe.

But then something happened that Koxinga had not foreseen. While Jing's regiment continued their efforts to provide the troops with provisions from the mainland, the generals in Peking resorted to an age-old trick to rid themselves of their last remaining food source. They ordered the coastal area between Canton and Nanking, stretching twelve miles inland, to be evacuated. A series of military forts was set up along the evacuated area to ensure that the orders were strictly enforced. All inhabitants within the area were forcibly removed, and any unauthorized person found within the twelve-mile no-go zone was executed to ensure that no one would be able to supply the rebels any longer. The whole area was to be burned to the ground.

There were many who did not hear of the edict. Some shrugged their shoulders and stayed, unable to believe that the edict was true, or that such an insane plan would actually be put into effect. There were those who stubbornly refused to leave, unwilling to give up their farms and land to such destruction. Those who were not executed for disobeying the edict were simply abandoned; they were the ones who starved to death.

Koxinga was astounded when he heard what had been done. The fertile farms, once a rich source of supply for vegetables and fruits, had been set alight, the crops destroyed, the farm animals stolen. Whole villages had turned into blackened ghost towns with nothing that could be of any use to his men on Amoy and the Pescadores. The entire region had become a barren zone. The once fertile lands of southeastern China, the rice bowl of China, now grew nothing but weeds.

Jing was now no longer able to feed his men. War vessels from the Qing were slowly encircling Amoy, preparing to attack it from two different directions. Jing had no choice but to leave the island and join his father in refuge on the Pescadores. With the additional troops to feed, the reprieve that the Pescadores had offered Koxinga and his men became even more temporary than he had anticipated.

Koxinga deliberately waited until the end of the northern monsoon. He calculated that with the winds against them, any Dutch ships in the area would not be able to send word to Batavia in time to request help. On the evening of April 21, 1661, a fleet of nine hundred ships of war and twenty-five thousand men crossed the Formosan strait toward the island once named by the Portuguese for its beauty.

It was a sight to behold. The fleet, consisting of Chinese war junks and ships forcibly taken from Western powers, was well armed with cannon and firearms that almost rivaled the weaponry of the Dutch. A day later, it reached the coast of Formosa.

PART THREE

18

Hostages

It was still early in the morning when Antonius heaved himself out of bed with a sigh, awakened too soon by the sensation of an overfull bladder. He got up clumsily, the stiffness in his bones worse than ever. Next to him Anna turned her back on him in indignation, muttering something unintelligible before embracing sleep once more. His youngest child, Hendrik, who shared the bedroom with his parents, didn't even stir.

Still groggy with sleep, Hambroek made his way outside to relieve himself in the outhouse. As the sea came into his field of vision, he stopped short. Thinking for a moment that the mist and early morning light were playing tricks on his eyes, he blinked, suddenly fully awake. He stared at the vast forest of masts along the shore in awe. The sea was alive with junks, vessels, and ships bearing down toward the coast.

"*God Allemachtig*." He urgently made his way to the outhouse, urinated in sloppy haste, slammed the door shut behind him and ran back to the house.

"Anna! Johanna! Wake up the children! Get dressed! Quickly!" His booming voice was enough to wake the whole household. His startled wife soon appeared at the top of the stairs, her brown curls escaping from under her sleeping bonnet.

"Antonius? What in the name of heaven is going on?"

"Just look through the window!"

The tousled Hendrik climbed out of bed and stood on his toes to see through the window facing the sea. He gasped at the sight that greeted him.

"What's the matter, Papa?" a yawning Johanna asked as she walked into the bedroom. Her mouth fell open when she, too, saw the armada that had gathered along the shore.

"Get yourselves dressed as soon as you can and make your way to Fort Provintia. Warn everyone else on your way. I don't know for sure what this means, but I'm afraid we will find ourselves in harm's way if we're not quick." He ran to the stables for his horse. He ignored the old Chinese peasant who squatted against a tree and regarded him with smug amusement.

Still in his nightshirt, he mounted the horse and galloped away, breaking up two mangy dogs in their attempt to mate and scattering chickens before him. He made his way past several elderly Chinese doing their strange but graceful taijiquan dance in the shade of the trees. They hardly seemed to notice him, their heavily lidded eyes discreetly following him as he went. They proceeded with their early morning routines as if the coming of the Chinese fleet was nothing out of the ordinary.

Antonius used his considerable voice to maximum capacity to rouse his colleagues from their beds.

"Cruyf! Mus!" he bellowed as he passed their houses, steering his horse along the dwellings to rap his fist on their doors. The horse whinnied nervously, sensing the urgency of the rider on his back.

"Raise everyone from their beds!" he shouted as a pale Mus appeared in his doorway, dressed in his long nightshirt. "Look yonder!" He pointed toward the sea. Mus squinted into the poor light of dawn before his face twisted in shock.

"*Grote God*," was all he could mutter, rooted to the ground.

By the time Hambroek reached Fort Provintia, he had left a trail of bewildered settlers behind him, many of them still in their nightshirts. They all stared at the Chinese fleet moving along the shore. Men and women shouted incoherently, running in and out of their houses, unsure of what to do.

At the officers' accommodation, Deputy Governor Jacobus Valentijn had already been alerted. Antonius dismounted when he saw him, and together they watched, disconcerted, as the dense forest of ships' masts bore down upon them.

* * *

Frederic woke at the sound of someone beating on his door. He had no idea what time it was as he swung his legs over the side of the bed, although he could see from the light escaping between the drapes that it must be dawn. The sound was repeated, urgent now.

"Mr. Coyett!" A voice shouted from somewhere inside his house. "Governor!"

He got up and peered down from the landing, where Captain Pedel looked up at him. "You'd better come with me, sir. Ships of war."

"What?" he muttered something under his breath as he rushed downstairs and pushed the curtains aside. "God's blood," he breathed.

From the landing above him, an alarmed Helen appeared in her nightgown. Their slave, who had been woken by the commotion, stood by dumbly, her unruly hair standing out in all directions.

"Koxinga, sir," the captain said. "He has come, just like you said he would."

Frederic was transfixed as he stared through the window. "God's blood, let it not be so," he muttered, turning to Pedel. "Well, captain. The good Lord knows I would have preferred to be wrong on this one." He pushed past him and ran back up the stairs, passing his bewildered wife and children.

"Come on up, captain!" he shouted over his shoulder, and Pedel made his way up the stairs, apologizing to Helen for his discourtesy.

"He isn't going to attack us," Frederic said, his face grave as he took off his nightshirt to expose a lean midriff. Pedel waited by the door as Frederic grabbed a pair of breeches hanging from a chair and stepped into them.

"He will probably ask us to leave, but he won't attack us. Not yet, anyway. He would lose face before his men if he attacked us unprovoked." He pulled on a shirt, still working the buttons as he walked down the stairs. Pedel followed close behind. "I know how this man thinks. He will likely send a messenger."

At the door he turned around one last time and addressed his wife. "Helena, wake Balthasar and get dressed as swift as you can. And don't leave the fort, whatever you do." Helena nodded, frowning, and hurried back to their bedroom.

As he came outside, Lieutenant Gerrit was already there waiting for him.

"Get all the women and children to the safety of the fort and have all the food supplies not yet within the fort's walls moved there at once!" he ordered. "Captain Pedel. Dispatch out one of our fastest gunboats to warn Batavia. Do it now!" he bellowed, half at a run.

"Sir, the winds have changed. The monsoon...."

"I know that, lieutenant! We have no other option. It's a risk we'll have to take. We have to send word to Batavia; it's our only chance. Send the signal to the *Hector*! It's vital that one of our ships anchored outside the bay breaks through the blockade!" he said, gesturing at the Chinese war junks. Most of the hostile ships had veered toward the bay's entrance, trapping the Dutch ships that lay at anchor there. They had nowhere to go.

"Right, sir!" Pedel replied, who got on his horse and was gone. Frederic stared after him as his horse spurted away, the mud clods flying from its hooves. For a moment, he wondered at the strange turn of events. The three VOC warships that he had commissioned from Van der Laan, the *Hector* among them, had been too large to pass through the bay's two ever-shrinking entrances. As a precaution, he had sent them away from Zeelandia to be anchored along the coast of the Formosan mainland, south of Saccam. It had turned out to be a prudent move. He hoped to God that the signal banners would be seen in time and that at least one of the ships would be able to break through to warn Batavia.

The entire village of Zeelandia was now fully awake. Dutch women, dressed in their long skirts and white bonnets, pushed their children with some urgency in the direction of the fort, their infants pressed against their hips as they glanced at the Chinese armada with growing unease. Dogs barked nervously, the women's voices were shrill with anxiety.

Frederic watched as the Chinese laborers discarded their farm tools and left the paddies to swarm toward the beaches, elated at the sight of the Chinese junks. Emboldened by the sight of the large numbers of their countrymen, they looked at the Dutch settlers with undisguised contempt. Two men hawked noisily and spat at his feet as they passed, their hostility tangible. Hundreds of Chinese peasants waded into the shallow waters, laughing and waving as the ships' crews landed on the shore. They were Chinese, their own people. No doubt they now felt strong and unafraid. This was what Frederic had feared for so long. It was only natural that the local Chinese would support Koxinga during an invasion such as this. How many times had he not warned Batavia that this might happen?

The officers and soldiers milled around him, their arms crossed in a show of feigned confidence. They did not know what to do in the face of such an invasion, and truth be told, neither did he.

Everyone jumped at the sound of the first cannon blast. Women shrieked in alarm and all the bravado that the men had just displayed evaporated. If anyone had been under any doubt, they now were no longer. The Dutch colony of Formosa was under attack.

From the fort's ramparts Frederic, his staff of officers and Christian Beyer watched the battle in the bay unfold. Having the great advantage of numbers, hundreds of enemy ships had maneuvered toward the mouth of the harbor, blocking its entrance to trap the ships inside.

He thanked Heaven that the *Hector*'s captain had seen the signals sent from Zeelandia. The captains of the *'s Gravelande* and *Maria* had also heard the first gunshot reverberate along the coast, and knew what they had to do, at all cost. The majestic *'s Gravelande* turned in time to fire its guns from starboard, its cannon finding an easy target as the enemy milled around. Junks exploded into the air, timber flying everywhere as scores of Chinese sailors were blown into the water.

The *Hector* managed to break free from its trap, sinking the junks that sacrificed themselves in an attempt to block its path. Its guns blaring, it covered for the smaller yacht *Maria* to turn and break through the opening it had created. Its sails barely hoisted, the *Maria* veered right into the path of hundreds of junks, its guns firing away. Using the northern winds to full advantage, it picked up speed as it headed straight for the blockade, crashing and sinking smaller junks in its wake as it gained momentum.

The crew had to run for cover as a cascade of burning arrows came veering their way, but most arrows thudded onto the deck without doing any real damage. Once at full sail, the *Maria*'s speed was too great for any of the junks to turn around and give chase.

"Look! The *Maria* has broken through! Thank God!" Gerrit shouted in relief.

Frederic closed his eyes briefly as he, too, said a silent prayer of thanks. Next to him, Christian Beyer let go an uncharacteristic yelp of delight at the small victory. The *Maria* had escaped and was on its way to Batavia.

Frederic lifted the brass telescope in order to estimate the number of enemy ships. The scale of the invasion had truly stunned him. He surveyed the scene around him, trying to discern the ships' maneuvers. As he observed the enemy's movements, he noted that the soldiers who had landed on Baxemboy, the isle across the channel, carried a variety of weapons. It was of little consequence: the colonists had deserted the isle after the only fort there was destroyed in a typhoon a few years earlier. He could pick out the archers, their equipment hanging down their backs. Some carried only a sword and shield, while others wielded what looked like battle-axes attached to long sticks. All the troops wore protective scaly armor, which covered the upper body and reached down to the knees, leaving the arms and legs bare to allow flexibility. He had never seen anything like it.

"What in blazing hell are they doing?" he asked, as he saw that they had begun shooting from afar.

"Do they honestly think to harm us with those small guns from that distance?" he asked Pedel.

"For all their numbers, sir, this only confirms that the Chinese are not a warfaring nation. They have no idea what they are up against," Pedel said with confidence. "They are probably unfamiliar with the power of our cannon."

Once more he tried to assess the number of enemy vessels. It was impossible: the concentration of junks was too great. For the umpteenth time, he cursed Jan van der Laan for the obstinate son-of-a-bitch that he was, having left them at their mercy while everything had indicated that this might happen. He also cursed his superiors in Batavia for their pig-headedness in ignoring his many warnings.

"Sir! Look!" Lieutenant Gerrit exclaimed. "There! On the beach!" They all stared at the troops landing along the shore near Zeelandia. The beach was suddenly crawling with soldiers.

"Don't trouble yourself, governor," Captain Pedel said with forced lightness as Frederic watched with increasing concern. "These men cannot fight," he said. "They are sure to run at the first whiff of our gunpowder."

Frederic said nothing. He admired the captain. Pedel was one of the few officers with the strength of character to speak his mind to his superiors. Yet somehow Frederic didn't share his optimism.

There was great turmoil at the gates of the fortress. Frightened Dutch settlers still came pouring in with their wives and children, while a frenzy of unorganized troop movement gave the place a feeling of utter chaos. In the bay the initial clashes between the two nations' ships had developed into a true naval battle.

Still, Coyett knew they would be safe within the fortress's walls. Fort Zeelandia was strong, well equipped and specially built to withstand an attack from the sea. It was strategically located on a hill overlooking the harbor, and defended by four bastions. The governor's residence, the warehouse, and other company buildings were all enclosed by its impenetrable walls, which had recently been fortified at his orders. He silently praised himself for being stubborn enough to proceed with the reinforcements without Batavia's approval. The fort would be able to protect the settlers of Zeelandia for some time. He wondered how Fort Provintia would hold up in Saccam, knowing full well that it was much weaker in its defenses. Silently he prayed that it, too, could hold out.

* * *

Antonius had leapt in fright when the first cannon had been fired at Zeelandia. He knew it would only be a matter of time before the Chinese army would reach Saccam, so they didn't have a moment to lose. He gathered his family, and urged all the Dutch colonists in Saccam to take refuge at Fortress Provintia. From the bastions of the small fort he saw how the otherwise quiet, picturesque bay had become the stage of a major naval battle. Just across the water they saw how Pineapple Isle was being besieged. Stranded along the beaches, the numerous war junks spat out an alarming, endless stream of soldiers. As yet, he could not see the Chinese digging any trenches, nor did they busy themselves building up gun batteries. But they still kept coming in great numbers, ever closer.

Once all the settlers were inside and the sentries had hermetically closed Fort Provintia, the soldiers positioned themselves along the various bastions, their muskets armed and ready to fire. From the speed at which the enemy troops advanced, Hambroek guessed that they would find themselves surrounded by noon.

"Mr. Valentijn, sir!" A sergeant appeared at the top of the stairwell. He looked pale and grim.

"What is it, Sergeant Stockaert?" Deputy Valentijn demanded.

"Bad tidings, sir. It appears…." The man hesitated, unwilling to be the bearer of unwelcome news. "It's the supplies. They've gone missing."

"Missing? What do you mean?"

"The food supplies. The grain. All the emergency rations that were stored in the warehouse, for just such an event. It's vanished."

Hambroek and Valentijn exchanged frowns, perplexed. Then Valentijn turned red with fury.

"Those confounded bastards!" he blazed. "It's the Chinese merchants. Those thieving, untrustworthy bastards! We should never have trusted them near the warehouse." He cursed himself inwardly.

"What about drinking water?" Antonius inquired in a low voice. "How long will that last us?"

Sergeant Stockaert gulped uncomfortably and looked at the ground. "With all these people here, I'd reckon a day or two. At the most."

Valentijn and Hambroek regarded each other in stunned silence.

"Then Provintia will be lost," Valentijn said under his breath, as he stared in the distance at the ever-increasing number of troops and enemy ships that threatened to surround them from all sides. It was a disturbing sight. Baxemboy, which was normally deserted, was now crawling with soldiers. Its undulating dunes were suddenly covered with what looked like dark molasses. The troops had also landed on the north of Pineapple

Isle, just near Zeelandia. Long boats had managed to cross over to the main island, where they emptied themselves of scores of soldiers, coming in their direction.

His officers had already given the order to start firing, if only to keep the approaching enemy at bay. The instant the first Chinese soldiers went down, they were replaced by others. The regiments moved forward in disciplined ranks, oblivious to the guns aimed at them. Some took hits from the Dutch musket, but still they pressed on, undaunted by the danger.

The faces of the officers around Valentijn were grim, their lips moving silently as they calculated the enemy's numbers and considered their chances. He was not a military man, but he, too, knew that they would not be able to withstand such numbers for long. He estimated that there were thousands of them.

"We can still leave," Valentijn suggested. "The Chinese haven't taken the south of Pineapple Isle yet. We can take the horses and head for the Narrows passage, where we can wade across for the safety of Fort Zeelandia. It is far stronger, and I know it is well stocked. That, or we can remain here and face certain death, either at their hands or through starvation."

The others looked at him dubiously.

"Then I suggest we leave now," Sergeant Stockaert said. "Afore we find ourselves completely surrounded."

Even as they spoke, they saw how two sentries on the north-eastern bastion were felled by a deadly shower of arrows. The first group of Dutch settlers, headed by Stockaert, fled from the fort's back entrance under the armed escort of several dozens of soldiers. Antonius remained with Valentijn and the other officers. They followed the movement of the fugitives until they finally disappeared behind a dune.

With one hundred troops remaining to defend the fort, Hambroek, Valentijn and their families were the next to leave. They hastily took the remaining horses that had been brought in from the stables. While the soldiers held off the attackers at the front by way of distraction, the small party of men and women made their way out of the back as fast as they could.

Clutching Hendrik tightly around the waist, Hambroek galloped at full speed through the dunes. Anna followed closely behind with Elisabeth. Johanna, already sixteen, rode by herself, her horse taking off as if with the devil in pursuit. Hambroek murmured a prayer of thanks that Cornelia, their oldest, was already safe within the walls of Zeelandia.

From the corner of his eye he saw that Jacob Valentijn rode just behind him, his nine-year-old daughter pressing into his back. Young Ben seemed to be holding onto the horse's mane for dear life. Valentijn's wife, her face panic-stricken, clung to her horse as it followed the others. Antonius knew that they had left Provintia just in time. Those who had remained would now no longer be able to escape.

The arrows struck down onto the earth with a thud, ever closer, barely missing them. He said a prayer once more, this time that they would make it to Zeelandia in time. They spurred their horses to go faster, their hooves kicking up loose dirt as they went. Just a few more miles, and they would be able to cross the Narrows and get to Fort Utrecht. The sentries there would cover them for the last several hundred feet to enable them to safely reach the gates of Fort Zeelandia.

Then something caused Johanna's horse to stumble, throwing the girl off, landing her flat on her back. Valentijn sailed past her, unable to check his horse without risking his children falling off.

Antonius reined in sharply, jumping down as he did. Gingerly he helped the dazed girl back on her feet. "Go! Ride on!" he yelled at his wife, who hesitated. "Go to the fort! Take Elisabeth and get away from here!"

But then he heard the ominous sound of something hissing through the air at high speed, just above his head. *Tzuk!* He heard a cry of alarm as he watched Valentijn's horse come down whinnying in anguish, an arrow shaft embedded in its flank. Valentijn only just managed to pull the children clear of the animal's crushing weight.

Ahead of them, sunlight caught a flash of steel. One of the escorting soldiers whirled when he saw a movement on his right, his musket taking aim. He was stopped short when an arrow struck his chest, a trickle of blood oozing from his mouth. Valentijn's wife screamed.

Another Dutch soldier gasped as a steel blade ran him completely through, the body held up by the blade.

Then they found themselves surrounded. Without giving it a single thought, Antonius launched his bulky body at one of the Chinese. His intended victim dodged him easily and hit him hard on the temple with the hilt of his sword, knocking him to the ground, leaving him momentarily stunned.

"Father!" he heard Johanna cry as she rushed forward to help him. In a daze he saw a Chinese soldier grab hold of her arm, laughing. It was the first time that he had looked an enemy soldier in the face. Somewhere in front of him, Valentijn's riderless horse dashed away, whinnying in sheer panic. Then Valentijn appeared, running past them, his son tucked under his arm. He didn't get very far. Two Chinese soldiers stepped in front of him, their bows poised in threat. From behind, another Chinese soldier belted his weapon hard against the calf of his leg. Valentijn cried out in pain, only just managing to put down Ben before his knees buckled and gave way.

"Papa!" Ben's scream resounded eerily through the woods. A soldier pulled the weeping boy away from his father.

Antonius was roughly dragged to his feet, his arms pinioned behind his back. Still recovering from the blow to his head, he heard a woman shriek. He did not know whether it came from his own wife or Valentijn's. The youngest children were crying hysterically, terrified of what was happening. As his eyesight sharpened once more, he saw Hendrik staring at him in shock, his left arm in the tight grip of his captor's hands. The boy's small fists opened and closed, opened and closed, utterly helpless.

Antonius searched for his wife and Elisabeth, but they were nowhere to be seen. Somehow, they had managed to get away. He threw Hendrik a quick glance, their eyes locking. The boy had also seen that they were gone.

The commanding officer barked an order, upon which the soldiers tied their hands behind their backs and prodded them along with angry shouts. They soon came across the horses, which had not strayed far after their scare. The animals were quickly recovered by the soldiers, who took the animals along as their prize.

The youngest children, pale with fright, were put on the backs of the horses as the Chinese sentries took hold of the reins to lead them. Everyone else was forced to walk. Antonius tried to stay upright in spite of the dizziness that he felt, Johanna supporting him at his side. The path was strewn with lifeless bodies of the Dutch. His heart in his throat, he scanned the corpses anxiously, fearful of finding those of his wife and daughter. But theirs were not among them. He recognized the bodies of the soldiers sent ahead to scout the area. Johanna looked away, biting her lip to stop it from quivering. A poke in his ribs prodded him on. Gnashing his teeth, he soundlessly said a prayer for each of the dead men they came across.

"We have prisoners, my lord," one of the men announced when they dragged Antonius and Valentijn into the tent unceremoniously, leaving the women and children outside wailing in protest at being separated from them.

"Ah. What have we got here?"

"Two males, two females, one of which is young, and three children. I believe one of the men might be a senior company officer, my lord. We also managed to capture their horses."

"Excellent work, soldier."

Both men were instantly forced to their knees. Valentijn lifted his head to see who had summoned them, to be brutally struck on the shoulder. The offending officer shouted something at him that he could not understand. Yet his meaning was clear: they were not to look up at the man standing in front of them.

Antonius knew instinctively who they faced. This could be no other than Koxinga, lord of the imperial surname.

"Ah, this is good, your excellency," a familiar voice crooned from a distant corner of the tent. "The man with the hair the color of fire is the missionary man who forces his one-god religion on the people. The skinny one is Coyett's second in command, the deputy governor. He is a prize indeed!"

Careful to keep his eyes downcast, Antonius glared in the direction of the voice.

Valentijn cussed venomously as he, too, identified the voice.

"Ting-bin, you motherfucking treacherous bastard!"

"Tut, tut, tut," Ting-bin cooed softly, enjoying the moment from the safety of his corner, nodding at the sentry standing over Valentijn. On cue, the sentry lifted his club, aiming it at the deputy governor's already maimed leg. Valentijn's back arched before he fell groaning on his side, his face a sickly green.

"So," the man in front of them said. "You are the governor's second in command."

Antonius heard Ting-bin's voice translate for their benefit.

"Do you know who I am? Ting-bin, tell them!"

Ting-bin happily obliged, informing them of Koxinga's full title with all the honorifics.

"I have a job for you. Both of you. You! Second in command! Look at me."

Valentijn worked his way up to a sitting position, wincing, and warily looked at the man of which they had heard so much. Antonius lifted his eyes with caution. He saw a hard, lean man in his thirties, his skin badly affected by a fiery rash.

"What is your name, second in command?" Koxinga demanded.

"Valentijn. Jacob Valentijn. I am deputy governor of the island Formosa, which is under the sovereignty of the VOC." He spat out the details of his function with pride, in spite of his pain. Ting-bin translated his response with relish.

"We shall see about that," Koxinga said, somewhat amused. "And you, missionary man?" He stopped in front of Antonius, who still had not stopped glaring at Ting-bin.

"I am Reverend Antonius Hambroek. I have been commissioned by the VOC as head of the mission on Formosa to spread the word of our one true God."

"One true God. One true God," Koxinga repeated ponderously. "One God, and yet two faiths. My father pretended to worship your one true God, did you know that? He pretended in order to be able to do business with the Catholic Portuguese, otherwise they would not deal with him. He even took on a Christian name. Nicholas Iquan, that's what they called him." He laughed out loud. "He fooled them, as he fooled you. Did you honestly, for one moment, believe that he would cease to worship the spirits of his ancestors, the gods of his own religion?" He laughed again, then suddenly he went quiet, his face solemn. "Like I said, I have a job for you. You, second in command, will write a letter to your governor, in your hand, that I will dictate to you. You will tell the governor that he must surrender. And if he does not surrender, then you will tell us all you know about the defense of the fortress."

"I will do no such thing," Valentijn retorted. "You may kill me as you wish, you filthy pirate, but I won't do it. I don't answer to you!"

Koxinga moved in closer and looked down at Valentijn, assessing the man. "Perhaps you do not mind if we hurt you, even kill you," he breathed. "How very brave of you. But what about the women and children outside?"

Valentijn cringed.

"That's your woman out there, isn't it? And the children? Are they yours? I thought so. You won't mind if we hurt them, would you?"

Valentijn face fell, rivulets of sweat streaming down his temple. He swallowed hard, shaking his head slowly. "You wouldn't!"

Koxinga snapped his fingers at one of his officers, giving him a short order. The man moved to leave the tent to return with Ben, Valentijn's five-year-old son. Ben's eyes went wide when he saw his father kneeling and bound in front of a strange Chinese man who stood towering over him.

"No! Please, no!" Valentijn pleaded.

Antonius wondered if Koxinga was bluffing, whether he truly intended hurting the child. At a nod from Koxinga, one of the soldiers made a show of drawing his short sword just outside the trembling boy's field of vision.

Valentijn watched with horror as the ugly brute moved his sword in the direction of his son's head. Predictably, his resolve broke, the bravado now gone. He reared up suddenly, but was held back by his crippled leg and bound hands, which caused him to fall back on his side, screaming with pain and frustration, the muscles in his face strained with emotion.

"Not my children, no, not my son! Ben! Don't hurt him, please, no!" he blubbered piteously, the spittle escaping from his trembling lips.

Koxinga watched him stoically. Valentijn's resolve had been broken. He was no more than a hopeless heap of misery. Antonius could not bear to watch the man in this state, but neither could he look away. Ben stared at his father, scared and confused, the tears leaving streaks of clear skin through the layers of dirt.

"I will do anything," Valentijn sobbed. "Just please don't hurt my family. I beg of you! I will write your letter, I will help you with anything you wish, tell you anything you wish to know. I ... just don't hurt my children!" He was crying unashamedly now, his pride gone. Ting-bin began to interpret, but Koxinga held up his hand, smiling. No translation was necessary.

Antonius wondered if Koxinga really had it in him to hurt a child, or whether it had just been an effective ruse. Whatever the case, it had worked, he thought grimly. He had broken Valentijn's resolve with hardly any effort.

"Excellent. Now we are accomplishing something. You help me, I will help you. Guard! See to it that his family is well treated and fed. You!" He pointed at another. "Remove second in command's restraints and get him paper and ink!"

While Ben was taken back outside to be reunited with his wailing mother and sister, a guard released Valentijn of his restraints. He rubbed at his wrists, which were bruised and swollen from his ordeal. His hands shaking, he took a fine brush and parchment from the guard, unsure of himself.

"Sit down there. At the desk," Koxinga ordered, motioning toward the low makeshift table that sat in the corner of the tent. "Write!" he said imperiously as Valentijn sat on his knees in front of it, wincing at the throbbing pain in his leg.

"I, Zheng Chenggong, lord of the imperial surname and supreme military commander under the mandate of the Ming empire, write to you, Governor Coyett." He cleared his throat theatrically. Ting-bin interpreted sentence by sentence.

"I will give you and the people of your nation the opportunity to surrender your fortress before I aim my guns at its walls. Should you surrender, then not even the smallest blade of grass shall be harmed. If you and your army leave so that mine can enter, then you, your people and all of your worldly possessions will be spared." Koxinga was silent for a while as Valentijn wrote the words with unsteady hand. "Let it be known that my destiny was determined a long time ago. That my fate is entwined with that of Formosa. It is with fair warning that I should inform you that I,

Lord Koxinga, am destined to conquer this island, as was once foretold. I therefore advise you to surrender." He looked over Valentijn's shoulder and summoned Ting-bin to check the letter's contents.

Ting-bin studied it for any deliberate errors, then nodded sagely that all was well.

"Good, second in command. I will personally see to it that you and your family are well taken care of. I might require some information during the next few days. You will be willing to provide me with that, won't you?"

Valentijn was drained and exhausted, there was no fight left in him. He nodded wordlessly. It was a mistake. Koxinga smashed his knee into the man's temple. Valentijn had to make an effort to remain upright.

"You will answer me by addressing me as 'Lord Koxinga.' Is that clear, second in command?"

"Yes, Lord Koxinga," Valentijn muttered, all his dignity gone.

"Good. Take them both away. I want to talk to the missionary man later."

Antonius was led back outside, where he was tied to a tall pole that had been hammered into the ground, his hands tied behind his back. Together with Johanna and Hendrik he watched as the soldiers released Valentijn's wife and children, and how they were handed food and water right in front of them. Parched and hungry as they were from their enforced journey, it was a calculated cruelty.

Antonius could tell from Valentijn's pallor that he was badly shaken, and suffering. He leaned heavily on his wife for support, the blood oozing from an open wound on his forehead. Valentijn glanced briefly in his direction, and just before they led them away, their eyes met. The deputy governor had quickly averted his face, but that fraction of a second was long enough for Antonius to see the shame that Valentijn felt. For his weakness, and for the betrayal he was about to commit. Hambroek looked back in silence. He could not judge the man for what he had done. Then he considered his own children, and his heart cringed. His turn was yet to come.

An hour later, the soldiers came back for him.

"Father!" Johanna cried as he was brusquely lifted to his feet. Hendrik started crying again.

"Be brave, children. We shall endure this! Johanna, look after your brother," he said, and allowed himself to be taken away, leaving his children behind in their distress.

"Missionary man! Welcome." Koxinga walked up to him, assessing him closely. The Chinese commander cocked his head as he tried to size him up, the hint of a frown appearing on his forehead. Antonius said nothing.

"Your deputy governor Va ... Val...?" He looked at Ting-bin.

"Valentijn, your excellency," Ting-bin said helpfully.

"Your deputy governor Va-len-tijn is a wise and smart man. He has seen that I am a man of honor and has accepted that it is my destiny to rule this island. He has decided to cooperate with me. As a reward, he and his family will be treated well."

Again, Antonius said nothing but merely swallowed, his Adam's apple moving visibly as he did. Koxinga noticed and smiled, then bent over to look him in the eye.

"I think you are far smarter than Valentijn," he almost whispered. "But then again, so am I. Valentijn has written a letter for me, addressed to your beloved governor. I need you to deliver it to him, to convince him that it is in his best interest to surrender. You see, this island is part of my destiny."

Antonius lifted his head to face him. "I answer to no one but the almighty God and the honorable governor of Formosa, Mr. Frederic Coyett."

"But they are not here now, are they? Now you answer to me. Remember, I have your women and children." Koxinga walked to the tent entrance and opened the entrance flap to observe the lovely, slender Johanna and the younger Hendrik. They looked back at him, their eyes fearful under his gaze.

"The young woman. She is your wife?" he inquired appraisingly.

"No. She is my daughter," Antonius answered, his heartbeat rising.

"Pretty girl. Where is your wife?" Koxinga asked.

Antonius shook his head. "She died a long time ago," he said, knowing that God would forgive him for the lie. He prayed desperately that Anna and Elisabeth had made it to Zeelandia.

"That is most unfortunate," Koxinga muttered, suddenly deep in thought, as if lost in some dark memory. Antonius looked up, somewhat confused.

The man actually seemed sincere. Then the Chinese commander snapped out of his thoughts, his expression hard once more.

"You will be my envoy," he announced. "Your children will remain here in my safe-keeping until you return from your mission. Then I will let them go. I don't think I have to tell you that I cannot guarantee their safety if you do not come back here within twenty-four hours. My men are lusty fellows."

Ting-bin giggled as he translated the last sentence. Antonius gave the interpreter a look of undisguised loathing.

"But you will be back. I can tell you are a man of honor. Tell your governor that I do not wish warfare and I advise him to listen to wisdom. Tell him, persuade him to surrender."

Antonius looked Koxinga hard in the eye. "I will be your messenger if you so wish, if only to protect my children. I will hand him your letter. But as God is my witness, I will not tell my governor to surrender. It is not up to me to tell him what to do."

"Fine. That is your choice." Koxinga said calmly, allowing his respect to show. "My men will see to it that you and your children are given food and water. Then you will leave on your mission."

To prevent him from falling prisoner to their own patrolling troops again, Antonius was taken to the outskirts of Zeelandia, upon which the Chinese sentries withdrew. He took a deep breath as he walked up the hill toward the fortress, recognizing some of the Dutch sentries standing guard atop the heavy gates.

"Reverend Hambroek!" one of the guards gasped as he was recognized, quickly letting him in.

"My wife and youngest daughter! Did they arrive?" he asked urgently.

"Yes, reverend, they made it back safely, thanks be to God. They're likely to be in the kitchen below. And Miss Cornelia, she's on duty at the hospital, God bless her," the guard added, his eyes shining.

Antonius breathed a sigh of relief and grasped the man by both shoulders in gratitude. His daughter Cornelia worked as a nurse at the Zeelandia hospital and had become an attractive, buxom young woman. Unfortunately for the young guard, his oldest daughter was already betrothed to Frans van der Voorn, one of the mission's schoolmasters. He thanked the young guard again and ran down the stairs to the kitchen, taking three steps at a time.

He saw Elisabeth sitting by the open fire, huddled in a huge blanket that someone had wrapped around her. He rushed forward to take her in his arms. "Blessed be to God," he murmured into the softness of the child's hair.

"Antonius!" his wife cried out as she saw him. He released Elisabeth in order to embrace her.

"They let you go. Thank heavens!" She pushed him away when she saw his bleak expression. "Where are the children? Hendrik, Johanna. Where are they?" The immense relief she had just felt was gone, only to be replaced by fear. "Antonius, tell me! Where are they?" Her eyes searched hopefully in the corridor behind him.

"They still have them, Anna," he said softly. "They are holding them hostage. I am meant to deliver this letter," he touched the pouch he was carrying, "to the governor."

Anna's face crumpled, her hands flew to her mouth in dread. "Oh, no! My poor, defenseless children. Alone with those monsters!" she wailed, nearly falling into a faint. The other women in the kitchen turned to look at her in sympathy.

Antonius caught her by the shoulders, holding her tight. "Anna, listen to me. As long as I do what they ask, they shall not be harmed. I actually believe they will release them when I return. It may sound strange, but I think this Koxinga is a man of his word."

"What about you? They'll probably keep you hostage when you go back! Or worse. They might kill you," she cried, her eyes darting in their sockets.

"Then so be it. We will all have to be strong now, Anna. Abide with me. We must endure."

"Scores of our people have already been killed! We came across some of the others who left Provintia before us. We had to wade through the bay so we wouldn't be seen by the Chinese soldiers." She spoke rapidly now, then lowered her voice. "They've got Frans, Antonius. Cornelia doesn't know yet. I didn't have the heart to tell her."

His heart sank. Frans van der Voorn was one of the most popular schoolmasters, and his oldest daughter's fiancé. These were going to be hard times for them all.

"I will tell her," he told his distressed wife. "But I must see the governor first."

"I'll be coming with you," she told him. The look on her face told him there was no use arguing.

The governor was in his office, together with Chief Merchant van Iperen, Christian Beyer, Captain van Aeldorp, and Sergeant Stockaert. Frederic came immediately to his feet as Antonius and Anna entered.

"Antonius! You made it through. God's blood, what did they do to you?" he managed to say as he saw the cuts and bruises. Ever the doctor, Beyer came over to inspect his wounds. But Antonius pushed him away and shook his head. "Later, Christian."

Frederic's exuberance faded when he saw the look on his face. "Sit down, Antonius. You had better tell me all that has befallen you."

Anna rushed forward, speaking out of turn. "That man Koxinga. He has taken our Johanna and Hendrik as captives."

Frederic looked from Antonius and then back to Anna, appalled. "What?"

Antonius reached inside the bag he was carrying and extracted the letter, handing it to Van Iperen. He knew the contents, and was unable to convey the message himself.

"You'd better read this."

Van Iperen looked up, surprised. "This is Valentijn's hand. Jacob Valentijn wrote this."

"Yes," Antonius said. "I'll explain later."

Van Iperen scanned over the contents, half muttering to himself, reading the occasional passages aloud. "'I, Zheng Chenggong, lord of the imperial surname ... under the mandate of heaven accorded by the emperor of China, write to you, Governor Coyett ... will give you ... the opportunity to surrender.... Should you surrender ... then not even the smallest blade of grass will be harmed.'"

Beyer scoffed at the last sentence as Van Iperen finished reading. Frederic took the letter from him, reading the contents for himself in silence. Then he looked up, scowling.

"Jacob wrote this under duress?"

"Yes. He wasn't going to talk ... until they threatened to harm his kin."

Frederic nodded, the corners of his mouth drawn down grimly. Antonius knew what he was thinking: the governor had a son of his own. He would probably have done the same.

"Frederic, they released him, and his family. They are treating them well. It's in the cards that he will cooperate with them to keep it that way. He's likely to provide them with all they wish to know. You have to consider that possibility."

Their eyes locked. They were both painfully aware what harm Valentijn could do by providing them with valuable information, exposing their weaknesses by telling them what he knew.

"Frederic, there is one more thing you should know," Antonius said. "He Ting-bin is out there, with Koxinga."

"Ting-bin? That treacherous bastard!" Van Iperen growled as Captain van Aeldorp slammed the doorpost with his fist, his jaw set with anger. Frederic absorbed the information in silence.

"Well, that was to be expected," Frederic said. The situation was growing worse by the minute.

"He has your children, Antonius. When did he tell you to be back?"

"He gave me but twenty-four hours. He said he would not be able to vouch for their safety once that period has expired." He fell quiet, suddenly feeling very old. Beyer shook his head, muttering something under his breath about the man being pure evil.

"Then you should go back without delay," the governor said. He scratched the back of his head, the stress beginning to show. "God's wounds. We find ourselves in a terrible predicament. I need some time to confer with my counsel. We shall give him our response. When we have decided...." He took a deep breath.

"We shall put up the signal from the fort. The red banner will be raised if we decide to fight. Or the white banner if we surrender," he added with a low tone, glancing at Anna with compassion.

"No, Frederic," Antonius said quietly, following the direction of his look. "I will not let you do it. You must not even entertain the thought. I will not allow you to surrender for my sake." His voice dropped an octave. "Not even for my children's. May God forgive me."

Anna's eyes flew wide open at his words. "Antonius! No!" she wailed. "You cannot go back there, they will kill you. The girls.... Frederic, I implore you, do not listen to him!" In utter despair, she flailed out at her husband, striking at his chest, crying hysterically. Antonius caught her wrists and pulled her to him. Beyer walked up to them, gently extracting the sobbing woman from Antonius' arms and led her to a chair, where she collapsed in sheer misery. The men looked at her, feeling useless in the face of such grief.

"I propose you write that letter now, Frederic," Antonius said. "I want to get back there as quickly as I can, for the children's sake. He said he would release them upon my return."

Frederic looked at the chief merchant. "Van Iperen, how do you vote?" Van Iperen turned pale and gulped, the question causing him great distress. After a moment's hesitation, he nodded. "I say we fight."

"Captain van Aeldorp?" The captain swallowed hard, but didn't hesitate. "Fight, sir."

Then Frederic looked at the doctor, who shook his head wearily.

"No Frederic, you will not have my vote on this. I am a physician. I will not have a war on my conscience." He left the weeping Anna for the moment to approach the governor, his voice a whisper as he grabbed his arm. "But I must warn you, Frederic. Do not underestimate this man, or his armies when making this decision. His armies are as well disciplined as they come, and the man is obsessed with this destiny affair. He believes it was prophesied. It will be a long, hard battle if you choose to fight." He hesitated. "Many shall perish if you do."

Frederic looked away. He was caught between two options, neither of which appealed to him in the slightest. Antonius watched his face, knowing that as the governor of Formosa, this decision was his to make, and his alone. He did not envy the man one bit.

"Very well," Frederic managed to say. "I will have the letter made up straightaway. We will have you escorted on horseback so you won't lose any time."

* * *

Koxinga waited as General San-ge held out an imperious hand to take the letter from the Dutchman, but the missionary ignored him and stepped right past the general to hand it directly to him. The man even had the nerve to look him boldly in the eye.

He got up and regarded Hambroek, inclining his head slightly at the man in a manner of grudging respect.

"Bring in his children," he ordered, without breaking eye contact.

Minutes later, the adolescent girl and the young boy entered the tent. The boy rushed to his father and threw his arms around his waist, his eyes tightly shut in an admirable effort to keep from crying. His daughter bit her lip as she clung to him, the strain beginning to show on her tear-streaked face. The missionary held both his children in a desperate embrace.

Koxinga handed the letter to Ting-bin, who quickly read its contents. His expression betrayed his disappointment.

"What does it say?" Koxinga demanded.

" 'We have received your letter in due course as brought to us by the esteemed Reverend Hambroek, head of the Christian mission on Formosa,' " Ting-bin translated. " 'We fully understand the message you wish to convey to us, however, we can only give you one possible response. Our answer is that, by the honor of our powerful and one true God, our nation and the directors of the Dutch East India Company, we have sworn to defend this castle and fortress with our lives. The soldiers that you will order to attack us will report to you the strength of our resolve. We will stand by our decision. Frederic Coyett, governor of Formosa.' "

Ting-bin scowled. He had expected the Dutch to surrender and thought that this was an unexpected setback. But Koxinga had not. He had known all along that Governor Coyett was not the kind of man to give up the island so easily. Of course he resisted. He would have done the same had he been in his position.

He walked up to the missionary, stopping only inches away from him. Hambroek reluctantly let go of his children and straightened up to look him right in the eye.

"You told your governor to fight, didn't you?" Koxinga asked.

"Yes, Lord Koxinga. I did indeed."

Koxinga pondered this information for a moment, pursing his lips and stroking his goatee beard. Then he gave a sign to his general that Hambroek could not quite place. San-ge nodded in understanding.

"Take the missionary man and his son away," the general ordered his men. "Leave the girl here with me. That is the price her father will have to pay for his foolishness and stubborn pride."

Ting-bin's mouth opened involuntarily, and then shut again, shocked.

"Ting-bin! Translate what I just said!" the general growled.

"The girl is to stay here with Lord Koxinga," Ting-bin almost mumbled.

Johanna's eyes shot to Koxinga, not understanding. But her father understood only too well. Without a moment's hesitation, he lunged forward at Koxinga in a fury, but two soldiers grappled him from behind.

"No!" he shouted, once restrained. "No! Leave her be. She is but a child!"

"She does not look like a child to me. Pretty young thing." Koxinga walked up to the trembling Johanna, reaching out to touch her cheek, his hand caressing his way down her neck in a highly suggestive manner.

"Don't you dare touch her, you monstrous creature! You'll burn in hell for this!" He struggled wildly, for a moment breaking free from the grip of his guards. The momentum caused him to stumble to the ground, whereupon the guard pounced on top of him.

"Take him away!" Koxinga hissed. "Everybody out. Except you, Ting-bin. You are to stay here." Ting-bin blinked, somewhat startled at the order, but did as he was told and stepped back into his corner.

"Johanna!" Hambroek was dragged out of the tent, still screaming abuse at his tormentor. "You touch her, and I swear you will burn in hell for it!"

Koxinga hardly blinked while father and son were lifted out bodily, Hendrik's legs kicking futilely in the air, mimicking his father in his use of language.

"Father! Hendrik!" Johanna tried to rush out after them, but one of the soldiers easily caught her by the arm, holding her fast.

When she stopped struggling, the soldier released her, giving her a slight push in Koxinga's direction.

"Your prize of war, my lord!" He smacked his lips salaciously as he grinned at his commander, beholding the red-haired girl with a roving eye before he took his exit.

Koxinga turned to Johanna, examining her closely, fascinated by her exotic grey-green eyes and the silky hair the color of fire. Most probably she had not yet been deflowered, such was her youth. She stood in front of him, trembling like a reed, the tears flowing freely down her cheeks. Then without warning, he grabbed her by the waist, his face close to hers, and pushed her onto the futon, heaving himself on top of her. His hand went to the clasp in her hair, releasing a cascade of fiery color. He grasped at it, pulling back her head sharply. She cried out in alarm as his hands next tore at her bodice, displaying one pale breast. Koxinga stared at the soft flesh for a moment and touched it, mesmerized. Then his hand reached down, pulled up her skirt and as he looked her in the eye, he ripped the cloth with a tearing sound to display a smooth, freckled thigh.

For a brief moment he struggled to pull down her undergarment, positioned his hips over hers, and willed himself to look her in the eye as he prepared to penetrate her. This was his right, his prize of war. But what he saw stopped him dead.

He no longer saw the red-headed daughter of the missionary man as the girl lay weeping beneath him, terrified and helpless. What he did see was his own mother. His own mother, as he imagined her being raped again and again, by a whole army of sweaty men, their oily queues dangling in her face as they pushed into her to satisfy their lust, her screams and sobs futile and unheard. Then that same image came back to him, that image that had haunted his nights for so long, the image of his mother's body dangling from the tree, the rain mingling with the blood running down her bare, bruised thighs.

Then, as suddenly as it had come, the illusion was gone. Gone with it, was his sexual arousal. Frustrated and embarrassed, he shoved away from the girl, covering his manhood in shame as he stood.

The girl looked up at him, completely baffled. Koxinga turned to Ting-bin, who had turned his back in discretion.

"Look at me!" Koxinga yelled at him. Ting-bin did as he was told, raising his eyes to his commander with caution.

"You ... you shall never speak of this," Koxinga hissed at Ting-bin in a low, dangerous whisper. "On pain of death, you shall never speak of this. As far as my men are concerned, I ravished the girl. Is that understood?"

"Oh yes, sire. I fully understand," Ting-bin said.

Koxinga turned back to Johanna, who was still frozen in position, half-lying, half-sitting, her upper body resting on her lower arms. "Ting-bin! Give the girl some tea." Relieved, Ting-bin quickly obliged, pouring the steaming hot liquid into a tin cup. Koxinga helped the girl stand up and took the cup from Ting-bin, passing it on to Johanna. She took it from him with unsteady hands and gulped from it gratefully, not once taking her eyes off him.

"Drink. It will do you good," Koxinga pressed, sitting down on the ceramic stool. The girl took several more gulps of the scalding tea until the cup was empty. Koxinga stood up again, took the cup from her hands and placed it on the stool. Bewildered, she looked on as Koxinga reached down to the dirt floor, grabbed a handful of dirt and while holding her by the waist, proceeded to smear it across her back and her bottom. Finally, as a finishing touch, he spat in his hands and smeared the remaining dirt across her cheeks. Then he took a step back to admire his handiwork.

Johanna raised a trembling hand to her torn bodice, completely at a loss. From his corner, Ting-bin observed the curious ritual with interest.

"That should convince them. More tea!" Koxinga ordered. Ting-bin handed him a fresh cup, and Koxinga sat down again, his expression sullen. Johanna had now dropped her eyes to the floor, her arms making a half-hearted attempt to cover one exposed breast.

"Your father will believe that I bedded you. My men expect me to." He stared into his cup, as if in shame. Ting-bin translated hesitantly.

"I simply cannot do it. My mother was raped by the enemy, as were all the female servants. They also killed my little sister." He paused. "They probably raped her, too, the beasts. My mother hung herself after that." A long silence filled the tent after Ting-bin finished translating.

"Your father is a fool," he told the girl. She blinked at him, unable to say anything. "A fool, but a brave one, and one to be admired. He is risking a great deal to save his people. Even you. I can respect that." Johanna swallowed visibly, her eyes still fixed on him like those of a sika doe caught in the glare of a tiger about to pounce. He continued to stare into his cup, downing the remains in one swallow.

He turned away from her gaze. "Your people, the Hollanders, are not my enemy. They are simply in the way. They don't belong here. But your father made a serious mistake when he encouraged your governor to resist my armies. He should have used his common sense, and advised the governor to surrender. He should not have interfered. I had hoped there would be no war." He looked suddenly weary and got to his feet. "Guards!"

The two men that entered the tent came in grinning slyly, eyeing their lord with envy as they saw Johanna, her hair undone, her face and clothing smeared with dirt and her bodice and skirt torn. Koxinga could almost read their thoughts: "Ah, the lord of the imperial surname is so lucky to have had his way with the girl!" She was so exotic, after all. The reddish hair, the pale, freckled skin.... He grimaced, satisfied with the illusion that he had provided.

"Take her to her father. Show her to him, but keep them apart," he ordered his men. As they left, he turned to Ting-bin, his eyes dark with warning. His whisper was low. "On pain of death."

"Yes, my lord," Ting-bin said with an emphatic nod of his head.

Koxinga got up and left the tent, closely following Johanna and the guards. He wanted to see the missionary man's face when he saw his daughter like this. Ting-bin stepped up right behind him, obviously eager to witness the scene he knew would follow.

* * *

Antonius had purposely been held within earshot of all that went on inside the tent, an intentionally cruel move. For fifteen minutes his daughter had been left alone with that monster, but those minutes had seemed like an eternity. He had been able to hear her every cry, her every gasp. The sound of her anguish conjured up images of his daughter being brutally raped. He cried, frustrated by the helplessness that had overwhelmed him, tortured by his doubts and the guilt that he felt. He had done this to her. Whenever he had heard her cry out, he wanted to put his hands over his ears to shut out the sound. But his hands were tied behind his back, and he had been forced to listen to it all.

She suddenly appeared. "Johanna!" He looked at her, appalled at her disheveled, smeared appearance, her torn bodice and skirts.

"Johanna! My child! My little girl. This is my own undoing. Forgive me, I never meant…." He fell to his knees again, crying pathetically. Then he saw Koxinga, and lunged himself forward again in anger, ignoring the searing pain of the rope cutting into his wrists. "You despicable bastard! You will burn in hell everlasting for this!"

Koxinga stayed where he was, his face impassive.

"Father!" Johanna cried out, trying to get to her father, but the guards held her in place. "Father, look at me!" He looked at her, the tears of rage and regret almost blinding him.

"No, father, papa! No! It's all right. It wasn't…. He didn't…. It's all right." She willed him to look at her again. "He didn't," she almost mouthed to him, shaking her head to emphasize her message.

Finally she had gotten through to him. He stared at her in disbelief. Then his look went to Koxinga standing by the tent's entrance. The man merely returned his gaze, as if he had played no part in what was happening. Antonius looked at his daughter, whose appearance confirmed his worst fears. He couldn't understand. Yet she was trying to tell him something. Through a haze of hot tears, he tried to focus on his daughter's face again. Johanna shook her head at him.

"*Nee.* No. He didn't. It's all right," she mouthed at him again.

For the first time Antonius became aware of the officers' and soldiers' eyes on his daughter, her bosom half bared, the flesh of one leg showing.

They were making rude gestures of debauchery, laughing, and applauding their commander's sexual appetite. Then something dawned on him. He had no way of knowing what had really just happened in the tent, in spite of his daughter's cries and appearance. Whatever it was that had occurred, he instinctively knew that Koxinga hadn't actually touched her. Not in the way that he feared.

Perhaps this was all just a show. A show calculated to pain him, to punish him for the fact that he had encouraged the governor to fight instead of urging him to surrender. But if it was, then it was also a show to deceive his officers and men. They all expected their commander to ravish the daughter of the man who had stood up against him. That was his prize of war. It was deserving of his status and his power. And it had been to discipline him: he was probably one of the very few men who ever dared deny Koxinga anything.

Antonius calmed down somewhat and stopped straining against his bindings, his breathing still laboring hard. Johanna could see that he had understood. She, too, became calmer.

"My precious Hannah," he mouthed, his heart still racing. She mimicked back, echoing his sentiments.

"Take the missionary man's children away," Koxinga ordered. "Tomorrow at dawn, you will release them. Make sure they are escorted safely back to their people by the eighth hour."

A few of his men frowned, puzzled at this.

"The missionary man is a man of honor. He has courage," Koxinga announced out loud for the benefit of those around him. "He has returned to us and has therefore kept his word. Now I, too, shall keep mine."

19

The Siege of Fort Zeelandia

JUST after the eighth morning hour, shortly after Johanna and Hendrik Hambroek were tearfully reunited with their mother at Fort Zeelandia, a very pale Van Aeldorp burst into the governor's office.

"You'd better come see this. Something is happening on the beach. It's the Chinese. They've got some of our people down there."

Frederic hurried after Van Aeldorp toward the northwestern bastion. A sentry handed him his telescope and pointed in the direction of the beach, just where Pineapple Isle bent inward to point toward the bay. Pressing the instrument against his brow, he searched for the movement he thought he had seen with his naked eye. There, he found them: tiny figures in the distance, no more than five hundred yards or so from where he stood. This was unusual, because they appeared to be almost within range of the Dutch cannons. With bated breath, he watched as he could make out the numerous Chinese soldiers and officers walking to and fro with deliberate purpose. But then he saw the others. They were dragged, pushed and shoved forward, their hands tied behand their backs. They were his people, Dutch colonists. Then they came to a halt, the prisoners forced down to their knees. His blood ran cold as he realized what was about to happen.

"It looks like they are going to execute them," Van Aeldorp whispered hoarsely.

Frederic swallowed hard. "May God help us." He stared down at the beach, shocked. Next to each prisoner stood a soldier with a broadsword, waiting. They were going to execute all of the prisoners, in full view of the fort.

"There must be around twenty of our people down there." He fiddled with the telescope, trying to focus on the prisoners' faces. "I can see them. Petrus Mus, Frans van Voorn, Antonius Hambroek.... May the Lord have mercy on them!"

Even at such a distance, he could see the characteristic full head of hair that belonged to Frans van Voorn, the way he was dressed, the way in which he held his head. All the prisoners had been lined up and were on their knees, their heads down. He saw Antonius raise his head to look up at the fort. He must have known that they could see them. The missionary was struck harshly on the head by the soldier standing behind him, who swore at him angrily.

Frederic lowered the telescope to his side and muttered something in despair.

Christian Beyer and Van Iperen joined him. Their faces somber, they followed the disturbing developments on the beach. The sound of women's voices made them turn around. Shrill, frightened voices, hysterical voices. A steady flow of women streamed from the various staircases onto the bastion. They, too, had been alerted of what was happening on the beach. He could not blame them. Many of them had husbands, sons, or brothers unaccounted for since the siege had begun. They moved toward the wall, terrified at the thought of what they might see beyond it, yet pushing and jostling for a sighting of their loved ones, even if they knew it might be the last.

Frederic spotted Anna Hambroek and her daughters Cornelia and Johanna. Helena had also made her way up the stairs. He tried to catch his wife's eye, and as he did, she hurried to him and grasped his arm, her eyes questioning. Gesturing with a subtle movement of his head toward the beach, she followed his gaze. When it dawned on her what was about to happen she gasped.

"Dear God. They've got Antonius. And Frans van Voorn."

Frederic nodded, turning his attention once again to the many women milling along the wall. He sought out Anna and Cornelia as they tried to push their way through. He had lost sight of Johanna.

"Go to them," he said to his wife. She nodded with a frown, squeezed his arm and disappeared among the crowd in an attempt to get to the Hambroek women.

A chilling, unnatural silence fell as the crowd grasped at the horror of it all. Some of the women began to weep. Others could only stare ahead, numb with shock, while others turned their faces away, unable to watch.

Frederic saw that Helena had managed to reach Anna and Cornelia. She was standing in their midst, her expression grave. Johanna had joined them too. The girl had her hand tightly clasped on her mother's arm, determined not to be separated from her again in the turmoil.

Cornelia stood frozen at the wall, her eyes filled with dread. Frederic followed her gaze to see what had riveted her so. The young teacher to whom she was betrothed struggled violently as he was being led forward and forced to his knees, the executioner's heavy broadsword unsheathed and dangling right next to his head. The high-pitched sound that escaped Cornelia's throat cut through Frederic like a knife and left his ears ringing.

Anna Hambroek, alarmed by her daughter's scream, scrunched up her eyes to discover what had caused her daughter's distress. Supporting herself with one hand, she stood on her toes to see over the side of the wall. Though her eyesight was no longer sharp, she too, stiffened from what she saw. Her mouth fell open when she not only recognized her daughter's fiancé among the prisoners but also her husband.

Helena glanced back at him, helpless. There was nothing that she could do but be there for them and help Anna and her daughters through this terrible ordeal. Frederic hoped to God that Balthasar had stayed downstairs. He did not want his twelve-year-old son to witness this.

His heart beating wildly, he forced himself to look through the eyepiece again. Some of the prisoners put up a fierce struggle, so that it took several soldiers to hold them down. Frans van Voorn looked deathly pale, his mouth wide open in a soundless scream. One prisoner had started wailing piteously. The same, awful sound was repeated over and over again, like that of an animal in distress. Someone fainted. One of the soldiers stood above him and undid his breeches, urinating on top of the unconscious prisoner as his comrades hooted with laughter.

And then the man appeared of whom he had heard so much during the past few years. The man who had now proven that their fear of him was justified: the lord of the imperial surname. Even at such a distance, he distinguished himself from all the others: his long stride, his confident, authoritative bearing. When he reached the beach, he planted his feet firmly on the soft sand and crossed his arms in defiance. Then he looked up at the bastion of the fort, searching, until he finally found what he was looking for.

Frederic could feel Koxinga's eyes resting on him, although he had never met him in person. Tasting the foul bile in his mouth, he suddenly had the sickening sensation that this spectacle was entirely for his benefit. And that the show was about to begin.

Two Dutch sentries, no longer able to restrain themselves, began to fire. But the distance was too great, their action futile. Captain Aeldorp had to box their ears and shout at them to cease fire to save their ammunition. Lieutenant Gerrit and Van Iperen tried to calm the distressed women, and attempted to move them away from the scene, without much success. Dr. Beyer attended to those women who had fainted, dragging them out of harm's way from the trampling feet of others.

Then Frederic spotted Balthasar. His face was ghastly pale. The boy stood less than twenty feet removed from him, his toes gripping onto a ledge, allowing him a better view over the women's heads. The direction of his gaze was fixed on the beach below. The boy blinked in confusion at what he saw there. Frederic had an overpowering urge to rush to his son and remove him from the scene so that he would not have to see this. But the milling, panicking crowd kept them apart. He knew that he would never be able to get to him in time.

He turned to Lieutenant Gerrit. "Fire the cannon," he ordered quietly, wondering if their target was even within range. "Do it now." Better to have them die from our cannon and take a number of the enemy while they were at it than for their people to die so cruelly at their executioners' hands, he thought.

The guns, already manned and prepared, roared from the fortress walls, leading to more screams from the women. It was no use. The guns were out of range. He watched the distant figure of the Chinese commander, who did not even flinch at the sound of the cannon. He and his men had apparently done their homework when choosing the location for their grisly display. Either that, or they had learned this from the defected soldiers, or their prisoners, whom they had probably tortured for that information.

Down on the beach, the Chinese waited for the gun smoke to clear. It was plain that Koxinga wanted to make sure he had the full attention of his Dutch audience. Frederic watched, mesmerized, as the Chinese commander gave a sign, upon which the executioners took up their positions behind the row of prisoners.

"Frans! Don't look at them!" came Antonius' booming voice from below. "Look up! Look at the fortress! God will receive us." They were the last words that would ever escape the reverend's lips. The executioners raised their swords in unison and simultaneously swung down.

Some of the heads gave way on impact, rolling in the sand for some distance. One or two remained dangling from a grotesque combination of sinew and muscle. Dark pools of blood stained the sand, even before the bodies slumped to the ground.

The eerie silence that had fallen around him lasted for just a fraction of a second. A low, collective moan of horror escaped the throats of the women. Anna Hambroek closed her eyes for a brief moment as she held Cornelia, who trembled like a leaf. Helena and Johanna stood unmoving, engrossed by what they had just seen.

In utter disbelief they watched the executioners wipe the blood from their hands and lower their stained swords in the cleansing surf. Cornelia fainted. Helena and Anna caught her just in time, struggling with the momentum of her weight. Frederic rushed forward to help them, and together they lowered the girl gently, placing her back against the wall. When he stood up he found himself facing his son.

Balthasar! His face was streaked with tears, his shoulders shaking with every sob. The boy had been so well looked after by Antonius and Anna after Susanna had died, and he knew how fond he had always been of Antonius. He looked at Balthasar, and at an utter loss of words, all he could do was open his arms. The boy threw himself against his frame, and as he held him tight, he could feel the boy's intense grief wash onto him, threatening to overwhelm them both.

After Frederic had extricated himself from Balthasar's desperate embrace, he handed him into Helena's care. Then he forced himself to look down once more, and found himself staring right into the upturned face of the man he knew to be Koxinga.

He felt the penetrating gaze, as if to make sure Frederic understood. He swallowed, gasping for breath, all at once aware of how deep his nails had dug into the palms of his hands. Every one of those men who had just died down there, he had known them all. Cornelia, who he had known as a child and watched as she grew up to become a young woman, had lost both her father and her fiancé. Antonius had been his friend. For the briefest of moments, he imagined that Koxinga nodded in his direction. Then, without another glance, the Chinese commander turned on his heel and strode away, his senior officers in tow.

The executions of the Dutch prisoners devastated the morale of the besieged. After witnessing the killings, Cornelia Hambroek went into a state of hysteria followed by a trance-like shock. Christian Beyer's heart went out to the poor girl, so he decided to look after her himself.

Anna Hambroek, grieved though she was at her husband's death, tried to remain strong for her children's sake, especially Cornelia's. When Johanna and Hendrik had returned to Zeelandia unharmed she had cried, hysterical with a manic combination of relief and distress. She was relieved that Koxinga had kept his word in that he had spared her children, but she was devastated that he had taken her husband from her forever.

At Frederic's urging, Christian Beyer had led Johanna aside, examining and questioning her in the presence of her mother on what she had endured during her captivity. He had relayed to Frederic that, apart from what had seemed to be Koxinga's half-hearted attempt at sexual molestation, the girl appeared to be fine.

Not for the first time, he thanked God for Helena. She had been a tremendous comfort to Balthasar, and she turned out to be a rock when it came to supporting the Hambroek women in their grief. She had buried her first husband not too long ago, so she knew well what they were going through. He would have to put aside his own grief, as there was no time for him to mourn.

The killings also had an effect on the Dutch troops. Out of sheer fear, several soldiers and officers defected to the Chinese, who had probably welcomed them – and any useful information they could give them – with open arms. One of the officers who had mysteriously disappeared overnight was Sergeant Stockaert, who had been stationed in Saccam. Frederic was surprised, as he had never expected it of him. Perhaps the sergeant had defected because he was married to a Chinese; as the years had passed, more and more colonists had married local or Chinese women. He understood that some of these men might struggle with their loyalties.

It was a disturbing development nonetheless. Still, he had little time to concern himself with this, as Koxinga had shown absolutely no mercy since his troops had besieged the island. The killings had only confirmed what they already knew: that the enemy who had declared war upon them for their refusal to capitulate was a cruel and determined one. This only strengthened his resolve to hold the fort for as long as he possibly could.

In spite of what they had witnessed from the fort's bastions, Frederic found that some members of his military staff were still convinced that the Chinese did not have it in them to fight like a true army. After holding a war council, he sent the *Hector* and *'s Gravelande* out on an expedition to obstruct the enemy's progress. The two warships set sail from the coast south of Pineapple Isle, where their orders were to destroy the junks that blocked a strategically important sandbar. It soon became clear that the captains had underestimated the war junks' defensibility. Horrified, Frederic and his staff watched as the largest of the Dutch warships, the *Hector*, found itself surrounded.

"God, no," he breathed. Enemy ships fired at their quarry from all directions, and an instant later, the *Hector* was ablaze, its deck and sails burning like a floating funeral pyre. The *Hector* was lost. They saw the *'s Gravelande* take a serious hit, its flammable ammunition catching fire; somehow, the ship's crew managed to douse the flames. Injured, she sailed to the open sea, never to return. The two smaller Dutch warships had no choice but to retreat to Zeelandia.

Stunned by this setback, Frederic tried to decide their next move. Captain Pedel, who had spent many years on Formosa and who knew the geography of the Tayouan region well, volunteered to lead an expedition to recapture Baxemboy. He reasoned that if they succeeded, they would be better able to guard the bay's only other entrance, just north of Baxemboy, and prevent the Chinese from entering. He had been among the junior officers who had quashed the rebellion in 1652, and he was confident that victory could be theirs once more.

Frederic was less optimistic. "Do not underrate this man and his army, captain. These men have managed to hold back the Manchus for years. They are abundantly trained and battle hardened."

"With all due respect, governor, I am well familiar with these men," Pedel said. "They cannot fight. They might have won against the Manchus; but those miserable Manchus are nothing compared to our soldiers." He smiled reassuringly. "Trust me. Twenty-five Chinese men are no match for one of ours. They will run at the first blast of our guns."

After a favorable vote, the expedition was approved. They all agreed that not taking any action simply wasn't an option. If they sat back and allowed the Chinese to surround the fortress without putting up a fight, then they wouldn't last long either.

Pedel divided his two hundred and forty men into two companies and addressed them, repeating the arguments he had used to convince the council. The men were inspired by his charismatic presence and confidence, and they set out to meet their enemy in high spirits.

The Dutch troops, armed with muskets, boarded their long boats, and covered by the guns of Fort Zeelandia, crossed over to the southeastern tip of Baxemboy. There, some four thousand fully armored men awaited them.

The first salvo was fired. At the forefront of the ranks, the musket tore into flesh, killing and wounding dozens of Chinese soldiers. The second salvo rang out, the thunderous sound reverberating against the dunes. Still the enemy did not fall back, but continued to press on in tight formation. More men went down as the lethal muskets found their targets. With growing dismay Frederic felt that something wasn't quite right: this was too easy. A third salvo rang out, felling more men, their bodies piling on top of those who were sacrificed before them. Then without warning, they saw a whole regiment of enemy soldiers drop down low on their knees. Instinctively he knew what was happening, even before the eerie sound filled the air. Thousands of arrows shot up into the sky. From the height of the fortress walls the movement of the silver cloud was almost gracious, like a shoal of shiny fish that moves as one. They could only watch as the arrows found their zenith, to dip and speed their way to earth, spurred on by the force of gravity.

The Dutch soldiers tried to run for cover, only to find there was none. Even from where he stood, Frederic could hear the thickening sound of metal thudding into flesh. He could see the blood gurgling from the men's mouths. Those who had escaped the first salvo of arrows ran or turned their guns on the archers, who were still in position, their new arrows in place. A second *whoosh* filled the air. Those lucky enough to escape the deadly showers were suddenly confronted by a whole regiment of enemy troops that had enclosed them from behind. They were trapped. Convinced as they had been by their bold and courageous captain that the Chinese were cowardly and spineless, they had expected the enemy to turn and run.

Now, they were confused, terrified, and totally unprepared for the onslaught that followed.

The soldiers of the Dutch regiment were easy prey for the disciplined Chinese army, who set upon them with a fury.

Only half of Pedel's regiment lived to leave Baxemboy that day. Those who survived the battle had escaped by wading through the waters of the bay and made it back to the fort exhausted and dejected.

While Captain Pedel lay dying after his attempt to recapture the isle, Captain van Aeldorp and Lieutenant Gerrit had taken their men to Saccam in an attempt to reinforce Fort Provintia. There, too, they had underestimated the sheer numbers of the Chinese. Once they realized what they were up against, they had retreated hastily to Zeelandia. Fort Provintia was now lost to them, Fort Zeelandia was their only remaining stronghold.

No one was still under the illusion that they faced an easy enemy. They had all seen that these soldiers were nothing like the poorly armed peasants they had dealt with in 1652. Captain Pedel had been mistaken. These soldiers were men who had gained their experience on the battlefields fighting warriors of equal if not superior strength.

Based on the size of the grain reserves in the warehouses of the fortress, the Dutch had estimated they would be able to hold the fort for two years at least. All they could do now was wait, and pray. Pray that the *Maria* had gotten through and that relief forces were on their way.

Not long after, a junk arrived with a dispatch from Koxinga. Frederic was surprised to see that Koxinga had sent none other but He Ting-bin. His former interpreter handed over the letter from his new employer, skittish at having to face him once again. Frederic glared at him with undisguised contempt as he snatched it from his hand. He felt sorely tempted to arrest and imprison Ting-bin for his betrayal, but he realized the futility of such an action. Apparently relieved that he had completed his mission, Ting-bin left Zeelandia as quickly as he had come.

Frederic listened to the translation of the letter in silence.

"You have now seen with your own eyes how your brave but foolish captain was defeated and killed on the battlefield," the letter said. "His men, who are fools like him, looked upon my armies with disdain at first. Did you not see how they threw down their weapons at the first sight of my warriors, only to await the punishment that was their due? Is this not enough evidence of your incompetence? Does this not prove that you are unable to face my army and fight my soldiers? You and your fellow Dutchmen are full of ill-placed pride and have very little sense. You are not even worthy of the mercy that I am about to offer. If you continue in your foolhardy attempts to resist my forces with the handful of soldiers who now take refuge in your castle, then you will be severely punished by my forces.

"Listen to wisdom," the letter continued. "Let your losses be a lesson to you, and remind you that your forces are but a thousandth part of mine. If you insist on this path of action, and decline my repeated call to surrender, then I shall soon order that your castle be attacked. We will assault, conquer, and destroy it till not one stone is left standing. Be warned that if I should so wish, I am able to move heaven and earth, for I am destined to win. Take heed, and consider my words carefully."

Frederic felt all eyes upon him as the contents of the letter had been read out to them. As taunting and provocative as the letter was, it only had the opposite effect on him.

"Surrender is out of the question," he declared gruffly. "We will stay and fight to the end."

* * *

Because of the high seas and perilous monsoon winds, the *Maria* took more than seven weeks to reach Batavia, not arriving there until June 24. It barely missed Klenk van Odessa's *Carolina*, which had departed for Formosa a few days earlier. The *Carolina* had made great speed as the southern winds carried it to its destination, and the two ships had passed within twenty miles of each other, unseen and unaware of the other's mission.

Governor-General Maetsuijker paled visibly when the captain of the *Maria* told him of the invasion of Formosa. For months, he had chosen to ignore the signs. He had taken Coyett's repeated warnings and requests for reinforcements as the exaggerations of a paranoid man. But now he realized that he had allowed himself to be influenced by men with their own agendas, bitter men with personal scores to settle. Why hadn't he been able to see this? Had he been so blind? He had seldom been so terribly wrong.

He cursed Admiral van der Laan for misinforming him and Nicolaes Verburgh for making him doubt Coyett. But most of all, he blamed himself for listening to them, for allowing them to cloud his better judgment. He was, after all, the one responsible for making this fateful decision. He gave orders at once for a fast yacht to overtake Klenk van Odessa to inform him the island was under attack. The moment the yacht had left, he decided to send a fleet to Formosa to aid the besieged colonists. Maetsuijker, however, had great difficulty in finding a suitable candidate to head the fleet, as hardly any of the officers were willing to undertake such a thankless task.

Finally, through sheer lack of alternatives, he commissioned the one man willing to take on the job: Jacobus Cauw, a lawyer by trade, a man with little wartime experience. Cauw had a serious speech defect that often made him the subject of ridicule, in spite of his keen mind and knowledge of the law. Fed up with being continually sidelined in his career, Jacobus Cauw decided to take on the challenge, and set sail with a fleet consisting of ten ships and seven hundred soldiers.

In the meantime, heavy seas seriously hampered the messenger yacht's progress, and it was unable to even get close to the *Carolina*. By the time it finally did, Klenk had already reached the shores of Formosa.

* * *

For the fifth time during the journey, Klenk van Odessa went through the instructions given him by the governor-general with eager anticipation. It was up to him to inform Frederic Coyett that he was to be dismissed from his duties as governor. With him, he carried a letter from Maetsuijker for Coyett. Both he and Valentijn would be expected to report to Batavia upon arrival to answer for their actions.

So he would now be in charge of Formosa. During the voyage, he re-read the letters and documents he was to deliver to Coyett that would relieve him of his function more than a dozen times. His mind went over the words that he would say to him, practicing a regretful look appropriate for the occasion. He thought of the power his new position would bring, and studied the few books and maps on China and Formosa that Nicolaes Verburgh had given him, determined to make a success of his posting. He was going to make it quite clear to the people of Formosa that the VOC had been unaware of the hard and unrelenting rule that had been Coyett's, and he wished to make amends.

Within twenty miles of his destination, he carefully filed his instructions for the last time, and supervised the packing of his belongings in his trunk. As he did so, he became aware of a considerable commotion on deck. Puzzled by the shouts and the sound of running, booted feet above, he went up to the deck, where he collided with a frowning captain.

"You'd better see this, sir," he said, handing over his brass eyepiece and gesturing toward starboard.

"*God allemachtig*!" Klenk van Odessa gasped. "There's an entire armada out there!" For several miles along the coast, the sea was an almost solid line of masts and sails. He gulped uncomfortably. "What are those ships? And where are they from? Can you tell?" he asked as he handed back the instrument. The captain dutifully pressed it against his eye.

"Chinese, sir," the captain said levelly, without lowering the piece. "Without a doubt. Hundreds of them, as far as I can determine. Perhaps a thousand."

"This cannot be. What does it mean?"

"Looks like a siege to me, sir. If we're to believe the maps they've provided us with, there are only two ways to enter the bay. But the Chinese have completely blocked both entrances. We couldn't get through there even if we wanted to. See for yourself!"

"Have they spotted us, do you think?" Klenk asked. The captain took another long hard look. Five war junks had sailed out in their direction, forming a barricade between their ship and the coast, but they didn't seem intent on attacking them.

"Yes, sir. But it looks as if they're letting us be. Till now. They do seem pretty determined to stop us from getting through, though."

Stunned, Klenk looked across the waters at the many junks facing them, their maroon sails as exotic as dragons' wings.

"Sir, if you wish I can lower the anchor near one of the beaches further south. We could send a sloop with a messenger to the governor to let them know that you've arrived."

Klenk didn't hear him, his heart rate well above normal. In the haze of his ambition, he had accepted Van der Laan's assurances that there was no military threat facing Formosa; and not knowing the Swede personally, he had taken Verburgh's views on Coyett's incompetence as the truth. He had never even remotely considered the possibility of finding the island actually besieged. If this armada belonged to that pirate Koxinga, then he must have declared war on the colonists. Engrossed by his dilemma, Klenk scarcely noticed that the captain had just asked him something.

"What? What did you say?" he almost stammered, trying to win time. This was a highly unexpected turn of events, and he was painfully aware that this situation was quite beyond him.

"Sir, I asked if you wished to land further south, so we can lower a boat and get a message to Governor Coyett."

Klenk just stared at him. The captain remained surprisingly cool and practical.

"Yes," he said, recovering fast. "Yes, do that, Captain." He turned back to look at the staggering number of war junks filling the horizon. He still had no idea what he was going to do.

* * *

"Governor Coyett, sir!" Lieutenant Gerrit said, visibly flustered. "Word has arrived from Batavia. Come quickly," he urged, walking ahead in great strides toward the square.

A group of well-armed men awaited them in the square, several native guides among them.

"Gentlemen. God bless you all for coming to our aid," Frederic said, immensely relieved. "You managed to get through the blockade."

"Yes, governor," one of the men said. "Your native guides helped us reach Zeelandia without being seen. I am to hand over this letter to you, sir, from Mr. Klenk van Odessa. He is here, aboard the *Carolina.* She is lying at anchor just south of Pineapple Island. "

"What? Klenk van Odessa? He is here? He came to Formosa? With how many ships did you arrive?"

The man hesitated, looking decidedly unhappy. "With one ship, Mr. Coyett. Just the one ship."

"What? With just one ship? The man is out of his mind! What is he doing here? Didn't Batavia receive word...?" He became conscious of the curious eyes of the people in the square, intrigued by the pitch of his voice. "I think we had better step into my office. Please follow me."

They all walked up the stone steps and crowded into his office. Van Iperen, Captain van Aeldorp and Lieutenant Gerrit took their usual positions, their expression solemn.

"The *Maria*," Frederic pressed the messenger. "Did the *Maria* not come into harbor before you left Batavia?"

"No, sir," the man said without hesitation. "It did not. I merely have instructions to give you these."

Frederic took the official documents and hurriedly unsealed them. He read the contents with growing astonishment, his lips moving in silence as he did. Shocked, he sat down on his chair. Then his mouth formed a twisted kind of smile.

"This I find interesting," he said. "Listen to this. I have been accused of 'sabotaging our well-planned attack on Macao and causing unnecessary panic among the people.'" He snorted cynically. "Well, well. It looks as if I am being dismissed from my post, gentlemen. The esteemed *Mijnheer* Hermanus Klenk van Odessa is here to relieve me from my duties and succeed me. Such fortunate timing."

Then, as if on cue, Coyett, Gerrit, and Van Iperen all turned to the large window facing the Formosa Strait, which was black with enemy ships. On the other side of the channel, Baxemboy was crawling with Chinese troops. There was a stunned silence.

Perhaps it was the comical, perplexed look on their faces that did it, or the sheer irony of the situation, but Frederic simply couldn't help himself and suddenly burst out laughing. The others looked at him in consternation. They exchanged looks, and all at once they, too, bellowed with laughter.

The unexpected mirth released some of the strain they had been under, and it felt good. Van Iperen and Coyett both wiped away their tears of mirth. Every time their merriment was about to subside, they caught sight of each other, and burst into peals of laughter once more. And all at the expense of the poor messenger, who looked dumbly ahead of him, feeling very foolish. The irony of the situation was not lost on him.

Frederic was the first to recover. With a grand, theatrical gesture, he took out a fresh piece of parchment and dipped his quill in the inkwell at the corner of his desk.

"'Esteemed colleague,'" he read aloud as he wrote, enjoying the moment, "'It has been brought to my attention that you have arrived in these waters with the instructions to replace me as governor of Formosa. I commend you on your new assignment and warmly welcome you to the island.'"

Van Iperen, unable to help himself, grinned again. This set off the others once more, their shoulders shaking.

Frederic tried to focus on the letter, and shook his head with a smile. "'It pleases me to invite you and your officers to come ashore so that we might consider the present state of affairs —'" he glanced through the window at the many enemy vessels that filled the bay "'— and to enable you to assume the responsibilities of your new post.'" His eyes twinkling, he signed it with a flourish, blotted out the excess ink and handed it to the messenger, who took it from him glumly. Frederic almost felt sorry for the man. He got up from his chair and slapped him on his back. "Come, my dear man. There's no need to look so sober. Can you not appreciate the humor of the situation?"

The man nodded, allowing himself a warped smirk as he tucked Coyett's letter into his folder.

"Convey that to the new governor, if you would be so kind."

As a last chuckle escaped Van Aeldorp's lips, Frederic approached the window to remind himself of the seriousness of their predicament. Sobered by what he saw, he took a deep breath, all the hilarity now dispelled.

"Lieutenant Gerrit, see to it that this man and his escort are given a proper meal and some rest before they return to their ship."

Three hours later, while their visitors made their way back to the *Carolina*, Frederic joined his staff of officers on top of the bastion to assess their situation. With a strategically placed cannon they had managed to block the main entrance to the bay, but they had been unable to defend the one north of Baxemboy. Much to their alarm, Koxinga's ships had succeeded in entering the bay at high tide through this northern entrance, which would have been only just deep enough. Here they had been able to sail through, out of range of Zeelandia's cannons. And there they had stayed, lying in wait for any movement the Dutch might make.

The fortress had been surrounded for almost a month and was crowded with all the inhabitants of the village, as well as those who had survived the siege of Fort Provintia. That fort had proven to be worthless in its defense, its walls weak and thin, with food supplies sufficient only to last them a few days. The troops who had remained to defend the fort were either killed or captured.

In contrast, Fort Zeelandia was large and well built in the style of the Renaissance, a layout that had been thoroughly tested over the ages. The fortress was well stocked with warehouses and permanent access to wells that provided fresh water. Sufficient livestock was penned in the square to feed even these unaccustomed numbers. The superior guns and cannon were enough to hold the enemy at bay. In the first attacks following their arrival, the guns had killed hundreds of Chinese soldiers, whose bodies, much to the consternation of the Dutch, were not removed. The corpses piled up at the bottom of the fortress walls, the stink of the carrion overwhelming. Yet for every Chinese soldier that died, it seemed there were ten to take his place.

There never seemed to be an end to it, Frederic thought as he looked at the position of the lowering sun. According to his calculations, Klenk van Odessa should be able to reach Zeelandia tomorrow before dawn. He dispelled the gnawing uncertainty that he might not come, and reprimanded himself for not giving his appointed successor the benefit of the doubt. He wondered how many troops he had brought with him. God knows they could use all the help they could get. While he discussed the matter with Captain van Aeldorp, they were interrupted by an excited sentry.

"Captain, look! Over there!" He handed the eyepiece to Van Aeldorp, pointing at the south, along the coast. The fleet of war junks had obscured it earlier, but now it was unmistakable.

"It's a Dutch ship, sir. Look."

The captain peered through the instrument, squinting. "Hmm," he murmured before handing it to Frederic. He scanned the horizon, and then he saw it too. The enemy's fleet had obscured it earlier, but now there was no longer any doubt.

"It's the *Carolina*," he said with certainty. "Klenk van Odessa's ship." He handed the telescope back to Van Aeldorp, who looked through the instrument once more.

"No. It cannot be. I don't believe it."

"What, lieutenant?" Frederic demanded, more brusquely than he intended.

"It looks as if —" Van Aeldorp paused to make sure. "It appears to be leaving." His tone was more definite now. Frederic snatched the telescope from him and searched the waters for the ship. Then he saw it. The sails were fully hoisted, gathering wind and picking up speed. It was definitely leaving. Coyett quickly did the math. The messenger and his escort could not possibly have made it back in time. Klenk van Odessa was leaving, and he had not even bothered to wait for his messenger to come back with his response.

"The coward," he muttered under his breath. "The bloody, godforsaken coward."

* * *

On board the *Carolina*, Hermanus Klenk van Odessa knew that he was abandoning his countrymen on Formosa as the crew prepared to set sail. He was not proud of what he was doing, and he could not justify it, not even to himself. He argued over and over again that Coyett and his officers knew the island and its people, and that Coyett would be better equipped to deal with Koxinga's army. He shuddered at the thought of having to take the helm in the midst of such an invasion. He simply wasn't up to being a wartime governor, or a hero; and he now knew he would never be. It shamed him to admit it, but that was the way things were.

"Depart, sir? Do you not wish to wait for Governor Coyett's response, at the very least?" The captain's tone was incredulous, almost accusing. It didn't make Klenk van Odessa feel any better about himself.

"You heard me, captain. Depart!" he snapped at the captain angrily, and stormed toward the stairway that would bring him below deck. Anywhere, as long as he could get away from these men, knowing that they would probably respect him no more. He could feel the looks of contempt burning on his back.

"Do we head back to Batavia, sir?" the captain called after him, trying to sound respectful.

Klenk van Odessa half turned, hesitating. Returning to Batavia would be like a mongrel dog running at the first sign of trouble, with its tail between its legs. His reputation would be tarnished, his career in ruins. Men of influence and standing would no longer wish to associate themselves with him. He could not face that.

"No," he said. "We're heading for Nagasaki." Unable to look the captain in the eye, he hastily made his way down the stairs.

* * *

In spite of the almost unlimited manpower at his disposal and the fighting spirit of his men, Koxinga was beginning to feel frustrated. In truth, he had not been surprised when, on the day of his arrival on Formosa, he had watched the blood-red banner being hoisted above the fortress. It only confirmed what he had already suspected: that the Dutch would not give up the island without a fight.

This he had anticipated: he had not expected otherwise. But it now it appeared that the fortress was far more difficult to conquer than he had originally thought. Worse than that, he and his men had not found the fort to have any real weaknesses. Up to now the Dutch had managed to ward off their attacks. Their heavy guns were strategically well placed along its walls, and every shot had killed scores of his men. Attacking the rear of the fortress at the southwestern side, from where the colonists still seemed to be coming and going, was much too dangerous. This side was covered by guns positioned on a redoubt, a small defensive tower built high on a dune, just a stone's throw away from Fort Zeelandia. The redoubt had a superb view of the back of the great fortress. According to his men it could even turn its guns on its interior.

No, he had to admit that they were not making any real progress. He well remembered Sun-Tzu's words in his *Art of War*: not to besiege walled cities if it could be at all avoided. He grimaced. Sun-Tzu was right, of course, as always. But the way he saw it, they didn't have any choice.

What concerned him most was that the food supply for his numerous troops was dwindling. In one of the warehouses in Saccam his troops had managed to find grain to feed his army, but according to his general it would not last them a month.

Leaving his generals to continue besieging the fort, he took a company of men and ventured inland to capture the fields and farms in a quest to find new sources of food. But the captured farm fields provided no real solution, as they were too scattered and the season for harvesting was too far off.

Instead, he went on to pacify the native population, hoping to win them as his allies. Koxinga found that their loyalty to the Dutch did not run deep. They must have seen the colonists retreat for the safety of the fortress, leaving them to fend for themselves. Most of the aboriginal villages were quick to side with him. They had been awed by his large, disciplined armies that came swarming across the island. Practical of nature, many of the villages did not even try to resist as they realized that the Dutch must be doomed to lose the war in the face of such odds, and quickly laid down their weapons in surrender.

He personally saw to it that they were well rewarded for doing so. Bales of silk and Chinese clothing were presented to the aboriginal chieftains, as well as the highly prized tobacco, which they eagerly received. As a token of their allegiance and acceptance of Koxinga's rule, the villagers did have to adapt to Chinese ways. The native villagers were given Chinese names, and were forbidden to use their Dutch names from that moment on. Everything that was remotely associated with the Dutch occupation, including the use of certain place names, was to be systematically erased from the island.

There was one thing that the Dutch had introduced that he did maintain: and that was the *landdag*, the annual gathering for all tribal chieftains. He invited them to an official banquet, and just as he expected, they all came to pay him their respect.

Within four days of his arrival, many of the aboriginal village elders had handed over their ceremonial staffs to Koxinga, as a symbol of surrender and of their newly placed loyalty.

During the first gathering, the tribal elders were asked to come forward, one by one. An officer called out their new Chinese names, names which came phonetically closest to their own, native ones.

"Malihe!" An officer prodded a wrinkled, wizened man in a curious mixture of clothing to step forward. He approached Koxinga cautiously, and was handed a parcel.

"From now on, you will be called Ma Lihui, and you are awarded the position of mandarin of the third rank," Koxinga announced. The man rolled his tongue over the unfamiliar syllables of his new name and received the clothing articles with reverence. The newly named Ma Lihui had been given the minor mandarin's blue tunic, which came with a silk cap, shoes, and sash, which were all symbolic of his changed status. The eyes of the old man shone with pleasure as he stepped backward to make way for the next. The other village elders gathered around him clucking excitedly, admiring and touching the finely woven silk and richly embroidered cap.

Koxinga was satisfied: his ploy to win over the aboriginal tribes had been successful. Not only were the natives easily convinced of the superiority of the Chinese forces over the Dutch, they were also impressed by the way that the Chinese troops treated them. The trinkets they were given worked like magic. It did not take long before word reached the other villages about the rewards they would receive if they offered their allegiance. Their elders soon came to Koxinga, to do just that.

Next, his men went further inland to win over the Chinese there. These could be migrants who had only recently fled the war in China, but also ethnic Chinese whose ancestors had come to the island generations ago. As instructed, the soldiers spoke of Lord Koxinga's goodwill and excellent leadership. They told stories of his heroism and his fairness, and announced that Lord Koxinga had come to save them from the tyranny of the Dutch. They made promises of fruitful harvests, fairer treatment, and greater wealth. They also spoke of how they would one day defeat the Manchu barbarians who had invaded their homeland, and of the freedom they would soon have to return to the land of their ancestors.

Just as he expected, the campaign was successful. To most of the Chinese on Formosa, Koxinga already had a reputation of mythical proportions. The stories that were being told came from those who spoke the same tongue, who shared the same ideology and culture. The local Chinese began to believe that Koxinga would be able to expel the Dutch and truly provide them with a better life. His long-anticipated coming brought them hope, so their loyalty and obedience came only naturally.

Koxinga lost no time in setting up a new civil administration system on the island. Accustomed to having to relocate from one place to the next in order to flee from the ever-advancing Qing troops, his administrators were experienced, and ruthlessly efficient. Farms were reorganized according to the age-old principles of Chinese agriculture. Here and there he confiscated land from the natives, allotting the plots to Chinese farmers to work upon. Before long, a civil administration similar to that which had existed during the Ming dynasty was established on Formosa. Along with it came new taxes that were collected in Koxinga's name.

* * *

Not all the villages surrendered as easily, or willingly. One of the exceptions was the village of Soulang, where the newly opened training seminary for reverends and schoolteachers was located. Over the years, more than a dozen Dutch families had settled there, and the vast majority of villagers were converts to Christianity.

As evidence of their allegiance to Koxinga, Soulang's neighboring aboriginal tribes, several of which were longtime foes, headed for the village and attacked it. Soulang's warriors put up a valiant defense; but against such odds their efforts were futile. The seminary and school building were set alight, the precious books and writing materials destroyed. Of the four Dutch school teachers stationed at Soulang, one was beaten to death with a crucifix. Two others were taken captive as hostages. Only one of them managed to make it to the sanctuary of Fort Zeelandia.

Any other villages in the area that still considered challenging Koxinga's armies now thought the wiser of it and laid down their arms. Pleased, Koxinga made sure that they were rewarded for their decision with silks and coral. Those foolish enough to resist, or anyone who showed the slightest hesitation about where their loyalties lay, was instantly put to death as a warning to all.

It proved harder to impose his rule in some other parts of the island, especially in the central western plains, which was the territory of the Kingdom of Middag. This kingdom was the result of an alliance between the many tribes native to the area. The Dutch had not made a real effort to bring it under their control, and the people of Middag had no quarrel with them. As long as the Dutch let them be, they ignored them, continuing with their centuries-old pagan ways.

Their initial reaction to the arrival of the Chinese forces hardly differed from when the Dutch had first come to the island. As long as they stayed well away from them, they mattered little. However, the people of Middag certainly had no intention of being subjugated to Chinese rule, just as they did not wish to be ruled by the colonists.

So when a large regiment of Chinese troops did venture onto their ancestral territories, the tribes felt threatened and their attitude changed. The Chinese, who had so far not come across any form of organized resistance on the island, suddenly found themselves ambushed.

Using the weapons with which they had hunted and fought for centuries, the native warriors attacked their new enemy with unsurpassed viciousness. The aboriginals knew the lay of the land intimately. Every tree, rock, and crevice was familiar; and they used that knowledge to their advantage. Some had blades, with which they hacked into their enemy. Others used spears, axes, and the muskets that they had stolen from the Dutch. Their archers were well hidden, their arrows appearing to come from nowhere.

When it dawned on the Chinese general that they were badly outnumbered, not even their discipline and training could save them. The soldiers scattered, running for their lives. They may as well have stayed where they were, for the warriors were hunters. Using all their skills, honed for millennia, they hunted down the soldiers like animals, killing almost everyone. Some two thousand Chinese soldiers were slaughtered during that attack.

* * *

When word reached Koxinga of the massacre of one of his regiments, he was livid. He had never anticipated this. It was the first time they had come across any real resistance from the natives: all the other tribes had transferred their loyalties to him so easily.

When Ting-bin mentioned that there had been a Christian mission in that area and that there might still be Dutch missionaries living among the northern tribes, he became convinced that they had incited the natives against them. He knew that the missionaries had considerable influence with the aboriginals, and he simply did not want to believe that they had turned against him on their own accord.

He became obsessed with the idea that the Dutch missionaries had been responsible for the attack. He strode around the tent swearing angrily, his head feeling as if it were about to explode.

"We shall have our revenge," he growled. "We will teach them not to turn the native people against us. I believe I can think of an appropriate punishment for these missionary men." He smirked at the thought. "Get those two hostages from Soulang."

The two Dutch reverends, who had not yet recovered from their violent ordeal at the seminary, were brutally dragged out to a rudimentary execution ground. There, the soldiers set about building crucifixes, to which they nailed the two screaming men. The crucifixes were then dragged to the beach, so that they could be seen from the ramparts of Fort Zeelandia.

"Kill them," Koxinga ordered quietly. The executioner lifted his heavy blade and struck at the men's bowels, after which the screaming finally ceased.

* * *

It was the manner of death of the two missionaries that shocked Frederic the most. That, and the sheer panic it had caused among the besieged Dutch settlers. Everyone wondered what fate would befall them if ever the fortress should fall. They often clutched at him, desperate for any reassurance that he might be able to give them as their governor. If anything, the murders made him all the more determined to hold out as long as they could.

The executions continued to perplex him. Since Antonius and the others had been beheaded on the beach after his refusal to capitulate, there had been no other killings. So far, he had been able to read Koxinga and predict his moves quite well, his actions fairly much in character of the man. Christian Beyer had briefed him thoroughly on this. He thought, with some cynicism, that some good had come out of the doctor being sent to Amoy to treat Koxinga. His acquaintance with Koxinga had so far proven very useful.

Frederic knew for a fact that the Chinese held many more of their people prisoner. Then why kill these missionaries from Soulang? And why had they been crucified? What did Koxinga mean to achieve with such an act? Somehow, he felt that the execution served as a gruesome message, directed at him. But what?

He felt the loss of Antonius more keenly than ever. As head of the Christian mission on the island, he would probably have had some insight that would help him understand. What would he have made of this?

Two weeks later, word reached him that a whole regiment of Chinese troops had been slaughtered by tribal warriors in the north. Antonius had once told him that there had been a mission post there in the past, but once the reverends came to the conclusion that these natives were impossible to convert, it had been abandoned. He had heard rumors that some of the older Dutch missionaries had chosen to remain there, but the company no longer had any dealings with those primitive tribes.

In spite of the warm May weather, he suddenly felt himself go stony cold. Things were finally falling in place. The crucifixions hadn't made any sense at first. Now he was beginning to understand. Did Koxinga think that the Dutch mission had incited the tribes against him? Had he blamed them for the massacre of his men? It would explain the crucifixions.

He could feel the hairs on the back of his neck rise as it dawned on him. Koxinga's motivation had been revenge. Simple, unadulterated revenge.

20

The Demise of He Ting-bin

KOXINGA was troubled by what he had done. He had ordered the execution of the prisoners in a moment of vengeful rage, but now he felt only remorse. It had been Ting-bin who had suggested that the Dutch missionaries might have been responsible for the slaughter of his men, and, in his fury, he had believed it.

Once that blinding red haze had receded from behind his eyes, he realized he might have been wrong. Perhaps the Dutch had nothing to do with the massacre of his troops in the kingdom of Middag. When he questioned his officers further, he found that they had not come across any sign of Dutch settlement in the territory, nor had there been any mission. It occurred to him that the Dutch may never have had any real grip on the warfaring tribe.

Then why in name of heaven had he ordered those men to be crucified? He knew enough of their Christian god and his alleged son, Jesus, of whom it was said that he died on the crucifix for all of mankind. He was aware of how important the symbol of the cross was to their faith, and he had made a mockery of it. His act of retribution had been downright childish. He thought of Dr. Beyer, for whom he had the utmost respect and whom he had begun to think of as a friend. He felt ashamed. What would the doctor think of him now? He had behaved like a barbarian.

But it wasn't just the crucifixions that he regretted. It was the face of Reverend Hambroek that had begun to haunt him. That determined, proud missionary who had given his life out of conviction, and one of the very few men who had ever dared defy him. Time and time again he was reminded of that moment on the beach, when he had looked up at the heavens, unafraid of the death that awaited him. The memory of it triggered his conscience and caused the foulest of moods.

His physical health was also deteriorating, although he did not care to admit this to anyone, afraid that his men might consider him weak, and that it would undermine his authority.

They had been on Formosa for four months now, but they had not come any closer to taking the fort, which was becoming more urgent with the growing food shortages. His sources, Dutch defectors included, had told him that the large warehouses at Zeelandia were stacked with plenty of grain. He needed to get to that food, but no matter what they tried, the Dutch continued to hold them off.

The pressing lack of food only served to highlight something else. He had been led to believe that Formosa was a lush and fertile paradise. He had been told that the fields were rich with rice and grain. The reality was that the farmed fields, separated by mountain ranges and deep, impassable gorges, were far and few between, and that the seasonal weather dictated the harvest times, just as it had in China. Pork was increasingly hard to come by and therefore expensive; venison had grown scarce due to over-hunting. The small amount of rice that was available to the troops was mostly of poor quality.

His administrators had already cautioned him that they would soon have to reduce food rations again. This concerned him greatly, as he was confronted daily by men who grew increasingly thin. Often, there was little else to offer his troops apart from congee, a porridge made from boiled rice.

His senior officers had already begun to complain that life in China had been much better, in spite of the danger that the Manchus posed. Besides, Formosa was even more humid than Fujian, and the heavy monsoon rains seemed to go on forever. Dozens of his men had already succumbed to scurvy, malaria, or other diseases that rampaged on the island.

Formosa was not at all what he had expected. Besides, he had never thought that the several hundred Dutch soldiers would be able to withstand his army for so long. It appeared that he had underestimated them after all.

Just when he was about to plan a major assault on the fort, he learned that a Dutch fleet of warships arriving from Batavia had broken through the blockade and had succeeded in reaching the south coast of Formosa. This enraged him. Matters were bad enough as it is, and this was the last thing he needed.

Frustrated with everything, he blamed Ting-bin. It had been Ting-bin who had convinced him that conquering Formosa would be easy, that the Dutch were cowards and would surrender within weeks, perhaps even days. It was Ting-bin who was responsible for conjuring up the image of a place where rice, vegetables, and fruits were plentiful all year round. Ting-bin had not told him about the humid heat that the summer months could bring, or the lethal swamp fever. Nor had he spoken of the formidable fortress, which seemed almost impenetrable, or about the barbarians' surprisingly willful nature. He should have told him, but he hadn't. And that was unforgiveable.

* * *

Ting-bin had no real taste for war. To him, it was all just an incredible waste of resources. Somehow, he had hoped – and expected – that the Dutch would be intimidated into immediate surrender, and that there would be no fighting. Then his work would be done and he would be handsomely rewarded for his efforts. He had looked forward to retiring in comfort, perhaps even acquiring another concubine. It now seemed that none of these things were going to happen.

In spite of the dwindling food supply and the primitive conditions that they now found themselves in, Ting-bin discovered a side to him that he had not known before: he was not entirely without compassion. In his function as interpreter, he often kept company with the captured Dutch soldiers and civilians, but not only because his work required it. Without being aware of it, he kept a close eye on their well-being, especially if they had treated him kindly in the past. He had been appalled by the beheadings on the beach and shocked when Koxinga intended to rape

Reverend Hambroek's daughter. He had even felt relieved when Koxinga had been unable to go through with the deed. Such things he had not foreseen when he had betrayed the Dutch and had sided with Koxinga; this he had never intended.

During Johanna and Hendrik Hambroek's brief captivity he often brought the children water or extra titbits of food, as Reverend Hambroek had always been good to him. When he felt that the Chinese soldiers were too harsh in their treatment of the prisoners, he would use his status and admonish them severely, whereupon they would back off for a while.

Even after Hambroek's children had been released, he had looked after the Dutch prisoners' interest. He played an important role in receiving defecting Dutch soldiers, most of them deserting out of sheer desperation, hunger, and fear for what Koxinga might do to them if the fortress should fall. He was usually the first to speak to them, in the first instance as interpreter, but often to help them find accommodation and secure them employment of some kind. He surprised even himself; and he wondered that he had perhaps worked for the VOC too long, that this might be the reason he felt compelled to help the colonists.

He had just woken from a brief nap in his tent after a meager lunch of congee and fish, and had barely finished relieving himself outside the tent when two sentries summoned him. He was to appear before Lord Koxinga straight away.

Startled, he dropped his cap, and when he stooped to retrieve it, his escort dragged him along brusquely. This unnerved him. Lord Koxinga must have been impatient and agitated when he had given orders to fetch him. He was only too familiar with his employer's temperament, and he tried hard to think what he had done to have caused him such dissatisfaction.

"My Lord Koxinga," Ting-bin said, in as modest a voice as he could muster.

General San-ge and one of his lieutenants were also in the tent. As soon as he entered, Koxinga rounded on Ting-bin furiously and hit him hard across the face. Ting-bin staggered back, barely keeping his balance. He blinked at Koxinga, stunned, feeling the warm blood seep from his nose. General San-ge looked on impassively.

"You lied to me!" Koxinga yelled as he stood inches away from him. He struck down at Ting-bin again, this time a dizzying blow that brought him to his knees. He heard Koxinga breathe hard, making an effort to control his temper. Ting-bin stayed on the floor, his eyes carefully averted. Much to his relief, Koxinga stepped back, but his anger had not yet abated.

"I should never have trusted you. You, who betrayed your Dutch employers so easily to save your own skin." Koxinga's tone was ominously low. "Double-dealing lowlife. Did you really think I would not find out what game you were playing with me? The only reason I allowed your deceit to continue was because I enjoyed watching your efforts to raise the money that you said the Dutch would pay me. You lied to them, just as you lied to me."

Ting-bin's heart stopped beating as he realized his ploy had been discovered.

"My lord –"

"Shut up!" Koxinga raised a foot and pushed Ting-bin over, so that he sprawled clumsily toward the floor, his dignity gone.

"You deceived me. You led me to believe that the Dutch had made a deal with me under the conditions that I had set, while they never actually had. You abused your position to let all of those poor people – my people – pay you money under the guise of a tax in my name! Did you honestly think I would not find out? Piece of turtle dung! Motherfucker!" He spat out the lowly insults with a passion. Ting-bin held up his hands to fend off any blows, shaking like a leaf.

"Lord Koxinga, I –"

"I told you to shut up! You lied to me, while I rewarded you so well for your so-called valuable information." Ting-bin remained where he was, frozen in his ridiculous position. "But your information wasn't very reliable, was it? You spoke of a mere handful of soldiers to guard the fortress. There are hundreds! You told me this place was abundant in food, a paradise. Yet my men are starving! You are utterly useless!" He lashed out with his foot, making contact with Ting-bin's shin. He cried out in pain. Koxinga waited for a moment, his expression dark.

"We are running out of food." He lowered his voice so that no one outside the tent would hear, scratching at his neck to relieve his itch, leaving pale marks where his fingernails had been.

"You have misled me. Had you been truthful about this place, I might have come up with a different strategy. But you were not truthful. You exaggerated, you lied. This," he made a sweeping gesture with his arm, "is all your fault!" He raised his voice again as he paced up and down, his two officers eyeing his movements stoically. "And now, new Dutch reinforcements have arrived. Did you know that? Have you seen the ships?" he yelled at Ting-bin, who shook his head slowly, shocked at the news. A Dutch naval fleet! So that was what all the commotion was about.

"No. You were probably sleeping ... or stealing our last remaining food. You're a liar, a thief, and a double-dealing traitor. You only think about what's good for you. You disgust me." Silence followed.

Ting-bin dared not move, for fear of another burst of violence. None came.

"You are useless. I am through with you," Koxinga said quietly. "You will no longer act as an interpreter, as an intermediary, or form any part of my counsel. You will be stripped of all your honors and titles, and you are never to show your face to me again."

Ting-bin gaped at him in bewilderment, swallowing hard. This is the last thing that he had expected.

"Lord Koxinga, please reconsider," he pleaded. "Please don't send me away. I beg you, I didn't...." He would have much preferred a serious beating, at least he could have borne that. This was the most terrible punishment. But Koxinga was not finished yet.

"There is a small thatched, abandoned hut on the beach where my soldiers will take you. There you shall live, alone. It will be expressly forbidden for anyone to visit you. If they do, they will be punished."

Ting-bin felt a shock run through his thin body as it dawned on him that he was being banished.

"My lord, please, no!" he wailed. "Forgive me, anything but that! Please, I beg you to reconsider...."

But Koxinga spat into the soil, turning from Ting-bin with a last look of contempt.

"Get him out of my sight," he ordered.

* * *

The sighting of the Dutch naval fleet caused a great deal of excitement among the Dutch colonists. Ten ships they counted. It seemed a pitiful force compared to the Chinese armada that lay in wait along the Bay of Tayouan, but it still gave them hope. For a very long time, nobody had even known whether the *Maria* had reached Batavia, or if help would ever come their way. Weeks had become months, and the waiting and the uncertainty had been testing for them all. Water and food had to be rationed with vigilance, and infectious diseases spread more quickly with so many settlers living at such close quarters.

Surrounded by anxious colonists within the confines of the bastion's walls, Frederic closely followed the maneuvers of the Dutch fleet to reach the coast. It seemed that the forces of nature were not on their side. A violent typhoon had forced the fleet to steer off course and harbor in safe waters, delaying their arrival. And now the heavy monsoon winds worked against them, while the Chinese blockade had thickened, hindering the fleet's progress. It took another month before Cauw finally landed and succeeded in getting his troops ashore.

Frederic welcomed Admiral Cauw at the fortress, knowing that his journey, hampered by storms and the ever-prowling enemy troops on the island, must have been harrowing. The poor man, whose eyes were circled with dark shadows from fatigue and stress, stuttered an apology that he had come with only seven hundred men. Frederic laughed at his modesty and nearly hugged the man for his courageous efforts.

During the next few days, he held military counsel with Cauw and his officers to consider their limited options. They soon came to the conclusion that with the relatively small number of troops that had accompanied Cauw, they should not wait for too long. They had to do something fast.

They finally agreed to send out Cauw's ships to rendezvous with the Manchu generals to try to form an alliance. In the meantime they laid out plans for a major counterattack, coordinating naval and land troops in a joint attempt to strengthen their position. They all knew that it was a highly ambitious plan; but they also realized that if they did nothing, their days on the island would be numbered anyway.

When the force and direction of the wind were deemed favorable, the three expeditions — two naval, one land — set out in a narrowly planned, integrated attack. Each expedition relied heavily on the success of the other. But nature turned against them once more, and everything that could possibly go wrong, did. All in all, more than a hundred and thirty men died on that fateful September day.

A month later, Frederic received word that the rendezvous between Cauw and the Manchus had never taken place. Koxinga had caught wind of their plans to meet with the enemy in China and had ordered his captains to attack any Dutch vessels trying to cross the Formosa Strait.

Cauw's modest fleet, carrying most of the reinforcement troops, was decimated. Those ships that had broken through the blockade sailed for Batavia, never to return.

Frederic felt deflated when he heard the news. Once again they were left to fend for themselves, to face a fate that seemed to grow more dismal by the day.

21

A Defector of Value

DOCTOR BEYER understood the need for Cornelia Hambroek and Geertje Hendricks to remain busy. After the sharp shock of bereavement that followed Cornelia's loss of both her father and her fiancé, she had returned to work at the hospital with a vengeance. Not only by way of distraction from her grief, but also to retain a sense of self-worth. He had been delighted that she had gone back to her duties so soon, and even more so when Geertje Hendricks, whose husband had been one of the two crucified reverends, had volunteered to come and help as well. The work appeared to be a bitter necessity for both women in order to remain sane.

Helena Coyett had also offered to do whatever she could at the hospital, but Beyer had persuaded her instead to provide moral support for all the freshly bereaved widows in the fortress. The governor's new wife had shown herself to be a strong, courageous woman who stood by her man in these difficult times in every possible way. And God knew they needed all the help that they could get.

Cornelia Hambroek and Geertje Hendricks both worked hard, and Cornelia's caring nature had a soothing and beneficial effect on the patients. The two of them moved about efficiently in the small, over-crowded hospital, changing dressings, providing water, and removing bedpans from the bedridden. Cornelia's buxom, radiant good looks had been replaced by a gaunter, sad kind of beauty that bespoke her tragedy.

Recently the two women had told him that they preferred not to think about the fate that awaited them. They were not the only ones, he thought. He often looked back on his days on Amoy and thought about the man he had gotten to know, the man who was responsible for their present predicament.

The small hospital was crammed with the sick, injured, and the dying, and they had run out of beds months ago. They had been forced to put the patients in every available space, many of them lying on the flagstones with only a blanket for comfort. Moreover, they had run out of medicine, so there was only so much that they could do to care for the sick. Wounded soldiers were brought in daily, and only the worst cases were provided with a bed or mattress. Initially Beyer had attempted to separate the wounded from the diseased to prevent infection, but he had given up as the number of patients had grown too large.

He was very fond of Cornelia, having watched her grow up on the island since she was a child. Now he admired the grim determination and spirit she maintained in spite of her terrible loss. She, in turn, looked up to him as a kind of mentor, which pleased him immeasurably.

"I feel so sorry for the poor man," she whispered to him one day at the large stone sink as they both scrubbed their hands vigorously. He insisted on absolute hygiene in the hospital, and woe to those he caught not following his strict rules.

"You mean Sergeant Radis?" Beyer asked, glancing over his shoulder in the direction of the sergeant. The man was sitting at the bedside of Youmei, his frail but lovely Chinese wife.

"Yes," Cornelia said softly. "Is there nothing more that we can do for her, doctor?"

Beyer shook his head. The young Chinese woman had come in coughing and wheezing several days ago, and she had had a high fever for days. The pneumonia that he had immediately diagnosed had quickly progressed, as she, like almost everyone else in his care, was weak with malnutrition. She had been struggling for breath since that morning, producing a high, tell-tale squeaking sound as she did. He did not expect her to make it through the night.

That entire afternoon, Sergeant Radis had followed him with his bloodshot eyes in silence, watching as he did his rounds with Cornelia. Beyer nodded to him sympathetically as he made his way to a patient two beds away from his wife's.

As if he had been waiting for him, the sergeant jumped up to intercept him, grasping his arm as he did.

"You have to save my wife," he whispered urgently. "I already lost my boy. Please, you must save her." He pulled Beyer by the sleeve to his wife's bedside. Feeling worn out, Beyer allowed himself to be led, gently removing the loose strands of hair from Youmei's face. He put an arm on Radis' shoulder.

"I feel wretched for having to tell you this, sergeant, but there is really nothing that I can do to help her."

"You're going to let her die because she is Chinese, aren't you?" Radis said, his voice breaking. "If she had been a Dutch woman you would have treated her. You just refuse to spend your precious medicine on a Chinese. She is a Christian, you know!" He had raised his voice to a near shout, causing some of the patients to turn their heads in their direction.

Cornelia quickly made her way toward the railing sergeant, concerned that he might disturb the other patients.

"Hans, please," she said, putting a gentle hand on his arm. "We all feel terrible about this, but Doctor Beyer is right. There is no medicine. Youmei has the sickness of the lungs. It has nothing to do with her being Chinese. We treat her just the same as everyone else. I will sit with you, we can watch over her together, if you like."

Radis brusquely shook off Cornelia's hand and stepped backward, giving her a look as if she were a witch about to practice her craft.

"No! Go away. You're the same. You're all the same. It's because she is Chinese, isn't it? Did you think I didn't know?" He ranted. She let go of him, dejected, reaching instead for an extra blanket, which she draped over the frail Chinese woman to protect her from the winter chill. Throwing a last compassionate look at Youmei, she returned to her other patients. Beyer nodded at her, grateful for her efforts. They both understood the desperation and grief that could come from the prospect of losing a loved one.

* * *

Youmei died within the hour. Sergeant Hans Jurgen Radis left the rear of the fortress, blinded by his grief. He ran, reckless of the danger, believing that they were all going to die soon one way or another. He cared not whether he would die of hunger or end up on the sword of one of Koxinga's soldiers.

He walked, ran, stumbling into the darkness until he came across a dune of which the beach side had been hollowed out, leaving it concave enough to conceal himself from patrolling Chinese troops. There he let himself fall to his knees, exhausted and drained. He tucked his legs into the comforting fetal position and fell asleep crying, oblivious to the soft churning sound of the surf as it rolled onto the shore. He did not even feel the light drizzle of rain that eventually soaked his clothes.

The following morning he woke with a start to find a Chinese man leaning over him. He got abruptly to his feet and backed away with an involuntary shout of alarm. He glanced around him to assess where he was, taking a fraction of a second before it dawned on him what had happened. The memory of his wife's death, his reckless flight from the fortress – it all came flooding back, the wave of grief engulfing him again.

He eyed the Chinese with suspicion. "I recognize you. Now where do I know you from?" He squinted, searching his memory. He noticed that the man was unarmed and not dressed in the gear of a soldier.

"You used to work for us, didn't you?" he asked in Chinese as he looked the man over. He associated this man with someone who always wore expensive silk tunics, whose goatee beard was well groomed, a man of standing and importance. The person he now faced looked scruffy, with unkempt hair and beard, and wore a faded blue gown whose embroidered sleeves were torn and frayed at the edges.

"Correct. I am He Ting-bin, formerly employed by the VOC as interpreter and intermediary. I was also a successful merchant, but no more." He sighed, lifting his chin in a small gesture of defiance. "Your Chinese is exemplary," Ting-bin said, impressed.

"My wife is...." He gulped as the truth hit home, hard. "My wife was Chinese."

"I know. I remember her. She is deceased?" Ting-bin asked with compassion.

"Yes. She died yesterday. The disease of the lungs."

"Ah. I offer you my sympathy."

Something triggered Radis' memory. "I heard things about you. That you deceived the company and that you extorted money from your own people. Is that the truth?"

Ting-bin bowed his head in exaggerated shame.

"Yes. I deceived your people. As I deceived Lord Koxinga, who is an honorable man, in spite of his reputation. But he found me out and I have been punished. Rightly so. I deserved it."

"You're still alive, though, aren't you?" Radis observed drily.

"Like I said, the lord of the imperial surname is an honorable man, and more compassionate than you Hollanders might think. I have done him great services in the past, and he knows it. He could have had me killed, but he banished me instead." To Radis' surprise, he grinned, a strange thing to do considering his revelations.

"You know, my banishment has given me time to reflect. The company has made me a rich man, it has always treated me well. You must understand that I had to succeed in the mission that the governor had given me. I had to do what I did in order to reopen trade. I had to succeed, at all cost. But I have paid the price," he said as a matter of fact. Then Ting-bin suddenly looked sorrowful. "The death of the good Reverend Hambroek, I ... I never intended ... you must believe me. He was a good man, always kind, always kind." He fell silent, lost in thought. Then he sighed and turned to leave, gesturing for Radis to follow him. "Come. There is someone who wants to meet you."

Hesitating, Radis followed the Chinese man in silence until they reached what looked like some kind of wooden shed. It was obvious that the boards had been repaired on more than one occasion, and in a ramshackle kind of way, at that.

As they walked toward the dwelling, a man appeared in the doorway, his hair cut short, the familiar moustache and beard gone. Radis gasped as he recognized the missing Dutch sergeant.

"Stockaert!" he exclaimed.

"Greetings to you too, Hans," Stockaert said sheepishly. "Ting-bin brought me here this morning upon finding you on the beach. What the devil are you doing here? If Koxinga's troops find you, they'll kill you. They're all over the place, you know that."

"I wouldn't care a fig if they did. Nothing matters anymore. Youmei died last night. They let her die because she was Chinese," he said with vehemence.

Stockaert nodded grimly to express his sympathy. Then he glanced around to make sure no one was there. "It'd be best if you came inside the hut," he said. "We'll talk there. You can trust Ting-bin; he's a changed man. And God knows we all need each other these days, no matter which side you're on."

Radis looked around the interior of the hut before he and Stockaert sat down on thick logs that served as stools. The inside of the hut was more comfortable than he had expected, Ting-bin had obviously made some effort to make the place livable.

"You went over to their side, didn't you?" Radis asked the sergeant.

Stockaert nodded. "I thought it was the best thing. As you know, my wife is also Chinese. My children are half Chinese, God bless them. If this stalemate goes on for much longer, we're all bound to perish. However much respect I have for the governor, he's a stubborn man. Sometimes bravery can be of no bloody use whatsoever."

The two men were silent as Ting-bin handed Radis a cup of boiled water. He downed it gratefully, after which Ting-bin refilled it and handed the cup back to him. Stockaert sat forward and looked at Radis intently.

"There isn't enough food. Koxinga will soon be unable to feed his troops if things continue like this."

"Surely they get supplies in from China? From the Pescadores?" Asked Radis, surprised. His former colleague shook his head. "No. The Manchus have blocked off the access to China, and even then, they burned everything.

Everything, I tell you. It's beyond belief. Farms, fields – all crops, burned to the ground. Such a bloody waste. And the Pescadores, what little they could grow there has already been depleted. They're getting somewhat desperate, I tell you."

Both Dutchmen accepted a morsel of dried fish from Ting-bin, chewing in silence.

"Why are you telling me this?" Radis asked. "This sort of information could strengthen the Dutch position. This will only make them more determined to hold the fort longer still."

Stockaert tore off another piece of fish with his teeth and washed it down with the remaining water in his cup. He and Ting-bin exchanged glances, whereupon the Chinese nodded, got up and left the shed. Radis could not help but feel that the moment had been planned.

Stockaert shrugged his shoulders. "You should come with me, Hans. I'll take you to Lord Koxinga. You're familiar with the ins and outs of the fortress, more so than any of us. God's wounds, you even helped build the place."

Radis looked at him, aghast. "Betray my own people? No, I cannot do that. I'm not like you."

Stockaert blinked and stared at the ground for a moment, digesting the insult. Then he shrugged his shoulders once more.

"I'm aware of that," he said, smirking bitterly. "You know, Lord Koxinga is not the monster they say he is. He can be cruel, but he is also fair. I'm convinced that he would be more than grateful to learn of your knowledge."

"I was only involved in the construction of Fort Utrecht, not Zeelandia."

"Indeed you were," Stockaert said pointedly, full of meaning. Then he was quiet once more, and they both stared out of the open door at the receding surf. "There are many more like me, you know," he said. "Berkhout, Danielszoon, Van Dongen, Valentijn...."

"Jacob Valentijn?" Radis asked, surprised. "So it's true? Deputy Governor Valentijn betrayed us too? I would never have believed...."

Stockaert shook his head briskly, somewhat annoyed. "You should try and look at it from another perspective. We just differ from people the likes of governor Coyett or Reverend Hambroek. Yes, they're heroes. We cannot all be, you know. I'll be the first to admit it. I just want to survive. Don't be too hard on Valentijn. He did it to save his family. He resisted at first, quite bravely, from what I've been told. But then they threatened to harm his wife and children, Hans. What would you have done in his place? Would you not have done the same? Or would you have played the hero?" He shook his head again. "I don't believe you would."

Radis bit his lower lip and stared ahead but said nothing. His family was dead: there was no one left for him. But he would have sold his soul to the devil himself if he could get his wife and son back again, and he knew it.

"So it's true, we gave up," Stockaert continued. "We defected, joined the winning side. That makes us weak and contemptible. But we're also realistic. Do you honestly believe that we Dutch can win this? That we would have the fortune of coming out of this alive? With your help, we can end this. Hopefully sooner rather than later; otherwise we will all die in this godforsaken place." He sighed despondently. "We should never have come here in the first place. This island doesn't belong to us." He said with a sweeping gesture of his arm. He got up and put a hand on his shoulder. Radis was still looking at the sandy floor. "I'll let you be to ponder this for a bit. I will be back here just before sunset. If you're no longer here, then I will know your answer and I'll respect you for it." With that, he thanked Ting-bin and left the hut, leaving the door open.

Radis put the last piece of rancid fish in his mouth, munching on it, lost in thought as he gazed at the repetitive roll of the waves. He had been on Formosa for years. He was a seasoned military man, one who had fought battles in both Europe and the Far East. For seven months they had been holed up, crowded together with terrified women and children. With fellow soldiers dying of the bloody flux, scurvy and dropsy as well as other diseases that were rampant among his people. He had witnessed the executions of his fellow Dutchmen, men he knew well. Some had even been his friends. The stories of Koxinga's cruelty terrified them all, and he, too, had nightmares about what would happen to them if the fortress fell. No, *when* the fortress falls, he corrected himself. Stockaert was right. Deep in his heart, he knew that it inevitably would. And now he had seen Stockaert. Defected, but alive and well, and that could not be said of many these days.

He knew that they could no longer count on help from Batavia. It was unlikely that Admiral Cauw should ever return, in spite of the hope that some of the colonists still held. He, too, had heard the rumors that the admiral had not succeeded in reaching China in an effort to enlist the Manchus to come to their aid. Where had he gone? Cauw had probably seen the light and fled the area, his tail between his legs. He couldn't blame the man. It takes one to know one, he thought bitterly.

Koxinga and his generals were becoming more aggressive by the day. Now that he knew Koxinga's food supplies were running out, he understood the increased desperation and ferocity with which they were attacking the fort. Koxinga probably knew about the grain supplies stored in the warehouses.

They had all been stunned when their attackers had recently brought in heavy cannons of their own. As they had not used these on the fort before, they had assumed that they had no such weapons in their possession. They had been wrong. It was only a matter of time before the fort would fall, and what would happen to them then didn't bear thinking about.

For hours, he sat on the beach, mulling things over. Two months ago he had lost his four-year-old son to the effects of scurvy. He had watched his wife shrink away in front of his very eyes; now she, too, was dead. Stockaert was right. He was no hero, but he could play a role in ending all this. If things continued the way they were now, they would all die and he could prevent that from happening. He did know the fortress inside out, aware of all its weaknesses and strengths. And he knew the layout of Fort Utrecht. Perhaps Lord Koxinga might be compassionate enough to allow the Dutch to leave the island, he thought. If that were the case, he would stay on Formosa. If he was actually going to do what he was now contemplating, then returning to Batavia was out of the question. They would probably hang him for desertion and treason.

* * *

Koxinga was highly pleased that Stockaert had brought in Sergeant Radis. It was a stroke of luck that they could well use. Although he was convinced that he would eventually conquer Formosa, he had never expected the Dutch to hold out for so long. The siege had lasted for over eight months, and still they had been unable to stop the colonists' comings and goings from the back of the fort. Covered by the guns at Fort Utrecht, they were still free to leave to obtain fresh food, medicine, and, most important of all, drinking water. General San-ge and his men had made various attempts to take Fort Zeelandia from the rear, but with every attempt, they had lost scores of soldiers from the guns that blasted from Fort Utrecht.

Koxinga knew that if they could capture the redoubt, its guns could be turned on the main fort, with devastating effect. The steep gradient of the hillock on which Fort Utrecht stood would make it impossible for Zeelandia's guns to fire back in defense.

The knowledge that the warehouses at Fort Zeelandia had ample grain supplies taunted him. His staff had managed to organize the Chinese farms on Formosa to maximize efficiency and production, but it was now December and they would have to wait for months until harvest time.

For weeks, he had eaten little but rice gruel, and many of his men were too weak with hunger to fight.

Koxinga had lost a lot of weight. They all had. Apart from the occasional wild pig and scraps of dried venison, there was hardly any meat. Manchu naval ships were regularly patrolling the coast; and even if Koxinga's ships could get through to Fujian, there was barely anything left after the Qing authorities had evacuated and scorched the once-fertile area. It was becoming more critical than ever that they take the fort.

The only good news was that his fleet had succeeded in discouraging the few remaining Dutch ships from sailing to China, where he knew they would seek help from the Manchus.

His junks had set chase after the Dutch, until the last remaining ship had given up and eventually sailed southward. His spies wasted no time in informing him that the small, decimated fleet had veered off to Siam and was seen heading for Batavia. At least that admiral had the wisdom to admit defeat.

Weather conditions had been very much in Koxinga's favor since he and his men crossed the strait, hindering the Dutch fleet from reaching Formosa. The winds had even been against the Dutch during their combined expeditions in the Bay of Tayouan, when it had suddenly died at the most opportune of moments, turning the Dutch ships into sitting ducks, easy targets for his war junks. The gods were on his side, and it only confirmed what he already knew: that it was his destiny to seize the island from the Dutch.

And now they had Sergeant Radis. Stockaert had told him that the sergeant possessed vital information that could prove to be the key to taking the smaller Fort Utrecht, and eventually Zeelandia.

He welcomed Radis to his tent with all the cordiality that a defector of his rank deserved. The Dutch sergeant eyed him warily, unsure what to make of him. Koxinga scratched his neck, conscious of the way the man stared at the fiery redness of his skin. The rash now covered most of his body. He tried to dress himself in such a way that they it be hidden, but the skin under his jawline remained exposed.

"Lord Koxinga, may I introduce Sergeant Hans Jurgen Radis," Stockaert said formally.

"Sergeant Radis," he acknowledged him with a courteous nod. "From your esteemed colleague," he motioned to Stockaert, "I understand that it took some convincing on his part for you to come to us. You have a conscience. That is a good and admirable trait."

Radis blinked. Koxinga saw that he was sweating heavily beneath the layers of his uniform, and smiled. Stockaert had told him that the man knew the lay of the fortress to the last detail. He could use the man well, so he had to choose his words wisely.

"It takes courage to do what you are doing. I understand that you married a woman from my country."

"Yes, sir. I did. My wife ... she passed away last night," Radis said, the pain in his voice audible.

"I am sorry to hear this," Koxinga said with sincerity.

"They let her die because she was Chinese."

Koxinga noted the bitterness in his voice and cocked his head at the Dutchman.

"The Dutch big-eared doctor, doctor Bei'er. He is the chief surgeon? He is still running the hospital?"

"Doctor Beyer? Yes, he is still there. He said he couldn't treat her. He just let her die."

Koxinga pondered this for a moment, then walked up to Radis, standing uncomfortably close.

"Then you are mistaken. I know Bei'er. He would never allow such a thing to happen. He would have treated your wife just like any other. You will not speak ill of him again, do you hear?"

Startled, Radis took a step back, paling.

"Yes, my lord. I beg your forgiveness. I ... I did not realize.... Forgive me."

"I am sorry about your wife," Koxinga said again, his anger easing once satisfied that he had made his point. "I also lost my family, so I know how it feels. For a long time, all I could feel was anger too." He sat down on a field stool facing Radis, who was still standing. "Your command of our language is admirable, sergeant," Koxinga continued. The Dutchman inclined his head, accepting the compliment.

"Listen," Koxinga continued. "If you help us, you could save a lot of lives. On both sides. I understand that you are in a position to provide us with valuable information that might bring an end to this stalemate. And this war."

"I know that you are as desperate as we are, Lord Koxinga. I understand that you're running out of food."

"Ah. So your old colleague and friend has been telling you our secrets." He looked hard at Stockaert, who guiltily dropped his eyes. Koxinga would let it go.

"Very well. I understand you are well familiar with the layout of the fort, and of the redoubt to the southwest of it. I also wish to know how many cannons and guns it houses, an estimate of the supplies of munitions, the number of troops that are stationed there. And the number of sick soldiers. Will you tell us what we wish to know?" All eyes were fixed on the sergeant.

Radis hesitated for a fraction of a second. "Aye, I will," Radis said. "But on one condition."

General San-ge cursed and advanced upon the Hollander for his impertinence, but Koxinga held up a hand. It stopped San-ge dead in his tracks.

"What condition might that be?" Koxinga asked. From the corner of his eye he could see Stockaert staring at Radis with open mouth.

"You are a man of honor, or so I'm told," Radis said. Koxinga raised an eyebrow at the double-edged compliment. "If I tell you what I know so that you can end this siege, I have only one request."

"That would depend on your request," Koxinga said gruffly.

"Then I ask you this: after you have taken the fortress, I beg of you to show mercy on the Dutch. That you will let them live once they have surrendered. All of them." He spoke the words rapidly as if to be done with it. Then he looked at Koxinga with frightened eyes, shocked at his own daring. Koxinga merely regarded him, pan-faced.

"Lord Koxinga, would you be willing to honor that request?" Radis asked again, his voice an octave higher this time.

They all tensed, waiting for his response. Koxinga stroked his goatee silently as he contemplated Radis' words. General San-ge appeared ready to pounce on the Dutchman, his face still dark with rage.

"You have my word. I will let your countrymen live. This is something that I have already considered. But they cannot remain here. You understand that they will have to leave. Formosa belongs to us now. There will be no place for the Dutch after this is over."

Radis was breathing rapidly now, his relief evident.

"Yes, Lord Koxinga. Of course. I would be forever in your debt," he mumbled, shaking like a leaf.

"Take heart, sergeant," Koxinga assured him. "By helping us, you will save your own people. Stockaert, take the sergeant with you," he commanded.

Stockaert stepped forward quickly, quite red in the face, half pushing Radis out of the tent in his eagerness to be gone.

And so Koxinga had finally discovered all that he wished to know, including the fort's weaknesses. In January 1662, General San-ge executed his orders. The attacks on Pineapple Isle intensified. The war junks closed in, firing their guns on Fort Zeelandia from both the sea and inside the bay. The artillery prepared several heavy gun batteries for an assault, while hundreds of soldiers set about digging trenches. Another unit was sent to attack Fort Utrecht. In the meantime the infantry pressed forward once more, unfazed by the heavy Dutch guns blazing from the bastions in defense. Everything was happening according to plan. With the knowledge that they now possessed, the end of the siege was near.

22

The Fall of Zeelandia

"WHERE the hell did those cannon come from?" Frederic asked sharply. "What the blazes are they up to now?" He snatched the telescope out of Van Aeldorp's hands and looked down from the southeastern bastion at the sudden increased enemy activity below.

"God's wounds!" he shouted as it became clear that they were setting up all the heavy gun batteries to target not Zeelandia, which would have been futile from that distance, but Fort Utrecht. The Chinese cannon were positioned just out of range of Zeelandia's guns and aimed in such a strategic way that it could only mean one thing.

"They know," he breathed, a chill running down his spine. "They know how many guns we have in the tower, and they know exactly where they are."

"Someone must have told them," Van Aeldorp said. "If they succeed in taking out the tower –"

"– then we will no longer be covered from the back," Lieutenant Gerrit added soberly. "We'll be completely surrounded. And what's worse, they'll be able to turn our own guns on us."

And we won't be able to cross the narrows for supplies, or to obtain fresh water when the wells run dry, Frederic thought to himself wryly. He didn't know what was worse.

So many of their soldiers and officers had disappeared, and it was difficult to know whether they had been killed in battle or captured, or whether they had defected to the enemy with valuable information. They would probably never know.

With growing anxiety, they watched as dozens of Chinese milled around each of the guns with dreadful efficiency.

"We could send out troops to engage them in battle, sir. Distract them. Stop them from bringing the guns," Lieutenant Gerrit suggested. Frederic thought he didn't sound very convincing.

Van Aeldorp looked somber. "No," he said. "By the time our men get to the batteries, they'll be dead. Then we won't have enough men to defend the fortress. We simply don't have the manpower. Look! Archers." He pointed at the regiment of archers that was taking up its position at the bottom of the dune. A large regiment of infantry also appeared to the southeast of Fort Utrecht, where they seemed to be taking up a permanent position.

Frederic's shivered, feeling suddenly cold, knowing that the incessant rain and the January chill were not to blame this time. He found himself surrounded by grim-faced men. They had all known that this was coming; it had only been a matter of time. Van Aeldorp ordered for his gunners to keep firing at the encroaching enemy, but to no avail, as the Chinese remained cleverly out of range. They knew that the impending attack on Fort Utrecht would be fatal, and that they would eventually lose this battle. And then all would be over. There was only one other thing left for them to do. They had to act now, while they still could. As the fortress's guns blared away to keep the enemy at a distance and by way of distraction, Dutch soldiers hurriedly carried out their final instructions, bringing large barrels of gunpowder to Fort Utrecht. The sentries at the tower were to hold out as long as possible.

* * *

The following morning, on January 25, Koxinga's men fired more than two thousand cannon balls at Fort Utrecht. The attack lasted for almost two hours. The Dutch soldiers who had manned the guns had fled the top of the tower, unable to fire back under such a relentless assault. Only twice did the endless barrage of cannon cease, but only to enable the enemy to reposition its guns on the crumbling target. Upon seeing the fleeing Dutch soldiers, the Chinese charged at the tower, the top half of which was in ruins. It now no longer posed a threat to them. The Chinese troops disappeared into its exposed entrances like a stream of ants.

Koxinga watched, accompanied by Hans Radis, whom he had appointed as his military adviser in the campaign. He was confident of the success he believed would soon be his. Feeling euphoric, he couldn't wait to see the strategic vantage point now that they had captured the tower. He strode toward the dune, but Radis grabbed him boldly by the arm.

"No! Wait!"

Koxinga pulled his arm free from his grasp in annoyance, but then it dawned on him. No enemy would be fool enough to relinquish such a strategic position without a last desperate strike. They fell back and watched the cold efficiency with which the Chinese soldiers emptied the redoubt of the Dutchmen's corpses. Unable to bear the carnage wrought on the countrymen he had betrayed, Radis turned away.

Koxinga's soldiers went back inside of what remained of the small tower, setting up their own guns. Satisfied, Koxinga watched as the barrels of the Dutch guns were redirected downward, to point at the southwestern walls of the once-impregnable Fort Zeelandia. The great fortress had never been so vulnerable. But then came the blast.

* * *

Frederic and his officers cringed from the enormous force of the explosion. Large pieces of debris were blown sky-high to land scattered before them. So his last orders had been properly executed. Down in the basement of Fort Utrecht, four large kegs of gunpowder had been strategically placed along the tower's foundations. Once the powder fuses had been lit, they had waited with bated breath, anxious that the smell of sulfur or the crackling hiss betray them and allow time for the fuses to be extinguished.

Fortunately that hadn't happened. Fort Utrecht was lost to them, but at least it had taken many of the enemy's soldiers with it. With grim satisfaction, Frederic and his men watched the flames rise amid the rubble of stone that had once been a tower. He quickly calculated that Koxinga must have lost more than fifty men in the blast. Not that it mattered any longer, he thought bitterly.

As darkness fell, the sentries reported that large numbers of Chinese troops had moved forward, enclosing the fortress like the claw of a crab. Van Aeldorp ordered the gunners to continue their fire. Throughout the night, the men fired at anything that moved, lighting up the skies in a constant series of bright explosions. Hardly anyone slept that night, kept awake by the endless, intermittent sound of the guns, their nerves frayed. They could no longer enter or exit the back of the fort. Frederic knew that with the loss of the tower, their sources of food and drinking water had suddenly become finite. What had once been a sanctuary had now become a trap.

The following morning, when the fire that had raged among the ruins of Fort Utrecht finally died, it became clear that the Chinese had taken the higher ground. It would not be long before their guns would be pointed at Fort Zeelandia, and then the walls of the fort would give way.

And yet Frederic refused to give up. He was the governor of Formosa: the island was his responsibility. Nine months they had held out, and he was determined to continue doing so. Without batting an eyelid, his voice calm, he proposed a counter attack. The other men looked at him dubiously, believing that he had finally lost his mind in all the madness that surrounded them.

"We could also just sit here and do nothing," he said. "Wait until the enemy walks in and slaughters us all. Is that what you prefer?"

"He's right. We have nothing left to lose," Van Iperen agreed. "We might as well die fighting."

It was a sentiment the others did not share. They put the matter to the vote, and of the twenty-nine men who voted, twenty-five voted against. Without the necessary support, his proposal was quickly dismissed. As governor he could now do two things: continue defending the fortress until its inevitable fall, and risk a complete massacre; or they could surrender now, and hope that Koxinga would show them mercy. It was a responsibility that weighed heavily upon him, and one that he would not wish on anyone.

On the eve of January 31, something decided the matter once and for all. A white-faced Van Iperen, who had been made responsible for rationing food and water during the siege, asked to speak with him privately. Frederic saw that his hands were shaking as he held his hat, kneading it nervously.

"Tell me, what's amiss, my good friend?"

"Grave tidings, Frederic." Van Iperen was almost stuttering. "It's the wells."

Frederic felt the hairs on the nape of his neck stand upright. He had known this was coming for some time. "The water is running out," he muttered, not needing to ask.

Van Iperen just nodded, his face a grimace of concern.

"How long do we have?"

"A week, perhaps ten days. And then only if we ration carefully. This is…." The chief merchant's words trailed off. The mere thought of a death caused by thirst terrified them both. Frederic turned away. "*God allemachtig*," he whispered, covering his face with his hands.

"Then it's finally over. For nine months we've held out. Nine bloody months! Only to run out of water…." He shook his head in dismay. During the past days, they had been able to hold off their attackers with their guns, their gunpowder's supplies enough to last them for a while longer. But their arms and guns were of no good to them once the water ran out. The two men stood in silence, each lost in their own train of thoughts as they considered the fate that awaited them.

Early the following morning, Frederic spoke to several hundred of settlers and slaves gathered in the square. They were restless, exhausted, and frightened. Rumors of the limited water supply had already started to circulate, and the thought of dying of thirst struck fear into the most hardened of them. He had already needed to place sentries by the wells to guard them.

His hands had begun to tremble the night before. It was the kind of constant, incessant trembling that came from prolonged emotional shock, and it had begun the moment Van Iperen had told him of the dwindling water supply. He fervently hoped that no one would notice. He was their governor, their leader, after all. They all counted on him. It would be wrong to show the fear that he felt.

But from Helena he could hide nothing; she knew him well, and very little missed her keen eye. The night before he had told her about the drying wells, and she had pressed his head against her ample bosom and comforted him like a child while he cried.

"So the time has finally come," she had said. He had nodded, unable to speak, infinitely grateful that she had remained on Formosa, with him.

"My brave, good people," he began from the top of the steps. He sought out Helena, who stood at the bottom of the staircase, encouraging him. Silence gradually filled the square as a woman gasped in awful anticipation. An infant cried piteously in a corner, and somewhere in the distance, a dog barked. They barely heard the guns firing, having grown so used to it that they had become numbed to the sound.

"For nine months we have held out against the enemy outside the fortress walls. This fortress has protected us, shielded us from Koxinga and his army. In our prayers we beseeched upon the Lord our God for his divine protection in these dire circumstances, in the hope that he would look kindly on our fate, and in the hope that he would send us aid to deliver us from the hands of our enemy. Yet Providence has decided otherwise. We now know that the aid that we prayed for will not be timely enough. The redoubt has fallen. Fort Zeelandia is now in great peril, as are we. As God is my witness, you have all shown tremendous courage and spirit, and you have survived." He looked at the many faces staring up at him from below: Anna Hambroek and her four children. Geertje Hendricks, who had begun to sob quietly. No one paid her much heed because all eyes were on him.

"You all know that since the fall of Fort Utrecht we have been made prisoners within these very walls." He cleared his throat. "That means that the resources available to us will run out at some point." His voice sounded weak to him, his mouth felt dry. "Our water is running out. We have no choice but to surrender."

Somebody in the crowd gasped. For a fraction of a second, an eerie silence filled the square. A man swore loudly, others scowled. Several women began to weep. Then a shout.

"No!" a man cried out, his eyes wide with terror. "It can't be! There is water. You're lying. If we surrender, they will slaughter us. We all saw what they did to Reverend Hambroek and the others. We must not yield to them!"

"He's right! We mustn't surrender!" a woman echoed. More shouts filled the square, adding to the protests.

Frederic had foreseen that this would happen. Two soldiers quietly made their way to the first man who had voiced his doubts, flanking him from behind. Their orders were clear. They were to neutralize anyone who threatened to provoke a riot.

"I speak only the truth," he went on, his voice firm once more. "We have water to last us for days, a week at the most. The enemy might breach the fortress walls before then." He paused. "It is true that we do not know how fate will take its course once we surrender. But it is not of our choosing. If we do not yield now, we shall surely perish. And I doubt anyone relishes the thought of dying a death of thirst.

"I do not believe that Koxinga will harm us if we surrender willingly. We must not forget that China is in the throes of war. Koxinga has brought that war to us here. He intends to claim this island. We are involved in this, whether we like it or not. But I am of the conviction," he looked around the courtyard, scanning the many faces, most of whom he knew personally, "I believe this Koxinga to be a fair man. I think he will let us go."

Whether he truly believed this to be true, he did not know. Then why had he said it? He only had his intuition to go on. That, and what Christian Beyer had told him about Koxinga. He saw the many anxious eyes fixed upon him. Everyone was alarmed by what he had just told them. There was nothing more that he could say. The people began to talk among themselves – whispers at first, but gradually the many voices rose to a crescendo that laid bare their growing fear. They all realized that they would soon be at the mercy of the enemy that had besieged them for the last nine months. That enemy had killed many of their husbands, sons, and fathers, sometimes right before their eyes. No one knew what lay ahead.

Frederic spoke again, his voice distorted by the emotion that his message entailed.

"At midday, when the clock strikes the twelfth hour, we shall raise the white flag of surrender. I must ask you to prepare yourselves for that moment. For now, I ask you to join me in prayer." He clasped his hands tightly together to stop them from trembling. "We pray to you, our benevolent and almighty God, to protect us from the brutality of our enemies. That they may show us mercy. We ask this of you from the depths of our hearts."

* * *

When General San-ge saw the white flag of surrender, he insisted on informing Koxinga himself. "My lord, it is over. The Dutch have surrendered."

"Yes," was all that he said. This was all part of the prophecy, after all. *Yes, foreigners. They not belong. Not easy, is difficult situation. But your fate, is on island. The strangers will leave, one day. Then island your destiny.* Yes, it had been difficult, much more difficult than he could possibly have imagined, but now he felt triumphant, euphoric. Not so much because victory was finally his but that the prophecy had been fulfilled, just as he believed it would be. His army would be able to celebrate their victory with the coming of the New Year, just three weeks away. It would be the year of the tiger.

He smiled. Ironically, his diviner had told him that the year of the tiger would not be auspicious for him, being a rat. The man had warned him that his duties would press upon him heavily and be damaging to his health. He had also advised him that the coming year would not be a good time to enter into dispute with any man, including members of his own family.

None of that mattered now. He thanked the gods that victory had come to him on time, before the coming of the new year. Given the circumstances of the past months, he had not been able to afford the luxury of listening to his diviner: he had ignored his warnings. That his health was poor, he knew well enough: no one needed to tell him that. Now that it was all behind him, he only felt immense relief. The time had finally come. Formosa was his at last.

"Fetch Ting-bin. We will need him for the negotiations."

"My lord?" San-ge asked. "But you banished him!"

"Did you think I had forgotten?" he said, slightly vexed at being questioned. "You heard me. Fetch him. We shall need to negotiate with the Hollanders. We cannot ask Stockaert or Radis to translate for us. They might arrest or even shoot them on sight for their treachery. I need Ting-bin. Get him."

"As you will, my lord."

* * *

They stood waiting on the beach, less than three hundred feet from where the Chinese delegation had taken up its position. Frederic's hands were still trembling, it simply would not stop. Next to him he saw that Van Iperen kept transferring his weight from one leg to the other, nervous like the rest of them. Any moment now they would be given the signal from the Chinese to come forward to meet them halfway. His staff pressed in close, as if they tried to draw comfort or strength from his presence. He wondered at the irony of it: it was a good thing that they could not hear the rapid beating of his heart.

In the distance he could see how a crowd of Chinese had gathered around their new leader, who was closely guarded by an armed escort, their weapons at the ready. Up to now he had seen Koxinga only from afar, so he could not be sure.

From the opposite side of the beach three men walked past them, their bodies silhouetted against the brightness of the sky. He held up his hand to shield his eyes from the glare. Flanked by two armed soldiers, a thin man tried to pick his way among the slippery seaweed. When they reached the delegation, the thin man dropped to his knees in front of Koxinga. Frederic squinted in disbelief. He barely recognized Ting-bin. The otherwise well-fed, even paunchy interpreter looked emaciated. His tattered faded clothing and unkempt appearance were a far cry from the immaculately groomed merchant he had not seen since the beginning of the siege. What on earth had happened to him? It must be a terrible loss of face to show himself in such a demeaning way.

"Is that not Ting-bin?" Van Iperen asked.

"Yes, I do believe it is." They gaped at their former interpreter, who now approached them with an official of high rank, probably one of Koxinga's generals. They were escorted by sentries. Ting-bin wrung his hands in his unease, his eyes cast downward to the soft sand before his feet.

The general stopped, leaving no more than ten feet between them, whereupon the sentries also came to an abrupt halt. They all had their hands on the hilts of their weapons in warning, alert but at ease. They were the ones in control now, and they knew it.

Frederic and his officers were all unarmed to show that their capitulation was sincere.

His heart beating wildly, he stepped forward to introduce himself. The general nodded curtly to acknowledge him and said something in Chinese. Ting-bin moved in closer, listening attentively to what the general had to say, his eyes averted. Frederic felt some satisfaction as it dawned on him that Ting-bin was no longer of any significance to Koxinga, and that he was just there as interpreter, and one who had fallen from grace.

"General San-ge wishes to introduce himself, excellency," Ting-bin began, his tone subdued.

"The general has come on behalf of the lord of the imperial surname and wishes to pay his full respect to you and your people for proving so admirable an adversary." Ting-bin's usual arrogance was gone, his manner humbled. Frederic could tell that whatever had befallen him over the past months had changed him.

"Lord Koxinga appreciates the determination and courage of you and your people," Ting-bin translated as San-ge went on. "You have succeeded in holding off his formidable army much longer than he thought possible, and he sincerely regrets any loss of life among the Dutch."

Frederic peered at Ting-bin closely. He had the appearance of a vanquished man, as if he had suffered a personal loss. Could he really be trusted? Yes, his words rang true. This time it would not be in his interest to twist the general's words. Then maybe there was hope after all. Perhaps their fate would not be as terrible as many had come to believe. He drew himself up proudly to address the general.

"I draw strength from these words, general. I am sure that Lord Koxinga will understand that it was my duty to protect the interests of the sovereignty of the VOC for as long as I deemed it possible."

General San-ge nodded graciously. "Lord Koxinga wishes you to know that he holds no ill feeling against you or your people. He insists that he has not come to wage war against the company or your country but has come to possess what is rightfully his." He paused for Ting-bin to catch up. It was apparent that Ting-bin's interpreting skills had become rusty from disuse.

"The Chinese people have lived on Formosa for some time now. We have allowed the Dutch to remain here only when we had no use for it ourselves. Now that we require this island, it is only just that you and your people should give it up to its rightful owners."

"What ... what does Lord Koxinga intend to do with us?" Frederic asked with bated breath.

"You will be spared. But you shall leave the island. All of you. You have ill-treated the Chinese people on this island far too long. You will have to leave."

Frederic felt his heart skip a beat. He dared not believe what the general had just told him. He heard Van Iperen exhale sharply, and Lieutenant Gerrit nearly lost his balance with the force of the relief that swept over him. Had Ting-bin translated the general's words correctly? For months, they had all been haunted by thoughts of what the Chinese would do to them once the siege was ended. None of them had dared hope that they would be allowed to live.

"What of the prisoners? Will you release them?"

"Yes."

"Jacobus Valentijn. Are you holding him captive?"

"He is your second in command?"

"He is the deputy governor, yes."

"He is our prisoner no more. And he is not likely to leave the island when you depart."

There was little need to say more. Frederic and Van Iperen exchanged meaningful glances. Valentijn must have negotiated that he would not be forced to return to his people after he had betrayed them, even if his betrayal was made under duress.

"Are there those who do not wish to leave with us?" he inquired.

"Yes," San-ge said. He did not elaborate. "There is more. Lord Koxinga has announced that, in spite of what you may think, he is no pirating thief and that he wishes to possess only that which is rightfully his. He wishes to remain on good terms with your revered company and does not wish to enrich himself with goods that he does not require."

Frederic wondered what goods Koxinga felt he would not require, but he did not voice his thoughts. He had no illusion that Koxinga would claim the valuable goods that lay stored in the warehouses in Zeelandia. He wasn't going to haggle over the matter now. If anything, he was happy that they were all allowed to leave the island alive.

The final negotiations lasted for five full days. Frederic had immediately agreed to dismantle the cannons on the castle, surrendering them to General San-ge. Within two days, the fortress was emptied of everything for which Koxinga had no use. It was obvious that he intended to move into the fort as soon as possible. Frederic could hardly blame the man, after spending nine months of discomfort in damp tents.

On the fifth day following their capitulation, Koxinga arrived in Zeelandia Village in person, heralded like a king. The moment had finally arrived for the Dutch to meet the lord of the imperial surname, the man who had come to put an end to their occupation of Formosa.

Frederic stood on the steps the fortress, Helena at his side. Around him the colonists had gathered, huddling close together for reassurance, their eyes skittish. There were still many who did not trust Koxinga and dared not take his word, in spite of reassurances.

Meticulously shaven and attired in splendid ceremonial robes, Koxinga strode across the village square, surrounded by his personal army, officers, and staff. He stopped, the men around him halting the same instant. Taking stock of his surroundings, Koxinga nodded briefly to indicate where he wished to take up his position. One of his officers shouted an order, and within seconds, his soldiers rushed forward carrying a canopy, a dais, cushions, and a small field table. Koxinga sat down, settling himself comfortably on the raised dais that was covered by the canopy. The perpetual drizzle had given way to more steady rain. With the exception of the great conquering Lord Koxinga and his closest aides, everyone else's clothes were soon sodden.

Koxinga and his officers and aides were accompanied by a large, motley group of Chinese peasants, tradesmen, and merchants, all vying for a good position to watch the spectacle unfold while keeping a respectful distance.

At a sign from General San-ge, Frederic released Helena's hand and walked down the steps to greet him. Captain van Aeldorp and Lieutenant Gerrit preceded him, ordering the colonists to make way for their governor. They moved aside reluctantly, as if to delay the end of their time on Formosa.

Frederic strode purposefully toward Koxinga with as much dignity as he could muster. A minor Chinese officer signaled rudely with his hand for them to stop. Frederic halted, and he could not help but stare at the figure on the dais. From afar, this man had exuded an air of authority and power. His clothing, the size of his entourage and the comfort that now surrounded him had all made him look more impressive than he truly was. But now all he saw was a man with a thin frame and a gaunt face, grey shadows underneath his penetrating black eyes.

Of course he knew that his adversary must have suffered hardships, just as they had. He knew that Koxinga and his army had also faced a lack of food, fresh water, and medicine. Beyer had told him of the mysterious illness that tormented him. His nemesis, the notorious commander in chief of the southern Chinese army, the man he had come to know as the lord of the imperial surname, was as emaciated as any other on the island. He looked like an old man.

An unnatural silence filled the square as people from two so very different nations, who had fought each other for so many months, regarded each other up close for the first time. There he was, eye to eye with the man of whom he had heard so much. This was the man who had so marked the years of his governorship of Formosa and who had now come to bring it to an end.

Yet he could not hate Koxinga for what he had done to him, for bringing down his world. He understood. He knew of the war in China, of the many battles he had fought out of loyalty for a dynasty that had fallen. This man had been forced to leave his country behind, driven away by an enemy as determined as he was. If the stories he had heard were true, then his father had betrayed his land and emperor, while he had fought against the Manchus till the bitter end. He could almost sense the man's losses, his ordeals, and his pain, and could only speculate as to what disease Beyer had tried, but failed, to treat him for. How had his illness impeded him in his daily life?

In spite of everything, the constant rains of the last months, the lack of food for his men and himself, the diseases that ravaged his troops just as they had ravaged his own, Koxinga had never given up. His perseverance, his dogged determination and shrewd judgement had brought him to where he was now, here in Zeelandia. This man was not a greatly respected leader for nothing.

Koxinga had been more than fair in the negotiations, and so far, he had been a man of his word. He could have had them all slaughtered, just as he had the prisoners. He had killed so many of his fellow Dutchmen. He had taken Antonius from him, his good friend. He should really hate him for it. But now he was allowing them to leave the island unharmed, something that had been unthinkable and for which he would be eternally grateful.

* * *

Koxinga observed the governor with interest. He had to admit that he had seriously underestimated this man. When he had crossed the strait, he had expected the fortress to fall within weeks, perhaps even days. Who would have thought it would take nine months for these people to finally give up? How many lives had been lost in the futility of it all?

The governor and I are much alike, he thought. Had I been in his shoes, I would probably not have done things differently. He narrowed his eyes slightly as Coyett looked at him, more directly than almost any other man dared. This governor was worthy of his admiration.

Coyett faced him proudly, undaunted by the rain that had soaked his blonde hair. Then, ever so subtly, Koxinga inclined his head toward the Swede.

The governor blinked in surprise. Then, slowly, he bowed back. It wasn't the kind of prostration that Koxinga had come to expect from everyone, nor was it a very deep bow, but it was clear enough for all to see. It was a symbolic bow of submission, gratitude, but most of all of unconditional respect.

As several hundred weary, defeated colonists looked on as their governor surrendered to the Chinese man on the dais, a tremendous roar emerged from the throats of the Chinese troops. Victory was theirs. The formalities could begin.

Once the official documents concerning the capitulation had been duly signed, Koxinga personally saw to it that all articles detailed in the treaty of withdrawal were followed through. He agreed to return all the company ships that they had captured. Hostages and prisoners held on both sides were released. Many of the younger Dutch women and girls were returned to their people, some of whom were heavy with child. Those who had been lucky enough to be given to unmarried junior officers had been surprisingly well treated, as their pale ivory skins and soft fair hair had been prized as exotic.

As he had expected, Deputy Governor Jacob Valentijn had chosen to remain on Formosa, preferring this to being court-martialed and probably hung for treason. Other defectors and those who had married Chinese or native islanders had also been given permission to stay.

Koxinga wasted no time in having the VOC's white banner lowered from the highest point of the fort. With no small amount of drama that befitted his sense of destiny, he watched as the banner carrying his family crest was hoisted there for the first time, the cloth undulating gently in the breeze.

He took possession of all the valuable merchandise and goods that were stored in the warehouses, in spite of General San-ge's assurances to the Dutch that he did not wish to enrich himself. He did, however, allow company officials to keep a modest amount of money, and he ordered the Dutch administrators to provide him with a list of all the Chinese who still owed debts to the company to ensure that these were paid in full.

As agreed, he provided the former colonists with barges to ferry them and their goods to the ships that lay anchored along the ashore. Supplied with the necessary provisions which had been offered them at a reasonable price, the Dutch were permitted to leave the island fully armed.

While the subjugated Dutch sullenly prepared for their final departure, the rest of the island's population celebrated. Large crowds of curious

Chinese and aboriginals gathered to witness the exodus. They all watched what remained of the company's troops march out of the fortress, the drummers beating their drums, the banner bearing the VOC crest raised.

* * *

As nearly nine hundred Dutch soldiers and civilians prepared to board the *'s Gravelande* and the other remaining ships, the last of the Dutch prisoners returned. Their release meant joyful reunions for some, but despair for those whose loved ones were still unaccounted for. Many of those whose husbands or fathers were still missing refused to board the ships, choosing instead to remain on Formosa and face the displeasure of the Chinese in the hope that their men would come back to them in time. They were convinced that Batavia would send a ship to fetch them later. Frederic thought this doubtful, but he said nothing, not wishing to crush their hopes.

Helena walked up to him, two young women in tow.

"Frederic," she said, gesturing at the two women. One woman had an infant at her hip and the other had two young children clutching at her skirts. Their husbands had not been among the released prisoners, and no one seemed to know of their whereabouts.

"He will come! Truly, Mr. Coyett, we must wait for my husband, he will come if only we can wait for just a few more days." She motioned to the other woman, desperately seeking support. "Her husband hasn't returned either. They will surely come. I implore you, sir, let us wait!" The second woman grasped his hands and dropped to her knees, pleading.

His heart went out to them. The chances that their husbands would ever return to them were slim. All the prisoners had been exchanged, the bodies of the dead had already been identified and prepared for burial. But he simply did not have the heart to deny them their request. He pulled the kneeling woman to her feet.

"I will see what we can do. But you must understand that I cannot stall our departure for much longer. It is part of the agreement that we leave in five days. These people want us to be gone. You should know that our provisions will suffice for only the journey that is ahead of us. They will give us no more."

He tried to talk to the mediators, but Koxinga was firm and demanded that they sail within the time that was agreed. Those who still insisted on waiting for their missing family members were given permission to stay at Fort Provintia in Saccam. That fort had been so badly damaged from the siege that the place was of little use to Koxinga.

On February 9 Frederic finally gave the orders to depart. The *'s Gravelande* raised its anchors and veered away from the harbor, the other ships trailing behind in its wake. The colonists on board the ships were worn out and weary, but relieved that at least they were still alive and on their way to Batavia. Then, quite unexpectedly, within a mile of the coast, Frederic ordered for the anchors to be lowered once more.

"Sir?" Van Aeldorp said, perplexed.

"We shall wait here," Frederic said firmly. "We cannot desert these people just yet. Some of them may still return, and when they do, they can signal to us to pick them up in the long boats."

The ship's lookouts remained especially alert, but there was no sign of the missing Dutch, from Saccam or any other place. The passengers had at first been compassionate and understanding for those still on shore and they respected his decision to wait. But as the days went by, they grew more restless. His officers informed him that the people were complaining and becoming edgy, eager to leave the island from where they had been banished. Still, he ignored them, postponing their departure for as long as he could.

But with their quarters cramped, the uncertainty was beginning to gnaw at everyone. Knife fights took place over the most trifling of issues. There were those who threatened to jump overboard and return to shore if they stayed for one more day. Even Helena had voiced her concerns on what he was doing, but still, he would not listen. Instead, he had Van Aeldorp take preventive measures and ensure that the soldiers kept the passengers under control. He simply could not rid himself of the feeling that he would be abandoning his people if he left.

After more than a week of waiting, it was Christian Beyer who finally breached the subject. He saw Helena and Balthasar standing behind the doctor, expectant, hopeful, Helena's arm draped around his son's shoulder.

"Frederic." The old man put a hand on his arm. "We all admire your compassion, but this is madness! We cannot remain here. We've been waiting for ten days."

"No, Christian, we cannot leave these people behind," Coyett whispered. "About a hundred people are still out there. We cannot leave them at the mercy of the natives and the Chinese. We would be deserting them!" He felt his eyes stinging with tears. He refused to believe that it was truly over, that they would finally have to leave the island for good.

Beyer shook his head sadly. "What you are doing is noble and kind, but you must consider the others. We have more than nine hundred people aboard these ships. We are all anxious to depart. We wish to forget what has befallen us and move on with our lives, Frederic. Besides, we can always ask Batavia to send a ship to fetch them later."

Coyett scoffed at Beyer. "Do you genuinely believe that? They could hardly spare enough ships to aid us in our hour of need. Do you honestly think they will send out a ship for those poor wretches who are still out there?"

The old doctor looked away to gaze at the lush green shoreline that had been enveloped in a haze of fog. His silence said more than enough.

"Frederic, you did what you could. No one has come. These people are lost to us. Anything could have happened to them." He was whispering urgently now, glancing over his shoulder at a group of men who were eyeing the exchange with interest. "Frederic, I implore you to listen to me. We simply cannot wait any longer. We have a long journey ahead of us. There are sick people on board, and if we wait any longer we will have a food shortage on our hands. We already have to ration food as it is!"

Frederic swallowed hard, his eyes on the beaches, still scanning for any sign of the missing men and women. He turned to the physician, his eyes moist with tears. He had to admit that it wasn't just these missing people that had made him delay their departure. For thirty-eight years, the island had fallen under the sovereignty of the VOC. He had lived here for almost fourteen years of his life, and he had been the twelfth governor of Formosa, and the last, an epitaph he did not relish much. He looked toward the south of Pineapple Isle, at the cemetery where Susanna lay buried. There she lay, next to the child that she had borne him but who had never lived.

He turned away so that Beyer would not be witness to his despair ... or his grief.

"So be it. You are right, of course," he said with a voice choked with emotion. He wiped his eyes with his sleeve, taking one final look at the coast. An estimated sixteen hundred soldiers and civilians had lost their lives since Koxinga's army had besieged them. Not for the first time, he wondered if he had done everything in his power to prevent the loss of the colony. He nodded grimly, believing that he had. There was little he could have done to change the outcome. He wondered how things would have turned out if his superiors in Batavia had listened to him, heeded his warnings, and acted upon them in time. He shook his head. No, he thought. Perhaps they would have been able to hold out a while longer, but Koxinga's seemingly endless supply of troops and his fierce determination to take the island as his own would have led to the same ending, probably at the loss of even more lives.

He could just make out the Zheng banner swaying in the wind above the fort, its fluid movements slightly obscured by a thin veil of mist. He gazed at it, mesmerized, and felt strangely at peace. Now that he had made his decision to leave, he was relieved that Formosa had ceased to be his responsibility. The Dutch no longer reigned over Formosa, the VOC ruled it no more. As he gazed at the banner displaying the Zheng crest, he imagined that, somehow, it had always been there. As if it belonged. It was only right. The island was no longer theirs to occupy. It had never been theirs in the first place.

"Captain!" he shouted. Captain van Aeldorp rushed forward, an expectant look on his face.

"Yes, Mr. Coyett?"

"Give orders for the anchors to be raised. We are leaving."

23

The Loss of a Colony

The door to Maetsuijker's office was rudely opened by a junior clerk. "Your excellency!" the youth cried out.

The governor-general looked up with a frown of annoyance at the boy's barging into his office without knocking. He was in a middle of a meeting.

"Sir, four of our ships have been sighted coming into our waters. The *'s Gravelande* is among them."

Maetsuijker looked at him with a vague expression, his mind still struggling to switch from the complex legal matters he had just been poring over.

"Four ships?" He exchanged glances with the two men at his desk. He couldn't quite grasp what it all meant. Four ships, including the *'s Gravelande*. His jaw dropped as it dawned on him. He stared at the boy, his mouth agape. The *'s Gravelande*'s base had been Formosa for years. This could only mean one thing.

"The *'s Gravelande*. God almighty." With an effort, he got up from his chair, holding onto the armrest for support for what seemed an eternity. "That means that Formosa is lost to us."

Distressed and suddenly pale, he walked up to the window. He could no longer enjoy the otherwise breathtaking view that greeted him. All he could see were the dark clouds far on the horizon, carrying with them the rains that the wind would bring them later in the day. Those same clouds now seemed to be a bad omen full of symbolic irony. He had ignored the signs and Frederic Coyett's persistent warnings that an attack would be imminent. He had refused every one of Coyett's requests for reinforcements, and he had shirked the responsibility, expecting Coyett to deal with it. So the man had been right all along.

He lowered himself back onto his chair. He removed his glasses shakily and stared ahead, feeling older than ever before. He rubbed at his temples, where the tension had been building up over the past few days but where he now had a splitting headache. He was painfully aware that he was partly to blame for all this. But was any of this really his fault? Could he have prevented this? For months the *Heren Seventien* had put him under a great deal of pressure. Those wealthy, mighty men, respected by all and residing in their stately homes on the canals of cities such as Amsterdam, Rotterdam, and Delft. None of them had any idea how things worked in the Far East; a few had never even been to Asia. They didn't understand why the Chinese refused so persistently to grant the VOC the trade that it so badly wanted. But they would not listen. The only thing that they wanted was results.

Their impatience, the ongoing war in China, but also his failure to distinguish hard fact from the warped truth that Van der Laan and Verburgh had presented him with, as well as Coyett's inability to defend Formosa against Koxinga's army: they were all factors that had contributed to this, the loss of Formosa. He could only hope that Coyett had succeeded in bringing back with him as much of the company's valuable trade wares as he possibly could.

"Gentlemen, I think it would be wise to resume our meeting at some other time." The two legal clerks gathered their possessions and took their leave. Maetsuijker barely acknowledged the men as they departed, and got up again wearily. He remained by the window, his eyes on the clear blue waters of the Java Sea, where the remaining ships of what had once been a great fleet gradually made their way toward the harbor. There was scarcely any wind, so their progress was slow. To Maetsuijker it seemed as if the majestic ships were reluctant to come in, putting off what lay ahead for just a while longer.

With a heavy heart, the governor-general took a deep breath and exhaled as he began to realize the full implications of what had happened. A colony under his jurisdiction had been lost. This had not happened before: there was no precedent. Yet he knew what was expected of him. Protocol was quite clear on this.

* * *

The imposing *'s Gravelande* was the first to enter the harbor. As the gangplank was placed on the dock, three sailors nimbly made their way down to secure the ship. An endless stream of weary passengers scrambled to disembark, eager to set foot on land after more than a month at sea.

Frederic had insisted that Helena and Balthasar leave the ship together with the rest of the passengers. He himself stayed on board with his officers as they watched the former colonists disembark. Some of them were embraced by family and friends who had come to meet them, alerted of their arrival. He had already spotted the governor-general, who stood grim-faced behind an armed escort of officers and soldiers. He sought the old man's eye, but Maetsuijker looked away in something that was akin to guilt, or was it shame? He felt his heart lurch and the bile of panic rise inside of him.

After all the passengers had gone ashore, there was no longer any point in delaying. He went down reluctantly, his officers and staff in tow. The feel of firm ground beneath his feet was reassuring as he approached the governor-general, buoying his confidence somewhat. His officers paid their respects and fell back as Frederic addressed him.

"*Mijnheer* Maetsuijker, your excellency." He inclined his head, then drew himself up to face the governor-general with dignity. "It is my sad duty to inform you that after a siege of nine months, we had no option but to capitulate to the pirate's son, Koxinga, lord of the imperial surname and supreme commander of the Ming naval forces. The Dutch colony of Formosa is no more."

Maetsuijker looked him in the eye, obviously feeling he owed him that much, and nodded.

"I understand," the old man muttered. "*Mijnheer* Coyett, it is my unfortunate duty, to hold you, as governor of the colony of Formosa, responsible for its demise. I am left with no alternative other than to place you and your staff under arrest."

Frederic had warned Helena and Balthasar that this would happen. Of course he had known that he would be tried: he was well aware of the company's laws and protocols. According to VOC policy he would have to account for what happened and would be held personally responsible for its loss. But this situation was new to them all: no Dutch colonies had yet been lost in this way. Now the unthinkable had finally happened.

Frederic's trial and that of his staff lasted for weeks. Manfully, he insisted that his officers be released and exonerated, and that any blame be carried by him alone. This won him a great deal of admiration and respect, not only among the former colonists but also among the Dutch in Batavia.

During the trials that followed, scores of clerks racked their brains over the numerous registers and ledgers that had been brought back from Formosa. The plain truth of it was that the VOC had incurred major losses from the fall of the colony, amounting to 471,500 guilders – an absolute fortune. Someone would have to be blamed, and Frederic knew that he would be the one to bear the brunt.

Bitterly he wondered how the annals of history would have differed if he and his people had been massacred. Most probably they would forever be remembered as heroes. His name might have been glorified as the last heroic governor of Formosa, with stories told of how they had fought and resisted the cruel and merciless Koxinga till the very end. But fate had decided otherwise. Instead, Koxinga had allowed him and his people to live, to expel them, only for them to return to Batavia humiliated in a decimated fleet, its holds carrying very little of value.

He knew what to expect. According to the company protocol, the penalty for the loss of a colony under one's governorship was death. And this was the sentence that was passed.

* * *

With the Dutch colonists gone, Koxinga dedicated himself to rebuilding Formosa into an island modelled on the China that he had been forced to leave behind. For the first time, private land ownership was established on the island, and, as a result, agriculture flourished.

He started by firmly eradicating all traces of Dutch administration. He renamed the island Dongdu, meaning "Eastern Capital," still refusing to give up his dream that the Ming dynasty would live on, with himself as its sole custodian. Determined to renew attacks once they had regained their strength, he launched one last military expedition on China, but by now the Qing had taken firm control of the south as well.

Despondent, he returned to Formosa. Not long afterward he learned that the last captive emperor had been executed. Any illusions that he still held were finally dispelled; the curtain had fallen on the Ming dynasty once and for all. The China he had known was lost to him, conquered by an enemy from the northern steppes. The house of Ming, the dynasty that he had fought for so valiantly all his life, his reason for being, was no more. The halting, heavily accented Japanese words were repeated in his head: *You want very much, can do very much ... big ambition. But careful! Must not want too much. You must learn see truth....*

It was over. Everything was over. Depression and grief took a hold of him, feeling there was nothing worth living for. He withdrew into himself more and more, staying in his private rooms for days on end. There was little that was still of any interest to him. He would sit, hours at a time, just staring ahead. He could not bear to have his wife near him, and whenever she did enter, he would set upon her in anger. Even his favorite concubine no longer pleased him.

His health deteriorated further. He had no appetite, and he grew thinner and weaker by the day as the hardships of the past year, the siege, the hard living, and his malnutrition began to take their toll on his already diseased body. Yet he often refused to let his physicians attend to him; on those occasions that he did, they could only do so much to ease the pain that tormented him. He suffered terrible headaches, which were invariably followed by bouts of insanity. He knew this, as he could see it in the eyes of others once the bouts had passed. With each episode of madness, he realized that he had blacked out. He could not remember what had happened, or what he had done. It frightened those around him not nearly as much as it scared him.

Koxinga's sons brought him neither relief nor joy. Jing and Xi had long vied for his favor, their jealousy and distrust growing with the years. The two brothers feuded fiercely – for land, for their father's trust, and for the right to succession. To them, he was little more than an old man they suspected did not have long to live.

Jing might be his oldest and favorite son, but he was not the more virtuous of the two. In a twist of irony, Jing resembled his grandfather Zhilong – not in the way that he had attained mandarin status, or become a successful businessman, but as the greedy, unscrupulous pirate and the treacherous turncoat that he had turned out to be. Although Jing regularly visited him, he did so only to safeguard his interests, assuring him of his filial piety and loyalty. But Koxinga always saw right through him and found him to possess little integrity. To be confronted by his son's depraved personality, in which he recognized his own father, was bitter and harsh.

He knew, too, of Jing's notoriety as a womanizer. Just like his father, Jing had an eye for beautiful women and unable to resist their charms. At the urging of his wife, Koxinga had warned him in no uncertain terms that it would be better for him to seek his sexual pleasures far outside their home. But it was to no avail: Jing always did exactly as he pleased.

One day, Xi burst into his rooms, absolutely livid. Before Koxinga had the chance to reprimand him for his ill-bred manners, Xi held up an imperative hand, demanding that he let him speak.

"Father! That brother of mine, that lowly piece of horseshit –"

"Don't speak of Jing that way! He is your older brother!"

"I don't care who he is," Xi raged. "Father, that lowlife seduced the wet-nurse in my house. He fucked the woman from whose very breast my children drink. My own children!"

Koxinga listened to Xi's ranting, aghast. He knew the woman his youngest son spoke of: she was a much-liked, attractive young widow with an impish smile. Xi went on, saying that his wife had once remarked that the girl had grown fuller in the waist, but the wet-nurse had laughingly dismissed it, joking that the cook's food was making her fat. Though the lady of the house had had her doubts at the time, she had not pursued the matter further.

Unfortunately for the girl, for that was all she was, the baby had come sooner than she had expected and she gave birth in the house of her employer. As a result, the news of her baby son was as public an event in the household as could be, and many feminine voices began to whisper, speculating on the father's identity.

No more than an hour after the boy was born, the lady of the house visited the girl. Barely recovered from her labors, the young mother was in such an emotional, confused state that she didn't need any coaxing to tell her who the father was.

When Xi had finished telling his story, it all became clear to Koxinga. So Jing had just become father to yet another bastard son. Yet this child had been born in his brother's house.

Koxinga had not been in a reasonable mood to start with. His pains had worsened. The terrible hallucinations caused by the concoctions Wang made him drink at night had only become more harrowing. He hardly slept. He could barely tolerate Cuiying, to whom he spoke with a cruel tongue. But it was his sons' jealousy and open hatred for one another that had been a constant source of pain to him. And now this. Infuriated by this latest piece of unwelcome information, he sent two guards to fetch his oldest son.

Even though all the other members of the Zheng household had heard of the birth of the illegitimate child, Jing was still blissfully unaware. Ignorant of the source of his father's anger, and indignant at being so summoned, Jing was defensive the moment he entered his father's private quarters.

"You incestuous pig!" Koxinga growled as soon as Jing appeared, advancing on him with menace.

Cuiying screeched at her husband incoherently and grabbed hold of his sleeve in a last act of despair, her eyes puffy from crying. "No! I beg of you! He is just a boy!" she pleaded. He broke away from her clinging hands and strode up to Jing, striking him hard across his jaw. Jing staggered back as he brought his hand to his face. Cuiying remained where she was, her tremulous hand reaching out in a helpless gesture to comfort her firstborn, yet not daring to cross her husband.

"How dare you demean our family name!" Koxinga shouted, red with anger. "Siring a child with your brother's wet-nurse! Have you no respect? Could you not at least have picked another woman to satisfy your lust! You have gone against a sacred family principle. This makes you no better than some filthy beast!"

Jing gaped at him, stunned, then looked at his mother for help. But Cuiying shook her head wordlessly, her lips trembling pathetically. There was nothing she could do.

"Uncle Cai?" Jing turned to his father's cousin for help. But Cai just stared at him, a disgusted look on his face, refusing to intervene.

"Did you even know that the girl was with child?" his father asked, red-faced. Jing did not answer, but threw a hateful glance at his brother. Xi just stood there, watching the scene stoically.

Jing drew himself up boldly. "Father, as I remember it, you have sired children out of wedlock yourself."

"How dare you!" Koxinga shouted, the veins at his temples throbbing dangerously. "You do not talk to me in that way. I am your father! I'll tell you something more." He approached him, only inches removed from his face. "You are a weakling, devoid of morals or standards! You're nothing more than a filthy piece of shit."

"Father! I —"

"Don't you talk back at me! You do not even know your filial duties." He turned away. "You do not deserve to succeed me as ruler of this island. Xi shall succeed me instead."

Jing's jaw dropped, the whites of his eyes visible. "You cannot do that!" Jing stammered. "I am your oldest son. It is my fate to become king of this place when you die, and I will do all in my power to make sure that it happens!"

"San-ge!" Koxinga shouted at the top of his lungs for his general, his body shaking. The general, who had been hovering uneasily in the background, stepped forward, throwing a hesitant glance at the sobbing Cuiying.

"General! I want this man killed. He is guilty of treason and of plotting against me."

Cuiying began to wail piteously. She threw herself at her husband's feet, clawing at his robes in despair. He tried to ignore her, but soon he found her persistence oppressive. He grabbed her hard by the wrists and threw her aside as if she were a bag of dirt.

Jing stiffened, his hand on the hilt of his short sword. San-ge just gaped at his commander, shocked and unmoving.

"Seize him! I order you! He deserves to die!" Koxinga's eyes were wide and belligerent, oblivious to Cuiying's wails.

"*Aiya! Aiya!*" she repeated the same syllables over and over again.

San-ge blinked at him. "My lord, with all due respect, he is your son. What he has done was wrong. But it does not warrant a death sentence."

"You heard me," Koxinga growled at San-ge, who remained rooted to the ground. "Seize him! Now!" When he realized no one would follow his orders, he became enraged. He kicked at his pathetically cloying wife, his foot glancing across the side of her head. She sprawled across the floor, where she remained, a hopeless crying mess of a woman. Still, San-ge did nothing. Koxinga lunged forward and grabbed San-ge's sword, then turned to strike at Jing with a blood-curdling roar. The sword came down with force, but struck air: Jing had sidestepped the attack easily. Koxinga recovered slowly, and looked around him, bewildered that the weapon had met neither flesh nor bone.

This wasn't possible, he had never, ever actually ... missed. He reeled around, feeling quite unsure of himself. It was an unfamiliar sensation. He raised the sword once again, his fury unabated. But then he felt the weapon grow heavy, his movement sluggish. He felt suddenly faint, as if drunk. Still wielding the sword above his head, he stopped as a blinding flash of pain seared behind his eyes. His grip on the sword's hilt loosened, and the weapon clattered loudly upon the floor.

He stepped forward, reaching a contorted hand in Jing's direction. That very instant, his sight left him. The pain behind his eyes tore into him with vicious stabs, consuming him. Both of his hands went to his face. He had had this before. The pain, the blindness, the terror that came with it. But this time it was worse. He was only faintly aware that around him, people were shouting, panicking. He did not recognize their voices, they all seemed strange to him, distorted. Only the piercing scream, not far from where he stood, he knew he had heard before. *Aiya! Aiya! Aiya!* Those same screeching syllables, over and over again. He covered his ears with his hands, shaking his head forcefully, anything to shut out that sound. It hurt too much. He stumbled forward in the black darkness that was his alone, his arms reaching out in front of him, in search of his servants.

"My robes!" he muttered with an effort, pain stabbing him with every word he spoke. "My robes! Get me my ceremonial robes!" he screamed, thrashing about, desperate that he be understood. "Cai! My robes! Give them to me."

His own voice sounded weak to him, barely audible, he could feel the tears streaming down his face. Gradually, his sight came back to him, however murky and vague. He saw his servants, their eyes fixed upon him in fright and confusion.

Then Cai's face lit up in understanding. He rushed out of the room to return with his full ceremonial mandarin robes. His servants rushed forward to help him into the blue silk garment, ignoring the indiscriminate, weak slaps that he rained upon them in the madness of his agony.

Once dressed in the official robe, he stumbled out of the room, falling against the walls to hold himself up. His family and servants, preceded by San-ge and Cai, followed him with concern. As he threatened to fall once more, San-ge rushed forward to help him up.

"No!" He waved the general away, upon which San-ge backed off. They all watched as he made his way through the hall in the direction of his own quarters, bouncing from the walls and falling to his knees more than once. No one dared help him for fear of his mad rages. He drew himself up with an enormous effort toward the polished brass mirror.

He squinted. The warped image that stared back at him was strange to him. It should have been him, the great lord of the imperial surname. But all he saw was a frightened old man, gaunt and thin, with a look of madness in his eyes, wearing his own robes of ceremony. Disgusted, he turned his back on his reflection and clawed toward the family shrine that was the heart of his personal chambers.

"Go away!" he screamed at those who followed him. He did not recognize them, they were nothing but strangers. Supporting himself, he turned toward the displayed ancestral tablets. He reached between the tablets with shaking hands, extracting a faded old scroll from a vase in their midst. This was his most valuable possession, given to him by Longwu, the emperor who had once adopted him in name and given him his title. The scrolls contained poems written by the founding emperor of the Ming, the illustrious emperor who had expelled the Mongols, bringing an end to Mongolian rule. That emperor had reconquered China. His China, which he now knew he would never see again. *The strangers will leave, one day. Then island your destiny. But pay price. Big price.*

He pressed the precious scroll to his chest. He closed his eyes, and muttered something as he recalled the day on which he and his father had prostrated themselves before Longwu. Somehow, he sensed his father's presence next to him, as vague as it was compelling. His eyes flew wide open, suddenly aware of those around him. The strangers stared at him, their mouths agape as if he were a demon. Then a final, searing pain ripped through his torso and he felt his limbs beneath him give way.

* * *

My dear, beloved son Balthasar.

It was a delight to receive your letter with the news that you have arrived in Batavia safe and well, and that you are now in the employ of the VOC. I am convinced that a promising future awaits you, and it reminds me of my own youth, when I, too, began to work for the company.

From your letter I understand that it troubles you to think how I might feel about your appointment with the VOC, with regard to all that has happened. I will be the first to admit that I have long borne a grudge toward the company, but this will not stop me from congratulating you on the respectable position you have managed to obtain. Times have changed, and I too have learned to deal with all that has occurred, and have eventually succeeded in putting it behind me.

I have fond memories of Formosa. It was where you were born. Your own mother, my beloved Susanna, is buried there, as is the stillborn child to whom she gave birth. If I remember correctly, you were but twelve years of age when we were forced to leave the island, a difficult age to be removed from one's trusted environment.

I cannot recall the exact moment when I realized that Formosa would be lost to us. I knew long before the wells had begun to run dry within Fort Zeelandia. I knew even before my appointed successor, Hermanus Klenk van Odessa had reached Formosa's shores, only to turn around and sail back to Batavia with his tail between his legs, leaving us to our fate. In fact, I knew before Admiral van der Laan had left the island, with the intention of taking Macao. By then, I knew that help would not be on its way, that it was all over. And yet I refused to give up. I refused to give up because I wanted to hold off the enemy for as long as we possibly could, even if I knew deep in my heart that he would inevitably be victorious.

Exactly what is it that pushes a man in spite of the knowledge that there is really no hope, to hold out in such difficult, testing circumstances? Is it some ill-placed sense of honor? Stubbornness perhaps? There are many who would call me stubborn. They are probably right. When a man is forced to live in solitude for a prolonged period of time, he has no choice but to turn to self-contemplation, only to be confronted by his virtues, of which there are often few, but most of all, his flaws.

I do not blame warlord Koxinga for what has happened. From the many letters I have received over the past years from our friends who spent time with us on Formosa, I understand that he was mourned on both sides of the strait. Apparently he was much praised and hailed as a hero. The Chinese people must have seen in him a loyal countryman, and a fierce and formidable champion of the Ming. He must have given them hope to the very last in his loyal defense of a dynasty in its decline. On Formosa, he will most likely be remembered for the legacy that he left its people: an island freed of the VOC, liberated from the Dutch who once occupied it.

You may know by now, Balthasar, that a sense of injustice can make a man bitter. God will know that I have done all that I could to prevent Koxinga from taking Formosa. And He will also know that the company is just as much to blame for the colony's fate as I allegedly was. I, too, had my enemies. Nicolaes Verburgh, for one. In his envy of others, he was unable to place the company's interests above his own. Admiral van Der Laan was another, he could simply not bear the fact that I obstructed his mission and the achievement of his dream of the conquest of Macao.

I thank the Lord for my friends and family, although there were often times that I believed that same Lord had forsaken me, especially during my banishment. It was you and your stepmother who have pleaded my case for many years, just as my brother did, your Uncle Peter, who, as a diplomat, attempted to mediate for me. Unfortunately, he died before his correspondence with the Courts of Justice could bear fruit.

It is also the former colonists of Formosa to whom I feel grateful, even if there were those among them who took offence to the respect I showed to Lord Koxinga by bowing to him during the capitulation. These individuals are simpletons who cannot see the Chinese commander-in-chief as anything but the enemy. They are not capable of judging him as a man like any other, who was a victim of his time in history, just as I was.

Fortunately, most of the colonists came forward to give testimony in my favor. They insisted that it was in fact I who had been the strongest advocate of fighting to the end, and confirmed that we would never have had a chance against the armies of the formidable Koxinga, whose cruel exploits they described with exaggeration and fervor.

All of them were heard. But what probably saved me most of all was my own administration. With a premonition of what must lie ahead, I had been prudent to box all my ledgers and logbooks and had insisted that they be brought on board of the *'s Gravelande.*

The company clerks spent long days reading and processing my carefully sorted records, which brought to light transcripts of letters both sent and received to Batavia that went back years, written by governors long before my time, disclosing many poor decisions made in Batavia with regard to Formosa's security and safety. My defending counsel pointed out that the Batavian council had systematically ignored my warnings – and those of my predecessors. Time and time again, we warned Batavia of the dangers Koxinga posed. And every time, their answers were the same: that I should deal with the matter myself, without providing me with the means to do so.

The day came when my accusers had to concede – however reluctantly – that Batavia had been just as much to blame for the loss of Formosa as I was. Governor-General Maetsuijker, whose conscience must have troubled him in the knowledge that he, too, had played a role in Formosa's fall, had to admit that the death penalty was too severe, and he intervened, whereupon my sentence was changed to one of imprisonment.

No doubt you will remember that I was then imprisoned for three years in Batavia's jail. I am grateful that, during all that time, you and your stepmother continued to lobby for my release. There were many others, prominent and influential citizens among them, who openly questioned the severity of the punishment of a respected man as myself who had committed no real crime. Alas, the Heren Seventien were unrelenting: they accused me of not doing the utmost to ensure that the company's valued wares were returned to them. If I am truly to blame for this, then so be it, that is something I can live with. We were fortunate to be able to leave the island alive as it was.

My imprisonment remained a delicate issue within the then small, tight Dutch community of Batavia. From your stepmother and my loyal friends I learned that it had become quite an embarrassment to Maetsuijker, who was much criticized on my account. It must have been difficult for him: he could not release me, as he was under pressure from the Heren Seventien, who, far removed from all that had happened, demanded a scapegoat. Eventually, Mr. Maetsuijker converted the sentence to lifelong banishment to Pulau Ay, the remote, isolated island of the Banda group of islands.

Only my closest relatives were permitted to join me there. As you may remember, I insisted at the time that you and your stepmother remain in Batavia. The memory of it stays with me till this day: you refused to stay behind, you wanted to come with me. But I did not want either of you, in particular you, Balthasar, to suffer the consequences of a banishment to such a remote place, with so little to offer.

Balthasar, you are my son and only child. It was my wish that you should attend a good school, that you be surrounded by civilized, literate Christians, and receive a proper education, so that you would have a future. I thank God that it appears that you have been granted this. The knowledge that you were in good hands in Batavia has made the solitude that I had to endure during those many years away from you and your stepmother more bearable.

Happily, you visited me there often. And when you came, I felt revived. During those long, lonely years spent on Pulau Ay, I had ample time for reflection. Isolated as I was, and far removed from the civilized world as we know it, there was nothing else for me to do but write my memoires, aided by the boxes of letters and documents that I had taken with me.

I have always known that you were unable to accept the injustice of the punishment that was meted out to me. Of course, I feel indebted toward William of Orange, for signing the annulment of my sentence. But it was you who ceaselessly petitioned for my appeal until the annulment was finally granted. For this, Balthasar, I owe you my gratitude.

After nine years of banishment, I was granted a full pardon, and my honor was restored. In spite of this you will know, as no other, that I still felt resentment toward the VOC for a long time. In the package that I have enclosed with this letter, you will find one of the first printed copies of my memoires, called *Neglected Formosa.* Although I wrote this partly to rid myself of the bitterness that has come from my experience, I also wrote it for you, so that you will know what truly happened. You will find that I have used a pseudonym. I did this in order to protect the good name of the publisher, but also to protect yours and the family's.

My dear Balthasar, you can rest assured that I am immensely proud of you, and I wish you all the best in your career with the VOC. In the meantime, I very much look forward to receiving your next letter.

With much affection,
Your father,
Frederic Coyett
Amsterdam, November 1675

Epilogue

On that humid June night, only five months after defeating the Dutch and expelling them from the island, Koxinga breathed his last. He was only thirty-eight years old. His sense of destiny that Formosa would one day be his had not failed him. But he could never have foreseen that his fate was to be linked to that of the Dutch colony. The full prophecy that had been made in his youth had come true. The Dutch had come to the island in the year of his birth, and he died within months of the colony's fall. He had conquered Formosa, but the price he had to pay for this was indeed high.

Upon his death, his two sons continued their bitter feud. Eventually Jing succeeded in taking the throne, and he named himself king of the island, which he remained until his death almost twenty years later. Following the dynastic rules, Jing's twelve-year-old son followed in his footsteps, but the young boy was incapable of dealing with the responsibilities. The youthful king became the pawn of ambitious court officials and relatives, who bickered and feuded on the issue of who should give him counsel.

When word reached Peking of the chaos that had taken hold of the House of Zheng, the Qing court lost no time in taking advantage of the situation. The Manchus launched a major attack on the island, sending its entire war fleet to its shores. The boy king had no alternative but to surrender. And thus, after only twenty-one years of rule on Formosa, the Zheng dynasty ended.

The name Dongdu, a last remnant and reminder of Ming opposition, was quickly replaced by "Taiwan," named after the bay at Zeelandia. It was the name the island had been given by the Chinese long before the Portuguese had first sailed into its waters.

When news reached Peking that the island had been conquered, the Qing emperor barely cared. It had been the fall of the Zhengs that he had sought, not the island itself. To the emperor, the name of the island conjured up images of barren mountains and muddy swamps that were rampant with disease. He even proposed that all his subjects unfortunate enough to live on Taiwan abandon the place altogether, suggesting that they return to China.

"That place is no more than a ball of dirt. What will we gain by possessing it? Nothing! It hangs alone in isolation beyond the seas, far removed from our shores! Our empire is surrounded by the seas. The seas form its natural border in the east and the south. It has always been this way, and so it will remain."

His general, well acquainted with the island, was shocked at the suggestion that they abandon it, as he could see the advantages of annexing Taiwan. But the emperor scoffed, unconvinced.

"Sire, I beg you to hear me out," the general countered, "The island is strategic territory for the empire. If we abandon Taiwan, it will attract pirates, perhaps even another foreign power. The Dutch might even return to occupy it again. It would be far wiser if the island were to remain under our control. This way, the Strait of Taiwan will be a safer place for our people, our ships, and our goods."

Eventually, the emperor agreed, and the island of Taiwan was made a prefecture of Fujian Province. For the first time in history, the island was part of the Chinese empire.

As the years went by, the general died, as did the emperor. Thousands of miles from the court of Peking, the island prefecture was soon forgotten, and it fell back into the state of isolation in which it had been before the Dutch had arrived.

Through an odd twist of fate, history would come to repeat itself. More than two hundred years later, the island would fall into the hands of a foreign power yet again, this time to an Asian empire far closer to its shores. For fifty years it would remain occupied by the Japanese, until they finally relinquished it, to leave it altered and with an identity of its own.

Not long afterward, a war on the Chinese mainland would bring change to the place once more. The island would again serve as a place of refuge for an army fleeing the mainland from a victorious enemy. And thus the island's history would come full circle.

Author's Note

Over the centuries, much has been written in Asia about the mythical exploits of Koxinga, lord of the imperial surname, champion of the Ming and the only man able to drive away the Dutch colonists from Formosa. Due to his mixed heritage, his heroism has captured the imagination of many a Chinese historian and Japanese playwright, who were keen to romanticize the events in his life and portray him as a great man. As usually happens, the myth has outgrown the truth and quite a few sources are thus less than reliable.

In many of the (Chinese) dramatized versions that are based on his life, Koxinga's story heavily overshadows that of the Dutch. Their story might have been dealt with to a limited extent, but usually they were stereotyped as "ugly, redheaded barbarians," or simply "the enemy." Even in the Netherlands, it is little known that the Dutch once colonized Taiwan. This is hardly surprising, as the VOC's neglect of Formosa and the dramatic way it was lost was something that was best forgotten. Dutch history schoolbooks may devote a sentence or two to the episode, but a lot of people don't realize that the former colony of Formosa and Taiwan are one and the same island.

Lord of Formosa is closely based on historical events: most of the characters described in this book truly existed. As I did my research, however, I often found that the various sources I consulted conflicted. The exact circumstances surrounding the rape and death of Matsu Tagawa, Koxinga's mother, for instance, differ somewhat according to the source, although they all imply that she died at the hands of Manchu soldiers. Also, Zheng Zhilong's defection to the Manchus is often denied by official Chinese historians, as this would cast a shadow of doubt across the man's character, who was, after all, Koxinga's father. It is, however, the most documented and likely scenario.

The actual cause of Koxinga's death remains something of a mystery. Of course we can never be certain, but there are medical experts who agree that, considering the symptoms described in historical sources, syphilis could well have been possible (see Antonio Andrade, *How Taiwan Became Chinese*).

Not wishing to fall into the trap of merely following romanticized versions that stereotypically glorify Koxinga, I have followed my instincts and chosen this version of events, which I believe to be the most probable. This way I hope to have portrayed him as a man of flesh and blood.

Where there were no sources, as these are often lost in times of war and chaos, I have used my imagination. However, Koxinga's obsession with the idea that it was his destiny to rule over Formosa was quite real; many sources mention this. It is very plausible to assume that such a prophecy was made at some point in his lifetime, and that Koxinga truly believed this.

Frederic's Coyett's *Neglected Formosa* was a major primary source of the Dutch point of view; but because it was written under a pseudonym and Coyett was an embittered man and not without enemies, I was wary of following it blindly. Coyett returned to Amsterdam, where he bought a home on the stately Keizersgracht (number 485) in 1684. He died at the age of seventy-two and lies buried at the Westerkerk. His son Balthasar had a prosperous career within the VOC, becoming governor of both the Banda Islands and Ambon.

As already mentioned, all the main characters described in this book are based on historical figures and were real. I have attempted to breathe life into them by giving them a voice in order to tell the story from their perspective. It is this that makes *Lord of Formosa* a novel.

Unsurprisingly, many historians have drawn parallels between Koxinga's flight to Formosa and the exodus of Generalissimo Chiang Kai-shek's army to Taiwan in 1949, which only emphasizes how the geographical location of an (is)land can influence the course of its history.

There have been profound changes in the geography of Tayouan Bay over the past centuries. The bay has gradually filled with sediment due to the strength of the currents and the countless typhoons that affected Formosa. Pineapple Isle and Baxemboy have gone: these have merged with the numerous surrounding sandbars and eventually with the Formosan mainland. However, many traces remain in Taiwan of the Dutch occupation, the ruins of Fort Zeelandia (Anping) and Fort Provintia among them. In Tainan there is a shrine that was built by Koxinga's oldest son, Jing, in honor of his father. Tainan also has a prestigious university named after him.

The People's Republic of China has also given Koxinga a prominent place in its history. On the small island of Xiamen, formerly known as Amoy, there is a larger-than-life size statue of him that stands overlooking the sea.

A Word of Thanks

The first person who deserves a place here is my cousin Julia Hines, who was willing to perform the monstrous task of proofreading the raw English draft. It was she who wrote the first review of the unpublished English version, which led to my virtual "meeting" on social media with Michael Cannings of Camphor Press; and the rest is, as they say, history.

I am very much indebted to Michael for taking on the publication of this book, as I am indebted to my sharp-eyed and ruthless editors John Grant Ross and Mark Swofford, who did a brilliant job of lifting the book to greater heights.

I would like to thank Tonio Andrade and Lisa Black of Princeton University Press for granting permission to use the reconstructed map of Tayouan Bay on page 51, slightly altered from its form in Andrade's *Lost Colony*. Tristan Mostert I owe a lot for his encouragement, friendship and support. Tristan's Dutch translation of *Lost Colony* (*De val van Formosa*) was an excellent, more recent source of information, maps, and beautiful illustrations, and I consulted it often. I also want to thank Gerrit van der Wees for his tremendous support and for writing a book review on the Dutch edition of *Lord of Formosa* (*Formosa voorgoed verloren*) in the *Taipei Times*.

I would like to thank my children, Jessica and Michael MacLaine Pont, for their patience and understanding when writing this book, as the years I spent doing so comprised a relatively large part of their lives. In spite of their teasing remarks that this story would probably never see the light of day ("keep dreaming, Mum!"), I suspect they are proud of me nonetheless, as they don't seem to mind their full names appearing at the end of this book. In spite of what they may have believed at times, I always put them first above anything else. I owe much to our beloved dogs, Aukje and Astor:

they saw to it that I could start with a fresh mind every morning and made sure that I did not turn to stone behind my writing desk.

I thank my husband, Alexander, my knight in shining armor, for his patience, support, and encouragement. He was the one who took me to distant, exotic lands, where I finally had the time and opportunity to write this story that had burned inside of me for so long.

In my youth I lived in various parts of the world, spending most of my teenage years as an "expat" child. I regard this as a tremendous privilege for which I am thankful. Back in 1982, my parents persuaded me to join them for a "gap" year in Taiwan, if only to give me the chance to find out which direction I wanted to take with my life. Even then I was intrigued by the fact that the Dutch had once colonized Taiwan.

I am particularly grateful to my father, Jan Bergvelt, who is no longer with us, for passing on to me his immense thirst for knowledge; his love for books, history, and the Far East; and his passion for writing. He died twenty years ago, just before he was able to achieve his own life-long dream of writing a book of his own. This book is dedicated to his memory.

Sources

Andrade, Tonio. *How Taiwan Became Chinese.* Gutenberg, Columbia University Press, 2005.

———. *De val van Formosa: Hoe een Chinese krijgsheer de voc versloeg.* translated into Dutch by Tristan Mostert, Uitgeverij van Wijnen, Franeker 2015.

Blussé, Leonard. *The Source Publications of the Daghregisters (Journals) of Zeelandia Castle at Formosa 1629–1662 Interim report.* European Association of Chinese Studies, Rome 1979.

Boxer, C.R. *Fidalgos in the Far East.* Martinus Nijhoff, The Hague, 1948.

Campbell, William. *Aboriginal Savages of Formosa.* Ocean Highways, April 1873.

———. *An Account of Missionary Success in the Island of Formosa vol 1.* renewed edition, Taipei 1972.

———. *Europeans in Formosa.* Hong Kong Daily Press, 10 Dec 1901.

———. *Formosa under the Dutch.* Kegan Paul, Trench, Trübner & Co. Ltd, London, 1903.

Candidus, Georgius. *Short Account of the Island of Formosa*, renewed edition, 1744.

Clements, Jonathan. *Coxinga and the Fall of the Ming Dynasty*, Sutton Publishing, London 2004.

Colenbrander, H.T. *Introduktie van de Koloniale Geschiedenis* vol 1, 1925.

Coyett, Frederic. *'t Verwaerloosde Formosa* (Amsterdam, 1675).

Croizier, Ralph C. *Koxinga and Chinese Nationalism*, East Asian Research Center, Harvard University 1972.

Davidson, James. *The Island of Formosa*, MacMillan & Co., New York & London, 1903.

Edmonds, I.G. *Taiwan, The Other China*, Bobbs-Merrill, Indianapolis 1971.

Fairbank, John. *The Chinese World Order*, Cambridge-Harvard University Press, 1962.

Fitzgerald, P. *The Southern Expansion of the Chinese People*, Praeger, New York, 1972.

Gemeente Amsterdam Stadsarchief. www.amsterdam.nl/stadsarchief.

Goddard, W.G. *Formosa: A Study in Chinese History*, Imperial Books, Taipei, 1966, second printing 1983.

Goddard, W.G. *The Makers of Taiwan*, China Publishing, Taipei, 1963.

Gommans, Jos & Diessen, Rob van. *Comprehensive Atlas of the Dutch East India Company, volume VII: East Asia, Burma to Japan*, Atlas Maior, Nationaal Archief, KNAG, Universiteit van Utrecht, 2010.

Groeneveldt, W.P. *De Nederlanders in China: De Eerste Bemoeiingen om de Handel in China en de Pescadores*, Martinus Nijhoff, 1898.

Horst, van der, D. *Verre Naasten Naderbij*: "De Eerste Nederlanders in China" Rijksmuseum voor Volkenkunde, Leiden, March 1976.

Hung Chien-chao. *Taiwan under the Cheng Family: Sinicization after Dutch Rule*. Georgetown University, 1981.

Keene, Ronald R. *The Battles of Koxinga*. London, 1951.

Kemenade, van, Willem. "Made in China", NCR Handelsblad 27 Nov 1982.

Last, Jef. *Strijd, Handel en Zeeroverij: De Hollandse Tijd op Formosa*, Assen, 1968.

Paske-Smith, M. *Western Barbarians in Japan and Formosa in the Tokugawa Days 1603–1868*, Paragon, New York, 1968.

Phillips, G. "Notes on the Dutch Occupation of Formosa." *The China Review*, 1882.

———. "Dutch Trade in Formosa." *The China Review*, Shanghai 1885.

Purcell, Victor. *The Chinese in Southeast Asia*. Oxford University Press, London & New York, 1951.

Stevens, E. *Formosa, Its Situation and Extent, Discovery by the Chinese, Occupation by the Dutch, Their Government and Expulsion by the Pirate Koxinga*. (Chinese Repository).

Sun Tzu. *The Art of War*. Lionel Giles, trans. Hodder & Stoughton, London, 1981 ed.

Taiwan's Economic History, vol. IV, Taipei, 1956.

Toorenbergen, van, J.J. *On the Dutch Mission to Formosa 1624–1661*. De Gids, volume 56, 1882.

Valentyn, Francois. *Oud en Nieuw Oost-Indië*. Joannes van Braam, 1723.

Verhoeven, F.R.J. *Bijdragen tot de Oudere Koloniale Geschiedenis van het Eiland Formosa*. The Hague, 1930.

Wills, John E. Cambridge History of China, vol. 8, *The Dutch Period in Taiwan History: A preliminary survey*. Cambridge University Press, Cambridge, Massachusetts, 1972.

———. *Pepper, Guns and Parleys: The Dutch East India Company and China, 1662–1681*. Cambridge University Press, Cambridge, Massachusetts, 1974.

Zeeuw, de, P. *De Hollanders op Formosa* . W. Kirchner, Amsterdam, 1924.

Zhang Weihua 張維華. 明史佛郎機呂宋和蘭意大里亞四傳注釋 (Notes and Annotations on the Four Chapters on Portugal, Spain, Holland, and Italy in Ming Dynastic History). Harvard-Yanjing Xueshe, Beijing, 1934.

CPSIA information can be obtained
at www.ICGtesting.com
Printed in the USA
BVHW04s1432060618
518396BV00001B/41/P

9 781788 691390